OTHER TITLES BY CHRISTI CALDWELL

Wantons of Waverton

Someone Wanton His Way Comes

Lost Lords of London

In Bed with the Earl
In the Dark with the Duke
Undressed with the Marquess

Sinful Brides

The Rogue's Wager
The Scoundrel's Honor
The Lady's Guard
The Heiress's Deception

Wicked Wallflowers

The Hellion
The Vixen
The Governess
The Bluestocking
The Spitfire

Scandalous Affairs

A Groom of Her Own
Taming of the Beast

Heart of a Duke

In Need of a Duke (A Prequel Novella)
For Love of the Duke

Scandalous Seasons

Forever Betrothed, Never the Bride
Never Courted, Suddenly Wed
Always Proper, Suddenly Scandalous
Always a Rogue, Forever Her Love
A Marquess for Christmas
Once a Wallflower, At Last His Love

The Theodosia Sword

Only For His Lady
Only For Her Honor
Only For Their Love

Danby

Winning a Lady's Heart
A Season of Hope

The Brethren

The Spy Who Seduced Her
The Lady Who Loved Him
The Rogue Who Rescued Her
The Minx Who Met Her Match
The Spinster Who Saved a Scoundrel

Brethren of the Lords

My Lady of Deception
Her Duke of Secrets

Nonfiction Works

Uninterrupted Joy: A Memoir

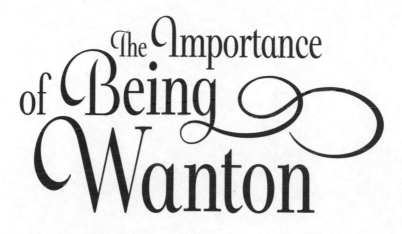

The Importance of Being Wanton

CHRISTI CALDWELL

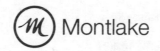
Montlake

Published by Montlake, Seattle

www.apub.com

Amazon, the Amazon logo, and Montlake are trademarks of Amazon.com, Inc., or its affiliates.

ISBN-13: 9781542027991
ISBN-10: 1542027993

Front cover design by Juliana Kolesova

Back cover design by Ray Lundgren

Printed in the United States of America

For Doug . . .
Not a single story would have ever been written if you
hadn't supported me as you did, and as you continue to.
Thank you for allowing me to lose myself in my stories.
You are my most perfect hero.

Prologue

1812

This was hell.

There was nothing else for it.

Or Charles Hayden, the Earl of Scarsdale, was being punished.

Or his parents hated him.

Or, perhaps, it was a combination of every given factor.

Either way, this was where he drew the absolute last line.

Gasping and out of breath, Charles raced along the dew-slicked grass.

"*Chaaarles!* I am *calling* you!"

Yes, the whole damned county could hear as much. That pursuit was also the reason for Charles's flight. He clenched his teeth. Well, not just that pursuit. The reason behind it.

All of it, really.

The Marquess of Rochester was entirely to blame.

The soles of Charles's leather shoes proved another enemy to him that day. He went skidding and sliding forward. On a gasp, Charles shot out his palms and caught himself against the trunk of the ancient yew. His heart pounding from the race he'd just run, he leaned against the enormous tree.

Mayhap his father wouldn't find him here. Mayhap—

Something struck Charles in the chest, and he glanced down. A small rock rested atop the tip of his shoe. *What in hell?* He whipped about, searching for the source of that missile. It would seem he was under attack from a number of foes this day.

His father's voice grew increasingly closer. *". . . aaaarles . . . !"*

His panic swelled, replacing his momentary distraction, and Charles scoured the horizon.

A mere speck appeared in the distance. There could be no doubting, however, the identity of that figure drawing nearer.

Nay, those *two* figures.

Tossing aside one shoe, Charles reached for his other. Haste, however, made his fingers clumsy, and he fumbled with the damned thing.

At last, he managed to get the Blucher boot free.

"I said . . . get back . . ."

He firmed his jaw. By God, if they wanted him, they were going to have to catch him.

Hopping up, Charles climbed onto the old, gnarled limb a foot from the ground, then used the enormous yew as his ladder toward freedom.

He'd reached the sixth branch, some seven feet from the ground, when they caught up to him.

The illustrious Marquess of Rochester skidded to a stop similar to his son's, with Charles's mother arriving close behind.

Hunched over, his long white hair tousled, Charles's father gasped for air. However, even with his hands resting on his knees, he still somehow managed to glower *up* at Charles.

But then, that was the way of the marquess. Capable of commanding with a single look. Of ruling all. Including one's son. *Especially* one's son. Alas, Charles had been ordered about for the last time.

"What in thunderation are you *doing*?" his father cried.

"I think that should be fairly clear." Charles paused. "I'm climbing a tree." *And hiding.* But he'd be damned if he used those words.

His breath having resumed a semblance of normality but for the intermittent gasp, the marquess straightened. "Get down here before you kill yourself and I am left heirless."

The hell he would. Charles made no move to abandon the spot he'd secured himself. "You've plenty of hair. Far more than is fashionable," he called down. "In fact, I have always been stunned that someone as stringent as you in terms of society should—"

"I meant *heir*-less." His father scowled. "As in without an heir."

Charles smirked. It was entirely too easy.

"I believe he was making a jest," Charles's still-winded mother explained to her husband. Cupping her hands about her mouth, she spoke loudly enough to make the marquess wince. "Isn't that right, Charles?"

Charles gave a little mock salute. "Indeed."

With a pleased smile, she turned back to the marquess. "See? As I said. Merely a jest." Yes, because she had always had a sense of humor and often was left attempting to explain even the simplest quip to the staid, humorless, duty-driven marquess. Betrothed as children, the pair had been married forever, and had known each other even longer.

Charles shuddered. It was the last fate he would ever want, that medieval manner of marriage. And the one he desperately sought to escape now. "Though technically, you'd not be heirless, either, Father," Charles gleefully pointed out. "You'd be *spare*-less, as there's always Derek to fill the role." Derek, who, by his fortunate entry after Charles, would never be saddled with the hell Charles had.

"This is not the time for games or jests or technicalities . . . or . . . or . . . *tree-climbing*," the marquess sputtered.

All the while, Charles's mother proceeded to murmur calm platitudes to her husband.

"He is being unreasonable, Aster." His father spoke as if Charles weren't even present.

"I'm being *unreasonable*?" Charles called, climbing another branch higher. "*I* am?"

3

"Come down this instant. You are too old for climbing trees, young man," the marquess bellowed. "Tell him, Aster."

There came a slight rustle and a grunt, and Charles looked all the way down just as his mother pulled herself onto the first branch, and then the second. "*Your father* says you are too old for climbing trees," she said, and the slight emphasis she placed on those first two words brought Charles his first real smile of the whole miserable day. Catching his eye, she winked.

His grin widened.

Alas, that smile also proved short-lived.

"The guests have already begun arriving, Charles," his mother said from where she balanced on a lower branch. "Emma's father is asking to speak with you before the ceremony."

Charles's stomach lurched, and by the way his belly turned, he was pretty certain he was going to cast his morning biscuits down below. Which . . . might not be an altogether bad thing. Surely his father would cancel the whole damned day after such a horror?

The marquess shook his fist. "I am not going anywhere. If you don't come down, I will bring the damned ceremony to you. Is that clear?"

Charles peered down at his father. "Ah, but doesn't the ceremony require two?"

"She's gone exploring, as she's wont to do. You know that." His mother rolled her eyes. That was likely something Charles should have known about his intended. And perhaps he would have if the betrothed in question weren't six, and if, instead, he were a grown man, marrying a grown woman of his choosing. "In fact, she's likely already been found. If you'd just come down . . ."

As the marquess shouted up his demands, Charles's mother spoke just two words down to her husband. "Dear heart." There was something in her quiet voice, calm enough to break through the blustery tirade.

"I know that . . . I'm not . . ." The marquess sighed. "Very well." He opened his mouth to say something else to Charles, but his wife gave him a long look. "Very well," Charles's father mumbled once more, and with a last glare for his son, he marched off.

The marchioness waited several moments for her husband to leave before drawing herself higher up onto the tree.

"Mother!" Charles called down warningly as she continued to make the high climb. When she gave no hint of stopping, he immediately scrambled down several branches, meeting her halfway.

As if she were greeting any of the expected guests for that day and not on a high perch some eleven or twelve feet from the ground, his mother seated herself on the wide branch. "And this from someone who was adamant that age shouldn't be a tree-climbing deterrent?"

"You're a lady."

"And if you're speaking like *that*, then I've failed in my role as a mother," she said drolly.

No, she hadn't. Quite the opposite. She'd been loving where his father had been removed. She'd been supportive where his father couldn't have been bothered. And yet, even with all that . . . she'd still attempt to come up here and compel him to wed.

"She's a lovely girl, Charles," his mother said with a quiet insistence, as if she'd followed the very thoughts he'd spoken.

Yes, that was it, exactly. "She is a girl. A little girl. A *babe*."

"Yes, yes, but she won't always be, and then she'll be grown up and you'll suit one another very nicely. You will."

He cast his mother a sideways look, searching for a sign that she was jesting, because *surely* she was.

"Why, I married your father, and we were betrothed as babes. And look at *us*." She smiled widely, and he took a moment to realize that she was deadly serious. That her words were not spoken with sarcasm or in kidding.

Far be it from him to point out that their comfortable, tedious arrangement accounted in large part for the reason he'd resurrected his tree-climbing skills.

With a sigh, he looked out between the enormous yew branches to the rolling green hills he so loved. A place that would now forever be tainted with this thing his parents would have him do. Because if he couldn't reason with his mother, there was absolutely no hope. Still, he tried one more time. He forced his gaze away from the countryside and over to the one parent he had always thought valued his opinion and would let him have a say in his future. "You are really going to make me do this?"

"Oh, Charles," she murmured with such pity and regret that they served as answers enough. She moved closer to him, and he reached out a hand to steady her, to make sure she didn't go tumbling below and break her neck and destroy this day even further.

His mother, however, waved him off. She wrapped her arms over his shoulders and lightly hugged him. "The truth is, Charles, sometimes we have to do things we do not want to."

"Like marry the Gately girl?" he spat, vitriol pulling that surname from deep within his chest, from a place where resentments would forever dwell.

"Like marry the Gately girl," she confirmed, giving no indication that she'd heard his hate-filled tone and disallowing him even that small satisfaction of her acknowledging those feelings. "Furthermore, I would be remiss if I did not point out that I think she perfectly suits you."

And he managed the impossible that day. Charles burst out laughing, that amusement so unexpected and fulsome that he was the one who lost his balance, and the only thing that kept him on his perch was his mother's quick and steady hand.

Except she winged an eyebrow and gave him a long look, confirming she hadn't been speaking in jest.

"My God, you are serious," he choked out.

"Well, I'm not your god, just your mother. But I am sincere. Very much so. You should have a care, Charles; she may be a child, but as I said, she won't always be. The little ducks grow up and become swans.

And remember, Charles . . . swans are capable of flight. As such, you would do well to not stray so far from the pond."

Charles puzzled his brow. What in thunderation was she talking about?

Leaning over, she pressed a kiss to his cheek. "If you are clever and wise and honorable, you'll be fortunate to never know what I mean. Now, how much time?"

"An hour?"

She shook her head. "I cannot manage that."

"Thirty minutes?" he asked.

"Twenty." She reached over and brushed back a damp strand that had fallen over his brow. "And another twenty to see yourself presentable," she murmured, ever so lovingly and tenderly adjusting his rumpled cravat, perfectly fixing the folds, and smoothing the lapels of his jacket. Then with the same impressive ease with which she had scaled the tree, his mother found her way down, and lifting her hems, she headed off to meet her husband. The pair spoke for several moments. Or rather, his mother did. His father listened, periodically nodding. Raising her hands to his mouth one at a time, he placed a kiss upon her knuckles before they took their leave.

Charles stared on at them, walking hand in hand; it was a relationship he'd never understand. Because there couldn't be two people more different than his parents: his mother, warm and nurturing and loving. And then there was . . . his father. Charles's father, who spent most of his days in his office with a magnifying glass in hand as he read whatever ledgers or books a man such as him bothered with. Still, for all the differences between the Marquess and Marchioness of Rochester, for some unexplainable reason Charles would never understand, his mother not only *loved* the surly marquess but was also happy. Blissfully so.

He scrunched up his mouth. His mother and father together, and their happiness, formed a riddle he'd never solve, and one he didn't even care to.

Perhaps, though, that was why she expected Charles should find himself like her.

But he wasn't. He never would be. Because unlike her, he would forever be filled with resentment and anger at that which they had forced him to do.

At last, his parents' figures disappeared from view, and Charles began to count. He counted the seconds as they became minutes. The moment he reached the agreed-upon twentieth minute, he waited another second, allowing himself that control, and climbed back down.

The moment his feet hit the ground, he donned his shoes, then started on the same path his mother and father had when a figure in the near distance snagged his notice. Her tiny frame clad in ridiculously large-for-her skirts, her golden hair limp around her face, the child stood amidst a small army of mute swans. In her white garments, she nearly perfectly blended in with those creatures that filled his family's lake.

However, it was not the sight of either her skirts or the swans that struck him.

It was . . . her stare.

Even with the twenty paces between them, there could be no disputing the fiery anger in the girl's eyes. Burning, blazing hatred that he knew all too well. But somehow more . . . striking . . . when he saw it reflected back in the gaze of a six-year-old girl.

Charles gave his head a disgusted shake. His mother had spoken of his wedded bliss someday.

With that hellion?

Cursing to himself, Charles began the trek back to the manor, where he'd sign the betrothal documents binding himself forevermore to a child bride.

⌘

Seventeen years later

It made sense that she should have requested a meeting . . . beside a lake.

Albeit a different lake.

Not the private, secluded one of his family's Leeds estate.

Rather, the very public Serpentine.

Although not at this hour. At the five o'clock morn time, only a lone gent stole a ride through the graveled riding paths, and the pink pelicans glided lazily over the serene surface.

Within a few hours, the very path he now strode would be bustling with passersby, all pretending for a brief interlude that they were away from the cacophony that was the metropolis of London life.

And it was the first time in the whole of his seventeen-year betrothal that Charles found himself intrigued by something—or anything—about the woman he was slated to wed in one month, four days, and—he consulted his timepiece—a handful of hours.

Charles crested the rise, and stopped in his tracks.

For the sight of the young woman, with her lace-ruffled skirts, may as well have been a still life from that time, long ago. Then, she'd had messy golden hair that had hung about her shoulders. Now, she was notorious for her tightly drawn back hair and her features pinched in what he was convinced was a perpetual state of disapproval.

His earlier intrigue was swiftly replaced by the more familiar customary annoyance, one that he immediately concealed; as testy as she always was on the rare occasions they were together, she was still the daughter of his parents' best friends, and she was still to be his bride. In sickness and in health. As long as they both should live. Doffing his hat, Charles started forward. "Good morning to you, Emma." He called out that greeting, commandeering her Christian name, even as the lady despised it.

As he walked to meet her at the shore, he caught the greater tensing of her narrow lips and recalled the curt rebuke she'd dealt when he'd first called her thus at her Come Out.

Do not call me Emma. It is hardly proper. You do not even know me . . .

Though if he were being honest, shameful as it was, he quite enjoyed getting a rise out of the usually aloof, and almost unfailingly unexcitable, miss.

He reached her side, and dropped a bow. "I received—"

"You are late, Lord Scarsdale," she said tersely, giving him a harsh once-over. "But then, you've made a habit of it."

A habit of it?

A large part of him wanted to debate the chit on the point. Except, even as he wasn't one who was generally tardy, he wasn't altogether certain how carefully she'd been watching his comings and goings at *ton* events.

He flashed a smile. After all, she was his future bride, and his grin was the greatest weapon he had to thaw her.

She stared back coolly, proving herself once more wholly un-thawable.

Very well. Let them get on with whatever urgent matter had merited his presence for a morning meeting. Charles returned his hat to his head and adjusted the article. "You wished to see me to discuss our upcoming nuptials. I thought I was clear; matters pertaining to the flowers and breakfast arrangements and music selection"—and anything and everything else—"are entirely at your discretion."

"Yes, you were." Something flashed in her eyes, a glimmer different from the usual ice that filled the stares she directed his way. There was also a trace of . . . sadness . . . contained within. Gone so quick he may as well have imagined it. That, however, was enough to prod his guilt.

"Was there . . . however, something that you wished to consult me on?" he gently nudged, as he wasn't averse to offering his opinion if she wished it. But he'd also known well enough before that a woman such as his betrothed wouldn't want his interference in the arrangements surrounding the nuptials.

Emma clasped her hands before her primly, as if in prayer, laying the steepled fingers against the flat of her belly. "My mother was handling them."

Then something registered . . . A simple word choice, casually spoken and slipped in, one that signaled a tense that had passed.

My mother . . . was . . . handling them.

Ah, so there was a matter of her mother's intrusion. She'd ask Charles to involve himself in wrangling the planning away from their determined mothers. "And . . . you would like my assistance in . . . speaking to our mothers about their handling of those details."

She gave a slight shake of her head. "Not at all. I have since . . . handled my mother." She grimaced. "Or rather, it. I have handled it."

And for a second time that day, his intrigue was roused by the not-so-very-mousy-after-all Miss Emma Gately. Her mother, a leading matron of Polite Society, roused terror in most men. He couldn't have fathomed a situation where Emma Gately handled the determined viscountess . . . in anything. Until now.

Emma didn't require his assistance in the matter of their wedding . . . which begged the question: What had she called him here for?

"I trust you are wondering why I've requested your presence." The young lady not only correctly surmised his thoughts but also had come at him again with that unexpected, and welcome, bluntness.

He inclined his head. "I confess to curiosity." Intrigue. From the moment her missive had come—and in the dead of night—it was, and had been, outright intrigue. "I expect it has to do with our upcoming nuptials?"

Odd. His mind hadn't even been able to formulate a thought of that day, let alone speak one from his mouth, without sending his gut churning and his stomach muscles twisting. And yet . . . this time, that customary and bodily response . . . did not come.

"Yes," Emma confirmed. "I have had time to consider our arrangement. Seventeen years." She looked out over the Serpentine, her eyes a shade of blue he couldn't place for the many hues to them. "Seventeen. Years," she repeated.

Charles ran his gaze over Emma's tense face, too angular to ever lend itself toward classical beauty, but sharp of planes that gave a man pause to notice, drawing him in. Or . . . in this instant they did, and it drew Charles's focus to one key realization: he stood in the presence of a woman who'd carefully tracked the length of their arrangement. Until this moment, however, he'd never considered that she might be aware . . . in the same way. Which in retrospect had been rather narrow-minded of him.

A soft breeze stole over the Serpentine, rolling gently; it managed to tug a single straight lock of hair from her tight chignon and toss it against her cheek. He moved closer, drawn nearer by that errant strand, a paradox to the self-possessed woman before him. His fingers came up, reaching for that tress, and he brushed it, tucking it behind her ear. "Yes, we've both had time to think on it." He spoke quietly, and the young lady pulled her stare from the smooth surface of the river and over to Charles . . . Her lips parted, that narrow lower lip lending an upside-down pout to her mouth, and his gaze caught.

His breath caught.

And he, Charles, the Earl of Scarsdale, rogue amongst gentlemen, scoundrel of London, found himself completely enraptured by his future bride. Her endlessly long, flaxen lashes swept low, and Charles swallowed spasmodically. How had he failed to either appreciate or revel in the complexity of that contoured mouth before now?

He lowered his head, determined to rectify that past failing.

Emma took a quick, lurching step backward, catching herself at the edge, so close the water kissed her hemline. "And as such, having had time to consider our betrothal all these years, I have decided it would be in my best interest to sever the formal contract."

They were confounding words to make sense of when he'd been so very close to taking her mouth with his.

Sever the formal contract.

"Yes," she said with a tight little nod, confirming with that bob of her long neck and passionless utterance that he'd spoken aloud.

"You are . . . breaking it off with me." Shock lent a hollow quality to a question that didn't make sense. He should be relieved. A lot relieved. And only grateful. She would spare him of an arrangement he didn't want.

Except she had done . . . that which he'd never been able to manage. She would defy their parents. She would reject a union that had been preordained by those same parents, a betrothal she'd been bound to for all but six of her years.

He shook his head, and tried again. "I don't . . ." Tried. And failed. The words would not come. Because it didn't make sense. Nothing about any of this exchange, from the note to this sudden, unwitting fascination with her, to the almost kiss, to the reason for his summons, did. "I don't understand." There—he'd at last managed to get out a full coherent thought, one that demanded clarity.

"I am breaking it off. Severing the arrangement," she said matter-of-factly, as if they discussed this very fine clement spring they now enjoyed. Emma stared at him expectantly.

What, however, was expected of him?

"I . . . did not ask for the betrothal to be severed," he finally said when he found his voice and a suitable response.

"No. I know that." She patted his hand; her fingers were long and tan, as if the lady enjoyed shucking her gloves and feeling the sun upon them. Did she? Or did her skin contain the gift of her family's old Roman roots? Both details he didn't know about her. But he likely should have. "You needn't worry that you will be held responsible," she said, misinterpreting the reason for his silence. "My parents will not blame you, Lord Scarsdale."

He latched on to that. "You've not spoken to your parents then?" Because had she done so, that lent an added . . . finality . . . to all this.

"I have," she corrected, adding that final nail. "They are well aware that I am the one who wishes to be set free."

Set free.

It was . . . singularly odd to have spent the whole of his adult life resenting his betrothal and the woman whom he'd one day wed.

Only to have her use those very words.

When he, usually glib of tongue, remained wholly without.

Alas, upon this day, his betrothed had words enough for both of them.

"I understand that you are also likely"—he waited for her to supply a response for whatever it was she thought he was feeling—"concerned as to how your parents might receive this new change in our circumstances."

This new change in their circumstances.

Yet again, she spoke of their end with an absolute conviction, which stirred more of that odd panic for reasons that had nothing to do with what she thought they did. Or for that matter, even reasons he could make any real sense of. "I do not care what my parents think," he said tersely, finding himself, and finding his way. Giving her the truth. He'd lived a carefree life for himself, to spit in the face of the life they'd been determined for him to live.

She gave him a small, mirthless, and almost pitying smile. "Ah, but that isn't altogether true," she said gently. "Otherwise, you wouldn't have agreed to the match in the first place."

Color fired his cheeks and gave Charles his first blush from a lady in . . . in . . . well . . . *ever.* She was right. "I was a boy."

"Precisely," she jumped in, snatching his defense, stealing it for her own purposes. "Our family's history and friendship is deeply entangled, and I trust, therefore, that you have concerns on that score as well." She made a lot of assumptions this day, his betrothed did. His almost-former-betrothed. "My father will make it abundantly clear when he speaks to yours that the decision began with me." *Began with me* implied

Charles was of a like opinion. Again, those words didn't have the freeing effect they should. Instead, they left him oddly queasy. "Of course, there is the matter of the legal arrangement; however, I have taken the liberty of conducting meetings to review the formal contract."

He tried to imagine Emma Gately slipping about London, paying visits to various solicitors and posing inquiries about her—about their—betrothal. It didn't fit with her. It didn't fit with the passive creature he knew her to be. *How many other ways have you underestimated the young lady?* Charles forcibly silenced that jeering question in his mind. "You spoke to a . . . solicitor." And that rankled for all number of reasons. Not the least of which was she'd gone and discussed wanting to be rid of him with another fellow.

She nodded. "Several"—*that was another several fellows*—"to ensure a similar opinion, of course."

"Of course," he said dryly.

"After all, a person cannot rely upon just one legal opinion."

"What do you know of . . . legal opinions?" That question really wasn't relevant to the fact that she was asking to be released of their betrothal.

"Enough," she said vaguely, lifting her head in acknowledgment, and only further sowing the seeds of his intrigue.

He was learning in rapid order that she was . . . nothing like what he'd imagined. In command of herself and what she wanted. Capable of making a decision about the future she wanted for herself, when Charles himself hadn't been able to do so. Nay, she was . . . different, in every way.

The sun peeked over the horizon, casting a bright flash of light over the water, the gleam nearly blinding. She lifted her parasol and popped it open. "Based upon my research"—her research?—"the arrangement is not formally binding, and neither party, neither of us, need be concerned on the question of a breach-of-promise suit being raised, as that would require a valid betrothal."

"And ours was not valid?"

It was a question, and also one she apparently had the answer to.

She shook her head. "Promises of marriage when a member of the party is below the age of consent"—she paused—"which I was, *are* not valid." She was clearly winding down, that note of finality creeping back into her dulcet tones. Tones that conveyed she'd tired of this exchange . . . and him.

And it was . . . humbling.

To say the very least.

And it was also when he knew he wanted her in his life. And he was going to fight like hell to not only keep her but also convince her that they'd both been wrong about one another.

"The solicitors were all of the opinion that the contract was well executed, though, because of"—she gave him a look—"our *fathers*."

"Of course, our fathers," he said, holding her eyes.

They shared a commiserative look, their first bond forged, a kindred moment born out of the meddlers of their lives.

"And they were all of a like opinion on the archaism of an arrangement fashioned for mere children," she went on, putting a nail in the coffin of that brief connection.

"They don't know a damned thing," he snapped.

"Actually, they do. One was Mr. Duncan Eveleigh, famed for his defense of women, and even more noted for his work on the defense for Lathan Holman, rumored traitor." She eyed him like he'd sprung a second head. And mayhap he had, and the second head was also the one responsible for him fighting even now to keep her.

Not that snapping at the lady was going to do him any favors.

"I did not wish for it to come as a surprise to you," she explained. "Not that I expected you would care," she said, and the absolute absence of inflection somehow caused that cinch to tighten even more than had she met his indifference these past years with tears. "But it is a formal contract we were forced into, and as such, we should each be fully aware of the dissolution of those terms." Emma adjusted the frilly lace parasol at her shoulder. "I wish you all happiness you might have been otherwise prevented from finding because of our betrothal. Good day, Charles."

Charles.

It was the first time he should hear his name fall freely from her lips, and on this, a goodbye?

She stepped around him, and put two paces between them before he registered that to be the end of this discussion. Which hadn't really been a discussion.

"What if I don't wish to be set free?" he called after her.

The young lady missed a step, then jammed the tip of her parasol into the ground, righting herself. Turning back, Emma faced him. He could make nothing of her stoic features, nor of the gaze she moved purposefully over his face.

He crossed the remainder of the way to join her. "I asked, what if I do not wish to be free, or end"—he gestured a hand between them—"this?" Whatever *this* was. And whatever it was, it had become . . . so much more in this one exchange than in every other they had shared before now.

Emma's serious-as-always state moved over his face.

Then she laughed, the sound tinkling with a slight snort, unrestrained, when the lady had always been tightly laced. And the sight of her proud shoulders shaking under the force of her levity, of her cheeks flushing with added color, held him even more enraptured than the sight of her siren's mouth.

Had he ever heard her laugh? Before this? He searched his mind. Why hadn't he made her laugh? He made everyone laugh. But her? He'd not even managed to make her smile.

Because you never tried. And it is a little late, chum, to start trying now.

He knew that. Knowing, however, did not undo the sense that . . . if she left, and if they left it off with a severed betrothal, he'd somehow be missing . . . even more.

After the young lady's laughter had abated, she gave her head a rueful shake. "Good day, Lord Scarsdale. Thank you for the much appreciated levity." Emma rushed off, her strides long and as purposeful as any gent's, and not the mincing, tediously slow ones that society demanded of women.

By God, even her damned steps were intriguing. How had he failed to notice . . . any of it . . . before now?

When it was too late?

A pair of young ladies appeared in the distance, meeting Emma. One he recognized as her sister. The other lady proved unfamiliar to him.

He didn't even know . . . whom she called friends, and the truth of that hit him in the gut, like a fist-blow of evidence to his failings as her betrothed.

Charles watched on, an interloper amongst the supportive trio of friends and ladies united over his and Emma's breakup. He clenched and unclenched his hands at his sides.

The women spoke for several moments, with Emma periodically nodding.

It wasn't a slow or shaky nod that bespoke upset, but rather the vigorous shake of a woman so wholly at peace and in complete happiness at what had transpired this day. The trio fell into step, and with each one that carried her farther away, the pressure in his chest grew and grew, crushing, crippling.

He stilled as Emma tossed a look over her shoulder, glancing his way.

Charles froze, for even across the distance dividing them, he caught it.

Aside from wringing his first laugh from Emma Gately, he managed another first that day—she smiled. One of the young ladies flanking her said something, calling back her attention, and with that, she looked away . . . and continued on.

She'd smiled at him, after all.

And all it had taken was the end of their betrothal.

Chapter 1

London, England
Mayfair
1829

THE LONDONER

SCANDAL!

The Earl of Scarsdale and Miss Gately have severed their long betrothal. It is rumored society's most charming rogue and scoundrel broke it off, allowing the lady her dignity while maintaining his bachelor state!

M. FAIRPOINT

Charles Hayden, the Earl of Scarsdale, was under attack.

His household under siege.

Nor was it the first time the townhouse had been invaded.

But every time was terror-inducing.

And even more so when the assault upon his household came in the dead of night.

Heart pounding, Charles surged upright in his bed, and frantically blinking the sleep from his eyes, he looked around his darkened chambers. His gaze settled on the front of his rooms.

"I'm certain His Lordship . . ." His butler, Tomlinson, was giving it his usual great effort.

History, however, had proven there was only one inevitable outcome . . .

"Step aside, Tomlinson . . ."

. . . and that outcome never ended in Charles's favor.

"I have a meeting with my son . . ."

A meeting.

Was it really fair to call whatever this forced entry was "a meeting"?

Lectures. Debates. Arguments, yes. He'd had all those with his father, ad nauseum.

But discussions? Nay, never that. Since he'd entered the world, he'd suffered through some order or another, coming from the man now marching toward him.

The footfalls and voices grew closer and the servant's tone increasingly strident, elevated in what had come to be his way of preparing Charles as much as he could, for as much as he was able. "I trust His Lordship will be happy to meet you . . . when he has awakened for the morn—"

"This is a matter of urgency that will not wait."

Not, a matter that could not wait.

But rather, a matter that will not wait.

It was a slight but telltale distinction, belonging to a marquess who was unaccustomed to taking anything but what he wanted and expected as his due.

Scrubbing a hand over his face, the stubble on his cheeks scratching his palm, Charles sighed and swung his naked legs over the side of the bed. *Bloody hell.* It was too early for this.

The door, however, had yet to be breach—

"Step aside," his father bellowed.

The panel burst open with such force it slammed against the opposite wall. The marquess already had his cane up in anticipation, stopping the oak slab from connecting with his face when it bounced back toward him. "Charles," he greeted, as if it were any other social call a father might pay his son and not a storming of said son's household.

Wiping the sleep from his eyes, Charles donned a taunting grin. "Fath— Oh." *Bloody, bloody hell.* His father had brought reinforcements— diminutive in size but dominating in spirit . . . and wearing skirts.

"Charles," she said as she swept past her husband and laid siege to her son's chambers.

Charles cursed and scrambled to get himself under the covers. *"Mother?"* he croaked. This was certainly a new and even more ruthless tactic. And that was precisely why his father was a formidable foe.

He peeked out from around the edge of the blankets.

The marchioness smiled at Charles's butler. "Thank you for all your assistance, Tomlinson," she said, drawing off her gloves one at a time and handing them over to the servant. "If you would be so good as to have these left with my cloak."

Putty in her hands, Tomlinson went all soft-eyed. "Of course, my lady," the young servant said, and after sketching a deep bow, he headed for the exit.

"*Thank you,* Tomlinson." Charles called out that sarcasm-laden response loudly for his traitorous butler. "That will be all."

Tomlinson closed the door on the remainder of that droll reply.

The moment he'd gone, Charles's mother stalked forward. "You're drunk, aren't you? You're slurring your speech."

"It was a deliberate exaggeration," Charles said, and the closer his mother approached to him and his naked self, the deeper he inched under the blankets.

Alas, his mother ignored those assurances, looking to her husband. "He's drunk, isn't he?"

The marquess leaned over the head of his cane and shrugged. "He's always drunk."

"I am not drunk," Charles called, climbing all the way under the blankets. Not this time anyway. "Though receiving a visit from both my mother and father in the middle of the night, I rather wish I was."

"He's making a jest, isn't he, Aster? That was a jest, wasn't it?"

"Indeed it was, dear." She paused. "And a poor one at that, Charles," she said, though it wasn't clear whether the disapproval in her tone was a product of his supposed weak attempt at humor or the fact that he was also supposedly drunk.

There came the groan of a floorboard and the rustle of fabric.

His father instantly yanked the covers aside and tossed them to the floor.

Charles squeaked. What special hell was this? "Good God, man, have a care," he sputtered, grabbing a pillow and holding it protectively to himself, all the while avoiding his mother's gaze. He tipped his head pointedly in her direction.

"Why are you tilting your head like that?" his clueless-as-always father demanded. "Have you gone and injured your fool neck while you were drunk?"

"Oh, for the love of all that is holy, I'm not drunk, and I'm motioning to Mother." Abandoning his efforts there, Charles looked once more to the only parent who did not require everything be spelled out in terms of emotions, sentiments, or intentions. "If you would, please, Mother?" Lying down as he was, with his parents both hovering around his bed, certainly robbed Charles of any real authority when he spoke.

"Please, what?" she drawled, and from the corner of his eye, he caught the way she folded her arms at her chest and stuck out a foot, indicating in every way that she had no intention of taking herself off that easy. Or letting him off that easy, either.

She'd really make him spell it out? "Would you please excuse us? Given my current"—heat exploded in his cheeks, and he glanced pointedly at the feather pillow across his person—"circumstances?"

"Naked," she said bluntly. "*Those* are your circumstances, and secondly, that man, as you referred to him, is, in fact, your father, and I am your mother. And I assure you, I've seen everything there is to see where a man is concerned. Including your *once* very small bits, and—"

Grabbing for another pillow, Charles promptly dragged it over his head, muffling the remainder of those words. Alas, it was too late. The words his mother had uttered couldn't be unheard. They would dwell forever in his ears, as rotten as poison. "Very well. Would you *both* allow me a moment to dress myself? Then I promise we can speak about"—refusing to relinquish his hold on his pillows, he settled for shifting his head back and forth between them—"whatever this is?"

His father's eyebrows dipped. "Whatever . . . this is?"

Alas, Charles had said the wrong thing. Because he was apparently supposed to know just whatever calamity had resulted in his parents barging into his chambers at this ungodly hour.

With a sound of disgust, the marquess slashed a hand through the air and stalked off, as if he'd quit his son completely. But then he began to pace. "Tell him, Aster." And Charles rather wished the pair of them had quit him.

Alas . . .

His mother drew in a deep, heavy breath, then pressed her fingertips to her lips, shaking her head, not getting the words out. And for the first time since they'd stormed his household, he registered the drawn lines at the corners of the marchioness's eyes. Creases that revealed her worry. His mother, who wasn't given to histrionics and who didn't bluster and overreact.

Panic grew in his chest. Grabbing the blanket, he drew it over his legs. "Mother?" he asked, sitting upright, as there came the first real stirrings of dread. "What is it?"

Whatever it was that had brought them here was surely—

"Your brother has not seen Morgan or Pierce this week." That announcement exploded from her lips, and her shoulders sagged.

Emma's brothers? That was what this was about? Charles puzzled his brow.

Because of . . . that? He stared at them. This was why they'd roused him from his rest and visited this misery upon him? He waited for her to add something more than that. *"Annd?"* he asked when it became apparent she had no intention of doing so and he couldn't even begin to fathom why he was at the heart of this latest disappointment.

"And they are best friends." His mother released a sigh. "Surely that must matter to you. Why, imagine if you weren't speaking with St. John or Landon. *Hmm?"*

"If I weren't speaking to St. John or Landon, then you have my express permission to never do something as bothersome as darken Derek's door in the dead of night."

His father sputtered. "Why— Why . . ."

His mother held a hand aloft, quelling the tirade her husband couldn't get out. "And furthermore, what is this nonsense about the dead of night? *Hmm?* Charles Christopher Ashton Hayden, it is seven o'clock."

"Seven o'clock is an unholy hour for a soul to be up," Charles insisted.

"Especially when one was getting oneself completely foxed the night before, eh, boy?" his father said, looking him up and down disapprovingly.

Fortunately, he'd grown well accustomed to his father's disappointment. And yet . . . his father had welcomed that deficit in Charles's character when it served him. When it had served the family. Now, he'd expect Charles to simply . . . cease being what he and the world expected him to be. Nay, what his father had once needed him to be. "This is the problem right here," his father said, shaking a finger Charles's way.

Charles slumped on the mattress and covered his eyes with a hand. It was coming. In fairness, however, the marquess had waited a good deal longer for the customary lecture than he usually did during their visits.

"He's a rogue."

"I thought you appreciated my being a rogue?" Charles drawled.

Color suffused his father's cheeks at the reminder Charles leveled there, the one neither of them spoke about anymore because of the hint of risk that could come should anyone, absolutely anyone, overhear and learn . . .

The marquess quickly found himself. "When you were a lad of twenty-three. I didn't expect the charade to become real and for it to drag on for years and years beyond that. Now that you've lost Emma, you *must* take on a more proper role to make a good match. Why, you're past an age when most gentlemen wed."

Ah, so *that's* what this was about. Making himself respectable now, so he could find a wife.

"It no longer suits you for me to be a scoundrel, so I am to shift course to 'proper gent'?"

"Charles," his mother said admonishingly.

Yes, it was an unfair blow to level, given Charles had willingly taken on that persona for the end it had served. "Either way," he said, frustration creeping into his tone, "I'm not a scoundrel. I don't drink and wager . . . nearly as much as I once did," he added in fairness.

"My, how . . . honorable." His mother gave him a sad look that was somehow worse than the marquess's blatant condemnation.

Charles felt his cheeks heat with a blush. "I'm merely saying when compared with other gentlemen, my actions are not outrageously wicked."

"Not outrageously wicked," his father muttered to himself. "Is it a wonder she ended it?"

Charles winced.

Clapping once, his mother held up her hands between them. "Gentlemen, that is enough. We have *not* come to discuss the state of your betrothal."

His broken betrothal.

"You haven't?" he asked incredulously.

"No," his parents responded at the same time, suspiciously in lockstep.

"Well, *that*, then, is certainly unexpected," Charles muttered under his breath.

"We are here because Lord and Lady Featherstone have failed to invite us to a dinner party, Charles," she continued over him.

"And?" he prodded when it became apparent neither intended to say more. That this was it. The offense.

Both of his parents looked pointedly at him.

"And you know we've never not invited one another to one's events. They are our best friends."

"Or they were"—his father glared Charles's way—"before you went and made a blunder of *that*."

"Surely you aren't . . . suggesting *I'm* at fault?" he choked out.

The marquess and marchioness struck a like pose, folding their arms and sticking out an opposite foot and eyeing Charles from under arched eyebrows, their silence serving as his answer.

So they *were* suggesting he was to blame. "Well, that is as unfounded as it is preposterous." He gritted his teeth. "Whatever upset you might have with me, I am not the one who broke it off with Miss Gately." They could be upset with him for overindulging and wagering and for the company he kept, but this? "Take your upset to the Gately household, and perhaps you'll get yourself somewhere."

His mother looked at Charles for a long moment before speaking. "Jared?"

The marquess promptly headed for the door and let himself out.

"You really should teach me the skill of dispatching Father," Charles said when he and his mother were alone. "It would prove ever most useful."

Her expression was unwavering, revealing none of her usual warmth. "As much as I always enjoy your levity and jests, this is not one of those moments."

Bloody hell. He'd never been able to close his damned mouth. It was the curse of his existence.

Amongst a lengthy list of many.

Coming over, she seated herself on the edge of his bed. "I'm not happy about . . . a lot of this."

He tensed his mouth.

"And wipe that petulant look from your face," she chastised. "This instant. I'm not here to lecture you upon your drinking and womanizing." His ears went hot. "Or wagering. Though I'd be well within my motherly rights, were I to do so."

Charles sighed. "Very well. What is it?"

"I want the situation with the Gatelys resolved."

He swallowed back a curse. "I cannot marry someone who doesn't wish to marry me, Mother." That rejection, Emma's rejection, chafed still. Because he'd not appreciated what he might have had . . . until he'd lost it.

His mother angled herself on the bed so she was facing him more directly. "I'm not asking you to marry Emma. Not any longer. That proverbial swan has soared."

"More swan analogies?"

"*Always* swan analogies," she corrected.

Well, they made even less sense now than when he'd been a boy of sixteen about to make the matrimonial march to his child bride.

"You owed the viscount a discussion"—she raised her voice slightly, edging him out of a place to speak when he attempted to do so— "indicating that you cared about the arrangement and that you have regrets for how it turned out." Her lips pulled in a grimace. "Or rather, how it did not turn out. That you recognize your fault, and that you value our family's relationship with his." She hesitated. "That is, if you indeed feel those things?"

"Of course I do." He may have always resented being betrothed as a boy to Featherstone's young daughter, but Charles had also always seen the older gentleman as a second father of sorts.

Her shoulders sagged slightly. "That is reassuring, as I did not believe I had raised a son who was indifferent to such bonds."

"However," Charles went on, "neither do I believe it will serve any good for me to speak to h—"

"It will."

Charles ran his hands over his face. She'd have him pay a visit to the viscount and take complete ownership of his and Emma's failed betrothal? So much for the lady's assumptions that none would hold Charles at fault. "I thought a mother's loyalty was to her son."

"It was. That was before you went and broke me and Alice Featherstone apart. If you learn nothing in your life, Charles, know this: women shall not tolerate any man who comes between them."

"And I take it that rule also applies to one's own child?" he asked dryly.

"Is one's own child a man?" She didn't wait for him to answer. "Then yes. I would say, especially one's son." With that, she stood. "Fix it, Charles," she said. "Fix your reputation. Restore your image. Make yourself the respectable man I know you can be." She started for the door. "Just fix it," she repeated, not even glancing back. She swept out and closed the door firmly behind her.

Fix it.

As in make peace enough between his and Emma's families so that their parents and brothers could all resume their friendships, and he could set to work reforming himself and improving his reputation.

Perhaps it wouldn't be so very difficult, after all. With that in mind, Charles dashed off a quick note, then rang for his footman.

The young servant arrived almost instantly. "My lord?"

"See that this is delivered posthaste to the viscount," he asked, folding the note and handing it over to Wickham's care.

Then heading back to his bed, Charles burrowed into his mattress. It was done.

Chapter 2

THE LONDONER

SHAMEFUL!

After finding herself jilted, a bitter Miss Gately Is determined to bring that same suffering to other ladies of
the Marriage Mart . . . encouraging rebellion and dis-
avowing marriage.

M. FAIRPOINT

Two months ago, Miss Emma Gately had paid a visit to three scandalous ladies on Waverton Street, living on their own.

From Emma's visit had sprung the Mismatch Society, a group of
young women who met twice weekly for one purpose and one purpose
only: asserting themselves in a man's world and giving nothing to those
lords they'd been expected to wed . . . no matter how unhappy they
were.

This morn, however, seated in her family's Mayfair residence,
Emma headed up an altogether different meeting.

Her younger sister, Isla; Emma's best friend, Lady Olivia; and Emma's identical twin older brothers sat in a circle around a tray of refreshments that a maid had brought in some twenty minutes earlier.

Morgan, older than Emma by two years, and than his twin by an hour, was the first to move. Leaning forward, he reached for a chocolate biscuit from the tray.

Isla shot out a foot, catching him square in the shins, wringing a gasp from him and knocking the biscuit to the floor. The confectionery treat rained sprinkles of sugar and chocolate forlornly as it went before landing with a plop atop Morgan's boot.

"Whatever was *that* for?" he demanded.

Isla glared. "Because we are focusing, Morgan."

"And you think a man can't focus while indulging in a biscuit?" he shot back.

"Actually, I don't think a man can focus on anything, biscuit or not, which is why I thought it was a bad idea to have either of you"—Isla nudged a chin between the twins—"here."

At her side, Emma's best friend didn't even attempt to hide her smile.

Pierce bristled. "I resent that. *I'm* not the one indulging in biscuits."

Morgan tossed up his arms in exasperation. "Then why even have the damned tray if we weren't supposed to be eating from it?"

Isla sighed. "You really are bad at this, aren't you?" She looked to the other women present. "He really is terrible at this, isn't he? Let me explain, dear brother; it is for show. When there is a gathering of guests, they have refreshments, and it signifies a casual gathering."

Morgan stared blankly at her. "And when there are no refreshments?"

"Why, then we are discussing business and everyone knows it," the youngest Gately explained in tired tones. She followed up that pitying response with an equally pitying pat on his knee.

"Well, I don't believe that makes much sense," he said, eyeing the tray covetously before ultimately sitting back in his chair and giving up all attempts at one of those treats. "Any sense," he added under his breath.

Isla smirked. "Nor do I expect it to."

Morgan tossed a pillow across the rose-inlaid refreshment table, which Emma intercepted. Catching the frilly lace article to her chest, she set it down in the empty space beside her.

"Might I suggest we return to the matter at hand," she said firmly.

All assembled looked her way.

Emma pressed her fingers together, steepling and unsteepling them, then stopped. "Something is amiss."

Morgan was the first to respond . . . or he attempted to anyway. "What is—?"

"She's referring to Mother's and Father's persistence with Scarsdale." Pierce took mercy on Morgan, sparing him from asking the remainder of that question and earning more of Isla's ire.

"Scarsdale." Morgan spat the name like it was the vitriolic curse it had become in the household.

"Yes," Emma murmured. *"Scarsdale."* The name of the man she'd been betrothed to as a child, who'd become a rogue, living quite happily for himself, while she waited on the sidelines. Until she'd tired of it and cut him loose. Or free. One would have thought he saw it as the latter. Alas, he'd never been agreeable in any way. Even in this, their breakup.

Pierce sat up straighter in his seat. "I thought he gave up."

Isla frowned. "Did he even try to fight for Emma?"

The absolute lack of inflection from her sister proved all the worse.

Morgan tossed the other throw pillow, taking a wider arc around Emma, to catch Isla directly in the side of her head with that soft, feather-stuffed missile. "And I'm the problematic sibling? I wouldn't go about tossing salt in the wounds of our sister."

Emma shifted in her seat. "I wouldn't say it was salt in the wounds." She knew her siblings all meant well, but God, how she hated that all society, her family included, took her as a hurt and wounded woman. She had been. But long, long ago, before the betrothal had ended.

Isla whipped her gaze toward Emma. "Forgive me. I didn't mean to s-suggest . . . I wasn't saying—"

"No, no. It is fine," Emma assured. "You aren't wrong." Isla stuck out her tongue at Morgan. "Quite the opposite. You are entirely correct." After all, "gave up" implied Lord Charles Scarsdale had attempted to keep her. Which he hadn't. Not. Even. Close. What he had done was go to her father and make an appeal to . . . what? Move forward with a marriage he'd certainly never wanted and one that she had . . . She shoved aside the young, naive thoughts she'd once carried and returned to the matter at hand. "More importantly, however, I do not believe Father has relented on the prospect of . . . a match between us."

Already identical, the Gately brothers' features now also formed matching scowls. Isla might have questioned why Emma had decided to include their brothers in the matter of Scarsdale and her parents, but the truth was, there wasn't a more loyal pair than Morgan and Pierce.

"Fathers," Olivia spat. "They are terrible, too."

"Yes, well, fathers are still men," Isla pointed out.

"This is true," Olivia agreed.

Pierce, the more easygoing of the twins, turned a frown on her. "I take offense to that."

Morgan nodded hard. "As do I."

Pierce snorted. "You shouldn't. Everyone knows you are of a terrible sort." He glanced at Olivia and winked. "I, however—"

Olivia laughed. "Very well. With the exception of my brother Owen; Pierce; and on some occasions, Morgan, every *other* man is terrible."

"Thank you." Morgan scrunched up his brow. "I . . . *think?*"

It was the closest Olivia had ever come, and likely would ever come, to a compliment of the male species. The forgotten daughter of a Waterloo general who'd been titled for his bravery, Olivia had been largely ignored by her father. Her eldest brother, traveling as he did, had proven almost as invisible. Even Owen, the youngest of her brothers, as loving as he was, had been consumed by his work as a barrister.

Morgan brought them back to the topic at hand. "What has Papa said now?"

Emma drew in a breath. "Nothing."

The gathering of four spoke as one. "Nothing?"

She confirmed that question with a nod. "Nothing," she repeated. Emma came to her feet, and began to pace. "It has been seven days. An entire week. There have been no summons. No notes sent to my room. Not even angry looks at mealtimes."

"And this is a problem?" Pierce asked, sounding as befuddled as Morgan looked.

Isla sighed. "Of course it is a problem."

The twins looked at one another, then back to Isla.

"I'll help," Olivia said, sitting forward. "It means something is amiss. It means they have been plotting, and are intending to one day soon corner your sister and maneuver her into marriage"—fury sparked in Olivia's eyes—"with that . . . with that . . ."

"Scoundrel," Pierce supplied with all the resentment only a brother could manage.

"Cad," Isla suggested.

"Sard," Morgan muttered, earning shocked gasps from Olivia and Isla. Emma laughed for the first time that day, even as Pierce leaned over and slapped their brother on the back of the head.

Morgan flinched, glared at his twin. *"Oww,"* he cried, rubbing his injury. "What the h—*Oww?"*

Pierce looked pointedly among the three ladies. "You do not say that in front of . . . in front of . . . them," he whispered, as if the "them" in question weren't in fact watching on with equal interest and amusement.

Emma rolled her eyes. Yes, because heaven forbid a lady should hear a curse that referenced sexual relations. Even a word as old as the medieval one her brother had uttered.

"Well, I would rather think that three founding members of a women's society formed to break down marriage and advocate for an equal place in the world would appreciate our speaking to them as we would any other fellow."

Precisely. "I do," Emma assured him, and patted him on the knee. "Very much so."

"As do I," Isla muttered, sounding pained to have to make such an admission about the brother she always butted heads with.

"Oh, you shan't find me taking umbrage with naughty words, either," Olivia confirmed.

If Emma had been in possession of the gavel used to call to order the Mismatch Society, this would have been the perfect time and place to use it. Alas, she may have been the one who'd led to the formation of the society, but her skill set was certainly not keeping order of a group. Nevertheless, given the direness of her situation, focus was certainly required. "Now that we've settled the matter of *how* we might refer to Scarsdale, can we return to the situation of my parents?"

"I'm still not sure why you would assume something must be amiss. Perhaps they have simply moved on . . . accepted your decision"— Pierce waved a hand at Emma—"and all that."

"Unlikely," Emma said, already shaking her head.

Olivia raised her hand. "I agree."

"Two people who were so determined to see their daughter married to a particular man that they were willing to betroth her at the age of six are hardly ones to go about abandoning the prospect of that match," Emma explained for her brothers' benefit.

"It is true," Olivia agreed. Reaching over, she gathered a pretty porcelain plate and filled it with several biscuits.

"Wait . . . I am confused," Morgan began slowly, eyeing Olivia. "So now is an appropriate time for pastries?"

Pierce swiped his hands over his face. "Bloody hell, Morgan. Would you let it go with the biscuits?"

"I am just pointing out—"

"That our parents are scheming," Emma quickly interjected. "Yes, I believe you are correct, Morgan." Just like that she neatly massaged his ego and distracted him from his impending quarrel with Pierce, and kept the group back on the topic of Scarsdale. Or more specifically, her life and her happiness.

Perhaps she wasn't so very bad at this, after all.

"Mama and Papa have grown decidedly less combative," Isla remarked.

A series of assenting murmurs rolled around the room. In this, even Emma could not disagree.

Emma chewed at the tip of an already jagged fingernail. And yet she still didn't trust that her parents had relented. For several simple reasons. She didn't trust her parents. She didn't trust Scarsdale's parents. She didn't trust Scarsdale.

In fact, she didn't trust anything connected in any way with the name Scarsdale.

"I don't trust it," Emma finally said with a shake of her head. "There is no way they intend to end their lectures." Not when, according to her older brothers, their mother had hired nursemaids with the task of teaching Emma as a babe to speak the name Scarsdale as her first word.

The springs of the upholstered sofa squeaked, and the floorboards squealed, as Pierce made his way over. He dropped an arm around her shoulders. "Mayhap they've finally seen the way," he said gently. "Perhaps you're free."

"And then that would mean you're free to go back to idol-worshipping him." Isla sniggered.

Pierce blushed.

Yes, because everyone knew Pierce and Morgan had always adored the most popular lord in London. There hadn't been anyone Charles couldn't win over. Including any number of women whom he'd carried on with over the years . . . one of whom had given him a child. Emma clenched her hands, hating that the truth of that hurt still.

A knock sounded at the door, and Tess, a young parlormaid, ducked into the room. "The viscount and viscountess have requested your presence, Miss Emma."

Pierce dropped his arm. "Or perhaps they've not seen the way."

Bloody hell. "I knew it!" Emma exclaimed, jabbing a finger around the nonbelievers of the quartet; all but Olivia had not seen. "I told you all!" And here her siblings had believed she was searching for something in nothing.

"Certainly not a matter you should have wanted to be correct on," Olivia muttered.

Indignant, Emma let her arm fall to her side. "I didn't *want* to be." Far from it. In fact, if she never had to converse with her parents on the matter of Charles again, the happier she would be for it.

Isla gave her a look, and Emma folded her arms. "What? I *didn't*."

"Of course you didn't," Morgan said dryly, as the eldest twin and Isla likely found the first time they'd concurred in all of the younger woman's life. "You were just gloating for no reason."

Tess cleared her throat.

They looked to the young woman.

"Please, tell them I'll be along shortly," Emma said.

The young girl's shoulders sagged with a palpable relief, and she rushed off.

The moment she'd gone, Emma stood and began to pace. Yes, given Emma's role with Mismatch Society people, both servants and members of the peerage had begun to look at her as though she were now unpredictable, and in ways she never had been. Nor, for that matter, were they incorrect. Not entirely anyway. Society had a tendency to never look beneath the surface. They'd seen Emma and seen a dutiful and proper daughter. As such, the world had clearly come to underestimate her. Her parents included.

Her former betrothed especially.

And as one who had been underestimated, she well knew to not make that same mistake, certainly not where her mother and father were concerned.

"You can always ignore them," her sister volunteered.

"Yes," she murmured, tapping a finger against her chin. "I *could*." But then they'd seek her out . . . wherever she happened to be, and she'd come to find she rather appreciated being in control of the situation . . . where she could, of course.

"I could always shoot him?" Morgan piped in. Several creases lined his high brow. "That is, not Father. *Scarsdale*."

"That is . . . sweet of you." Emma flashed him a wan smile, touched by that show of support . . . , even if it was a rather morbid one. "Thank you for that offer, but I must decline."

"Well, it stands whenever you— *Oww!*"

Pierce slapped his older brother in the back of the head once more. "And leave me as the heir?" Emma's lips twitched. Most younger brothers would have been resentful at finding themselves the spare—especially by no more than fifty-five minutes. However, that had never been the case between Morgan and Pierce.

Morgan scowled, rubbing at that injured-for-a-second-time spot. "Bloody hell, Pierce. What kind of brotherly disloyalty is that? And for your twin, no less? Suggesting I would perish?"

"In a duel? Against Scarsdale? You would," Pierce said flatly. "Absolutely you would." He shot Isla a glance, looking to her for support.

Isla lifted her palms and shook her head. "You're on your own, Pierce."

"Fine. You're a terrible shot, and he's a great one, and—"

Emma slid herself between them, breaking up what was quickly escalating. "There is nothing else to do but face them." She brought back her shoulders. "And reiterate one more time that I will no sooner wed the Earl of Scarsdale than I would . . . than I would . . . Titus Oates," she exclaimed.

Her brothers shared a puzzled look.

"He was the dastardly English priest who fabricated the Popish Plot," Olivia explained.

"Ahh," the twins said in unison.

Morgan shook his head. "Why would you want to marry such a fellow?"

Isla let out a sigh. "She wouldn't, Morgan. That is the point. She's likening Scarsdale to Oates. Two villains."

Understanding dawned once more at the same time for the brothers. *"Ahh."*

And if she weren't moments away from facing off, yet again, against her single-minded parents, Emma would have managed a laugh. As it was, she needed all her wits about her. Angling up her chin, and her neck straight and her back even straighter, Emma marched for the door, the raucous applause from her quartet of supporters fueling her steps and firming her resolve.

Enough was enough.

She had been more than patient with her parents' interference . . . an interference that stretched back more than seventeen years, to when she'd been a girl and they'd been crafting her future. Without so much as a consideration given to what she wanted. Or didn't want. Without a thought that she should have a say in deciding which gentleman she might—or might not—wed.

It ended here.

This day.

Now.

Emma reached her father's office and, in one fluid movement, let herself in. Measuring her steps and pacing her stride, lest they take her as too emotional, she headed over to where her father sat at the front of the room. More than a foot taller than his wife, and seated at the head of the desk, that was where all pretense of power ended. Her mother, stationed in a thronelike chair to the right of him like some manner of aide to the king, had always been the one calling the proverbial shots.

As far back as Emma could remember, whatever the reason for her summons, be it daydreaming in her lessons or the biscuits she'd been filching in the kitchens, they'd always presented a unified front in every way, but it had been unfailingly clear who ultimately guided all decision-making.

"Mother," she greeted when she reached one of the giltwood side chairs opposite them. "Father." She didn't bother waiting for an invitation, but rather seated herself in one of the deucedly uncomfortable chairs. No one, absolutely no one, would ever convince her the decor option wasn't by design, a bid to distract or keep at a disadvantage whoever was across from them.

Well, not this day.

"Mother? Father?" her father demanded of his wife.

"I'll handle this, dear," the viscountess promised, patting his enormous hand. She turned a full frown on Emma. "We do not like your tone. 'Mothering' and 'Fathering' us. You do that when you're upset."

Emma, however, wasn't in a "Mama" and "Papa" affectionate frame of mind. She hadn't been for some time now.

"You wished to see me," Emma said. The last thing she intended was to allow them to distract her with their hurt feelings at being called by the proper "Mother" and "Father." "Nor do I believe my summons has anything to do with what I refer to you as."

Her mother's eyebrows met her hairline.

When issued a summons, none dared to challenge the viscountess. Emma pressed her advantage of the distinguished viscountess's shock.

"Before you say whatever it is this time about my betrothal—" She grimaced. Nay, that wasn't correct. That would merely fuel their relentless hope. "That is, my former betrothal. I have something I would like to say." A very lot of somethings. And she'd been organizing them in her mind for years and years, and the moment had finally come to speak her truth. "In the matter of Lord Scarsdale—"

"The marriage is not to be."

That statement from her mother brought Emma up short. She quickly righted herself, nodding. "Yes, precisely. E-exactly." Well, that was hardly satisfying . . . having her speech correctly predicted. She hurried to right herself. "That is precisely what I came here to say. He—"

"Scarsdale is *not* the man we believed he was, Emie," the viscount stated in such angry tones it took a moment to register what he said.

At five inches past six feet and some twenty stone, her father had always had the look and sound of a bear when he was upset. For two months that bellicose grumbling had been directed her way. Until now. This time, in the matter of her broken betrothal to Scarsdale, his disappointment was in fact directed not at her but at . . . Charles?

Emma opened her mouth, but promptly closed it, not even bothering to attempt for words that were not there. For . . . this was certainly not what she'd been expecting. Every carefully crafted argument as to why she'd never wed Charles—and every incisive arrow she'd intended to level about their regard for the gentleman—fell, useless.

Husband and wife reached for one another's hands, and clasped their fingers in that familiar, affectionate way. All the while, they continued to stare back at Emma. As she stared back at them.

Catching the underside of her chair, she inched the rickety seat over. "Come again?"

"Come *where* again?" her father asked perplexedly, very much Morgan and Pierce's sire. "We've not gone anywhere."

"You are telling me you see that Scarsdale is a scoundrel and that you no longer expect me to marry him?" she asked bluntly.

Her parents nodded, the gestures remarkably synchronized.

"I believe you have that right," her mother answered for the pair. "However, we've not used those exact words, per se."

"'Scoundrel' is rather harsh, Emie," her father said with a weighty disapproval in his deep, rumbling voice.

Now, this was what she had expected.

Emma folded her arms at her chest. "What would you call a gentleman who has kept on with any number of mistresses?" Including the notorious Misses Lee and Linden, two women he'd carried on with and been linked to over the years. "And who also had a child with one of his mistresses while being betrothed?" she asked, deadpan. A child he'd, at the time, not even allowed Emma, his future wife, to meet.

A blush filled her father's cheeks, and yanking a kerchief from his jacket pocket, he dabbed at his brow.

Her mother patted his hand, and murmured something that sounded very much like "I'll handle this, dear." Yes, because that was ultimately the way of the adoring couple's marriage: Emma's mother handled . . . just about everything, making decisions like some military general, her husband the answering footman who'd be sent to battle with her instructions guiding him.

"Now, the fact remains he is your father's godson, and there is and always will be a bond there."

"Apparently bonds to godsons are deeper than those to daughters," she muttered under her breath. "If that isn't the patriarchy, I don't know what is."

Her words were immediately met with such a wounded expression from her father Emma almost felt bad. Almost. There was still the matter of Papa's continued relationship with not only Charles's parents . . . but also Charles himself.

"I am sorry if you've felt less than supported," her father murmured. "That brings us to the reason for our meeting."

Emma dragged her chair all the way over until her knees brushed the front of the oak desk. Surely there was more at play here? "All right. Out with it, then?"

"Your Mismatch Society," her mother began slowly. "There has been increasing focus and interest in your society."

Emma's father, however, couldn't control himself anymore. "You are creating a scandal, and it is just that we want to be sure your involvement in this organization is . . . worth the attention. That it is something you truly want to do."

Emma looked between her parents and weighed her response. That was what this was about, then? They had relented on the matter of Charles. A lightness filled her, coming from the sense of freedom that brought. But there was also something more—determination. She'd tired long ago of being "poor Emma," and if she failed in this endeavor? Then she would be an object of pity and gossip once more, a pathetic figure to be talked about. "I appreciate your concern, and also your support. However, there is nothing else I want to do or be doing."

Her parents exchanged a look. Her father appeared as though he wanted to say more, but Emma caught the tight little nod her mother gave him.

"Now, is there anything else?" Emma asked, taking control of the remainder of this exchange.

"That is all." Her mother inclined her head.

Still, as Emma made the march across the room, she braced for them to call her back.

A lifetime of knowing these people gave her reason enough to be . . . suspicious.

And yet . . . she reached the corridor, and there were no attempts to summon her back.

The moment she reached the parlor, four sets of eyes immediately swung Emma's way.

Standing at the window, with his mouth stuffed with chocolate biscuit, Morgan hurriedly swallowed it down. "Well?" he demanded.

"It was a disaster," Pierce predicted, always the more cynical and skeptical of the twins.

Emma ventured deeper into the parlor. "Quite the opposite," she said, joining the group at the center of the room. "Mama and Papa merely wished to speak with me about the Mismatch Society."

Her loyal contingency exchanged looks.

Pierce snorted. "You're telling us that meeting had nothing to do with Scarsdale?" He answered his own question. "Unlikely." With that he grabbed himself a treat from the dessert tray, and headed over to where Morgan stood at the window, watching the passersby beyond those silk damask curtains.

She snapped her fingers in her brothers' direction. "I beg your pardon. I'll have you know they finally acknowledged that Scarsdale is a . . ." Not a scoundrel. Emma set her jaw. Her parents had not committed to language that strong.

The twins *would* choose that moment to direct all their attention back her way.

"That he's . . . ," Olivia gently prodded.

"No longer a suitable match for me," Emma substituted. And when there was still only silence, she turned to the greatest source a woman could for support: her best friend and sister. "They are done with him." Just as she was.

So, it would seem, was her brother.

"Oh, I find that hard to believe," Pierce drawled from his spot at the window.

She raised her chin a fraction. "And just what makes you say that?"

"Because Scarsdale is here . . ."

Her heart forgot its function of beating. It wasn't unusual for him to arrive. He'd done so with a regularity . . . since she'd broken off their betrothal.

". . . with his father and brother, this time," Pierce was saying.

"Indeed?" Morgan angled his head, looking out for his Eton and Oxford chum, and closest childhood friend. "Wasn't expecting Derek."

"Oh, would you stop," Pierce muttered. "He's not here for you. It is obvious why he's here. Scarsdale's come with reinforcements this time."

Emma sprinted across the room, yanking her brothers by the backs of their jackets, forcing them off to the side and out of view. She peeked around the edge of the green silk curtain, and angled her gaze down, bypassing the white-haired gentleman and dark-haired fellow in favor of just one . . . and her heart did a silly leap, for an altogether different reason. Several inches past six feet, in possession of a frame that showed off his love of riding and boxing, he was everything unlike the padded, soft fellows of Polite Society. The sun glinted off golden strands a fraction long enough to flirt with respectability. His jaw square. His cheeks chiseled. His nose a perfect slab of aquiline flesh. He was entirely more handsome than any man had a right to be. Emma tightened her mouth. Yes, he might be more beautiful than Apollo himself, but beauty didn't erase all the many flaws that made him the absolute last man she'd ever tie herself to. "It doesn't matter that he's arrived," she whispered furiously, as Barley drew open the panels to greet the earl.

The old butler said something, his back to them as it was, so there was no hope Emma could make out anything of what the servant was saying.

She squinted. *Wait a moment . . . ?* Emma pressed her forehead to the lead windowpane.

"He is smiling." A crooked grin that dimpled just one cheek curved Charles's perfectly formed lips. "Why is he smiling?" Emma whispered, ignoring the glance Olivia and her siblings shared. "Either way. It does not matter. Papa has ordered him—"

Barley nodded vigorously, and gestured with his hand.

Emma's eyebrows went flying up.

"Inside?" Morgan drawled.

"I expect it is only because the marquess and Lord Derek are with him," Olivia said unconvincingly. "He cannot go about sending his and Morgan's closest friends away. However, I should expect he would send Scarsdale away."

Yes, one should expect.

Emma gritted her teeth.

"Should" being the operative word.

Flipping his Oxonian hat back and forth between his hands like a damned master juggler, Charles took a step forward, then stopped. He glanced up.

Curses and gasps went up from the lot around Emma. Not Emma, however. She remained rooted to her spot. Yes, he'd caught her spying, but she'd be damned if she looked away.

His grin widened, and then he bowed his head.

"As if it is a bloody social call," she said to herself.

And then he followed Barley, disappearing . . . within her house.

Silence fell once more.

More tense. More tangible.

Emma released her hold on the corner of the curtain.

Pierce cleared his throat. "Well, I think *that* is what makes it safe to say Father has not relented."

Chapter 3

THE LONDONER

FRIENDSHIPS ABOUND

The Earl of Scarsdale has never met a person he couldn't charm, and that includes the Viscount Featherstone.

M. FAIRPOINT

Charles had known since he was a boy that he'd no wish, interest, or even curiosity in the woman his parents had betrothed him to as a babe.

It hadn't been until he was a grown man, watching her walk away, that he'd realized what a damned fool he'd been.

That did not mean, however, he'd given up all hope of wooing her back.

Charles let his cue fly, and cracked the balls upon the billiards table.

"Well done, Charles. Well done," Emma's father, the Viscount Featherstone, boomed, slapping him hard between the shoulder blades with an enormous hand that managed to shake even Charles. But then, the viscount was a mountain of a man . . . which made it rather fortuitous that he didn't want to separate Charles from any of his limbs for the broken betrothal. "Better than your father, you are. Not that that is much of a recommendation, eh, Jared," he jested, nudging the marquess beside him.

Both men jostled one another the way two jocular youths at Oxford might.

Charles's younger brother, Derek, slid into position beside him, and made a show of studying the billiards table. "*This* is how you've been spending your time," Derek said from the corner of his mouth. "Joining the older set for ribbing and billiards? You really are dicked in the nob since Emma Gately's defection."

Charles bristled. "What is *that* supposed to mean?"

"It means that there is no way you'd be here if it didn't in some way have something to do with your former betrothed."

The father to the lady in question came close to consider the placement of his last shot before continuing on.

Former betrothed.

Charles picked up his glass and stared briefly into the contents.

In the first weeks following their Hyde Park meeting, he'd not been able to even think those words without needing the help of a bottle to drown them out. Given he was driven to merely sipping from a modest snifter felt an improvement, indeed.

He and Derek remained silent, with Charles not again speaking until the marquess had taken up a place closer to the viscount. "Is it really so hard to believe that my being here has *nothing* to do with Emma?"

"Yes," his brother said bluntly. "In fact, I'd wager the only reason you're here is because of Miss Gately."

His brother was only partially right. Charles's daily calls to Emma's father had begun because of her, and might have everything to do with her. "It isn't so bad as all that." Far from it. "In fact, I've quite enjoyed myself," he admitted as their father took his shot.

Craaack.

"You?" His brother laughed. "You're enjoying . . ." He waved the tip of his stick at the two older men, who were pretend-jousting with the ends of their cue sticks as improvised rapiers. "Is it really so hard to believe that you, a connoisseur of fine spirits and finer women, have settled into domestic life, minus a . . . wife?" His brother snorted. "Yes, I do find that hard to believe."

"Quit your dillydallying, Derek," their father shouted. "You are holding up our game-play."

"Yes, quit your dillydallying, little brother." Charles ruffled the top of Derek's black curls in the way he'd always hated.

Swatting at his hand, Derek moved into position.

"Such is the way of second-born sons, isn't it, though?" Lord Rochester said commiseratively to the viscount, and both fathers went on to lament the inherent problems in heirs and spares.

"Oh, yes, jolly good fun, indeed," Derek muttered, bending over the table and aligning his cue with his ball.

Charles laughed, tossing back another drink of his brandy while his brother took his shot—one that went predictably wide, as Derek was predictably bad at the game.

"Come, I know it is hard to fathom that I might enjoy being here, but I have moved on from pursuing Emma as determinedly as I have." At least, enough that he no longer spoke of it daily. But he still wondered at what might be, and visited in the hopes that he could gather some way in which to earn the lady's notice that was more . . . favorable than it had been before.

His brother gave him a look.

Charles's neck went hot, but he'd be damned if he allowed any man, let alone his younger brother, to bring him to any more of a blush than that. "Very well," Charles allowed. "My visits *may* have begun as one thing, but that isn't the case anymore."

"*May?*" His brother was unrelenting.

Adopting an air of complete disaffectedness, Charles swirled the contents of his drink. The problem with wearing one's heart upon one's sleeve, as Charles had for as long as he had, was that anything he said about his relationship with Emma Gately—or rather, lack thereof—was suspect, at best. "I am not as devastated as I was," he said simply. At least, not to the point of making a public arse of himself. "In fact, I am grateful to Miss Gately for opening my eyes to some of the . . . simpler pleasures I'd previously been missing out on."

"Such as playing billiards with our father and the viscount?"

"Such as playing billiards with our father and the viscount," Charles said, drawing forth all the elder-brother patience he could.

Derek dissolved into a paroxysm of laughter, doubling over from the force of it.

"So nice it is, seeing your boys getting along so well," Emma's father was saying to Charles's.

"Oh, yes, getting along so well." When the older gentlemen's attention was firmly away, Charles turned up two middle fingers, and his brother howled all the more, the corner of his eyes leaking with tears of his amusement.

Muttering to himself, Charles silenced the remainder of the choice words he had for his brother and his explosion of levity. After all, it was hardly Derek's fault. When Charles had been five and twenty, he'd been of a similarly like and erroneous opinion about such things.

Or in Charles's case . . . wrong about far more. So much more. The crystal sheen of his snifter reflected back Charles's dark expression. As always, she slipped in, as she'd been two months ago . . . rushing off, away from the Serpentine and completely away from Charles. Taking another long, deep swallow of his drink, he grimaced at the sting of the liquid sliding down his throat. He set down his snifter on the side of the billiards table. "Either way, my being here has nothing to do with Emma Gately. I've never even caught a glimpse of her here." Not for lack of trying. Whenever he was ushered through the halls of the viscount's household, Charles skimmed and searched. Alas, the lady was as elusive as the smile he'd rarely seen her wear.

Which, of course, only lent to this deeper hungering to see her. "And even if I did," he went on for his benefit as much as his brother's, "I wouldn't be distracted from what brought me here."

"Oh, yes. The good fun to be had with our fathers," Derek said, his face a mask as, behind him, the two older men had shifted their attentions to light fisticuffs.

Resting a hip along the side of the table, Charles pointed his glass at his brother. *"Precisely,"* he said, taking another sip of his drink before setting down the snifter.

Derek glanced past him. "Do you know," his brother murmured, "I *do* believe I was wrong. This does promise to be good fun, after all." He nudged a similarly squared jaw toward the front of the room.

Charles followed that pointed gesture, and froze.

Emma stood there. Several inches shy of six feet, all willowy grace, she commanded even the enormous arched doorway.

The lady's gaze, however, was not on him, but . . . Charles followed her stare, and with a silent curse, he shoved his snifter across the mahogany so that it came to a stop against his brother's fingers, lest she see it and have confirmed everything she already believed about him.

"Very smooth of you, brother," Derek said with a wide grin as Emma marched forward with determined strides.

"Emma!" the viscount called warmly.

"Papa," she returned.

So that was why she'd come. Of course it was. She'd been clear she'd no wish to see him again, and—

His heart lifted a fraction as she continued forward in Charles's direction, and he, always effortless on his feet where the ladies were concerned, remained against the billiards table, tongue-tied.

Emma reached them, her gaze lingering upon his abandoned snifter. And for all their brotherly quarreling, Derek raised Charles's glass as though it were his own and drank down the remaining brandy there. And then popped up.

Derek gave him a swift kick, prompting Charles to move.

He straightened, and flashed a half grin. "Miss—"

"Miss Gately." His brother beat him to that greeting. Dropping a bow, Derek captured Emma's fingers and drew them to his mouth for a kiss. A lingering kiss upon her knuckles.

A smile formed on Emma's lips. "Lord Derek," she greeted warmly—with a greater warmth than had ever been directed *his* way. Having spent the better part of his young—and adult—years as a rogue, there'd been all too many telltale signs that his brother was headed along that same scoundrel's path. It was one thing, knowing that, and quite another altogether, witnessing one's brother turn the Hayden charm upon one's former betrothed.

Charles frowned.

His brother retained his hold upon her fingers, then . . .

Charles narrowed his eyes as Derek stroked his thumb along her wrist. "A pleasure as always," Derek murmured.

Folding his arms at his chest, Charles stuck out a foot and tapped the tip of his boot pointedly.

All the while, his brother and Emma pointedly ignored him.

"Likewise, Lord Derek." She inclined her head slightly, drawing Charles's attention and appreciation to that gloriously elongated swan's neck. "I trust you are enjoying my father's brandy?"

Derek blinked. "Miss—?"

She nodded to the glasses flanking either side of him on the table. "To merit *double* glasses."

Derek promptly released her fingers, a blush suffusing his cheeks, and Charles didn't even attempt to repress a grin.

"Getting your brother to take the blame," she chided, making for an all-too-brief triumph as she turned that displeasure back Charles's way once more. "*Tsk, tsk,* Lord Scarsdale."

"I didn't get him to take the blame. I was merely setting aside my glass."

He winked.

⸎

Young ladies were schooled early on in all the reasons to avoid a rogue, rake, or scoundrel. Along with those lessons came the markers of what posed the most danger to a lady's sensibilities and senses: The crooked grin. The kiss. The whisper of poetry. A forbidden caress.

Those lists had been proven remarkably incomplete and erroneous.

For it was . . . *the wink.*

That subtle glide of lashes sweeping down, but not before those depths of irises glimmered with wickedness, a transitory glimpse of a whole host of sentiments: mirth, interest. Desire.

Her lungs struggled to force out the air stuck there.

Desire?

Emma silently scoffed. Impossible.

Furthermore, it was not as though she'd *known* any of those others firsthand . . . not from this or any other gentleman.

Which perfectly recalled her to the very reason she'd stormed here in the first place.

"Your shot, Charles," Lord Derek called over.

"Might I speak with you, Lord Scarsdale?" she said tightly.

"He would be glad to, Emma," the marquess called out on behalf of his eldest son.

"But it is his shot, Fath—"

The marquess fixed a glare on the younger gentleman, effectively silencing him. "I said, he is free to speak to Miss Gately, Derek." He

52

pointed the end of his stick in Charles's direction. "He's free to speak with you, Emma."

Color filled Charles's cheeks, and he glanced in the direction of his always-meddling sire. "I can handle my own affairs where Miss Gately is concerned, Father," he said tightly.

The marquess snorted. "If that were the case, you wouldn't find yourself in the position you have, then, would you, my boy?"

Emma's father and his closest friend in the world dissolved into laughter, and she gritted her teeth. As if any of this were amusing, in any way.

"What are you doing here?" she demanded, earning a look from her father and Charles . . . which she ignored.

Charles held his cue aloft. "Playing billiards."

"Playing billiards?"

He nodded. "With the boys?"

"The boys?" she echoed. Her voice climbed a fraction. "The *boyyys?* They are ancient men."

"I heard that, Emie," her father chastised.

Lord Derek added his indignation to the mix. "And we aren't *all* ancient. Why, I'm younger than Ch— *Owww.*" A startled shout escaped the younger man when his father tapped him hard on the back with his billiards stick.

"Have a care, boy."

Cursing softly, she gripped Charles by the arm and steered him several paces away from the *boys* now playing.

Except . . . she had made the mistake of touching him. Her fingers curled reflexively upon the soft wool fabric, that softness at odds with the sinewy muscle under her palm. All the moisture leached from her mouth, leaving even her throat dry. Bloody hell, what was wrong with her? "They are not boys, Lord Scarsdale." She swiftly released him, and stole a glance up to ascertain whether he'd caught that moment of insanity. He continued to eye her from under a hood of golden lashes. "Boys are those scoundrels you keep company with. Speaking of, are they otherwise engaged that you aren't with your own sort?"

He applied chalk to the end of his cue. "I'll have you know, one of my 'sort,' as you refer to them, is, in fact, *married*. And happily so."

"Yes," she said softly. They had wed several weeks earlier. Her heart cinched. Where there should be only happiness for her friend Lady Sylvia, the cofounder of the Mismatch Society and a former widow who'd found love, there was also a pain she refused to let herself feel . . . for that which Emma had so desperately wanted. No more. Never again. "I am well aware." She steeled her jaw. "That doesn't change . . . who *you* are, however, Charles."

His brows snapped together, and his perfectly formed mouth tensed in the first-that-she-could-ever-recall hint of failure in his always-charming attitude.

Coward that she was, as tension ran through him and a palpable dark energy thrummed in the air around them, she wanted to call back her words.

"Oh?" Abandoning his relaxed pose, he moved closer, shrinking the space between them and making her feel instantly small in his tall, commanding presence. "And tell me, Emma, since you know so very much. Who am I?" A slight edge of steel coated that murmur, danger whispering up from both his words and a tone too deep to be considered a baritone.

She swallowed, her body pulsing, not at all born of fear, but coming, instead, from her heightened awareness of him.

"Hmm?" Charles leaned close, his mouth a fraction of a breath from hers, and it was the second time in her life that she'd been so near to this man. A kiss whispered in the air. A desire that defied logic and knew not of the distant activity unfolding in this room. Just like at the shore of the Serpentine more than two months ago, all she knew was a hungering for whatever promise he dangled with his nearness. "I would

love to . . ." He shifted his mouth so it lingered closer to the shell of her ear; the sough of his breath tickled that sensitive flesh, and brought her eyes briefly shut.

I would love to . . . ?

What? *Whaaat?* Her lashes fluttered open, needing the remainder of that answer from him.

Charles's lips curled in a taunting, knowing, confident grin, a smile that could be born only of a rogue's knowledge of the subtleties of a woman's quickened breath and rapidly beating heart. "Hear whatever opinions you've drawn about me, Emma," he teased.

He may as well have dunked her in water to douse her desire.

Bloody hell. "No, you wouldn't," she said flatly. "Your ego couldn't stand it." When would she cease being captivated by him?

"I have an ego, do I?"

He did, but one deserved because of his Adonis-like looks and his effortless charm. And she'd sooner slice out her tongue than feed into his deserved esteem.

"The truth is, Emma, you know nothing of me."

The casual way with which he said it struck her square in the chest. Charles couldn't have hurt her more had he taken the end of the cue stick he'd applied chalk to and jammed it through her chest.

I know nothing about you because you never let me. Because you never wanted to learn anything about me, she screamed silently.

Emma gave a flounce of her head, hating the absolute absence of curls that would have added a flair of emphasis. Alas, she'd never been in possession of the luxuriant tresses of the women he preferred. "I've known you the whole of my life, Lord Scarsdale." She infused her response with an impressive modicum of boredom, given he'd leveled a truth that had always caused the greatest of aches. "I *know* a good deal more about you than you credit." The most distant memories she carried of him included someone who had been friendly enough to her . . .

until the day of the mock wedding ceremony their families had held . . . when she had learned precisely how he felt about her.

His grin widened, and lifting his hands, he waggled four fingers of each. "All right. Out with it. Let's hear it."

The doors opened, and her brothers spilled into the room, studiously avoiding looking at Emma as they made a path to their best friend, Charles's brother, Derek.

The moment Pierce and Morgan had moved past them, taking a wide berth, she proceeded to oblige him. "You don't take anything seriously, Charles. Everything and everyone is a joke to you. You're notoriously late." From their betrothal on to every ball at which she'd ever been in attendance with him. "Should I keep going?"

The ghost of a smile grazed the corners of his lips. "Can you?"

He was amused? The lout. "You hunt!"

"And you . . . have a problem with hunting?"

She despised it. "It's cruel," she said flatly.

"It is the English way."

Emma's lips pulled. "Yes, domination is the English way, isn't it?" she muttered. God spare her from men who conquered. "People don't go about chasing you—" She stopped herself from completing the remainder of that wholly untrue thought.

He leaned in. "What was that, sweet?"

Sweet. And while the Lord was at it, let him save her from pretty words her former betrothed used on every woman.

"You drink too much," she said bluntly, getting to the heart of the list she'd composed prior to sending 'round the note to break off their betrothal. "You're a womanizer." She'd been but a girl when she discovered he'd gotten a child on a woman who was decidedly not her, and the adoration she'd secretly carried for the free spirit that he'd been had died a swift death. "You wager too much."

His golden lashes swept down, forming a hood that shielded the thoughts within. "And you pay too much attention to the scandal sheets, so I should say we're both in possession of our own character deficits, Emma-love."

Emma-love.

There'd once been a time she'd longed to hear such an endearment from this man's lips, one that was intimate, reserved just for her. And she didn't want the sound of her name tangled with that affectionate utterance to have any effect, and certainly not the damned "flutters," as she'd come to name the dratted sentiments. "And you're casual with your words of affection," she said softly, tiredly. "I'm not your love, Charles." He'd seen to that long ago.

Charles winced.

But neither did he make any protestations of the contrary.

Of course, what had she expected? The entire reason he'd fought to keep her was because of his wounded ego and his family's insistence, and a rejection he was so unaccustomed to that he didn't know what to do with how Emma had ended it.

Emma drew a deep breath. "I'm not even sure you are capable of the emotion," she said, for herself as much as for him.

He narrowed his eyes. "That is a bold presumption, Emma-love."

This time she didn't give rise to that deliberate endearment, one meant only to goad. "Is it? From a man who'll sire a child and not give his mother the benefit of—"

He surged forward, and Emma gasped, stumbling over herself in retreat, until her back collided with the wall.

"Do not mention Seamus," he seethed. "And do not mention things you know nothing about." Volatile emotion blazed from his eyes, burning her with anger . . . on behalf of his son. "Have I made myself clear?"

Laughter went up between their families at play; how could the world be so oblivious to the volatility of her and Charles's exchange that bordered on fire?

She gave a juddering nod. "My a-apologies. I didn't—"

"Know that I wouldn't want his name dragged about?" He cut her off.

Emma bit the inside of her cheek, ashamed and appalled . . . with herself, for having inadvertently done just as he'd said and raised his child as a cornerstone of her upset with Charles. "You are correct," she said softly. "I should not have mentioned him in such a way." She grimaced. "In any way, that is. It wasn't my intention to disparage the boy." But rather, to what? Highlight that Charles had failed him? And yet all these years, she'd believed Charles . . . indifferent to the boy. Only to find Charles was anything but. It was the first hint of a real layer of a person—a man who was protective of his son. And it was also the first she'd come to see that, as he'd said, there was perhaps more to Charles than she'd believed.

Charles nodded tightly in a silent acknowledgment of that apology. She drew in a deep breath, and forced herself to focus on the whole reason for seeking him out this day. "I want this to stop," she said quietly. It had gone on enough. "It is hardly fair for me to . . ." Have to see him daily. And be reminded of how little he'd wanted her before. And all the unlikely reasons he supposedly wanted her for his wife now. "Have you subvert my wishes by being friendly with my father and mother."

He frowned. "I've always been—"

"Stop," she hissed. "Just stop. They will not cease in their efforts until you cease in yours." And until they did, she would be forced to live in a perpetual hell where the only thing her parents spoke to her about or saw her value in was a potential marriage to this man before her.

Charles trailed a gaze over her face, one that had such shades of tenderness her heart quickened, the organ's unlikely reaction to the very favor she put to him now. Nay, not a favor. Demand. One that if he cared in any way, he'd honor.

Then, ever so slowly, with a languidness to his movements, Charles brought up his shoulders in a slow shrug.

She gasped. The gall of him. Emma lowered her voice when she spoke. "I am asking you to cease with all these friendly visits to my father." Because it was . . . impossible having him here daily.

He applied more chalk to that damned stick, which couldn't possibly require another bit of dust as long as it should ever be used. "Very well, Emma," he said quietly, and her eyebrows went flying up at the unexpectedness of that capitulation.

"Thank you . . . Charles." As he'd made a concession, she could certainly do so with something as simple as using his name.

He paired his rogue's grin with a wink.

And her heart did its characteristic leap in her breast. "If you'll excuse me. I have matters to see to."

Charles angled the cue stick, cutting off her escape. "I take it the important business you see to is, in fact, your club." And then it was as though she'd imagined that unexpected show of real emotion from him, as Charles dropped a shoulder casually against the wall, curving his body in a way that framed her perfectly and managed the impossible . . . to make Emma, taller than most men, feel dainty beside him.

She gritted her teeth. He'd choose this instant, of course, to keep her at his side.

"Do you need one of us to beat him, Emma?" Morgan called over, far more loyal than either of their parents combined.

"As if you could beat Scarsdale." Pierce snorted, and the twins promptly forgot about coming to her defense, should she need it, and instead sparred over the matter of Scarsdale's prowess.

Emma briefly closed her eyes. This, again, from her brothers? Their great fascination with duels and dueling. "Men," she muttered. Not that she'd require either of their help anyway. They'd all proven remarkably useless where she was concerned.

Charles leaned in. "What was that?"

She squared her shoulders and got back to the prime focus of her annoyance. "I'll have you know, we are a society." She'd opened her mouth to launch into a lecture when she registered the glimmer in his chocolate-brown eyes. She firmed her lips. "I see." She'd often read that he was one of the teasing sorts. But never had he engaged her so. She'd wanted him to. "You are making light."

An eyebrow went arcing up. "You're in the habit of recognizing jests now?"

Yes, because he'd taken her as one incapable of having fun or even a spirit. "It is rather hard not to when I have the biggest one before me."

He blinked slowly, and then those long golden lashes ceased moving altogether. Good, let him stew upon that.

"Furthermore," she went on when all their family members present were otherwise diverted. "You should have a care, throwing around willy-nilly jests about my ability to laugh or smile, Lord Scarsdale." Emma took a step toward him. "You never took time to learn anything about me. As such, allow me to advise you . . . I've always been capable of doing so, and were I you, I wouldn't go throwing about my lack of amusement in your presence, given you never provided me with a reason to laugh or smile. Therefore"—she stuck a finger in his chest—"I would also say it is a greater reflection of you, and a deficit on your character, more than mine."

With that, she yanked her skirts away and stalked off.

"What in hell have you done now, my boy?" The marquess's booming disapproval for his son followed Emma all the way out into the corridors.

And with her second victory in the matter of Charles Hayden that day, Emma smiled.

Chapter 4

THE LONDONER

FATHERS AND GUARDIANS BEWARE

The Mismatch Society poses a very real danger to Polite Society . . . and all the institutions it extols. At the start of their formation, they may have enlisted the honorable Viscount St. John to provide a veneer of respectability; however, the shine is well and truly off.

M. FAIRPOINT

Lots of people spoke disparagingly about Charles.

They'd done so when he'd been a wild youth in Oxford.

The words spoken of him had only increased after Seamus's arrival. But then, society never tired of whispering about those babes born outside the bounds of matrimony.

Charles had managed to let those unfavorable words roll off; people's opinions of him mattered far less than the well-being and happiness of his family . . . of any of his family: His parents. His brother . . .

His lone sister, whom he would have done anything for, and whom he'd also failed so terribly.

And Seamus.

In fact, Charles had believed himself immune to the ill opinions.

Only to be proven wrong that day by Emma's impressive takedown of him.

Why does it matter to you? She has made clear what she feels about you . . . and it is . . . nothing. Nay, it was worse than nothing. She despised him. She didn't respect him.

So why did he care so very much? Why did he hate that she thought him to be . . . the exact same thing the world believed him to be?

Because you saw in her, too late, a woman of spirit and strength and convictions, the likes of which you've known in no other person before her.

"You don't take anything seriously, Charles. Everything and everyone is a joke to you. You're notoriously late . . . You hunt . . . You drink too much . . . You're a womanizer . . . You wager too much . . ."

All the while, her opinion of you was . . . is . . . that.

Seated at his private table at White's, he glared into the contents of his whiskey glass, then set it down hard.

A shadow fell over his table, and he glanced up to find his two longest and truest friends in the world: Lord Landon, fellow rogue, and Lord St. John, the actual saint of their trio.

Landon grabbed a chair and seated himself, with St. John slower and more measured in doing so. "Good God, the foul mood persists," Landon greeted with his unflagging charm.

I was once the same damned way.

And Charles was more than tempted to grab his half-drunk whiskey and finish it off. Which he would have . . . had Emma Gately's accusations not been ringing in his head.

"Drink too much," he muttered to himself.

"Yes, I think that is my point," Landon piped in. "You're at it again, but this time in a foul mood." A servant came forward with two glasses, one the marquess grabbed up while St. John set his off to the side, with a word of thanks for the footman. "I thought it could not get worse than your moping," Landon remarked when the servant had gone. He helped himself to the bottle of whiskey Charles hadn't been able to bring himself around to drinking.

"I was *not* moping," Charles groused.

Both men looked back at him.

"Oh, fine. I was moping a bit."

"Well, angry-drunken Scarsdale is even worse than depressed-forlorn Scarsdale, isn't that true, St. John?"

"I'm not drunk." Charles only *wished* he were.

If that didn't require him fulfilling those low opinions Emma had leveled at him.

"I'd rather not see him angry *or* depressed," the viscount said as if Charles hadn't spoken to his own sobriety. He'd long been the reliable one of their group, and just then, St. John had that steady, concerned gaze trained on Charles. "What is it, Scarsdale?" he asked quietly, with a solemnity Landon had forever been incapable of.

Charles shoved his glass across the table. "She doesn't wish me to see her family."

The viscount's deep-set brow creased. "She?"

"Who the hell else do you think 'she' means, St. John?" Landon asked in exasperated tones. "His former betrothed," he said, removing a pipe and waving it in Charles's direction. "The estimable Miss Gately." Another footman rushed over and lit the wooden scrap before rushing off. Landon sighed, and rubbed four fingers along his right brow. "Oh, bloody hell. Let's get on with it, then. What has the lady done to upset you now?"

And that was why Landon, disreputable, in dun territory, and preferring his women and spirits too much, would always be a best friend. Because when it came down to it, ultimately he wished to help, and he cared about the people he called friends: Charles. St. John. "She doesn't wish for me to see her father. She insisted she doesn't want me to join the viscount for billiards or . . . anything."

Silence met his pronouncement.

St. John cleared his throat. "And?"

"And . . . I, well, I don't think it's her place to say."

"Because you of a sudden enjoy hanging out with elderly lords whom your father calls friends?" Landon asked without inflection, and also absent the sarcasm leveled Charles's way by Emma.

His friends' words danced close to the accusations Emma had tossed when she'd called Charles out before the bulk of their families. "Not that it is either here or there, but I do enjoy my time with my father and the viscount. Which is what I told her."

"And you're still trying to win her back?" Landon asked slowly. "Or have you given up on that?"

"The former," Charles confirmed.

Chuckling, Landon saluted him. "Then you're going about it a deuced funny way, friend."

"She's insisted she doesn't want you visiting with her father, and yet you've explicitly gone against her wishes?" St. John asked slowly.

"Because if I don't"—Charles dragged out each syllable—"then I'm not going to see her."

Landon pounced. "Then . . . find other places to see her, old chap."

"I don't know where that is," he said quietly, as her charges hurled at him came back to haunt Charles in this moment.

You should have a care, throwing around willy-nilly jests about my ability to laugh or smile, Lord Scarsdale . . . You never took time to learn anything about me. As such, allow me to advise you . . . I've always been capable of doing so, and were I you, I wouldn't go throwing about my lack of amusement in your presence, given you never provided me with a reason to laugh or smile . . .

"That is my point exactly," Landon was saying, casual through Charles's tumult. "Does she go to the parks? Which shops does she visit?"

Nothing. He knew none of those things about her.

"Find her there, and don't make it damned confrontational." Landon tossed back his drink.

"It would be a waste of time, given my latest meeting with the young lady," he said tersely. "She accused me of being unable to take anything seriously."

A damning silence met that revelation.

Landon and St. John looked between one another, pointing at each other . . . debating who'd speak next . . . as if Charles weren't staring back at the pair of them. "Fine," Landon mouthed. He turned back to Charles. "Why the great offense being taken? You *aren't* serious about anything."

Charles bristled. "Of course I am." When both friends were silent, he looked to St. John for support.

"You are a devoted brother," the viscount was quick to oblige.

A devoted brother.

Landon pointed his pipe Charles's way. "There you go."

Those words, coming from a man such as St. John, with six sisters and a widowed mother he cared for, why, there was no greater praise. And yet . . .

St. John had six sisters, and Charles just one . . . one whom he'd failed spectacularly. That always-with-him truth still hit like a kick to the gut. He gave up the battle he'd waged since arriving and grabbed his glass and swallowed down a large sip of his whiskey.

"That is all?" Charles asked, glancing between his suddenly silent friends.

Landon released a frustrated sound. "Do you want to know my opinion?"

"N—"

"Why should you want to impress the lady? It is over." *It is over.* There was such a finality to his friend speaking it that Charles's heart squeezed painfully. "And she isn't worth any more of your heartache."

Landon was wrong on any number of scores there.

Charles glanced down at the varnish of the same stale table he'd sat at year after year after year.

Emma, mastermind of a society to advocate for better lives of women, and a lady determined to exert control over her own life, *was* a woman worth the heartache, as his friend called it. Only it wasn't about impressing Emma. Not really. Yes, he despised that she looked at him and saw a wastrel, scoundrel, libertine. But he hated more the idea that . . . she was, in fact, right about him.

"Ahem." St. John made a clearing sound with his throat until Charles looked up.

"When it comes to matters of the heart, Landon," the more contemplative and measured of his friends said, "it is not your place to tell Charles or any man whether it is time to call something 'over.'"

"No, you are correct," Landon readily conceded.

Of course, St. John's assertion, they now knew, came from the fact that he had been secretly in love with the wife of their late best friend, the Earl of Norfolk. "Thank you, St. John," Charles said quietly.

The viscount lifted his head in acknowledgment.

For years, both Charles and Landon had been oblivious to the sentiments St. John carried for Lady Norfolk. Charles, however, had come to suspect something was amiss eventually—after all, the honorable St. John had completely turned his back on Sylvia, who'd been his friend, after her husband's death. That suspicion only grew when they reconnected.

St. John could speak better than most about unrequited regards.

Sighing, Landon dragged his chair closer, clamped his pipe between his teeth, and held two palms aloft. "Very well. I shouldn't be the one to tell you when to quit Miss Gately. You are asking for help, different help, then. It is like this . . ."

"Here we go," St. John muttered, choosing that moment to reach for the bottle and snifter.

"A man is either blithe"—Landon waggled his right fingers—"or . . . serious about life." He gave a wag of his left palm. "This"—the marquess held up the blithe hand once more—"is you. You must be one or the other. You have to pick one."

Pick one.

St. John rolled his eyes. "For the love of God, man, a person can be both."

"That's your wife's society speaking," Landon shot back. "It's not the way things really are."

Both men proceeded to launch into a debate. As they did, Charles contemplated the point they argued.

The way Landon spoke of it, there was a choice . . . a choice in how Charles had lived his life these past years. When for so long he'd not been afforded that option. Not really. Instead, he'd been forced to, as Landon said, choose one over the other, and Charles had done so gladly—to protect his family. And the secret his family carried.

Society had formed their low opinion of him.

All the while, he'd accepted his circumstance, but he'd also gone through life annoyed at the perceptions that surrounded his existence, and a decoy existence that he'd fashioned himself, at that.

As his friends chatted, he stared absently out across a crowded White's.

His mother's latest directives whispered forward.

"Fix your reputation. Restore your image. Make yourself the respectable man I know you can be . . ."

She'd charged him with the responsibility of *improving* himself, while Landon insisted it was an impossible task.

All the while, there'd been a woman such as Emma, who with her society was putting forward views that challenged the black-and-white opinions Landon spoke of now.

Charles's thoughts slowed, and then took off at a rapid clip. Emma had set out to start something . . . and she had done so in a way that expanded minds. The world saw one thing. And one thing only. And she'd identified that deficit. Just one group such as hers, however, would never be enough to undo the flaws steeped within society's perceptions of . . .

"My God," he whispered. It was the answer to so much: his mother's latest orders for him, and . . . Emma. "That is it!"

His friends stopped midconversation and eyed Charles with matching degrees of wariness.

"What?" St. John asked in hesitant, fear-laden tones.

Leaning across the table, Charles gripped St. John's face and kissed his cheek. "You are brilliant, man."

Charles released him quickly, then sat back in his chair.

"People are certainly going to talk about that," Landon said on a laugh.

Sure enough, any number of eyes had already landed on their trio. "Fine. Let all the bastards talk. That is precisely what this is about."

"I . . . I . . . am afraid I'm not following," St. John admitted. "Precisely what . . . *what* is about?"

"I confess, Scarsdale," Landon added. "For the first time, I've joined St. John here in the department of cluelessness."

Enlivened for the first time since Emma had ended their betrothal, Charles shared the idea which had taken root. "The ladies, your Sylvia, my Miss Gately—"

"She is not really your—"

Charles pinned a glare on Landon, effectively ending that unnecessary and unwise interjection, particularly as it was an unwelcome distraction in light of what had come to him.

Landon cleared his throat. "You were saying?"

Warming to the topic, Charles grabbed his chair and dragged it to the very edge of the table until the side bit into his stomach. "What Emma and Lady Sylvia have introduced was considered scandalous—a group of women coming together to discuss political ideas and opinions. They are no different from a salon during the Enlightenment. Hosted primarily by women. In fact, I'd say they are quite the same. Do you know the difference?" His friends stared back blankly. Charles grinned. "The difference is there was a counterpart—a male-oriented counterpart—the café . . ."

A slow understanding settled in St. John's eyes, followed swiftly by dread, as the other man managed nothing more than a slow shake of his head.

Oh, yes. In creating something such as that, it not only proved Charles was capable of being more than the blithe lord even his friends took him for . . . it was also surely something Emma could respect.

Landon kicked back his chair so it rested on two legs. "What do you know about . . . Enlightened thinkers?"

Yes, that would be the opinion. Nor, for that matter, was his friend truly off the mark. Charles hadn't involved himself in such scholarly matters. "I confess, not much. Everything I've learned has been from Seamus." Charles couldn't have been prouder.

"Then leave it to Seamus to one day do what you are thinking," St. John pleaded.

Confusion creased the place between Landon's eyes. "What is he thinking?" He shifted focus from St. John to Charles. Then horror lit his gaze. "My God, I've become St. John."

Both Charles and St. John ignored the other man's theatrics, carrying out a conversation all their own. "There has been a need revealed, thanks to your Sylvia and my Miss Gately—"

"Splendid! Then just say thank you and leave it be," St. John implored. "But do not do . . . what you are thinking to do."

"Oh, no." Charles shook his head. "Not 'thinking to do.'"

The viscount's shoulders sagged with a palpable sign of his relief.

Charles smiled again. "What I am *going* to do."

"Will someone *please* enlighten me in exactly what you two are talking about?" Landon paused. "No pun intended."

Waiting for the undivided attention of his audience of two, Charles spread his arms wide. "I shall also be offering a place for people to come together and discuss . . . matters."

"Matters?" St. John repeated.

Frowning at that underwhelming response from his two closest friends in the world, Charles waved his fingers in an emphasizing circle. "We shall work out those details as we go. But it shall be important matters, pertaining to . . . politics and life and society and—"

St. John cut him off. "And which exact 'we' will make up your society?"

Charles gave him a pointed look.

The viscount didn't blink for several moments.

Charles nodded slowly for the other man's benefit.

Horror filled St. John's wide eyes. With a groan, the recently wedded chap grabbed the bottle once more and splashed several fingerfuls into his empty glass. He paused, contemplated the glass for several moments, and added more of the spirits.

Charles and Landon watched as he downed his drink in a single long, painful-looking swallow.

"Ah." Charles wagged a finger. "And I should point out, *we* are not a society. *We* are a club. 'Societies' suggest stodgy groups who'd exclude people from their ranks."

St. John proceeded to dissolve into a fit, strangling on the last remnants of his brandy.

Leaning close, Landon slapped him hard on the back. *"This* is your idea to win back the lady?" he drawled while their other friend choked. "If so, it is a *terrible* idea."

"The w-worst," St. John managed to force out, and proceeded to refill his glass.

"I disagree," Charles said for the pair of naysayers. "Why, having established a club of her own, she may even appreciate mine."

His friends spoke in unison. "She won't."

Fair enough. She *might* not react favorably. Not at first, perhaps. After all, a gent could never truly be certain where a lady was concerned. "Well, at worst she'll be indifferent." As indifferent as she'd proven to be toward him these past months.

"That is not the worst," St. John said with a shake of his head. "At. All."

Landon stared at him incredulously.

"Nor, for that matter, is it entirely about winning back Emma." There was a small element of rehabilitating his reputation, which *might* have just a bit to do with his mother's last visit and . . . *also* winning Emma back. Charles reached for his drink.

Both men gave him a look.

"What? It isn't," Charles insisted, forgetting his snifter. *Some* of it had to do with proving—not just to her, but to all of society—that intellect was not reserved for a certain, select type of person, a person Charles had never been and would never be. Why should there be just the one group, and an exclusionary one at that?

"Well, let me spare you the ending. You're wrong," Landon said bluntly. "It is a rotted idea."

"Oh, no. It's not that at all. She doubts I'm capable of seriousness. I'm just as capable, if not more, of discussing and debating . . . things."

Landon snorted. *"Things?"*

Charles slid another glare his friend's way. "Laugh all you want . . ."

In the midst of drinking his brandy, St. John lifted a palm. When he finished, he held on tight to his glass. "Oh, I assure you, I am *not* laughing."

Nay, in fairness, the viscount sounded one more idea from Charles away from dissolving into tears. Charles could understand that. His wife was the head of the only club for the improvement of thoughts. "With the exception of St. John here, they've barred gentlemen from entry. They've meticulously selected their membership. Only certain women, fitting certain criteria, are allowed. Well, we shall be the alternative. A place . . . for all!" He shot out an arm.

Alas, his friends sat stone-faced, and visibly unimpressed. So much for the support of a man's best friends. Charles let his arm fall. "You think it's a terrible idea because of my intent to win back Miss Gately." He directed that at Landon. "And you . . ." He shifted focus to St. John. "Your real concern is how your wife will receive you joining an alternate club. You, who don't even attend her meetings anymore, because they are hers." When St. John's eyebrows dipped, Charles rushed to clarify. "I am not passing judgment. I am pointing out that you were only invited to join the ranks in the first place because they had a need of you . . . but when they received the legitimacy that your presence provided, and you were married to Sylvia, you ceased attending. You let them to their group, as you should have. However, people need choices," Charles pointed out. "Why should there be just one club? A need was identified . . . and as such, there should be many places that allow people to come together and share in ideas and frustrations and beliefs."

This time, a different silence met Charles's words, this one neither mocking nor confused, but contemplative. It was the sound of two men who recognized the truth in what Charles spoke . . . even as St. John was determined to resist it.

"It is a society," St. John said, desperation in his voice.

Charles grinned. "Well, again, we are a club . . . and we are going to be a club like no other. We shall meet, and our membership will include both men and women."

Always proper, St. John tried once more to interject his pragmatic reasoning to derail Charles's idea. "And just where do you think you are going to hold meetings for men and women, in a way that society isn't scandalized? You're a rogue," the other man said bluntly. "Landon is a rogue."

"*Ohhh*, I prefer rake." Landon kicked back his seat, balancing on the hind legs of his chair once more.

"And of a sudden," St. John continued purposefully over that amusement-laden interjection from their friend, "proper mothers are going to simply let their proper, marriage-minded daughters visit *your* household?"

No. In a world where a lady's unsullied reputation was the currency upon which empires were built, the *ton* would never allow it, and yet . . . there were . . . ways.

When St. John had concluded that diatribe, Charles wagged a finger under his desperate friend's nose. "Ah, you shall leave those details to me."

Raising his drink, Landon laughed, and touched the rim of his snifter to Charles's. "Oh, now *this* I am going to enjoy."

St. John dropped his poor head to the table, and proceeded to knock it lightly against the smooth mahogany surface. And with his head down, he raised his glass and touched it to Charles's and Landon's still-raised drinks.

For the first time in a very, very long while, Charles was enjoying himself, too . . . and all thanks to Miss Emma Gately.

Chapter 5

THE LONDONER

LADIES ARE FLEEING

The Mismatch Society has seen a fluctuation in their membership, which can be explained only by reasonable fathers, brothers, and guardians at last saying "Enough is enough" to the nonsense that has been tolerated far too long.

M. FAIRPOINT

Each meeting of the Mismatch Society began with a formal attendance being checked.

Given how precarious each lady's ability to participate in the female-centered group, in fact, was, verifying just who was amongst them and who was missing had been a vital part of each session. Because when members disappeared, there were specific reasons for those absences. Always, it had to do with disapproving parents or guardians or brothers serving as guardians, who eventually tired of "shows of spirit and disobedience" from a lady who was in attendance.

Such challenges had become less frequent following Sylvia's marriage to the much-respected and highly proper viscount.

Which made the abrupt and sudden change to their membership so stark and alarming.

For in a fortnight, there could be no doubting their numbers were somehow dwindling . . . by five, to be exact.

Lady Sylvia had called an emergency meeting—only the second since the Mismatch Society's inception. This time, however, the meeting had been called not at their usual location on Waverton Street, but at Lady Sylvia's new residence, also home to four of their members, the three eldest Kearsley sisters and their mother.

A din filled the parlor as the remaining seventeen ladies spoke loudly amongst one another, outrage lending their voices increased volume.

"It is shocking. And upsetting . . . ," Cora Kearsley was saying, dabbing at the corners of her eyes. "I so enjoyed Miss Dobson's c-contributions."

"There, there." The young lady's mother, the dowager viscountess, used a white kerchief to dab at Cora's damp cheeks.

Seated between Olivia and Isla, Emma watched the pair. From the moment the Kearsleys had joined the society, they'd been accompanied occasionally by the now dowager viscountess. It was a show of maternal support that continued to singularly fascinate Emma. As one whose own mother had betrothed her as a babe, it was a bond Emma hadn't known was a real one between a mother and a daughter.

Yes, Emma's parents had allowed her and her sister to attend . . . but they'd put up a fight whenever Emma went against societal norms. They'd allowed her to attend, but they'd not believed in what she'd helped found, or in the mission of their group.

"It is so predictable, is what it is." Brenna Kearsley stormed back and forth, pacing before the hearth. "Time and time again we will be expected to justify our purpose, and assure Polite Society that we aren't a threat."

Except . . . while the women around her spoke to one another, frantic in their mutterings and whisperings, Emma's gaze was on three amongst their ranks: Sylvia, Valerie, and Annalee, the ones who lived at the Waverton Street townhouse. Or, rather, the latter two ladies lived there, as Sylvia had recently wed.

Now, the trio sat silent. And then over . . . to Brenna, rightly ranting, and yet . . .

She puzzled her brow.

"What is it?" Olivia asked at her side.

"Anwen isn't here."

"Yes," Isla muttered.

"But . . . it does not make any sense. Her absence was included amongst the loss of our members, but it isn't . . . consistent with the others," Emma said, motioning with her hand.

Her sister, Olivia, and the ladies seated nearby followed that gesture over to where the dowager viscountess soothed the still-inconsolable Kearsley sister.

"And there is also Cressida," Emma noted. Miss Cressida Alby, their most recent member, a timid, quiet young lady whose brother had inherited a bankrupt title and betrothed her to a scapegrace lord, had approached Emma at Almack's when Cressida made her Come Out. Bonded by the fact that she'd also been betrothed against her wishes, they'd struck up a quick friendship, and Emma had taken her under her wing.

"We have a specific answer on her whereabouts. She sent a note," Valerie announced, brandishing a page.

Before anyone else could move, Emma was quickly across the room and rescuing the folded page. Breaking the seal, she read:

It is as I feared . . . the inevitable. Since I ended my betrothal, my brother disapproves and has forbidden my attendance. I've been unable to convince him. I don't have that ability. I'm not as strong as the rest of you. I shall miss you forever.

Emma crushed the page in her hands, cursing softly. This was to be their continued lot . . . women arriving, asserting themselves, only to be ripped out of their fold and thrust back into the neat societal role the world had for them.

"Is she lost to us?" Isla whispered.

"Yes," Emma said tightly. For now. She wasn't abandoning Cressida.

"That doesn't account for Anwen's absence," Olivia murmured as Emma reclaimed her seat. "What of *her*?"

Lady Sylvia sailed to her feet, so self-possessed she managed to command a room to silence with a stoic quiet of her own. "I suspect I know the reason for the changes."

When all the conversation had ceased, she stepped forward. "I've called an emergency meeting, as you know, and I've also requested the attendance of a former member who might be able to provide us with the details we seek regarding the current changes to our group and our group's membership."

The door opened, and Eris, at five the youngest of Lady Sylvia's sisters-in-law, skipped in. "I got him for you. Clayton is coming," she said in a singsong voice as she skipped over to Sylvia.

"Splendid! Thank you, Eris."

"Can I stay?" the little girl piped in hopefully. "Can I *pleeeease* attend this meeting?" she begged, clasping her hands together and looking to her mother.

"Oh, I think it would be a good idea for you to be here for this," the dowager viscountess allowed.

Olivia's brows came together. "Has Lord St. John rejoined our ranks?"

Something was amiss. The same warning bells that had chimed at Emma's mock wedding at the age of six blared loudly now. "Not . . . to my knowledge," she murmured. Best friend to her former betrothed, and yet as different from him in every way as it was possible for two men to be, Viscount St. John was nearly as tall as Emma's father and in possession of heavy features. He would never be called handsome, but he loved his wife with an enviable devotion. He was serious and supportive. Unlike Emma's own faithless, Michelangelo-subject-of-sculpture-worthy Lord Scarsdale.

A whistling sounded in the near distance, growing increasingly closer.

Lord St. John entered the parlor. "You summoned me, lo— *Ohhh.*" The viscount's tender greeting ended abruptly, as he moved an ever-widening gaze from his wife to take in the eighteen pairs of eyes upon him. "Hell," he finished, earning a series of shocked gasps.

Eris giggled.

His eyes widened. "Hello!" he quickly amended. "That is . . . I meant to say 'hell*oo*!'" He dropped a hasty bow.

Emma narrowed her eyes as suspicion stirred. "He knows something," she said out of the corner of her mouth. "And I'd wager it is not good."

"What makes you say that?" Isla protested.

"Oh, I don't know." Emma took in the exchange between the gentleman in question and the dowager viscountess. "The way in which he's darting his eyes around, looking for an escape, all the while his mother speaks to him." More specifically, it was the tense way in which Lady Sylvia watched him while he spoke. The intensity of the other woman's stare. As a lady who'd been hurt by a man, Emma had come to recognize the marks of an aggrieved or offended woman. And there could be no doubting . . . "Lady Sylvia is displeased with him."

Isla cocked her head. "I . . . she looks exactly as she always does."

"Then you're not paying close enough attention, little sister."

Isla made a face. "He's only been supportive of the Mismatch Society. From the start."

Emma slid a look her sister's way. How conveniently Isla forgot about the fact that he'd paid their meeting a visit once with the express intention of shutting them down. "From the start?"

Color bloomed in Isla's cheeks. "*Almost* from the start. When others were attempting to shut us down, he lent his name and presence to the Mismatch Society. And I know you are cynical, Emma." *About love and men.* Her sister didn't speak it, but her message was clear. Nor, for that matter, was Isla incorrect. As such, Emma didn't take offense. "But I refuse to believe that our founding leader's husband would have some nefarious, underhanded involvement in our demise." Isla turned to Olivia. "Tell her."

The other woman held up her palms. "I know better than to involve myself in your disputes."

And additionally, Olivia was second only to Emma in terms of her distrust and skepticism where men were concerned.

"Ladies," Lord St. John called to the room at large, lifting a hand in a gesture that signified both a salutation and a parting. "Forgive me. I was unaware you were meeting. I do not seek to intrude . . . If you'll excuse me?"

He took a step toward the door. An entirely too quick and also damning one. "You will do no such thing, dear husband," Lady Sylvia drawled. "I noticed it's been quite some time since you've attended any of our meetings; however, I thought you would join us today?" The leader of the Mismatch Society gripped a Venetian giltwood side chair and moved it into position at the center of the room.

The gentleman's swallow was audible, and also so wild his cravat moved under the force of it. "In-indeed? I had a meeting, however . . ." Sylvia winged up a blonde brow, and the gentleman promptly sat in the seat that was too small and too uncomfortable in its stiffness for the selection to have been anything but deliberate.

"Enough. Stop looking at him like that, Emma," Isla whispered furiously.

She'd do no such thing.

"You're going to upset Sylvia," her youngest sibling went on.

"Sylvia wouldn't want for Emma to blindly follow, either," Olivia pointed out.

Emma gave a decisive nod. "There you are. Listen to Olivia."

A sound of frustration escaped the younger girl. "I'll not be party to such disloyal discussion," Isla muttered, and in a marked display of distancing herself, she drew her skirts close and inched away from Emma.

To her sister's defense, Isla had never been betrayed or hurt by a man to know just how little they, on the whole, were to be trusted.

KnockKnockKnock.

Annalee banged the gavel, an intricately crafted piece designed by the husband of Mismatch member Lila, the Duchess of Wingate. A Lost Lord who'd been abducted as a boy, the former fighter had found his way back into the peerage, and had been supportive in every way of the Mismatch Society.

Annalee looked to Sylvia. "*This* meeting is called to *orderrr.*" Only the slight slur of that last word indicated the young woman, a survivor of the Peterloo Massacre, had already consumed a drink too many that day.

All eyes immediately went to Lady Sylvia.

Nay, not all of them. Lord St. John had his gaze firmly on the doorway.

Escape.

As one who'd fled her mock marriage ceremony and most meetings with her then betrothed, Lord Scarsdale, in the years to follow, Emma recognized that longing to leave. All too well.

"As you are aware," the lady began, "there is always a great concern when members leave our ranks. We've all come to know precisely what that usually means."

Murmurs of assent went up amongst the ladies present.

Yes, it meant that disapproving kin had stepped in and barred their daughter or ward from attending.

"And though that is the heart of the reason you've all been called," Sylvia went on, "there is another more pressing matter that merits a discussion prior to our lost membership."

Emma sharpened her gaze upon the viscount.

More blood leached from his cheeks, and he leaned forward in his chair, then sank back. Arching forward a second time like a baby bird practicing flight . . . and failing.

"I've recently discovered *by chance*"—Sylvia lifted her voice for just those two one-syllable words, drawing a noticeable attention to them—"the possibility a new society has been formed."

"What sort of society?" Olivia puzzled aloud.

Emma's suspicions deepened. What sort of society, indeed?

"Surely not a . . . rival organization?" Cora sounded so very close to crying that her mother produced another kerchief.

More murmurings rolled around the room, these more shocked and frenzied than the prior ones.

"Well, need it *realllly* be a rival?" St. John ventured. The gentleman wrestled with his previously perfectly folded cravat. "I mean, can it not simply be that there's an alternative place? Why should there be just one society? A need was identified . . . and as such, there should be many places that allow people to come together and share in ideas and frustrations and beliefs."

Well, that was *quite* the defense. Emma sharpened her eyes on the viscount, whose response was more than a rote deliverance. "That strikes me as very specific for someone who knows nothing of such a league," Emma said into the quiet, and all eyes swung her way. She grunted as Isla sent an elbow sailing into her side. "Ouch."

"Now that is unpardonably offensive," Isla said on a furious whisper, and then looked to Sylvia. She raised her voice. "I do not agree with my sister."

"You should," Sylvia drawled, and Emma felt her sister's pause and the tensing of her leg against hers, and as she looked to Emma, Isla's expression wavered.

"I . . . should?" she asked hesitantly, sliding a wary glance to the tense, pale gentleman at the center of the room and the discussion unfolding.

"Oh, yes." The viscountess placed her palms on either side of her husband's chair and leaned forward. "Isn't that right, dear husband?"

Sweat beaded the gentleman's brow, and he shifted back and forth in the too-small-for-him seat, the delicate scrap groaning under his movement. "I . . ."

"Are you uncomfortable, dear husband?" the viscountess went on. "If so, you have only yourself to blame." Fierce in her command of the moment, she straightened. "You do know something of it, and I'd ask you to share what you know."

His mother leaned forward, proffering a kerchief for her son, which he accepted, promptly mopping at his perspiring forehead. After he lowered the rumpled fabric to his lap, retaining his hold on it, he spoke. "I understand how you might perceive my support of a new society as a betrayal. Initially, I was of like mind."

"Initially," Valerie spat.

He frowned, and continued, "It was, however, pointed out that salons are not an original idea. Nor should they be reserved for one group of people. If there are others that would like to bring people together to engage in meaningful discussions, then who is anyone to suppress such opportunities?"

Silence rang in the uncharacteristically quiet gathering.

Annalee was the first to break it. "And I take it you've been attending these meetings?" she drawled, using the candlestick beside her to light her cheroot. The end sizzled ominously.

Except this time the viscount inclined his head, and appeared steadied by the justifications he'd provided the room. "I have."

Gasps went up.

His wife rocked back on her heels.

And Emma seethed. Another betrayal. This here, this meeting, was precisely why a woman would be wise to never fall in love. For there was no other way to look at Lord St. John's actions as anything other than a betrayal. As prettily as the viscount may have dressed up his actions, the truth remained: he'd been as disloyal as every other man. He was no different from the company that he—

She froze . . .

Her thoughts trickled to a slow stop, then resumed a rapid, water-fall-like flow, each thought after another crashing through.

No.

He wouldn't. He wouldn't dare interfere in this. Why, the idea even coming to her was preposterous. A man who spent his days at his clubs and his nights at his wicked clubs, Charles Hayden, the Earl of Scarsdale, wasn't one to go filling any part of his time with a pursuit such as the Mismatch Society. It defied logic and reason of the rules of rakes and rogues.

And yet, telling herself all that . . . she *knew*. She knew with the intuition only a woman was capable of—the same intuition that had told her at the age of six that he didn't wish to wed her.

Because she knew him. Even as he'd insisted she didn't. She knew how he thought. And following their broken betrothal, witnessing his dogged determination, she'd learned the depths to which he'd go to make her life an everlasting hell.

A curtain of red rage fell across her vision, briefly blinding . . .

"And who is the founder of this great society?" Clara, former cour-tesan turned countess and proprietor and a leader amongst the ranks, put that question to the viscount in a way that had him shifting once more.

"Scarsdale," Emma hissed, answering for the viscount and bringing everyone's focus back over to her. This had the earl's doing all over it.

Lord St. John hesitated, then nodded.

A curse exploded from her lips, the sound paired with Charles's name and drowned out by like curses from her offended sisterhood.

Sylvia clapped her hands. "You are excused, husband." The viscount promptly stood. "This has been most informative." She leaned up and kissed his cheek.

"You're not mad, then," he said, the tension leaving his shoulders.

"I did not say that exactly." The viscountess adjusted her husband's cravat in an intimate, tender moment Emma couldn't look away from. She'd wanted that for herself. And having always known what marital fate awaited her, Lord Scarsdale had slid into those imaginings, taking up a natural place in the romantic musings she'd once carried.

Seized by a regret that would always be there, Emma forcibly averted her gaze.

Lord St. John made a beeline for the doorway. He paused at the entrance, clinging to the threshold. "I should also point out the meetings aren't exclusively reserved for gentlemen," he said. "Women have also been encouraged to attend."

With that, he left.

Energy ran through Emma. It brought her to her feet, and she began to pace. The Mismatch Society fell to what was becoming a new quiet for them. And she felt all their eyes upon her as she marched back and forth across Lady Sylvia's floral Aubusson carpet. That was how it had always been: because of him, all eyes upon her. Not for any reasons that were good. But because she was the object of pity. And scorn. People saw his infidelities and the delay of their nuptials as a reflection of Emma, some imagined failings over which she'd had no control.

But this? This was different. This was him infringing upon something she had created. Nay, the first endeavor she'd ever had in the whole of her life. When Emma had first paid a visit to the three women living on Waverton Street, she'd stepped through the doors, there seeking guidance on how to change. How to earn Charles's affections.

Everything had changed that day. Nay, more importantly, Emma had changed that day. She'd looked at her reasons for being there. She'd considered everything that had been asked and expected of her . . . and had come to find she wanted no part of that. From the seeds of her resentment with her lot in life, the Mismatch Society had been conceived . . .

She seethed, her steps growing more frantic and frenzied.

Olivia stretched out a hand, and Emma ignored it, increasing her stride once more.

Now he'd simply start up his own *damned* society. And he'd sold it, so convincing in his reason for doing so that he'd swayed Lord St. John into thinking there was something more to it than there was.

And, of course, Charles's gathering included women. And, of course, those women would invariably attend. Because all society was endlessly fascinated by the charming rogue. But to know so many of the women she called friends had defected so? It was unconscionable. It was unforgivable.

"Is that where our members are going?" one of the newer members, Miss Lawlor, whispered.

"It appears that way," Sylvia said quietly.

"But . . . but . . ." Isla's eyes wavered as her illusions were shattered by the evidence of the truth that she'd mistaken as cynicism from Emma.

Alas, what else would one expect of a man linked to Scarsdale and Landon?

"How could Anwen?" Brenna seethed, each of them apparently directing their outrage in different places this day.

"Because she wants to get *marrrried*," Eris piped in.

Emma hardened her mouth. Yes, because after all, that was what this all came down to. Ultimately, women might scream for independence and speak about wanting a new place in the world, but when it was all said and done, the moment they had an opportunity to find love, off they went. Charles had been clever enough to see that. Clever enough to give women a society that wasn't anti-marriage, where they could meet gentlemen.

"Damn him," she whispered before she could call that telling curse back.

"Lord Scarsdale wouldn't," Cora said, and resumed crying once more.

Emma stopped her pacing and sat. "Oh, he did." He'd done precisely that.

"Or should we say . . . *they* did?" Valerie glowered at the chair Lord St. John had previously occupied.

"It is 'they,'" Little Eris piped in with an absolute lack of artifice only a child could be capable of. "Because we're angry at Clayton. And Scarsdale. I think we're probably going to be angry at Landon, too."

"Oh, undoubtedly," sisters Cora and Brenna said at the same time.

And then it came . . . whispered but loud enough through the din to be heard . . . and to be heard by all: "*Poor* Miss Gately."

There it was.

That one word spliced together with a name—hers.

And just like that, Emma found herself the object of what she'd been for so long amongst society—an object of pity.

Her hands formed reflexive fists, balled so tightly she drained the blood from her knuckles.

As everyone slid those benevolent glances her way, Emma sat stiffly through it. Those looks being directed at her, all the worse because they now included her sister and her best friend. Damn Charles. Damn him for doing this again to her, just in a different way.

Sylvia cleared her throat. "Now we've sorted through the mystery of our missing members and verified they are not waylaid by unscrupulous guardians and dastardly fathers, and that is what matters," she said quickly. "As such, I am adjourning today's meeting."

"But I wanted to yell more about Clayton," Eris whined as her mother came to her feet and took Eris's hand in hers.

"Come, come. There will be plenty of time and reasons to yell about Clayton," the dowager viscountess promised.

As the rest of the members took to their feet, lingering briefly to talk to the women seated beside them, Emma seethed.

Fury continued coming. Who knew anger had a taste, and it was fire on a scorned woman's tongue? "This is not to be borne," Emma bit out quietly to Isla and Olivia as they stood. First he'd made a pest of himself, striking up a friendship with her father. And finally, he'd plagiarized her idea and turned her into an object of pity amongst her friends. This? This was a step too far.

"What are you thinking?" Isla murmured as they headed for the doorway.

Emma was thinking this was unforgivable, and she didn't know what she intended, but—

"Emma, might I speak to you?" Sylvia called out.

Isla and Olivia looked to Emma, then quickly excused themselves until just Emma, Sylvia, Valerie, and Annalee remained.

The viscountess pulled the door closed. "I wanted to apologize. When I . . . called today's meeting, I did not think"—a blush bloomed on Sylvia's cheeks—"about how the others might respond, and I should have."

"Damned straight you should have," Annalee said.

"We *all* should have," Valerie pointed out, placing slight emphasis on that reminder.

"It is fine," Emma assured them. "It isn't your fault." Fault belonged with just one this day. She flattened her mouth into a line. Damn him.

Sylvia rested a hand on her shoulder. "Don't."

"I—"

"You are thinking to confront him. But doing so allows him back in your life . . ." The older, entirely too savvy viscountess cut her off, and called her out—accurately. "He's a rogue of the first order."

As the viscountess's last husband had been the best of friends with Charles, the other woman would know from experience.

Annalee pointed her cheroot at Sylvia. "She is right. You don't want this."

Nay, Emma didn't want it, but this was just one more piece in her life beyond her control because of her former betrothal. "If I do nothing, he wins," she said tightly.

"Some might argue that if you do something . . . and with him, you lose more," Valerie murmured.

Chewing at her nail, Emma stared into the empty hearth, contemplating her friends' words. They were not wrong . . . Charles merely sought to goad her. This all, ultimately, came down to her rejection of him. And yet . . . Emma faced her friends. "If it weren't Lord Scarsdale, and if the members hadn't reacted as they did today, would we have simply let this affront go?"

Their collective silence served as answer enough, and yet Sylvia confirmed it anyway. "But the fact remains it *is* Lord Scarsdale, and as long as we play whatever game this is to him, the ladies will continue to respond as they did." She shook her head. "And that is not what this place is about, Emma. This is a place to be free of the constraints that men and society bring to our lives."

Only it was just pretend. They might walk through the doors and share their views and live in that time, free of those constraints the viscountess spoke of. But it was just pretend. None of them could truly be free of the chains about them . . .

"I'm putting you in charge of our next agenda."

Emma whipped her gaze back to the viscountess. "But . . ." She was rubbish at speaking publicly in the group. Nor had she ever been charged with developing the agenda. "That isn't my role."

"Not before." Sylvia smiled. "It is now."

Blast and damn. It was an attempt to distract her and nothing more.

"It will be good for you, and the other members. You've never had the opportunity to lead a session."

And she hadn't wanted to. Having that focus trained on her left her nauseous in a different way than Charles's betrayal.

"But—"

"It is settled, Emma." The viscountess spoke with an air of finality. "We have competition now, and have to be even more creative in our content. Focus your attentions *there*."

And not on Charles.

That meaning was clear.

"Very well," she said stiffly. "Thank you."

The moment she took her leave, she let loose a stream of curses in her head.

Her friends might think to divert Emma with a new responsibility in the society, but they also underestimated her if they believed she was capable of just that. Nay, first, she was going to pay a visit to Cressida Alby and her brother, and when she was done with that, there was a certain call in need of her attention.

Chapter 6

THE LONDONER

BRILLIANCE ABOUNDS

A valuable addition to Polite Society has recently sprung: a club that provides a valuable means of bringing persons together to speak. Unlike the Mismatch Society, which takes itself too seriously and tries entirely too hard, it is no wonder so many are clamoring for a place within this new, exciting establishment, hosted by none other than the Earl of Scarsdale.

M. FAIRPOINT

White's was more crowded than usual, even for the afternoon hour. That fact was not just some matter of chance.

Reclining in his chair, Charles stared at the Baron Waldegrave. The young rogue, with his Brutus curls and deliberately unkempt cravat, wore a look Charles recognized all too well.

And he didn't trust him on sight for it. "State your intentions," he said, turning to an empty page in his notebook.

The fellow cleared his throat. "I . . . I thought . . . is this an interview?"

Landon snorted. "Surely you don't think our club would have such low standards that we wouldn't conduct *interviews?*"

Charles and Landon both leveled the younger man with a look that effectively doused the cocksure arrogance the boy had come in with.

Ducking his shoulders, the baron squirmed in his seat. "To join the club?"

"Is that a question?" Charles asked. He didn't wait, turning that query instead to Landon. "Was that a question?"

Taking that cue from him, the marquess shook his head disapprovingly. "It sounded like a question to me."

Lord Waldegrave immediately shot up in his chair. "Not a question. A request?" When both men continued to stare at him, he said, "An appeal?"

Charles shook his head. "Another question." He made a note in his book; feeling the younger man arching forward to examine the words there, he looked up quickly.

"*Tsk-tsk,*" Landon said, cradling his drink in his hand.

Waldegrave immediately sat back.

Then Charles got to it, the heart of the question that mattered most. "Why do you wish to join?"

And just like that, all the nervousness seemed to seep out of the young man's wiry frame. Waldegrave's lips formed one of those affected, crooked half grins that Charles knew all too well. Dropping his left elbow onto the table, the young man leaned forward. "I think that should be clear."

Charles sharpened his stare on this latest interviewee. Of course, the lad was too arrogant, and too young to lose his grin over it. "Say it anyway."

The other side of the boy's mouth completed his smile. "A room full of ladies without the benefits of their mothers present?" And with that, he waggled his eyebrows, holding Landon's gaze first, and then Charles's, a young rogue who recognized like company. But he was also too much a fool to know there was a difference between a rogue and a rake.

Charles and Landon looked at one another.

"Get the hell out, Waldegrave," Landon snapped.

"But . . . but . . ." The young man sputtered, struggling and failing to get his complete thought out in one piece. "I thought this was a way to get men with ladies who have a taste for passion."

Anger briefly darkened Charles's vision. "It's not," he snapped. "You really think I'm going to stage seductions between men and innocent women in my *mother's household?*"

Waldegrave hesitated. "Uh . . ."

"I advise you don't answer that." Landon helped the young man out, effectively saving his life. The young baron immediately closed his mouth. "Go."

Waldegrave jumped up and immediately fled.

"Who is next?" Charles asked before the rake had even gone. Skimming a finger along his sloppy notes, contained within what might have actually been an empty page in one of his ledgers, he settled his index finger on a name. "Beaufort."

Charles glanced over to the balding young gentleman hovering in the wings.

"This day has proven enlightening," he said, snapping his book shut. Of the seven interviews they'd conducted thus far, all but one had resulted in the same outcome.

Landon chuckled. "What did you expect? That you were going to have a sea of bookish lords interested in talking philosophy and life? Why, we're not all that different from any of those other ones." He nudged his chin at a table full of the gentlemen who'd assembled to commiserate over their rejections. All six of the men glared back their way.

Yes, it was a fair point. They hadn't been vastly different from all the men whose ulterior motives and interests were solely on interacting in ways that were noneducational with the ladies who made up his club. But neither had they preyed on unwed ladies.

Charles stared, frozen, vacantly at the cover of his notebook.

"Don't look so glum," Landon said, pouring him a glass of brandy and pushing it his way until the snifter touched his fingers. He consulted his haphazard notes, then glanced over to the young gent hovering in the wings. "We'll find the honorable ones. Rare though they are. Why, here is one now!" With that, he held up his hand in greeting, and Charles looked to the approaching lord.

Landon brightened. "St. John! Grab a chair. You're right on time. Almost anyway."

The viscount passed a horrified gaze over the cluttered table. "What in *helllll* is this?"

"Interviews," Charles explained, raising a hand and staying the approaching Lord Beaufort, holding on to their privacy a bit longer.

"Interviews?" St. John repeated.

Charles and Landon nodded in response. The other man continued to stare back blankly, his brow creased in lines of perplexity, before he at last availed himself of a seat. "Explain," he said with an ease that could come from only a man with six troublesome sisters.

Lord Beaufort pointedly cleared his throat. All three men shot up a hand, holding him at bay. The young gent, recently out of university, rocked back on his heels and remained there, waiting.

"I think it should be clear," Charles explained, shuffling through the first stack of papers, evening those sheets, and then arranging the others. "We're conducting official club business."

St. John shook his head, then several moments later, continued shaking. "And you somehow decided White's was the best place for official business?"

"Well, it couldn't very well be at Forbidden Pleasures. That would defeat the purpose," Charles said jovially, leaning over to pat his friend on the back. "It's the easiest way to assemble honorable gents and interested parties. Get them all in one place and—"

"Weed them out," Landon supplied. Reaching for the barely touched bottle of brandy, he proceeded to refill his glass.

"Let me get this straight: you two, leading rogues of Polite Society, are interviewing lords to see if they are . . . respectable enough." St. John paused, then promptly burst out laughing.

Landon grunted. "Quite judgmental of you, old chum. One should think you'd approve of us being careful in our process."

"Yes. No. I . . ." The befuddled gentleman dragged a hand through his hair, then began again. "Of course, I am pleased that you are placing such emphasis on the character of the members."

"Did you expect otherwise?" Charles asked, already knowing. Already knowing the opinion society . . . even his best friends and family . . . had of him. He was entirely deserving of it. But it chafed still.

"Of course not," St. John said unconvincingly.

"I'm allowing gentlemen to enter my family's household, the place where my sister and Seamus live . . . and where your sister and other men's sisters and wives will meet," Charles said. "Do you truly think I'll allow just *any* rogue to attend?"

Folding his arms at his chest, Landon stared pointedly at the viscount. *"Hmm?"*

Properly chastised, St. John bowed his head. "You . . . my apologies," he said quietly. "You are correct. I'm just . . . pleased to see the measures you've put into place."

Surprised Charles would do the right thing? It didn't need to be said. The meaning of those unspoken words was clear.

Coughing into his fist, St. John nodded for them to continue. "As you were."

Landon motioned for their next potential member to join.

Beaufort trotted over and hovered until Charles gestured to the last open seat. "Join us, Beaufort."

The young fellow promptly sank into the seat. "A-all three of you intend to interview me?"

"Is that a problem?" Charles, Landon, and St. John asked at the same time.

The boy's enormous Adam's apple leapt. "No," he croaked, his voice climbing several octaves. "Not at all. It is an honor." He swept his arms wide and dropped a deep, seated bow that managed to connect the lad's forehead with the corner of the table.

All three men collectively winced at that solid thump.

Blushing, Beaufort straightened.

"Now . . ." Charles's question faded as he caught sight of the latest addition to White's. His brother wound his way through the crowded floor, beating a purposeful path forward until he came to a stop at Charles's private table.

Derek doffed his hat, slapping it against his palm and sending a cloud of dust wafting.

"Hey, pup," Charles greeted. He stretched out a leg, using the tip of his boot to snatch one of the empty chairs from a nearby table and shove it over to Derek. "Joining the big lads, are you?"

Derek ignored that offering, his expression dark, his eyes troubled.

All Charles's fraternal senses went on brotherly alert. "Out of here, Beaufort," he said, cutting off the young man still in the midst of conversing with St. John.

The other man stopped abruptly and frowned up at Charles's brother. "I beg your pardon. I've scheduled my appointment, Hayden. You're stealing my time."

Derek blinked in confusion. "What . . . is *happening*?" he asked with the same confusion St. John had arrived with earlier.

"Nothing anymore. You heard the Haydens. Time to shove off, Beaufort," Landon said, pushing the smaller man's chair back with his right foot to edge it away from the table.

"Gentlemen, if you'll allow me a moment?" Charles said the moment Derek had seated himself.

As if at last sensing the tense shift, his friends looked between one another.

"Of course," St. John murmured, climbing to his feet.

As both men took their leave, Derek didn't offer so much as a parting goodbye, and the sense of dread only spiraled. "What is it?" Charles asked the moment they'd gone.

"I . . ." Derek averted his stare, the club's bounty of candles casting a bright glow over the room, highlighting his flushed cheeks.

"What is it, Derek?" Charles urged a second time, gently but firmly.

"I attended a club that caters to men and women." A wicked establishment Charles had frequented time enough in his youth, at first in the name of duty, and then because it had become easier to be numbed by the solace found in a stranger's arms than to confront directly how he'd failed his sister. Such clubs were dens of sin, and he despised that his brother had found his way into that world. "There was . . . a young woman there," his brother finished, glancing down at his feet.

Impatient for the details that had sent Derek racing here, Charles controlled himself, allowing his sibling the time he required.

"She wasn't dressed like the other women. She was attired like a proper lady, in modest garments. And she was pale . . . and"—Derek dragged a hand through his hair—"I managed to speak to her alone." His brother's mouth hardened. "Some cad told her he loved her, ruined her, and sold her. She is just seventeen."

She is just seventeen.

Oh, God.

Sweat slicked Charles's palms. His stomach roiled.

The past came rushing up to meet him, and he thought of another young lady who'd suffered such a fate. Not a stranger, but his sister, Camille. Who'd been differently but similarly ruined by the dissolute lord who'd inherited the ramshackle properties next to their Kent country estates. That rake, who'd met her secretly, had seduced her out of her virtue, then left her with a babe in her belly—the babe Charles had come to pass off as his own in a bid to protect Camille from the scandal and suffering that would await her as a single mother.

Since the moment he'd learned of his sister's fate, Charles had been left desperately trying to put together the pieces of something that could never truly be fixed . . . But even so, he'd tried like hell anyway.

"Charles? Charles?" his brother repeated a second time, more insistently, pulling Charles back from the abyss of so many regrets.

"Yes, forgive me."

"I couldn't get her out," his brother said tightly. "The chap was quite condescending, and I couldn't. I'm not a lord with any influence. I don't have the funds to even try. I—" His features spasmed, and he slammed a fist on the table, that thump an echo of his fury and frustration, attracting attention from nearby patrons.

"*Shh,*" Charles urged. "It is fine." He willed a thread of firmness into that assurance. "Tell me where they are. I'll coordinate what must be done."

"Thank you," his brother mouthed, his shoulders sagging, revealing just how young he still was.

A short while later, he and his brother rode for Cannon Street.

Chapter 7

THE LONDONER

SUSPICIONS ABOUND

The town agitator, none other than Miss Gately, pre-
suming to know what is best for all ladies everywhere,
has been spied gallivanting throughout different
ends of London, haranguing fathers and guardians,
attempting to bully those gentlemen into her way of
thinking. Is there no level to which this jilted miss will
not sink?

M. FAIRPOINT

Two murders had been committed on Ratcliff Highway.

Two families, within two weeks of one another.

In all, seven victims had lost their lives on these very streets.

Granted, those atrocities had been committed more than seventeen
years ago.

Never more did Emma Gately regret having listened to that omi-
nous tale told by Daria, one of the Viscountess St. John's sisters-in-law.

At the time, Emma had been fascinated by the telling, particularly by the young lady. Now she recognized her privilege, which had also blinded her to the fact that people lived in these parts of London.

That one of their members, Emma's new friend, Cressida, had lived there.

Did live here.

And riding through the clogged roadway of Artichoke Hill only heightened the sense of impending peril that hung in the air.

The carriage lurched to a jolting stop, and Emma gripped the edge of her bench to keep from being flung, even as her maid went flying into the side.

A moment later, the carriage door opened, and her family's driver, Tensly, looked up, his eyes reflecting her own concern. "Streets are too full," he shouted loudly enough to be heard over the circus of sounds outside. He doffed his hat and wiped at his damp brow. "Cannot get any farther than this, miss."

Emma leaned over and peered out. At her side, her maid, Heather, followed suit.

People filled the streets, vendors selling their goods.

It was, however, still broad daylight. How much peril could—?

A fellow in tattered garments with a ladder hoisted about his back shouted at Tensly. "Outta the damned way!"

As one, Emma and Heather immediately pulled back inside, with Tensly pushing the door shut behind them. "I don't know, miss," the young woman murmured, echoing Emma's own reservations. "It isn't the . . . safest place, and your parents would have my head if anything were to happen to you."

"No, they'd have mine, and know that I was to blame, and appreciate that you were good enough, at least, to accompany me."

"I don't know about that," the young girl muttered.

Emma chewed at her lower lip, warring with her indecision. The cowardly part of her said to forget this visit. The other part called her out for being not only a coward but also a privileged woman at that, who'd balk at visiting anyplace outside Mayfair.

In the end, those latter sentiments won out.

Heather groaned. "Oh, *missss*," she moaned, recognizing what Emma intended even before she confirmed it.

"I'll just be a short while," Emma promised, drawing up her hood.

"I'm accompanying you."

"No," Emma insisted. "It will be fine. How dangerous could it"— something struck one of the carriage windows, knocking the glass loudly, and they both jumped—"be?" she finished with a smile.

And before the girl took it in her head to follow, Emma let herself out.

Tensly was there immediately with a hand up to help her. Calling her thanks, Emma started across the street, zigzagging around passersby and people moving livestock along. Her feet dragged through the thick mud coating the earth, and yet . . . the scent of dung filled the sky, competing with the smoke and soot for supremacy. And when collectively roiled together, the people who visited these parts, who lived here, were left with an ungodly stench thick enough to suffocate a person.

Shamefully, it had never occurred to her how people outside of Polite Society lived. In this case, even people who found themselves counted among the ranks of the *ton*, as Cressida and her brother now did, found their lives . . . a struggle. And Emma was struck by the depth of her own narrow-mindedness of the world around her and the economic plight of so many.

Where Mayfair sipped tea at this hour, it would appear Central London bustled with workers. Emma skimmed the rows of townhouses, a mix of new, bright, freshly painted stucco and sorry, crumbling structures, searching for the markings. Anything to set the dilapidated structures apart and highlight the place she'd come in search of. Regent Street was, in short, an area in transition, on their way to becoming a fashionable, safe, inhabitable place, but still on a long path to that point.

Emma searched the townhouses, looking for the number of Cressida Alby's residence. She squinted . . .

And her heart fell.

Sandwiched between two gleaming white structures, Cressida's home boasted broken windows and rotted wood, with holes enough to let the elements sail through. The modest but fine garments she'd donned, however, had revealed no hint as to how she'd truly been living.

Catching her hem, Emma held the already grime-stained article aloft and dashed across the street. The moment she reached the door, she lifted the knocker, letting it fall several times.

And standing back, she waited, staring up at the run-down stucco unit belonging to Cressida's family.

From within, there came the shuffle of feet and the annoyed mutterings of a person on the other side.

The panel opened. An aging apron-clad servant with straggly, stringy grey hair gave Emma's garments a harsh once-over. "What ya want?"

Emma donned a smile. After all, Lila's household, run entirely by former street fighters and their families, had familiarized her all too well with the unconventional servant. "My name is Miss Gately." She procured a card from the reticule hanging on her wrist, and held it over. "I'm here to see Miss Alby."

The old woman looked her up and down. "Wot ya want with the miss?" she demanded, making no move to take the ivory scrap from Emma's fingers.

"Uh . . . yes," she said, stuffing the article back inside her reticule and closing the latch. All the while, she studied this gatekeeper to the latest member snatched from the folds of the Mismatch; the woman's sallow face proved an unreadable mask. Whether she was friend or gaoler to the young lady here in this household, Emma knew not. In the end, she opted for the truth. "I am a friend to Miss Alby."

"Miss Alby ain't got herself any friends," the servant said bluntly, and made to shut the door.

Emma shot up a hand, inserting her fingers in the opening to keep from letting that panel slam on her.

Or to get your fingers severed, a voice taunted.

She spoke on a rush. "I assure you, I am very much her friend. I'm one of the founders of a society of young women, which Cressida once joined. She is my friend, and I have come to pay a visit," she ended with a greater firmness. She'd not only come to visit, but more importantly, to ensure her friend was safe and well . . . and that she wasn't being forced into that miserable marriage she'd no interest in.

The old woman eyed her a long while through sunken eyes, made all the deeper by the way in which she narrowed them upon Emma's face. Then she glanced over Emma's shoulder to the streets beyond.

Emma turned, following her stare, then gasped as a wrinkled hand wrapped about her arm and jerked her forward.

The servant slammed the door behind them. "Ya ain't got much time with the miss," she said gruffly. And then without bothering to see whether Emma followed, she stalked off.

Emma looked around at the dark foyer, devoid of sconces or candles, and climbed her gaze up to the empty place where once had hung a chandelier but now remained a ceiling peppered with holes and damp spots.

"Ya 'eard what I said? Ya don't 'ave much time," the old woman snapped, and Emma sprang into movement, quickening her stride to catch up.

It was a short walk, down a narrow hall that had been stripped—and poorly, at that—of the wallpaper, peeled as if in haste by someone who'd had intentions of making over the walls, but had abandoned their efforts upon the struggle to remove the previous work. The chipped and faded oak panels had been all pulled shut, but for one.

They stopped before that lone open entryway.

Faded green velvet curtains had been drawn far back to allow light into the parlor; that same garish green adorned the pieces of Chippendale furniture that showed hints of once greatness and wealth, but had since been dimmed by time and lack of care.

Cressida occupied a room beside the empty hearth, busy at work, darning—

Emma's heart wrenched.

"Ya got company, gel," Emma's guide announced with a great tenderness and gruff warmth . . . the manner of which Emma'd not have expected possible of the servant.

The young woman's head went flying up; with stockings and darning needles in hand, she sprang to her feet. "Emma!" Surprise rounded her eyes. She was immediately across the room, her arms outstretched, but then caught herself, rocking back on her heels and denying herself and Emma that overly warm greeting. "It is . . . so very good to see you," she finished instead. Hanging her head, she brought her stockings and darning needles behind her.

With a grunt, the loyal maid plucked those articles from her mistress, dropping them into the front of her own apron.

"Won't you join me?" Cressida said weakly.

Emma smiled. Removing her gloves, she dropped them into her reticule. "I would enjoy that very much."

"Trudy, will you please bring refreshments for Miss Gately?"

"Oh, no, that won't be—"

"Ya know we ain't got refreshments," the loyal maid chided, and Cressida's face buckled.

"I don't require refreshments," Emma was quick to reassure. Collecting the younger woman's hands, she squeezed lightly. "Your company is the sole reason I've come."

Trudy's harsh features softened. "There ya go, gel. A real friend ya don't need to hide that rubbish from. Tea. We got tea," she said, and with that, the gruff, coarse figure shuffled off.

The moment she'd gone, Cressida motioned to a small, faded gold settee with slightly torn upholstery. "Won't you sit?"

Emma immediately took up a place on that bench, resting her reticule on her lap.

The other young woman claimed the matching settee across from her.

A brief, silent awkwardness fell. "Now you can see why he wished me to wed . . . ," Cressida murmured, clasping her hands upon her lap. "To sell me." This time, however, there was an acrid bitterness in her avowal.

So much resentment and hate filled Emma . . . for what Cressida Alby and all women endured.

"Regardless of wealth, brothers and fathers"—even the devoted ones—"are only interested in selling one's daughters. For gain. For wealth. For familial friendships." As had been the case with Emma's parents.

"Why have you come?" Cressida asked curiously.

Not for the first time since she'd arrived in Regent Street, Emma's heart pulled for the young woman. Did she truly not know she called her a friend? That she wasn't alone? By the rounded set to her shoulders and the sad glimmer in her eyes, the answer was likely the latter. "As I said to Trudy," she said gently, "you are my friend, and you have been missed. Not just by me, but the others as well."

"I'm sure no one even noticed," Cressida murmured, dropping her glance to her pale-pink muslin skirts. "I hardly contributed and really only listened." She spoke with a quiet sadness of someone who'd heard those words tossed at her, and now spoke them in rote remembrance.

"That isn't true." Quitting her place, Emma went over to join the younger woman. "That isn't true at all. You came and listened and wanted to be there with us. Because you believe in what we believe in and our mission for other women, that makes your contribution as meaningful as anyone else's." Unlike the members who'd so quickly defected because of a newer, brighter, shinier organization to come along. "Your role among our society isn't to be understated."

A tremulous smile formed on Cressida's wide mouth. "Thank you," she whispered through tears that shimmered in her pretty brown eyes.

Emma brushed the drops that fell from the younger woman's cheeks. "Come now, none of that! This is a happy time. We are reunited, and I've come to share all the latest developments with you." With that, Emma proceeded to provide her recently found friend with an enumeration of the latest developments, from the inception of Charles's new club to the loss of their members.

By the time Emma concluded, the earlier sadness in Cressida's eyes had been replaced with the sparkle that usually brightened them. "What do you intend to do?"

Emma lifted an eyebrow. "You assume I intend to do something?" she asked, touching a hand to her breast in pretend disbelief.

"I know you intend to do something," the other woman said, and they joined in laughing.

When their shared amusement had settled, Emma confirmed her friend's supposition. "I intend to confront him, of course."

"Of course." Cressida clapped her hands together, then sighed. "How I wish I might take part again in the society."

"You can, and you will."

Just like that, the light went out of the young woman's eyes. "You don't know my brother."

"I have two."

"Not like mine," Cressida said, her words so faint Emma strained to hear, and when she did, a chill traipsed along her spine. "I don't want to talk about that."

"But . . ."

"I'm not coming back. And I do not wish to speak further of it." Cressida spoke with a forcefulness Emma had never recalled from the girl.

"Of course," she said quietly. "We needn't."

Trudy arrived with a tray bearing three mismatched teacups and a chipped porcelain pot, which she set down before them. Instead of taking her leave, however, the woman settled onto the vacant settee, and helped herself to a cup of tea with an ease cementing that familiarity between her and Cressida.

"Trudy was our family's all-purpose servant," Cressida shared as she accepted the pot of tea from the old woman and poured first one cup, then another. "She is family." She handed Emma one of the cups.

"Closer than family," the old woman grunted, and sipped her drink.

Closer than family therefore also meant a confidante who might have a greater chance of succeeding where Emma had otherwise failed. "I was encouraging Cressida to rejoin me for the Mismatch meetings."

"Mr. Alby won't allow it," Trudy said bluntly.

Cressida sneered. "Baron Newhart. Do not forget he is now a baron."

"Don't care what 'e is," Trudy spat. "Always been a selfish sod. Now 'e's just a selfish one with a title and a sense of import, and 'e won't ever agree to the girl's attending." Trudy directed that last part at Emma.

"But . . ."

"'e's not pleased she went against 'im," Trudy went on. "Only way 'e'd likely consider it 'tis . . ."

If Cressida agreed to marry the man he wished so he could have the fortune he wanted. And even that wouldn't secure Cressida the freedom she needed from a rotter like her brother. "You'd simply go from one prison to another," Emma said tightly. "That will never do."

They sipped their tea in silence.

After they'd concluded, they resumed their discourse, with Emma filling Cressida in on other details she'd missed since she'd been forced to resign her membership. When their visit was concluded, Cressida alone escorted Emma to the door. "It has been so lovely to see you," she said wistfully.

"I shall come again, and will continue visiting until you resume your place." Emma smiled. "And then, even after it," she vowed. Trudy rushed forward with Emma's cloak, and she accepted it from the older woman. "It has been a pleasure, Trudy."

"The same," the old servant said gruffly. "Now go on with yarself."

Adjusting the grommets of her cloak, Emma stepped outside. The rush of sunlight, after walking the dim halls, proved briefly blinding, and she lifted a hand to shield her stare. She blinked several times in a bid to adjust her vision to the afternoon sun . . . and gasped.

A slightly soft-around-the-middle gentleman stood at the base of the steps.

The brother.

Raising a monocle, he peered at her. "Miss Gately," he said coolly.

Emma donned the same smile she had when first meeting Trudy; however, the baron proved even more unbendable than the maid. "Lord Newhart," she greeted, infusing as much charm as she could, finding herself with the opportunity she'd sought. Holding on to the wrought iron rail, Emma took the steps to meet him. "I had hoped to speak with you."

"Oh?" He doffed a hat so high it looked more a prop for a stage with a farcical production about some lord than an actual article a real, nonfictional man might wear.

"I don't know if you are aware, but I'm one of the founders of the Mis—"

He cut her off. "I know precisely who you are."

Hmph. So this was not going to be as easy as she'd anticipated. Not that she should have expected anything else, given how the male members of Polite Society had responded to the formation of the Mismatch Society.

"Now if you'll excuse me, Miss Gately?" The gentleman made to step around her, and she hurried to place herself in his path.

"If I might beg a moment of your time, Lord Newhart?" She added another smile to her appeal.

All the while her mind raced, running through everything she already knew about the man before her, as well as everything her friend and Trudy had revealed this day, about his pomposity, his regard for his title. She shifted tactics.

He grunted. "What is it?"

"It is just . . . your sister has been such an addition to"—his brows dipped, and Emma continued, careful to leave out mention of the name of the society that blinded this man and most men to anything but their resentment—"Polite Society," she neatly substituted. Some of the tension eased from his high brow.

"Oh?"

"Yes, yes. Very much so. I do not know if Cressida has mentioned, amongst her friends she includes the Viscountess St. John. The Dowager Viscountess St. John." There was a visible softening to the man's fleshy lips with every respectable title she dropped. "The Countess of Waterson and the Duchess of Wingate."

The pale planes of his rounded face tensed, and he thumped the bottom of his cane on the limestone step. That thumping inadvertently sent loose pieces of the stone flaking free. "A former courtesan and a street fighter's wife. My sister is above reproach and will not be keeping company with such shameful, wicked, wanton creatures." With every insult hurled, the color in his face deepened until his cheeks were splotchy red.

That red matched the rage that raced through her at the audacity of this man, who couldn't hold a candlestick to the women of strength and courage and convictions.

"Now, if you will excuse me," he demanded, this time sharper and harsher in that command.

"No, I will not." Emma dropped her hands onto her hips and blocked his efforts once more.

His already buglike eyes bulged. "I beg your pardon."

"You are making your sister a prisoner, and I am here demanding you set her free to spend her days as she would. And she would have those days spent at the Mismatch Society."

"You . . . you . . ." He surged forward, and Emma kept herself rooted to the place where she stood on the middle of his steps, even as under her skirts, her legs trembled and the nerve endings cried to flee. If she did, then the message would be sent loud and clear to bullying men such as the one before her that the women of the Mismatch Society could be intimidated. "Stand out of my way."

If bullied once, bullied a thousand times more in the future to come. "I will not, until you agree to let Cressida attend."

"My God, you are stupid."

Emma curved her lips in a slow smile meant to challenge and taunt. "I prefer brave."

He shot out a hand, gripping her arm so hard he pulled a gasp from her. And it only emboldened him. Cocksure and arrogant, as only a bullying man could be. He tightened his hold all the more, and tears pricked behind her eyes from the fierceness of his touch.

And then Lord Newhart smiled his first smile of their meeting. "No woman will ever dare come to my household and order me about. That is a mistake, Miss Gately."

Chapter 8

THE LONDONER

CAUGHT

Miss Gately has been spied bullying the brother of one of her former club members. After she physically accosted the poor gentleman, it was only the intervention and rescue from one Earl of Scarsdale that saw her poor victim freed.

M. FAIRPOINT

That same day, alongside his brother, Charles collected and settled the young woman Derek had found into the household with Miss Lee and Miss Linden: two women he'd been linked to over the years. It was a residence he'd come to studiously avoid. If he were discovered at their townhouse, it would not only fly in the face of the plea his mother had put to him, serving to resurrect gossip-filled rumors about his wicked association with those women, but also would add further fuel to Emma's ill opinion of him.

Mindful of the peril he'd find himself in, Charles adjusted the brim of his hat and quickly made his way out of the Regent Street townhouse.

Derek followed behind him. "Thank you," his younger brother said quietly as they left.

"Do not thank me."

"You paid a small fortune to secure her release, and I know what it will mean if you are discovered here . . . for your . . ."

Derek didn't finish, nor did he need to. "His . . . Miss Gately" had been the way all his family and friends had come to refer to her. Even as she'd never truly been his. Not beyond a document that she'd wanted even less than he had.

They started across the street to the two lads holding the reins for their horses.

"Have you considered telling her?" Derek pressed. Telling Emma? Emma, who already believed Charles couldn't be faithful to her, who believed only the worst of him . . . and that most of her reasons for doing so were entirely fair and accurate. "I believe if she knew—"

Charles stopped abruptly on the pavement and faced his brother. "That I've not been romantic with Miss Lee and Miss Linden, that she'll suddenly think better of me?" he shot back. "What about the other women before them?" Because whatever she might think or discover or learn about the women whose townhouse he'd visited this day didn't erase the sins he was truly guilty of. Or the mistresses he'd ultimately taken in his life. "*Hmm?* The ones whom I did carry on with in the very way she believes I conducted myself?"

His brother went silent, his gaze moving to a point beyond Charles's shoulder. "Miss Gately—"

"Bloody hell," he snapped. "Enough with—"

"No. Miss Gately," his brother repeated, and pointed, bringing Charles's focus across the street.

He squinted at the young lady in the midst of conversing with some gent who stood entirely too close. Surely not. *"Emmmma?"* Impossible.

Charles rubbed at his eyes, and the sight remained. But Emma . . . with some bounder who had a hand upon her arm. Fury blazed to life, devouring Charles with a hungering for the blood of the fiend who dared touch her.

Charles was already striding across the street.

"Go easy on him," Derek called after him, his voice indicating he attempted to keep up.

Charles, however, moved at a near sprint toward the pair. Emma . . . and the cad who'd lose a hand this day. Or his life. Likely in that order. Even with the paces between them, that fiery, bold challenge in the lady's eyes was one he recognized all too well. Lord knew it had been turned Charles's way enough. But this? Now, here, with a man who'd dare assault her?

He quickened his stride in a bid to reach her, cursing the cluttered streets that threw up barricades to his reaching her.

Charles wound his way around a pair of bucket-bearing boys, nearly knocking into the lads, keeping all his focus upon Emma. The cad took a step closer to her. "You there," he barked, but his calls were futile in the din of the afternoon activity.

The cad twisted Emma's arm slightly, a barely perceptible movement that Charles observed in his scrutiny, and his gut clenched, and with a shout he charged on ahead to save—

Emma brought up her knee deftly, and swiftly, catching the gentleman between the legs, instantly crumpling his form. The man cried out, and releasing the cane he held, he clutched at himself.

Slightly breathless from fear and shock, Charles staggered to a stop before the pair . . . just as Emma put a foot atop the bounder, locking him in place on the ground.

And Charles found himself breathless with something else: awe.

The pair looked Charles's way. Surprise filled Emma's eyes. "Charles," she blurted with no small amount of surprise—a surprise he understood all too well. And with her foot adroitly resting atop the gentleman's throat, where one forward press would kill the man, she would have ended any ill-timed movements on his part. "What are you doing here?" she asked, conversing as easily as if they met over tea and not with her in the middle of Regent Street, defending herself like some Spartan warrior woman of old.

He doffed his hat. "Uh . . . saving you?"

Emma widened her eyes.

"But not," he was quick to add. Clearly not. Yet again, his former betrothed had saved herself, and quite nicely . . . first from an unwanted betrothal, and now, it would seem, from some bounder on the street.

There came an animal-like whimpering, bringing Charles's attention back to the pale-faced lord. "Do I need to kill him?" he asked conversationally. "Or do you wish to see to the honor yourself?" The ghost of a smile danced on her lips, that beautiful tilt of her mouth so infrequently bestowed upon him that it sent his heart into an overtime rhythm.

The man moaned, turning his head slightly enough that Emma angled her heel down a fraction, halting any further movement. She hesitated a moment, then slowly removed her foot.

Charles leaned down, and taking the man by the front of his jacket, he drew him up by the lapels so the coward had no choice but to look him in the eyes. "If you ever go about handling Miss Gately, or any other woman, that way again, I will happily destroy you," he said, adding an icy smile that sent the man in his arms trembling. "Only after she's finished with you, of course. Is that understood?"

The cad frantically nodded, blubbering like a babe. Charles wasn't finished with him. Not until he heard the words. "Is that understood?"

"Y-yes! *Yeesssss!*"

Except Charles couldn't, and wouldn't, let off so easy a man who'd ever put his hands upon her. "Make your apologies."

His eyes darting over to Emma, the man swallowed visibly. "I'm s-sorry," the younger man said on a rush.

"Assure her that it shall not happen again."

"Never!"

"To any woman."

The coward under him quaked all the more, and also hesitated. Charles brought up his fist, and the scared pup whimpered.

"To any woman! To any woman," he cried, repeating that second promise all the louder.

Charles hesitated a moment longer, then released the whimpering fellow, lowering him back to his feet.

The moment he was free, the blubbering lord scrambled about, snagging the spectacles Charles, previously tunneled in on his fury, hadn't even realized the man wore, and a cane. The cad made a beeline for his townhouse, tripping and stumbling over his legs as he took the steps two at a time.

The moment he was inside, he slammed the panel shut.

In the aftermath of the moment, the battle, Charles's body continued to thrum. "You're certain—?"

"Oh, I assure you, I'm quite unharmed." She spoke quickly and with a greater steadiness and calm to her voice than he was capable of in this moment.

That would make one of them who was fine, then.

Emma glanced about, muttering to herself, and then her eyes lit. Hurrying up the steps, she collected a delicate white lace parasol and draped it at her shoulder.

Unlike Charles, who was unsteadied by the whole damned exchange, she was masterful in her strength. God, in her defense of herself, and in her absolute lack of need of Charles or any warm-blooded man, she was magnificent.

"Will you walk with me?" Charles asked.

⌘

Following the emergency meeting of the Mismatch Society, Emma had assembled all manner of words she had for Charles, and knew precisely how she intended to deliver them.

None of them had been warm.

None of them had even been remotely kind.

But then, all of them flew out of her head with that one question: *Will you walk with me?*

It was the first time he'd ever asked to do . . . anything with her.

Yes, they'd often danced at *ton* events, but only because his parents were standing over him, ensuring he remembered to ask for the next set.

But this? This was different.

This offering came with just the two of them together, Charles having rushed to assist her. Granted, she'd not needed assistance in that particular moment, but he'd let her handle all that—deciding on when her exchange with Lord Newhart was at an end—and that ceding of power was something she'd not expected of him. Or any man.

And . . . she didn't know what to do with the moment or with him.

She was, once again, the besotted girl just out of the schoolroom, all tongue-tied around Charles, the Earl of Scarsdale, and she hated herself for that weakness. Granted, neither could she do anything to break herself free of that weakness. She'd focus on her anger with him later.

His brow dipped.

"Yes," she blurted. "That . . . would be fine."

And falling into step, they began their stroll in the most unexpected part of London, on their first, and unlikeliest, of outings.

Charles's gaze went to the place Lord Newhart had touched Emma, and it was as though he sought to discover for himself whether that flesh, concealed by a cloak, bore bruises. She braced, expecting him to press her with questions about Lord Newhart's attempted assault. "Why were you there?"

"Lord Newhart is brother to one of my dear friends, a fellow lady of the society," she explained, without really explaining anything. "Miss Cressida Alby."

"That man has a sister," he said between clenched teeth.

She nodded. "He's not a sibling like any of mine or yours." Emma clenched and unclenched her fingers around the handle of her parasol. Equal parts pity and loathing for what the cad no doubt inflicted upon the girl sent rage rippling through her. "After Cressida broke her betrothal to a man chosen by Lord Newhart, he forbade her from attending the Mismatch Society." Emma's mouth hardened. "He took exception to her being a member, and severed her connection with the society." As so many other men had done to their daughters and sisters.

"And you were there, attempting to change the gentleman's opinion," he murmured. His words, however, didn't end with the upward tilt of a question.

It was a rule ingrained into women from the nursery: thou shalt not challenge a gentleman. Their egos were too fragile; women were warned of the perils of offending any man. Emma paused in the middle of the pavement, bringing Charles to a stop beside her.

"I trust you intend to lecture me on challenging guardians and brothers on behalf of their sisters." And she didn't make hers a question, either. "And venturing out without the benefit of a maid or footman?"

"Though I confess to wondering as to where your maid or footman might be"—his lips pulled in a crooked devil's grin that did funny things to her still unordered thoughts—"I'm hardly the one to go about lecturing anyone on anything." His smile dipped into a wistful, sad little smile. "And certainly not you."

His admission, however, brought her back on her heels.

Her brothers, her father, and certainly any other man would have been so offended at her being here, and handling herself as she had.

"If Miss Alby's brother would seek to control her and place his hands upon any woman, then she was wise to end an engagement supported by one such as him," he said tersely.

Emma started, whipping up a gaze to his ice-filled one as the truth of the moment hit her—he supported Cressida Alby's decision.

His mouth, previously wistful, formed a wry smile. "Did you think I should commiserate because I'm also a product of a broken betrothal?"

"I . . ." Heat rushed her face, for, well . . . she *had* thought that.

They reached a bustling corner of the street, made impassable by a not-so-small contingent of builders attempting to navigate four stacked, twenty-meter beams across the roadway. Charles faced her. "I would never hold Miss Alby's decision to command her future against her." His eyes locked with hers, the power within those depths so intense they robbed her lungs of air. "Just as I don't hold you responsible for making the decision about what you wanted." His lips quirked at the right corner, highlighting the dimple there. "Even if I wanted you to choose differently for entirely selfish reasons."

Emma fluttered a hand about her breast, before realizing what she did. She let her arm fall, and glanced about.

Charles looked off. "It is passable again," he said, holding out an arm, and Emma hesitated a moment before placing her fingers atop his sleeve and allowing him to guide her on the path they'd been traveling.

Stunned—or rather, shamed—into silence by his revelation this day, as well as by the palpable fury on the other woman's behalf, Emma focused her eyes forward . . . and tried to make sense of any of what she'd just learned about Charles. For neither had she believed he'd be one to stand there in wait, allowing her to handle a situation as she had a short while ago with the baron. Trusting her, but lending his presence for support should she require it.

She needed to process all these pieces of a man she didn't know. Not truly. For this? This was yet another first for her with this man . . .

As they walked, he picked up the discourse they'd left. "Your visit today, then, was to call out Miss Alby's brother?"

"No, to visit Cressida," she said automatically. "I wanted to ascertain she was well."

He shot her a look.

She wrinkled her nose. "*And* to speak to her brother."

Emma and Charles shared a smile.

They neared the place where her driver sat in wait, and she found herself oddly regretful that this time with Charles was coming to an end.

When they stopped, Tensly jumped down to greet them, but still, neither she nor Charles made a move to leave. To end the exchange.

The driver fell back.

Charles removed his hat, fiddling with the brim; it was . . . an endearingly distracted gesture from a man whom she'd believed to be imperturbable. He moved a searing gaze over her face, his eyes warm like the spring sun beating down upon them. And surely it was those rays which accounted for the heat unfurling within her. "You handled yourself . . ." A breeze stole across the bustling roads, and he paused. Reaching up a hand, he caught a loose strand that had become untucked during her earlier efforts with Lord Newhart. Charles retained his hold upon that lock, and had she not been studying him so closely as she was, were her body and mind and every part of her not so in tune with every passing moment of this exchange, she'd have missed the way in which he lightly rubbed that blonde piece between his bare thumb and forefinger, as if he were testing the feel of it . . . committing it to memory. "Magnificent."

Her breath caught, that swift inhalation lost on another wind gust. Did he speak of her hair, which was so agonizingly bone-dry straight she'd brought maids to tears trying to assemble the uncurlable locks? Or did he refer to how she'd handled Newhart? Everything was confused, just then.

At last, Charles brushed the strand back behind her ear, tucking it in place there.

But neither of them moved. They each remained locked where they stood, feet frozen to the pavement. Her family's servants in the wings, with a sea of workers passing by, and she couldn't bring herself to care about any of it.

"You were magnificent back there." He repeated the whole of the thought, and her heart . . . damn her heart for lifting at that praise, when most men would have been horrified at a lady acting so. At a woman not filling and fitting the role of meek lady in need of rescuing.

"The Duchess of Wingate's husband, as you know, was a fighter. He's provided lessons for our members so that we might be able to defend ourselves."

She searched again for some hint that her words were met with shock or derision.

Another smile formed on Charles's mouth. "You could school the men of Gentleman Jackson's, including Gentleman Jackson himself." Bowing his head, Charles stepped back. "Good day, Emma."

And with that, he left. Emma stared at his retreating frame.

All these years, she'd taken Lord Scarsdale as a replica of every last lord in London who chafed at women asserting and exerting themselves in any way. She'd expected he'd be like the men who wished for women to be seen and not heard.

And she didn't know what to do with this new glimpse of the man she'd almost wed.

Chapter 9

THE LONDONER

A RAGING SUCCESS

The Earl of Scarsdale's club continues to grow in membership, prestige, and greatness. Is it a wonder with such a leader at its helm?

M. FAIRPOINT

Over a few days' time, not only had Charles established his club to counter Emma and her Mismatch Society, he'd secured a respectable venue and attracted a number of also respectable members.

In short, everything was going along swimmingly.

And certainly merited the likely celebratory invitation Charles's footman, Wickham, held out.

Seated at the desk in his rooms, Charles accepted the sheet, and unfolding it, he made quick work of skimming the customary short, clever poem-like verse from his friend:

After the work you've done this week, it is a celebration we should of course seek. Glasses need be raised in toast, as we allow you that proper boast for everything achieved. Forbidden Pleasures at ten o'clock.
Be there.

L

With a laugh and wry headshake, he folded the note and set it down on the corner of his desk. "Please, send 'round my regrets to Lord Landon. I won't be joining him this evening."

Wickham, who'd hand delivered the missive and was already buried deep in Charles's armoire, filling his arms with garments for the evening's entertainment, glanced over his shoulder. "What?" Surprise lit the young man's voice.

"I will not be joining him," Charles reiterated, rubbing at the back of his neck, those muscles aching from the amount of time he'd spent with his head down, taking notes for his new endeavor. "If you would send on my regrets?" he repeated.

"Of course." The young man returned the garments he'd selected to their proper places and brought the gold-painted panels of the armoire shut. "As you wish, my lord."

Setting aside his notebook, Charles removed a sheet of paper, and dipping his pen into the inkpot, he dashed off a quick declination. After he sprinkled puce powder to dry the ink, then folded it, he handed it over.

Standing at his shoulder, Wickham continued to stare wide-eyed at the proffered response to Landon . . . as if he'd never before beheld a rejection of this sort.

In fairness, the young man hadn't. As such, that shock was certainly merited. It was the first time in the whole of Charles's adult existence that he'd declined to join his friend at their scandalous clubs.

Nay, the more wicked the venture, the more likely it was Charles would be there.

"It's all right," Charles said dryly. "It's not going to bite your fingers."

His cheeks flushing red, Wickham took the note and, with a bow, rushed off.

After he'd gone, Charles returned his attention to the place it had been for the better part of the evening: his work.

He dragged forth an old university notebook he'd repurposed, three-quarters of those pages dedicated to notes he'd made in his youth, the last quarter filled with hastily written potential agendas and topics.

Charles turned the page, updating the most recent changes to the attendance sheet.

From him, Landon, St. John, and Anwen Kearsley, the eldest of St. John's brood of sisters, the organization had grown.

Sometime later, his old university notebook nearly full, Charles stole a glance at the clock. Twenty minutes past one o'clock. It was a new, unfamiliar way to find himself . . . particularly at this hour. For more years than he could remember, his time had been spent out, living his most improper life.

His gaze snagged on his visage reflected back from the enormous gilded mirror hanging on the opposite wall, and he stared contemplatively at himself. Emma hadn't been incorrect in the charges she'd leveled his way—that was, with the exception of the one sin she and all society believed Charles guilty of. Over the years, he *had* drunk too much. And sat across from dealers at gaming tables, placing wagers.

Oh, with time's passage, he'd tempered those wicked pursuits. They'd lost their appeal. But the image, however, remained.

Just as the perception of him as a libertine had, too.

Nor was it Emma's fault for holding those ill opinions. Charles had stepped in and passed off Camille's illegitimate son as his own, and in so saving his sister, he'd also shaped a narrative in which he was a reckless rake who'd not taken proper precautions to ensure he didn't litter bastards about. Nay, Emma took him for the manner of man who'd leave some woman to the shame which came from birthing a bastard, and never offering that woman his name . . . because in short, that was what he'd done . . . on the surface.

And he'd do so again gladly. Protecting the sister he'd failed had been all that mattered.

However, he'd not properly considered . . . Emma. Nay, he had not considered her in any way—how such a scandal would reflect upon her. And more importantly, how she would feel at his having a by-blow son. In large part because at that point, she had still been a child and, in larger part, because he failed to see her as his eventual wife. Resentment and the age gap between them had made it entirely too easy to disregard how Emma would feel and be impacted by the lie of Seamus's birth.

Given those reasons alone, why should her opinion of Charles ever be favorable? In fact, it was a wonder she'd not broken their betrothal off long before she had.

All this time, however, he had filled his days with largely empty pursuits. Until now. Until these past ten days.

What had begun as a way of challenging Emma's views of him had morphed into something more. The short time in which he had begun his work in the Club D'égalité had been some of the most productive and rewarding, and also humbling.

For he'd not anticipated just how much went into the creation and organization of such a pursuit . . . and how little he, in fact, knew about it. Even more shocking had been the discovery for Charles that . . . he didn't hate it. Not at all. Oh, he wasn't good at any of the organizational details of the club. There was still a greater hint of chaos than order to the weekly meetings . . . which might or might not have resulted in a greater interest in his club than the actual content being discussed at this point. The structure of the meetings was not fully set.

But he was learning, and the Club D'égalité was growing, and . . . there had been an unexpected sense of . . . accomplishment . . . to it all.

Closing his notes for the day, Charles adjusted the leather notebook so it sat framed in the very center of his desk.

He patted the top of it, the gold lettering of his initials faded by time. And pushing his chair back, Charles stood and headed across the room. He shucked off his shirt and tossed it aside as he went; his trousers followed suit as he littered a path of garments on the way to his bed.

And climbing under the covers, he slept.

As a young child, Emma had been far from a dutiful, proper young lady.

Far from it. Swimming naked on the lake at her family's estate. Fishing in the dead of night until she'd cleared out her father's stock, then transporting those creatures to another pond so they might be saved from giving their fish-lives in the name of sport.

Dampening the powder used by her father and his guests on their hunts.

Undoing all the traps that had been set for those hunts.

The list went on and on, of scandals that had brought her mother to tears and her father to lecture and her siblings to amusement. Every last one of those outrageous acts had taken place before her twelfth birthday.

That was the year when everything had changed. She had changed. She'd been saddled with Miss Finch, a governess who'd praised Emma's intelligence, schooled her in the art of using one's mind, and urged her to present an image of solemnity to the world.

Until Miss Finch, no one had spoken to Emma about her mind mattering.

That stern, solemn instructor had reshaped every way that Emma wanted the world to see her, and the way that she chose to present herself.

Rather . . . she'd been . . . fascinated.

From that moment on, she'd presented herself in a way that she could be proud of. What she hadn't anticipated was that she'd also become someone her betrothed could not stand being with.

As such, in the whole of her adult years, she could count on just one hand the number of outrageous actions or activities she'd taken part in. Really, she could count on just one finger: the visit she'd paid to Waverton Street, which had led to her cofounding of the Mismatch Society.

And from that moment, all manner of impropriety had sprung.

Perhaps her founding the Mismatch Society, however, had freed her in some way. For here she sat, poised to do something so shocking it made the formation of the Mismatch Society look like a Lady Jersey's approved, sanctioned tea.

Yet, seated in the crowded hackney in the dead of night, with most of respectable society firmly in their beds for the evening, she didn't feel the dread or horror or any other proper sentiment she should. Nay, with Olivia and Isla crammed on the seat beside her, and Owen stationed across from them, she found herself filled with an anticipation.

Alas, the indignation and anger she'd felt after learning of Charles's rival society hadn't been quite . . . what it was since he'd come upon her on Regent Street.

Stop being a ninny. Would a man feel any such compunction about calling out one's rival? Would a gentleman let one mere interaction— even if it had been a special one such as what she'd known—allow his course to be altered?

No. Get your head clear, and remember, he is your nemesis.

Granted, a nicer nemesis than she'd taken him for. But still a nemesis all the same.

With that, Emma reached for the latch to let herself out. Olivia's brother swiftly covered it, intercepting her efforts. "D-do you care to talk it out one more time?" he croaked. "Perhaps we . . . can come up with some other idea?"

Olivia slapped his fingers. "Oh, hush. *We* didn't come up with anything." She gestured between Emma, Isla, and herself. "*We* did. Now, if we may continue?" Even in the darkness of the carriage, Olivia's eyes lit as only an angry sister's eyes could.

"Yes, yes." The more-loyal-than-they-deserved Owen promptly sat back in his seat. "Of course, forgive me. Carry on. As you were."

Olivia peeked out the curtains at the impressive stucco, center-unit structure occupied by one Lord Scarsdale. "Are we even certain he is home?"

"If he's not, I'll wait," Emma murmured, peering over Olivia's shoulder. But for the sconces flanking the black lacquer doorway and the hint of light radiating from the foyer windowpanes, Charles's townhouse had been largely doused in darkness.

"And you've prepared everything you intend to say?" her friend asked . . . for a third time since they'd set out.

"Yes." She'd carefully scripted every part of her plan, and every word she'd say.

"I'm still not certain how you're sure you'll gain entry?" Isla asked with skepticism that could come only from a young lady's naivete.

For Emma well knew how to gain entry into the household of a gentleman such as the roguish Earl of Scarsdale. All she need do was knock on the front door, gain entry, and . . . *Risk your reputation and scandal, all in the name of boldness,* a voice taunted at the back of her mind. Nay, it was more than that. In the name of the Mismatch Society, the future and success of their organization. She was fighting for their survival, and fighting for her members.

Owen cleared his throat. "You do know friends generally talk friends out of risky escapades?" he pointed out, edging away from Olivia before she could deliver another blow.

"Ah," Isla said. Holding a finger aloft, she waved it in the direction of the fourth member of their party. "But I am a sister, and sisters cheer sisters on through every boldness."

Olivia favored her brother with a glare. "And I may not share Emma's blood, but we are as close as sisters. Isn't that right, Emma?"

"Absolutely."

"Fine. However, if I may," he began, earning groans from all but Emma as, every bit the solicitor analytical in his business, he launched into a lecture. "I should like to point out—"

"No," Olivia and Isla said in unison.

"One," he continued over that interruption, as he ticked up a finger. "The risk to Emma's reputation." That for so long had been something she'd cared very much about. How much of her life, however, had been wasted worrying about what others might say, instead of focusing on what she truly wanted . . . and deserved? "Two, Scarsdale is a terrible chap. A libertine. A rake."

"Those are the same," Olivia pointed out.

Owen nodded so quickly his spectacles slipped all the way off his face. As he spoke, he fished about for them.

Bending down, Emma retrieved the wire pair and, cleaning off the smudged lenses, returned them to his face.

His cheeks went red. "Many thanks. Where was I?"

"You were wishing me the best of luck?"

His smile dipped, and he blinked in confusion. "No. No. I don't think it was that. At all," he said, with his endearing inability to recognize teasing. "I think I was attempting to convince you this is a rubbish *id-aahhh*." Owen let out a quiet groan as his sister caught him hard in the shins.

"Do hush, Owen," she admonished. "You have one purpose here and one purpose only—"

"Protection," he muttered, rubbing at his injured leg. "I know. I know." Olivia's brother, a de facto friend of Emma's over the years, looked past his younger sister and to Emma. "However, I would be remiss if I did not add my voice of reason to the mix."

"No, you wouldn't," Olivia and Isla said at the same time.

"You are not of the *same* mix," Olivia added.

Owen bristled, his glass spectacles slipping again over the bridge of his slightly too-narrow nose. "I beg your pardon?"

"You're not a woman, Owen." Olivia sighed her exasperation. "You are merely a stand-in for potential footpads and other unanticipated dangers that we might encounter."

And it was an unlikely role, at that, for him to be assigned. Near in height to Emma, he was even more painfully thin than Emma herself. A strong gust could knock over the young solicitor. And a strong gust in the form of his sister's slight nudge between his shoulder blades when she was displeased with him, in fact, had toppled him. An air of frailty had always clung to the young man, who'd battled yellow fever as a boy and grown up with his books for company when the other boys were . . . well, doing what other boys did. Thin, bookish, and usually buried away in his work, that still hadn't prevented him from accompanying the three ladies in a mark of his goodness and loyalty. "Are you certain you— *Owww*," he cried out as he was dealt a third strike.

Touched that he'd brave his sister's wrath on her behalf, Emma leaned over and patted him on the knee. "My apologies for your sister's ruthlessness."

And before he could launch another attempt to talk her out of an already dangerously bad decision, she adjusted the hood of her crimson cloak, drawing it up and pulling it forward so the deep folds shielded the whole of her face. Reaching past Olivia, Emma pressed the handle and jumped down.

The moment her feet hit the uneven cobblestones, each leg rolled outward, and she tossed her arms wide, steadying herself. When she had her feet properly under her, Emma began the short walk to Charles's residence.

Nay, to Lord Scarsdale's.

Visiting the gentleman in his residence at this hour required that degree of formality between them. And as much as she wished to be reviewing the script she'd prepared, Emma found all her attention was required on the perilous path that came from the heeled satin articles she'd donned.

She silently cursed.

What woman would prefer a blasted heel?

God give Emma a comfortable, smooth flat slipper over the ridiculousness of such a shoe any good English day of the week.

"I told you, you should have practiced more," Isla whispered scandalously loudly behind her, before Olivia grabbed the younger girl and dragged her into the carriage and out of possible sight.

Yes, and it was the first time she'd truly considered she risked not just her reputation but her sister's, as well. And Olivia's. Granted, Owen was there, and his presence would salvage his sister's some. But . . .

Stop.

Get in.

Say your piece.

Get done what you need to get done, and get out.

That quick, and in that order.

And yet . . . it wasn't that simple. She'd spent the better part of her adult life thinking about her eventual future as Charles's wife and . . . imagining being in his life.

In his bed.

Even as she'd known all the while that he'd never desired her. Or wanted her, or been attracted to her in any way. Which was perhaps why she'd spent the better part of the day *also* considering precisely what she'd wear for this upcoming meeting.

As Emma reached the bottom step of Charles's townhouse, she climbed her gaze up the center unit, sandwiched between a bright-orange stucco residence trimmed in black paint on one side and a pale-green one on the other. Charles's, constructed of pale-white limestone, extended some fifteen feet above the ones that flanked it. And for all the ornate luxuriance of those other structures, Charles's possessed an urbane elegance, perfectly suited to the sophisticated occupant who called this place home.

When she'd first arrived in London and learned he kept a bachelor's residence, she'd had her family's driver take her riding by . . . several times. All the while, she'd peered from around the edge of the gold velvet curtain, considering this very townhouse. She'd wondered if it was the place they would one day call home together, because a man such as Charles wasn't one who'd spend all his time at the country properties. But neither were the townhouses in these streets those ones frequently lived in by husbands and wives. Instead, they were well-known residences of bachelors.

She'd gone back and forth. Wondering. Trying to answer those questions in her mind.

It had been on the fourth carriage ride by that she'd seen it.

Nay, not it.

Him.

Or, rather, them.

Charles had been meeting his family at the doorway—his sister, his parents . . . and the small boy who lived with his parents.

His son.

She'd stared at that small boy, holding the hand of his aunt, as the family filed inside.

It had been the first time she'd seen the child, her husband's illegitimate son. Tiny. Blond. The very image of Charles. And it hadn't been *resentment* she'd felt for the boy, born through circumstances he'd had no control over. But rather . . . the searing, red-hot burn of . . . jealousy and shame, all rolled up together. Over the fact that Charles had created a child with another.

All the while, he'd been assiduously avoiding any and every interaction with Emma. It had felt like the greatest failing on her part, the absolute inability to make the man she was slated to marry care about her—in any way.

Charles had looked up, and she'd promptly released the curtain, pressing herself against the back of the carriage bench . . . as she'd been confronted with all the ways in which she'd deluded herself about a marriage between her and Charles.

It had been a reminder that, where she'd spent her childhood and young adult years wondering about their future, her someday husband had been living a life without a thought of her in it.

No, he'd never expressed an interest in a relationship with her. Any interest at all, really.

Until that day at the lake.

Until she'd broken it off.

Until now.

"Get on with it already," Olivia called in a furious whisper from across the street, jerking Emma out of the past and into the present.

She used the rail to steady her legs the remainder of the way; the unevenness of her steps now having less to do with the fine articles on her feet and everything to do with her impending meeting, she climbed up the seven steps.

Raising her hand, she lifted the polished brass fleur-de-lis door knocker and brought it down hard.

That metal clang echoed damningly loud down the still of the nighttime streets.

And as she stood there, huddling in her cloak, images filled her head of people poking their heads out to find her on Charles's stoop. Not that, in her satin crimson cloak and arriving at the hour she had, they would suspect it was her. And yet . . . that reassurance brought little calm.

There came the shuffle of approaching footsteps on the other side of the black lacquer door panel, and then fiddling on a lock.

The door opened, and a sleepy-eyed butler looked about; his gaze settled on her, then widened.

Emma husked her voice and spoke. "I am here to see Lord Scarsdale."

How many times had such similar words been uttered at this very threshold? And why, if she didn't care about Charles and she'd moved on from his betrayals, did the idea of it still hurt?

"I . . ." Charles's butler scratched at his tousled hair.

"He is expecting me," she lied, taking advantage of the servant's sleep-dulled mind.

Except the young man seemed to find himself. "His Lordship isn't taking visitors at this time. Said he isn't to be disturbed." He made to shut the door, but Emma slid around him and let herself into the foyer.

Her heart raced faster as she found herself that much closer to the goal with which she'd set out that night. "Oh, trust me. He'll want to see me."

And he would, even if she had to go search him out herself.

"If you would be so good"—she lowered her voice another shade, attempting those sultry tones likely belonging to every woman who'd entered through these front doors—"as to provide His Lordship word that he has a very important guest, one who is very eager to see him."

The butler hesitated, moving his gaze over the textured layers of her crimson cloak, then swallowed audibly. "If you'll wait but a moment, madam?" With that he bustled off, climbing the curving staircase and heading down the hallway that fed off the right side of the main landing.

The moment he was out of sight, Emma hurried into movement and set herself on the same path to Lord Scarsdale.

Chapter 10

THE LONDONER

GENTLEMEN WILL BE GENTLEMEN

Even as the Earl of Scarsdale is seen frequently at his clubs, well into the early-morn hours, his personal club continues to thrive. Is there nothing he cannot do?

M. FAIRPOINT

RapRapRapRapRapRap.

An incessant banging cut across Charles's slumber . . . and forcing his eyes open, he blinked and wrestled back the fog of sleep.

His gaze took in the inky-black cover of his chambers, the low fire in the hearth, the crack in the curtains that revealed the dark night sky.

Stretching an arm sideways, he grabbed the small, ebonized table clock from his nightstand and dragged it close to his face so he could make out the silvered numbers.

Two o'clock in the morning.

RapRapRapRapRapRap.

There was no escaping them. That rapid, determined knocking was the one that signified his butler's panic, and his parents' arrival.

Bloody hell.

Charles searched about for the Tulipwood nightstand, depositing the timepiece.

What in hell was it now? Dragging a pillow over his head, even as he knew his efforts were futile, he ignored that rapping . . . as long as he possibly could.

"My lord?" Tomlinson's voice came muffled by the pillow and the panel. "You have—" The butler's words ended on a loud gasp.

Really? After ten years employed by Charles and well accustomed to the marquess and marchioness's nighttime visits, he'd still not learned the lay of the land?

Well, the last damned thing Charles needed was being caught in the buff by his mother.

Giving up on sleep, he tossed aside the pillow and hurriedly swung his legs over the side of the bed.

He made it only two steps before a pale-faced Tomlinson opened the door and staggered into the room. "Company," the young man croaked.

"For the love of God, before they come up here, go back and tell them I'm not . . ." Charles's words trailed off as a person sailed through the door, neither of the ones responsible for his birth. A woman in a crimson cloak with a deep, black velvet-lined hood. *Blast and damn.* Charles quickly headed for the other side of his bed, to the garments he'd left littered about. The last thing he needed was for Emma to learn he'd received a nighttime visitor so that she could only further her bad opinion of him. "I've said no women in my townhouse," he said tightly. His nephew visited often, and he'd not have the respectability of the household questioned by carrying on with women under that same roof.

The minx, however, seemed to take that as an invitation to stroll deeper into his rooms.

"How . . . honorable of you, Lord Scarsdale," she said.

Charles froze. He knew that voice. Husked even as it was, there was no disguising the lilting, lyrical quality to it. Nay, impossible. After he'd discovered her emasculating Lord Newhart, he'd thought of her. He'd imagined her as she'd been . . . and then in ways that broke the bounds of everything respectable. He'd imagined her here . . . as she was now.

"It is so good of you to be bound by *some* rules of respectability."

It was the smile; who knew a voice could smile? But hers did, and it pulled him back to the moment.

Cursing, Charles dived for the bedding and became tangled over the damned boots he'd shed hours earlier. Coming down hard on his arse, he grabbed for the sheets. Yanking at the coverlet, he tugged it down from atop the bed.

"My lord?" Tomlinson called over. "Should I fetch a constable—"

"Get out," he croaked. "You can get out, Tomlinson. I'll receive . . . *her*." For all his rules about not allowing women in his household, for her he'd make an exception.

Her, as in his former betrothed, in his bedchambers, cloaked like a siren, with him naked as the day he was born.

There came the rushed footfalls of Tomlinson's bare feet as he retired from the room, and then the click of the door closing behind the servant. Silence fell, punctuated by only the crackle of the slowly dying fire. Sprawled on his back, on the floor, with only the quiet for company and absolutely nothing happening . . . he found himself blinking back the haze of confusion. Mayhap he'd merely dreamed the whole exchange, after all. Because nothing else explained why Emma would be here, and attired in a shimmering, suggestive cloak befitting a woman who took delight in seducing scandals. Scrambling onto his knees, Charles caught the edge of his mattress and raised himself slightly, peeking over the side.

Emma shoved back the deep hood of her cloak, revealing a pleased smile and a teasing glimmer in her eyes, the pairing of which knocked the breath from his lungs. Before he registered . . . this was *Emma* staring back at him.

His innocent, virginal, almost-was bride.

Cursing, he dived back to the floor and dragged the sheets atop him once again. Then he stretched up, grabbed a pillow for good measure, and held it protectively between his legs.

The click of her heels upon the hardwood floors resonated as she drew nearer. He looked up. Emma peered down at him with a mix of glee and boredom. It was an unexpected blending of emotions, as contrary as the woman before him. "What are you doing here, Emma?" he squeaked, his voice climbing to a pitch it hadn't attained since he'd been a boy of fourteen.

With slow, languid movements, she peeled off her gloves, shedding the black leather like a snake he'd once observed with Seamus at the Royal Menagerie, coming free of its bothersome skin. "You can rest easy, Lord Scarsdale," she drawled, gesturing to his prone form with her gloves before tossing the articles upon his bed.

"I don't think I'll ever rest easy again," he said hoarsely. Not after this. From this moment forward, any time he entered his townhouse, and these rooms, he'd see her here. See her as she was now, looking ripe for seduction.

Emma laughed, the sound low. Throaty. Charles swallowed hard, or he tried to. Alas, who could have known the simple sound of a woman's laughter could cause Charles's shaft to rise and throb as it did now.

"No need for modesty." Lowering her hands to her knees, she bent over him, leaving her cloak gaping, and revealing the low-necked crimson gown she wore behind that garment, the daring neckline which forced his eyes to those gently rounded breasts on perfect display. His mouth went dry, and he cursed the fire that had dimmed for failing to illuminate her body as it should, for denying him the true shade of that flesh. "It is not anything I've not seen before," she drawled.

His gaze fixed on an intriguing crescent mark on the top of her right breast, it took a moment to register the words the young lady had spoken.

Nay, not the young lady. His betrothed. His former one anyway. But still.

Emma straightened and started away from him. Charles stared after her retreating frame, watching her as she took a small tour of his room.

It is not anything I've not seen before . . .

Which implied she'd seen . . . men. As he was now. Naked. Fury edged out the desire that had been coursing through his veins, a red-hot anger fueled by jealousy.

She thought she could simply deposit that revelation, and not speak any further on it?

Charles shoved himself up onto his elbows. "Which . . . men have you been seeing?" he asked with all the calm he could muster at the thought of Emma with . . . anyone. He'd choke the life out of the bastard. And then he'd revive him so he could kill him all over again. That nameless-for-now man his former betrothed had seen.

Or men?

Emma stopped her perusal of his room and glanced over her shoulder. Her lips pulled up at the right corner, in the hint of a smile. "You, Charles," she drawled. "I've seen you."

He opened and closed his mouth. Before . . . now?

Her crimson lips tipped up at the other side, forming a complete smile, bewitching him completely and freezing his breath in his lungs.

"Before now," she said, following his silent questions with an unerring and unnerving accuracy.

"I don't . . . recall that."

"You should pay greater attention to your surroundings, then." With that matter-of-fact set-down, she loosened the large crystal clasp at her throat. It gave with a faint click, and the garment slid in a noisy, shimmering heap to her feet.

Charles stilled for the second time since she'd stormed his chambers.

The daring red gown clung to her form, a figure he'd once taken as coltish, too foolish to see . . . and appreciate . . . her lithe frame, which conjured a warrior woman who, with her regality, grace, and strength, transcended time. Her legs that went on forever. The understated curve of her hips served only to accentuate lusciously curved buttocks. She was the very reason sailors dashed themselves against those jagged rocks.

"When?" From where he still lay sprawled on the floor, he asked that question quietly. "When did you . . . see me?" When really, the question that *needed* to be asked and answered was how in blazes had he been so much a fool to have been naked before Emma Gately, and been so oblivious to her nearness?

She caught one of the posters of his bed, and wrapped her arms about the mahogany pillar, studying Charles from around that carved wood. "The better question is how many times."

He'd still argue his previously unasked question was the better one.

"You made something of a habit of swimming nude at your parents' house parties, did you not?" Emma didn't give him a chance to answer, clearly already having one. "And here I'd been so certain those swims had been deliberate, to raise their ire, and yet if they had been, surely you'd have recalled them."

Actually, she had been correct.

"Alas, it was not a habit you quit, though, did you, Lord Scarsdale?" she murmured in contemplative tones. "There was the time two years ago . . . I came upon you . . ."

She left that to dangle in the air, a memory she had that included Charles, but one which he had no memory or knowledge of.

And . . . he wanted it. He wanted so very desperately to reverse time and find himself in that moment with her . . . creating a future recollection that they two shared. What would it have been? What could it have been?

There was, however, no going back. Hell, at this point, Charles wasn't entirely certain there was any going forward with Emma, and that acknowledgment he made for the first time to himself struck in his chest. But he'd also be damned if he didn't try, still.

"Did you?" he asked, adding a layer of huskiness to his response.

"Oh, yes," she said, with a little lift of her shoulders in a bored shrug.

Charles narrowed his eyes on the saucy woman he'd almost wed.

Emma pushed herself away from the poster and took a step closer. "I had quite a view of . . ." She dropped her gaze to the blankets—nay, more specifically, square between his legs.

Heat crept up his neck, and he squirmed, his bare ass cold on the hardwood floor. Surely she was not looking at—

"Your bits and pieces."

Charles choked. There was something utterly horrifying in hearing the woman he desperately wished to wed use that same term his own mother had in these rooms about his . . . about his . . . *bits and pieces.*

Emma flicked a bored stare over his person, and with a yawn, she resumed walking.

By God, she had . . . yawned at him. Because of him? And about his, as she'd called them . . . bits and pieces? It was really all the same. And it also happened to be the first time in the whole of his life that a woman had done so.

That heat continued its climb all the way to his cheeks.

Emma flared her eyes. "My goodness, are you *blushing*?"

Nearly pitch black as the room was, the minx missed absolutely nothing.

"Hardly." Charles clenched his jaw. "I am . . . merely *hot.*" He wasn't given to lying, but he also wasn't one who was readily going to own a blush.

The young lady cast a glance over her shoulder, giving him a cursory up-and-down look before resuming her turn about his room. "Given you aren't wearing a stitch of clothing, I'd say that is rather hard to believe." She moved with ginger steps. Careful ones. All the while she did, she passed her gaze over the items assembled upon his desk, and the furniture situated around the room, as if all of it were infinitely more interesting than Charles himself. Which, given how she'd initiated their breakup and received his pursuit following it, wasn't that hard to believe. Still, her indifference chafed. Emma's ankle turned ever so slightly, and she immediately righted herself, so quick with that correction that had he not been studying her as closely as he was, he would have missed it.

She cleared her throat and, carefully lowering herself to a knee, grabbed his trousers. Straightening, Emma tossed them down at Charles.

Refusing to give up the death grip he had on his sheet, Charles made no effort to catch the garment. Instead he let it hit him in the chest.

Wordlessly, she presented him with her back and made her way over to his desk.

As he stood, he kept his gaze upon Emma. Emma, running her fingers over his book. His inkwell set. There was an intimacy to her exploring those particular items, even deeper than her being in his rooms. "It does occur to me, since you stormed my household, you've not provided the reason for your . . . late-night appearance," he called over, clutching the sheet carefully about him.

"No." Emma released the corner of his notebook and faced him; there wasn't the blush he'd worn moments ago, which he would have expected any young lady to be in possession of, given his state of undress. Rather, standing with the hearth at her back, the fire casting a glow about her, Emma's sharp features were a study of concentration. "No, I have not."

He waited for her to say more.

Alas, he could have kept waiting until Boney was revived from the dead and made the march on back to Corsica.

Very well. Charles sighed. He knew why she'd come. What her visit here was about. "You were angry at my seeking out your father. I promised to no longer do so, and I've not. Your father paid me a . . ."

Her lashes swept low, her eyes forming narrow pinpricks. So she'd *not* known, and he'd said too much.

"You didn't come to see me." Sadness stole the previously spirited glimmer from her eyes. "Let us be clear. Every time you called, you came to my father."

"Is that what it was about?" he asked quietly, that possibility sinking in. After all, she was a founding member of a women's society where ladies came together, demanding more of a place in a world so determined to prevent such a reality for them. "Had I gone to you that first time," he murmured, "would your answer have been different?"

"No," she said, so softly, her reply so confident, so assured . . . so . . . automatic, his face heated for a second time that night.

Emma resumed her stroll, and no, he'd not imagined it. Her steps were slightly unsteady, and as he released his sheet and shoved a leg into one of the holes of his trousers, he peered at her. Periodically, as she went, she shot out a hand to steady herself. And that uneven gait was why she occasionally gripped items about his chambers: the bed poster. His desk. He glanced down at her heeled shoes, and when he returned his focus to her face, he found her eyes upon him.

Adjusting the front falls of his trousers, he started across the room, and stopped before her.

A few inches shy of Charles's six feet two inches, Emma was taller than most men and any woman he'd ever known. And yet, even as all she needed to do was tilt her neck back a fraction to meet his eyes, her gaze did not meet his, but lingered instead upon his bare chest.

And close as he was, he not only saw that but heard the rhythmic movement of her swallow.

And he reveled in it. Finding himself, once more.

Charles brushed two fingers down the curve of her cheek, exploring those angular planes that had come to be an endless source of fascination for him.

Her breath again hitched, and she raised her gaze to his.

He lowered his mouth close to the shell of her right ear. "So then why are you here, Emma?" Though he wished to know that answer, he'd no regrets at her being here. Alone, with him, in this moment. "Why have you come?" He whispered the question, arranging those words in a different way.

Her body curved into his. Her flaxen eyelashes dipped a fraction, and he exulted in the telltale evidence of her desire for him. That triumph proved short-lived.

"Why . . . why . . . ?" Emma widened her eyes. "Never say you're trying to seduce me?" She burst out laughing.

And he was so distracted by the sound of her laugh, full and bold and husky, seductive in sound, and so very different from when she'd laughed that day in Hyde Park, that it took a moment for it to sink in.

He bristled. "Are you *laughing* at me?"

"Y-y-yes," she stammered, her mirth doubling, and this time she bent over and promptly lost her balance, landing on her knees.

Charles's frown deepened. Oh, well, this was really enough.

Still, her amusement didn't let up. She dabbed the tears of hilarity streaming from the corners of her eyes, and using her palm to leverage herself from the floor, she attempted to get to her feet.

Charles was immediately there. Leaning down, he swept an arm about her waist, and the other under her knees, effectively killing her mirth, as it ended on a shuddery gasp. He made to release her; sliding her body slowly down his frame, Charles set her back on her feet.

Emma pressed her hands against his bare chest . . . as if to push him away? And yet ever so slowly, her fingers unfolded, as soft as a butterfly's caress, upon him, curling and uncurling in the whorls of hair that matted his chest.

His heart pounded hard, his hunger for her blazing all the stronger.

"I could, you know," he said huskily.

"You would have to do far better than that, Charles." Her rebuttal emerged as a breathless whisper, one that dared him, challenged him to do just that.

Chapter 11

THE LONDONER

HURT FEELINGS?

With the Earl of Scarsdale succeeding as mightily as he is with the operation of his new club, his former betrothed, Miss Gately, is certainly seething with the jealousy only a woman is capable of.

M. FAIRPOINT

You would have to do far better than that?

Where had those words come from?

And which had they been? A challenge or plea?

With her body pressed against his nearly naked one, everything for Emma, in this moment, had become jumbled, twisted in her mind.

Her reason for being here clouded by that simple husky promise he'd made: *I could, you know.*

For actually, she hadn't known it. She hadn't known he'd have cared either way about wanting to . . . or trying.

He angled his lips lower, placing them near her neck, his breath a teasing, ticklish warmth that sent her belly dancing and her senses spinning. "Is that a request, Emma-love?"

Her body trembled and her eyes slid shut.

Stop!

He's merely playing at seduction. Just as he'd played at wounded betrothed after she'd called it off.

Emma scrambled away from him, her ankle wobbling slightly under its heel as she hastily put a much-needed step between her and Charles, and whatever effect he was having on her. "You robbed from me, Charles Hayden, and I'm here to order you to cease, this instant, or be prepared for the consequences."

His brow furrowed.

Was it the fact that he'd failed in his seduction? Or the charges she'd leveled? Either way, she felt a rush of triumph at having turned the tables on him.

Calling forth the script in her mind, Emma continued on the offensive. "You have made a scandal and embarrassment of me for the last time, Charles. I won't allow it." *Not this time.* Not when she'd put up with society's scorn since she'd made her Come Out and the world had delighted in reminding her that she was the unwanted future bride of the sought-after, charming Lord Scarsdale.

He shook his head slowly. "I am afraid I do not follow, Emma?" He spoke haltingly, his words ending on the uptilt of a question.

Emma cut him off. "Oh, come, Charles," she scoffed.

"Wait . . . you are . . . offended because of my *club*?"

Oh, if that wasn't a false surprise better suited to the ultimate actor on the London stage.

"You think I would be happy that you created a rival league?" she shot back.

"Well, I confess I didn't think you'd necessarily be *un*happy." He flashed one of those lazy smiles, surely meant to disarm. "But neither did I believe it would merit this reaction. I did consider the possibility you might even be . . ." Charles held out both his palms, balancing them back and forth like the scales of justice, perfectly framing his heavily muscled chest, his flat, defined, contoured belly. Emma's stomach fluttered as she found herself briefly transfixed by the sight of him.

"Indifferent?" She managed to supply him with that hated word. The irony of it was not lost on her, as she was fighting to keep her thoughts ordered over the mere sight of him.

He brightened, and let his arms fall. "Yes, precisely. That was the very word I had in mind."

Yes, precisely. Because she, Emma Gately, was nothing if not indifferent . . . about everything. It was how the world had come to see her, because, well, that was how she'd allowed herself to be viewed. She'd affected an air of indifference to conceal the hurt that came from having a betrothed who was just that—indifferent to her. Steeling her spine, she took a step toward him, cursing the shoes she'd selected that slowed her pace. "Well, I'm not, Charles," she snapped. "I'm neither happy nor indifferent . . ."

He cleared his throat, his briefly relieved expression fading. "Which suggests 'angry,' then."

Emma brought her hands together in a slow, deliberate, and sarcastic clap. "Precisely, Lord Scarsdale." In fairness, he'd not known she'd be upset. Now that he did, he would end this foolish enterprise.

"Yes, well, I am sorry for that, but I've no intention of ceasing my operations, if that is what you are asking," he said bluntly, effectively killing that delusion she'd allowed herself.

Emma strangled on her response. "You . . . you . . ."

Charles stared back patiently.

"Demanding!" she shouted. "I'm not asking. I'm demanding you cease."

Then he yawned.

She flared her eyes. "Did you just . . . did you just . . . ?"

"Yawwwn?" he offered, a second one of those tired expressions stretching out his syllables as he completely turned the tables on her this time. "Indeed."

Emma gasped. My God, he'd gone and stolen her affected boredom as well. "You are unconscionable, Charles," she hissed. Had there ever been a thought that he truly wished to resume their betrothal, this was the decided death knell. Because no gentleman would dare go about stealing her ideas and her affected mannerisms.

"Because I yawned?" He flashed a pearl-white smile that shone even brighter in the dark, and wrought the havoc it always had upon her heart. "Given you yourself did so just moments ago, Emma, and given the late-night hour, I thought you would be completely understanding if I were to do something as rude as— *Oomph,*" he grunted as Emma stuck a finger in his chest.

She bit the inside of her cheek to conceal the pain inflicted upon the digit by that solid wall of muscle. "Listen here, and listen good, Charles. I've put up with a great deal where you are concerned over the years, but I absolutely draw the damned line at you stealing my idea."

"Do you want to know the truth, Emma?"

She dropped her hands upon her hips. "Always."

"Your idea is not original. You're no different from a café or salon, a place where people go to come together, and if you encourage free thought as you say and suggest, then it's fairly hypocritical to go about ordering similar clubs to close."

That blunt, inflectionless charge pulled a gasp from her as she staggered back.

And then promptly tripped over her slippers and came down hard on her buttocks. Of course.

This damned night. It hadn't gone at all as she'd planned. But then it never had where Charles was concerned, and the reminder of it only filled her with the sudden, unexpected urge to cry.

The floorboards groaned as he joined her . . . as he joined Emma in her humiliation and shame.

"I'm fine," she said, her voice thick to her own ears, still unable to get to her feet . . . or look at him.

As effortlessly as before, he swept her into his arms and carried her over to the leather folds of his desk chair. With an infinite gentleness, he lowered her into the seat, the leather groaning with the addition of her weight.

Dropping her head along the back of his seat, she stared overhead at the ceiling and let her shame be complete. "It is these blasted slippers." Before he could speak, Emma shot out a foot, revealing the satin scrap upon it. "I don't know what I was thinking." Except, she did. She'd known that the women he kept company with were the scandalous, sophisticated sorts who wore the most daring garments.

Charles, however, proved polite enough to not challenge Emma on her lie.

"Ah, but surely you know there is a good deal to be said for a comfortable slipper," he murmured. Sinking to his right knee, Charles reached for her skirts.

Emma sat completely motionless as he inched the fabric of her red satin gown up.

Up.

Up.

Up.

Higher still, until the heavy fabric pooled about her knees and the cool night air kissed her bare limbs. Her translucent silk stockings, purely ornamental, did nothing to ease the cold. Nay, they added a heightened sense of awareness to the air around her. And his touch. That, too.

Unlike before, when Charles had been flippant and teasing, a change had overtaken him.

The energy in the room grew heavier and keener as he raised her foot, cradling it in his right palm, and with his left, he drew the end of her laces, pulling at that silk thread with a deliberateness that sent her pulse clamoring. Never taking his eyes from hers, he loosened the other side of her lace, and then drew off her heeled slipper.

"There," he murmured. "That is better, is it not?"

So much better. A little moan spilled from her lips at the exquisiteness that came with that freedom . . . and the tenderness of his touch. So very much better. But not even for the reasons he suggested, comfort seeming an irrelevancy compared with the heat pooling low in her belly. Somehow, Emma made herself nod, the gesture feeling shaky and uneven.

She needn't have bothered; he'd already returned his focus to her feet.

The next slipper followed suit until her feet, but for her silk stockings, were bare, and he looked down at her exposed legs.

She bit the inside of her cheek, never wanting this moment to end. Wanting him to continue holding her . . . And he curled his left palm into the high arch of her foot, then slowly massaged that aching flesh.

There was a purposefulness to his caress, one that sought to rub away the hurt, and yet . . . Emma swallowed hard. For there was more to whatever this was. Her body came alive, her senses tingling to life, and from nothing more than his touch. Then he pressed his thumb into that tender spot.

Her breath caught noisily.

He glanced up, and his gaze fixed on her face, his eyes darkening. "You like that."

It wasn't a question, but a statement from a man who knew the subtleties of a woman's body.

It was, however, the first he'd ever made an attempt to know hers. *Oh, God.*

Emma nodded once more. "I do." She dampened her mouth. "Are you . . . attempting to seduce me?" It was . . . too preposterous to believe. To believe this man who'd avoided her for years should desire her . . .

"And if I was?" he asked quietly. "Would you allow it?"

Would she allow it? Would she be able to resist? Emma closed her eyes as a battle waged within her, that over which her body longed for, and that which her stubborn pride insisted she deny at any cost. In the end, she proved weak. Or mayhap it was that she was strong in knowing what she wanted. Emma held his gaze squarely. "I allow it."

Not: she would.

She did.

And in this moment, she tossed her seduction over to this man and this moment with him she'd secretly hungered for.

Charles went still. From the way he gripped her dress, his white-knuckled fingers clutching her hem, to the tension of his broad shoulders and the fire in his eyes, Emma knew one thing with an absolute certainty. He was a man not so very much in control. Not so very much, at all.

Or mayhap Emma just projected the turbulent sea of disorganized thoughts and sensations onto him.

Something changed in that moment, in his touch, and in the very air around them. For ever so slowly, Charles unfurled his fingers and glided them along her kneecap, and down ever so slowly, tracing the line of her calf, all the way to her ankle and her previously sore, pinched toes.

Had they truly hurt? Everything was so confused in this moment. Every fiber of her had been reduced, tunneled, to simply sensation and feeling.

Charles reached the end of that distracted caress, then pausing ever so briefly at the arch of her foot, he resumed an upward stroke, following that same path his fingers had just taken.

Emma's breath grew shallow, and her skin radiated, tingled under that simplest of touches.

Only there wasn't anything simple about it. Not truly.

She should leave. She needed to. There was a carriage full of friends awaiting her, and ruin also lying in wait.

God help her. She couldn't bring herself to care. Not enough. Not as she should.

Closing her eyes, she allowed herself to focus only on that wildly illicit touch. Then, his eyes holding hers once more, he reached for her stockings, and proceeded to lower one.

Oh, dear.

His gaze heated, the glint there a knowing one, belonging to a man well aware of the effects he now had upon her, and she couldn't bring herself to care. Pride was an overestimated commodity in this instant.

Using the palms of his hands, he rolled that silk article lower, baring all her leg, and with a surprising care, he set aside her stocking. He set to work on the second, showing it the same tender care and attention.

This was a peculiar alteration of her body's sensation, and the ability of her nerve endings to process them, where the cold was now a balm, a sough upon her heated flesh.

Of their own volition, born of an understanding as old as Eve and Adam's joint fall from grace, she let her legs splay, opening for him, and then he lowered his head between her legs.

Emma hissed. Surprise, shock . . . and a shameful bliss sent her hips shooting up.

Charles looked up at her. "Trust me, Emma."

Trust me.

They were the last words this man was deserving of.

And yet in this moment, she was hopeless to do anything but follow where he led.

Still, he waited. Allowing the decision to be hers. Not taking more than she was willing to give. Not taking anything unless she granted it. And that power proved the headiest aphrodisiac, as she nodded and surrendered to her own wants.

Charles filled his hands with her buttocks, urging her closer to his face, and then he put his mouth to her.

In this, her first kiss of any sort.

This manner of kiss she'd never known.

Hot and wet there, between her legs, Emma should probably feel a sense of shame or embarrassment. That was surely what any decent lady would feel.

And yet . . .

Her eyes slid shut, and she moaned, the sound wanton and wicked and wonderful to her ears, as he with his lips worked a sorcerer-like magic upon her. Never had she been more grateful to have surrendered her worries about propriety and properness. He flicked his tongue over the sensitive bud, teasing her, suckling at that flesh, until Emma's hips moved of their own volition, lifting into him.

His large hands sculpted her buttocks, squeezing that flesh as he brought her closer to his ministrations.

Charles dragged his tongue over her, tasting her sodden channel.

"Mmm," she keened, her speech having dissolved, as she was capable of nothing more than animalistic, primitive sounds to encourage him to not stop. Never stop. She'd not survive, and yet as he plunged his tongue in and out of her channel, feasting on the folds, she cried out, not entirely certain she could survive if he continued taking her to whatever place she now journeyed.

A place where pleasure morphed with pain, and then blended into some glorious torment that cast out all reason and left her centered on only one place, that sharp, throbbing ache between her thighs.

"You are so wet for me," he praised, his voice hoarse as he dragged a trail of kisses to the inside of her thigh.

She whimpered, lifting her hips and seeking his efforts where she wanted him most. Where she needed him most.

He proved as elusive in lovemaking as he had in marriage, withholding that which she wanted and torturing her instead with a slower, teasing caress of his lips, kisses that he swept in a path lower, his hot mouth, wet from her essence, leaving a trail all the way to her knee. And then he came back up.

"Please. Please. Please," she panted, thrusting her hips furiously in a bid to have him there.

"Like this?" He slid his hands under her buttocks and lifted her closer to his face, then paused with his mouth a hairbreadth away from her burning center.

She arched her hips, seeking him, but he edged away, continuing to deny her.

"Tell me," he whispered, his husky baritone teasing and taunting. "Tell me what you want, Emma-love."

Emma-love.

Her eyes slid closed once more. It was that endearment. Had she ever really despised it? How, when in this moment, there were no more perfect words melded than those two, together?

"Say it," he urged, this time more harshly, all hint of lightness gone, replaced with a layer of darkness born of passion and suppressed want.

Using her elbows, she pushed herself upright so he had to angle his head up to meet hers. "I want your mouth on me," she said in clear, even tones that were at odds with the rapid rise and fall of her breathing.

His eyes darkened, and then with a growl, he took her.

He took her as she'd been hungering for him to, with a searing intensity and almost violence that liquefied her from the inside out.

Emma slumped in her chair, and tangling her fingers in his hair, she gripped those glorious, luxuriant golden strands. And she gave herself over freely to feeling everything he'd unleashed within her.

She rocked her hips against his mouth, and then he slid his tongue within her slit.

"Charles." Emma hissed his name, her thighs tightening reflexively about his neck, even as she simultaneously ground herself against him in a bid to ride to the peak of whatever pinnacle he drew her higher and higher toward.

He responded by suckling her nub all the harder, and then he slid a finger inside her.

Emma cried out.

"You like that, don't you, love?" His breath rasped against the damp curls between her legs.

"Mmm," she whimpered.

"I want to hear you say it. I want to hear the words." And then he teased her by sliding another finger inside. He stroked her, tormenting her in a new, forbidden way.

Emma's back collapsed as she went limp once more in her seat. He wanted her to speak those words, surrendering to him, but god help her, she couldn't form a thought coherent enough to string together a single sentence.

And then, he stopped.

Emma cried out at the loss, her hips surging up to call him back.

"Mm. Mm," he teased, and then those hands massaging her buttocks ceased even that delicious temptation, and her body wept for the loss of him. "I want to hear the words from you, love." Charles straightened, and she shot out her arms to bring him back, but he was only dragging a trail of kisses higher, to different parts of her body that had previously been neglected, punctuating each word he spoke with a kiss. "Every. Single. Word."

Emma gasped as he reached the bodice of her gown, the air caught in her lungs, trapped with a breathless anticipation.

Ever so slowly, he lowered her neckline, until her breasts were bared to his gaze and the night air.

"Lovely," he murmured, and with a reverence that brought her lashes sweeping down, he palmed that flesh, filling each of his large hands with her breasts.

She whimpered.

Charles glanced up. "Do you like that?" he asked as conversationally as if he were inquiring about her preference for tea.

Emma managed a shaky nod before she recalled what he wanted. What he expected to hear. What he demanded to hear.

"V-very much so." The husky quality of her response was foreign to her own ears.

His brown eyes darkened, passion deepening in those fathomless irises, and holding her gaze, he proceeded to run the pads of his thumbs over her nipples. A delicate circling that sent her hips rising and falling again.

Charles leaned forward, and before she knew what he intended, he closed his mouth over the tip of her right breast.

She cried out as he suckled and teased and worshipped that sensitive flesh. And then he switched his ministrations to the previously neglected peak, laving it with a like attention. Charles swirled his tongue around her nipple, playing with the tip as if it were his for the taking. And in this moment, it was. All of her, any part of her he wished, was his, if he would just assuage the ache pulsing between her legs.

Emma rested a hand on his head, and Charles paused; again, he looked up at her through thick, hooded lashes.

"I want your mouth on me as it was before. I want to feel your tongue there, Charles."

His breath hitched, and then with another one of those animalistic growls, he fell to his knees and kissed her where she'd urged him.

Closing her eyes, she released a contented little sigh before the pleasure of what he did became too much, and keening cries and moans spilled from her lips and echoed off the high ceilings of his chambers.

Charles suckled at the folds of her flesh. He stroked his tongue within her. Again and again. Those expert glides brought her higher and higher, to that pinnacle she'd been seeking to climb from the moment he'd first begun worshipping that place between her legs.

Emma stiffened; she used her palms to leverage herself in her seat, to get higher to that elusive goal, and closer to Charles and whatever magic he wove. Charles continued a steady pace within her. The pressure built.

Emma stiffened as her body exploded, as she fell from that cliff. And she screamed, capable of just one word: his name.

"Charles!"

Over and over again she screamed it, as she bucked her hips against his mouth, thrusting herself into him, wanting the moment to go on forever and ever. Never wanting to not feel the magic that was making love with this man.

He continued to worship her, not letting up on pleasuring her, coaxing every last drop until she collapsed into the folds of his seat, replete in her surrender.

Her heart racing, Emma lay sprawled there, certain her pulse would never find its way back to any semblance of a normal pace.

Charles fell back on his haunches, and reaching for his nearby shirt, he wiped away the remnants of her pleasure that still glistened upon his mouth.

The sight of it . . . the sight of him, however, cleaning himself, proved starkly sobering.

And with that, the heady magic that had held her ensnared lifted.

Oh, God. Emma briefly closed her eyes. Years ago, between his indifference and the child he'd had with another woman, her heart had been shattered. All she'd had left after her broken betrothal had been . . . her pride. And in so taking this moment for herself, giving herself up to passion in his arms . . . it threatened to weaken her in ways she couldn't afford.

What have I done?

"I trust you're feeling very s-smug." Her voice quavered as she spoke. "That this was some sort of t-test."

Finding another clean portion of his lawn shirt, he brought it between her legs and gently, tenderly cleaned her. "Hardly smug," he said gruffly. "And never a test." His eyes locked with hers. "Never that, and never in this w-way."

Her lips slipped apart, that slight tremble of his last spoken word there hinting at a man as shaken as she'd been by their exchange. And . . . that unsteadiness bonded them in a way that sent her flying to her feet, nearly toppling him in the process.

"I have to go," she said.

"Sadly, yes." This time there was the hint of his rogue's drawl that somehow restored her semblance of thoughts, and reminded her that he was still the same roguish Charles he'd always been.

Emma hurried off to fetch her cloak.

He intercepted her efforts, collecting the garment first. He snapped it once, and brought it about her shoulders. "I should see you h—"

"I'm not alone," she hurried to assure him. "My sister and Olivia wait below." Outside in a miserable hackney, while Emma had been learning the wonder her body was capable of. Heat bloomed on her cheeks.

She clasped the latch at her throat and headed for the door. She made to raise her hood.

"Emma?" he called.

She paused, staring questioningly at him.

Charles strolled over to join her at the door. He reached up, and her heart hammered as he set to work righting her chignon, brushing the loose strands back behind her ears. "I am sorry if I offended you earlier . . . in what I said," he murmured, lowering his hands, and she silently mourned the loss of those intimate ministrations he'd performed. "That was not my intention."

And not for the first time that night, Charles stole her breath. He'd . . . apologized.

"Thank you," she said softly.

For so much.

She might resent his past treatment of her, but he'd shown her passion that she'd not believed to ever know, and had done so without judgment. And as much as she might regret losing any part of herself, his had also been a gift. One that left her at sea, attempting to sort through a balance between the pleasure she'd wanted and the pride she sought to protect. Because she could not have both. At least not with Charles Hayden, the Earl of Scarsdale.

"Emma?" he called, cutting into her panicky musings. Charles grabbed each of her forgotten slippers in his hands and held them up. "And your slippers?"

"Ah, there is a good deal to be said for a comfortable slipper. And there's even more to be said poorly about an uncomfortable heel. They shall only slow me down."

He grinned . . . and despite all the terror reality had brought, Emma found herself smiling in return.

And with that, barefoot, Emma left.

Chapter 12

THE LONDONER

A RENAISSANCE MAN

Notorious rogue the Earl of Scarsdale continues to be spied in London bookshops. Between his rumored hunting, shooting, and boxing skills, he epitomizes a true Renaissance man. It is no wonder the dour, unsmiling bluestocking Miss Gately was unable to make good on their betrothal.

M. FAIRPOINT

Over the years, Charles had all manner of thoughts about Emma Gately, his one-day bride, whom he'd known since she was in the cradle. He'd believed she was an impossibly wild little girl, who'd grown into a woman who was proper and staid, and who dutifully did whatever it was her parents expected of her.

And yet in just over two months, he'd come to find all the ways in which he'd been wrong about her.

He'd failed to see—and appreciate—her spirit. Her biting and clever wit. Her strength and courage that had allowed her to do whatever it was she wished, despite her parents' opinions about those decisions. She'd proven a surprise in every way.

But last evening, her clandestine nighttime visit had marked his greatest shock where Emma was concerned.

Someday, hopefully a day a long way from this one now, when he drew his last breath, he'd do so with a smile, recalling her as she'd been in those shimmering crimson garments. The rustle of those articles as she'd walked, her siren's song that had lured him.

And when she'd sat in that chair, laid possession of the seat in his chambers . . . and splayed her legs for him, she'd been beautifully unapologetic in her passion. She'd thrown herself into her desire.

God help him; after she'd marched off like a goddess warrior leaving a battlefield behind her, sleep had been impossible as he'd thought of nothing but her and her cries of surrender.

Following her barefoot exit last evening, he'd not been able to think of anything but her. Those memories followed him still the next morn as he walked down the cobbled streets toward the Old Corner Bookshop with his nephew, Seamus, prattling at his side.

"I've decided to leave Eton."

"Hmm." As a gift, she'd left behind those translucent silk stockings, those languorous articles that still bore the rosewater scent of her.

Seamus gripped his arm and steered Charles around a pair of approaching young ladies and their chaperones. The quartet all walked with their gazes down . . . unlike the bold woman who'd laid siege to his household last evening.

"I'm also going to join a circus. I've always been rather good at somersaults, you know."

"Yes." And her crimson laced, heeled shoes had been abandoned in her departure. He would forever . . . "I know . . ."

Seamus held up his arms toward the overcast London sky, then made as if to spring forward.

Wait a moment . . .

Slowing his steps to a stop, Charles blinked in confusion. "That would be a terri—" He caught the teasing light in the boy's eyes too late. "You're ribbing me."

"It was easy to do." With a grin, Seamus winked, the very wink he'd pleaded with Charles to teach him on one of his weekly visits. "You weren't paying attention."

Nay, because his mind had been firmly on Emma Gately and their late-night meeting. Details which, of course, couldn't be shared with anyone. Ever. And especially not his almost-eleven-year-old nephew. "I was paying attention," he lied. "You . . ." He furrowed his brow. Charles turned, and dropping to a knee, he faced the little boy. "Aren't truly thinking of leaving Eton?" he asked, searching his nephew's heavily freckled face. Seamus loved his studies. Nothing short of sheer misery would make him quit attending the school he'd always longed to go to.

His nephew stared back with a somberness better suited to a man sixty years his senior. "I think of it quite regularly." The boy paused. "And joining the circus," he added, a slow grin forming on his lips.

"Not paying attention, you say? See, I heard everything you said." Charles reached out a hand.

His nephew ducked out of the way, attempting to dodge his efforts, but Charles looped an arm around Seamus's narrow shoulders and pulled him close. Forming a fist, he lightly tousled the top of the boy's head until Seamus snorted with laughter.

Charles ignored the sharp stares shot their way from passersby who sniffed their disapproval at the air.

Seamus immediately sidled closer. "I don't like that people look at me like that," the boy confided after they'd resumed their walk down the pavement.

Charles tensed. That disapproval followed whenever he and Seamus made their way about society. "It doesn't matter what they think," he said tightly, hating the world for turning their unkindness upon a boy. Hating himself for not being able to do anything to prevent it. It was generally why Charles opted for places where there would be less of that scrutiny: less-traveled areas of London. Hyde Park in the early-morn hour. Shops that were not the most popular ones.

Seamus scrunched up his small brow. "Perhaps." An anger that Charles had never observed before from the boy flashed in his green eyes. "But I still don't like it. It isn't fair." His nephew spoke with all the truth only a child was capable of.

It isn't fair.

"No." There could be no truer words uttered about everything surrounding Seamus's birth and Camille's broken heart. "It's not." None of it was. For any of them.

Fortunately, they reached his nephew's favorite place in the world, and the conversation found a natural, if abrupt, end. As he opened the door and Seamus went scurrying off, Charles stared after the little boy as he disappeared behind the enormous shelves.

Or mayhap it was just that he let the matter rest because he was a coward. But God help him, he'd no idea how to handle . . . any of this in terms of Seamus's reception.

Upon Seamus's birth, Camille and his parents had insisted the boy be hidden away as much as possible. At that family meeting, they'd disagreed with Charles's opinion that Seamus would be better served confronting whatever was directed his way, and preparing for that unkindness. Years later, wanting to protect Seamus as he did, he'd come 'round to understanding his family's desire.

He closed the door, and the same tinny bell that had announced their presence jingled once more.

At the front counter, the proprietor, Mr. Garrick, glanced up and lifted a hand in greeting before returning his attention to the exchange with a pretty, dark-haired woman and her husband, the Marquess and Marchioness of Drake. The lady speaking with the young proprietor balanced a babe on her hip, speaking animatedly with her husband and Mr. Garrick. All the while, around them, three small children spoke over one another, the two little boys engaged in a pretend sword fight and the lone little girl mediating between them like she was the nursemaid that noisy crew so desperately needed.

In short, it was a loving, noisy family . . . the manner of which Seamus had been deserving of.

Charles may have protected his sister's image and reputation, but he'd not been able to do that in the same way for Seamus. Just as he'd never be able to provide the boy with the respectability he craved and the family he deserved.

And what of what you *wanted . . . ?* a voice at the back of Charles's head prodded.

A happy family, including a wife and a parcel of children, was not something he'd really ever given any consideration to. Because it had been a given, much the same as waking up and breathing. Because of that, he'd never thought about marriage. Just as he'd never thought about the family that he and Emma would have had. A bride for him had always been there.

Until she hadn't been.

And now, seeing that happy family before him . . . and imagining, too late, what might have been with him and Emma . . . left a sharp ache in his chest, the very place where his heart beat.

Just then, the marquess glanced over and frowned.

Charles's neck went hot at being caught watching the familial tableau; he bowed his head and resumed walking deeper into the bustling shop.

The shop hadn't always been bustling. When Charles had first begun taking Seamus to the out-of-the-way, dusty old establishment, he'd done so because of the lack of crowds and patrons. Seamus had been allowed to run about freely. With the passing of Mr. Garrick's father, however, the shop's new proprietor had slowly and steadily transformed the place into a busy one. Charles and Seamus's history with the shop, and the familiarity they had with the proprietor, made it impossible to seek out a quieter, safer-for-Seamus replacement.

Charles continued on through the establishment, familiar enough with the place and his nephew to know precisely where he could be found. Reaching the far recesses of the shop, he located Seamus sprawled on his stomach as comfortably as if he were before the hearth in the Hayden family home. It was the same way he'd perused the texts in this place since they'd begun visiting; however, that had been before . . . when there hadn't been patrons filing about.

Seamus picked up his head and frowned. "Go," he said, waving an arm in Charles's direction.

"Perhaps we just purchase it?" he suggested. As it was, the world talked enough about the boy, and Charles would spare him further scrutiny where he could.

"It's not the same reading at home as doing it here." Seamus patted the book. "I have to make sure I like it."

Charles tried once more. "But—"

"Go, Scarsdale." His nephew cut him off, and then lowering his chin onto the floor, he resumed reading.

Charles gave his head a rueful shake. In moments such as these, he was rather certain he was receiving a taste of what his own father had contended with over the years in terms of Charles's own displays of disobedience and rebellion. Granted, Charles's displays had extended more to mischief-making than *actual* trouble.

Not that he'd not enjoyed his studies. He had.

But neither had he been a natural academic, as his nephew was. In fact, all society needed to do to see Charles wasn't the boy's real father was to look at how easily academics came to his nephew. Possessed as Seamus was of a keenly focused mind, one that wasn't distracted, as

Charles's had always been, that would've been all the proof the world needed. But society didn't look closely. They didn't look at all. They were content to see only the surface, and as such, it was remarkably easy to convince the world Camille's son was in fact Charles's.

Seamus, however, with his flawless ability to focus on his studies and academic pursuits, was very much his mother's son.

Unlike Charles. There'd always been more a distractedness to Charles's lessons, with his mind shifting and twisting to some other different and, in the moment, more interesting endeavor.

Perhaps that was why establishing his own counter-club to Emma's had proven so damned difficult. Because it required that focus he'd always been fighting to find within himself.

Strolling the empty aisles, Charles scanned the books' spines, examining the titles. The overwhelming inventory of books made it nearly impossible for him to focus on finding one that might aid him in his new endeavor. It was like so much noise that he couldn't crowd out.

And it was one of the reasons he'd come to so admire Emma. Not only had she managed to create something, but she'd made it look remarkably easy. When Charles knew it was anything but.

It did not mean, however, that he didn't intend to try. Or that it couldn't be done.

Distractedly, he studied the gold lettering of one particular title. Charles quickly snagged the book and pulled it from the shelf.

Jane Austen's *Pride and Prejudice*.

He fanned the pages, his eyes skimming the words as they fluttered slowly by, and then they stopped.

His gaze passed over the passage upon the middle of the page, and he continued skimming.

And then stopped.

Frantically, he worked his eyes up . . . searching . . . and then he found them.

"I declare after all there is no enjoyment like reading! How much sooner one tires of anything than of a book! When I have a house of my own, I shall be miserable if I have not an excellent library . . ."

Charles stared contemplatively at the words written there. Over and over.

. . . there is no enjoyment like reading! How much sooner one tires of anything than of a book . . .

He went absolutely motionless as an idea cut through the previous confusion of his club. The idea broke free and blared strong.

Whistling a jaunty little tune, he began to read.

Chapter 13

THE LONDONER

DOWN WITH BOOKISH LADIES

Miss Gately is rumored to be single-handedly responsible for the surging interest amongst young ladies on matters of politics and business. For shame!

M. FAIRPOINT

Twelve hours after Emma's early-morn rendezvous with Charles, she was certain she was never going to be able to clear the haze left by those stolen moments of bliss found with him.

He'd opened her eyes and body and soul to passion, which she'd never before thought to know.

And now she was never going to be the same.

Her world had been shaken. After all, what did it say about her that she'd faltered as she had in Charles's rooms?

If she wavered in this way, she'd lose all that she had left where Charles and society were concerned—her pride.

Emma gripped the fabric of her skirts. No one could ever know.

An elbow collided with Emma's side, snapping her from her reverie and bringing her back down to Earth. Or as Earth would have it . . . the uneven cobblestones of Watling Street.

"We are in a pickle . . . ," her sister was saying.

Having lost the ability to think of anyone and anything but Charles and that passionate exchange, Emma knew her sister wasn't wrong on that score.

"It is hard to say what is most dire about the situation. The fact that . . ." Isla stopped abruptly and slanted a sharp, assessing glance Emma's way. Her eyes flared. "Are you paying attention?" she demanded with a no-nonsense quality to her tone.

"Of course," Emma lied, her cheeks burning up.

Fortunately, one of the privileges enjoyed by eldest-born sisters everywhere was the freedom from being lectured.

Alas, Isla seemed not to have gotten those important notes.

"No, you are not!" she charged.

Or mayhap it was more a product of the Mismatch Society's influence upon the previously measured girl. For she'd not ever been one to challenge Emma, and certainly not openly in the presence of company. Albeit Olivia and Owen . . . but company, still.

Isla marched at an impressive pace better suited to a military general. "You have no idea what I've been speaking about since the carriage ride. Do you?" she demanded of Emma.

It was one thing for Emma to acknowledge to herself that she'd been woolgathering. It was quite another to hear it from her younger sister, and youngest sibling. For it confirmed the very fear she'd carried, that the world would see all the ways in which she'd weakened toward the last man she should be weak over.

Her stomach muscles twisted.

No idea? In truth, she'd no blasted clue what her sister spoke of. Since Emma had taken her leave of Charles in the early-morn hours, she'd been incapable of thinking about anything beyond—

Isla gasped. "My God, you are either woolgathering or clueless as to what I have been saying about your role in saving the Mismatch Society."

Emma bristled. This time she had been more . . . silently worrying than woolgathering. "I resent that. You are my sister. You should have faith in me to know I'd never woolgather, and that I am taking my current responsibility very seriously."

Her youngest sibling gave her a dubious look.

"And furthermore," Emma went on, "you are being melodramatic."

"Then you aren't paying attention."

"I settled the matter . . ." *Last evening.* A blush singed Emma from the tips of her toes to the roots of her hair, and she hurriedly pulled her bonnet into place to conceal that telltale color that came with the resurrected memories of everything Charles had done to her.

"Are you fighting?" Olivia called from behind them.

Emma and Isla spoke at the same time.

"Yes."

"No."

Unfortunately, Isla's denial came louder, clearer, and more emphatic.

"Well, it behooves me to point out that, given the state of the Mismatch Society, we can hardly afford to have contention between our remaining members." Olivia scolded better than any of the stern nursemaids and governesses Emma and Isla had suffered through over the years. "And that includes the both of you."

So it wasn't only Isla who feared the current state of their society. "I've already told you." Emma attempted to reassure her naysaying sibling. "We needn't worry any more about Charles's group. That matter has been settled."

Her sister snorted.

Do not take the bait . . . do not take the bait . . .

It was futile.

"What?" Emma asked, unable to tamp down her exasperation.

"If you *think* the same gentleman who's been doggedly paying visits in the hopes of winning you back wouldn't show the same tenacity in *this*?" Isla shook her head. "Then you have learned nothing about Lord Scarsdale and what he is capable of, and the Mismatch Society is destined to perish."

Emma winced. *Destined to perish?* And worse, her sister suggested the inevitable failure was in part because of Emma's failings. This time, Emma's cheeks heated for altogether different reasons, at being called out in the one endeavor in which she'd taken pride in . . . in . . . well, the entire course of her life. "You are wrong." About both Charles and the doomsday-like quality of Isla's warning.

"I certainly hope so," her sister allowed. "But in the event I'm not? *Hmm?* What do you intend to do to see that we don't continue losing members?"

Had Isla always been this . . . unrelenting? "I have . . . *some* ideas." None. She'd absolutely no thoughts as to how to focus the next meeting, her first real role of leadership since the inception of the society.

Not breaking stride, her sister pointed a finger her way. "I *heard* that."

"Heard what?" Olivia called from behind them.

"It was a pause."

"I heard no pause," Owen volunteered, and Emma cast a grateful smile over her shoulder for his defense.

Undeserved though it may be.

"Then you weren't listening hard enough, Owen Watley," Isla shot back, and taking Emma's arms, she commanded her sister's focus once more. "Assuaging your ego should hardly be your concern. Our society is under siege. Everything we've created, and everything we hold dear, is being threatened, and as one of the founding members charged with righting the faltering ship, well, it requires at least *some* attention from you."

Well. That was quite the verbal takedown.

"Thank you for your faith in me, little sister," Emma drawled.

"It isn't that I don't have faith in you," her sister protested. "It is simply that—" Isla abruptly stopped talking as a handsome couple with their small army of children filed past, and a nursemaid, trailing close, approached. The moment they'd passed, Isla resumed, this time speaking in a barely audible whisper. "It is simply that you've been uncharacteristically distracted . . ."

Emma held her breath, braced for the completion of that thought.

. . . *since last evening* . . .

Since she had dashed barefoot from Charles's household after he'd made love to her. Except . . . she still had her virtue. Or anyway, Emma did in the *strictest* sense of the word. Was it really, therefore, the same to classify whatever wonderful wickedness she'd experienced last evening as— "Ouch!" she squeaked, rubbing at the forearm her sister had just pinched.

"This. This is what I'm talking about," Isla said flatly as they came to a stop outside the Old Corner Bookshop. She drew Emma by the elbow away from the entrance so that they were framed by the sparkling windowpanes. Isla ran a concern-filled stare over Emma's face. "You've just created something so special, and something so wonderful, and I would hate to see all your efforts for naught because . . . because . . ." *Of him.*

Emma stiffened.

This time, there could be no doubting those unspoken words. Rather, this time, a name.

"Emma?"

They both looked over.

Owen stood with the door open, and Olivia poised on the threshold, staring back, a question in her eyes for Emma.

"We'll be along shortly," she promised, waiting until Olivia and Owen had continued ahead, leaving Emma and her sister alone.

The moment the Watley siblings had disappeared inside, she turned her attention back to Isla.

"You are . . . not wrong," she conceded, because she respected her sister too much to lie any more than she had. "I am no more distracted now than I've been since I ended it with Charles," Emma said quietly.

Her sister smiled sadly. "That is hardly a ringing endorsement of your focus, nor any real indication that you've moved on from him."

That charge brought Emma's fists curling. She wanted to lash out at her sister. To call her out for having dared think the thoughts she had.

And yet this was her sister, and sisters oft knew a woman better than the woman knew herself, and this moment proved no exception.

Her gaze snagged on the happy family that had passed them earlier, the handsome gentleman lifting each child up into the carriage, their merry mirth and happy laughter a touching scene of everything Emma had secretly longed for with Charles. Then he caught the pretty brunette by the waist, and—

It was too much. Emma forced her stare away from that intimate exchange, and she found her sister watching her once more.

"I am doing the best I can to put him from my thoughts, but it . . . isn't as easy as all that. We have been betrothed since we were children. I have seventeen years of thinking my life would be one way with him, and just two months of readjusting to this new norm." Emma caught her sister's hands and squeezed lightly. "But just because I am, does not mean I'm incapable of helping to make the Mismatch Society everything I, you, and every other woman wish it to be."

Isla's throat moved furiously as fury burnt through the worry that had been there in her sister's eyes. "I do not doubt you are capable of doing anything, and saving our society, at that. I just don't want to see you give him any more of yourself than he's already had. He was *never* worthy of you." Those words came as if torn from deep within Isla.

Emotion swarmed Emma, and she fought the sting of tears. "Thank you," she said past a thick throat.

Her sister went up on tiptoe and kissed her cheek. She hesitated and, by her still-troubled eyes, appeared as if she wished to say more, before finally hurrying inside the bookshop.

Emma stared after her, taking a moment to order her thoughts. Though she believed Isla exaggerated several points she'd made this day, her sister was also correct on any number of other scores. Emma had not been putting proper attention where her attention was due.

As she entered, Emma loosened the lace strings of her bonnet, lowering the article.

She was to be the one organizing the topic of the next Mismatch meeting.

As such, she should have been devoting her full attention to developing the agenda for the first full session she would be organizing and moderating. Emma headed past the enormous collection of gothic novels and romance tales to the philosophical section at the far corner of the shop that she frequented when she came. She wandered down one of the narrower, empty aisles. Absently, she plucked a copy of Rousseau's *Du Contrat Social* from the shelf.

Alas, since she'd fled Charles's house and boarded the hackney home, she'd been unable to think of anything . . . but him. And the passion he'd awakened. And her sister was right. It was past time that she put her efforts where they should—

"It's no wonder he won't even buy a book for you . . ." A child's voice cut through her silent musings, and Emma picked up her head.

"He will," another boy shot back. "He would. He offered. I chose . . . stop it!" Those words came more strident, more desperate than commanding.

There came the distant sniggering.

Emma narrowed her eyes. It was a sound she knew all too well. Not a true laugh, but more a taunting cruelty disguised as mirth. Shifting course, she followed those voices. Those jeers and sniggers grew increasingly louder.

She stopped, at last finding a trio of children. Two tall, gangly boys of similar height, but one in possession of bright crimson curls and the other ink-black hair, stood over a much smaller child, who sat on the floor. Even seated as he was, Emma could make out the slight, painfully slender form, a good deal smaller than the ones now confronting him. Even so, there was an impressive strength and courage to the cornered child, who, behind spectacles that appeared too large for his face, glared up at his detractors.

Fury for the child, and on the child's behalf, sizzled in her veins as rage briefly blanketed her vision.

"He doesn't even like to be seen with you . . . ," the redheaded boy jeered.

"You're wrong. He's here. He's—"

The other nasty child kicked the book out of the smaller boy's fingers, sending the volume flying back into his face and knocking his spectacles loose. The literary missile landed hard on the floor, knocking into the small stack of leather-bound titles that had been sitting there.

That pile tumbled over, toppling forlornly open upon their now-wounded spines.

That was really enough. "You there." Three sets of gazes swiveled her way as Emma stormed over. "You miserable little cur." She looked between the two bullies. "The both of you."

The ginger boy, the clear ringleader of their pair, flushed as red as the hair on his head. "I'm not little," he blustered, while his still cruel but somewhat wiser friend edged away from Emma.

Resting her hands akimbo on her hips, she ran a condescending stare up and down each of their persons. "I'm a woman, and I have you pegged a good six inches shorter than me."

The color on both children's cheeks deepened by several shades. "I'm not done growing," the mouthier of the two shot back.

She snorted. "That remains to be seen. In fact, who is to say you haven't stopped already?" Emma continued marching forward until both boys, this time, retreated from the silent, wide-eyed child on the floor.

Mouthy Boy and his follow-along friend backed square into the shelving until she had put an effective end to their retreat and had them anchored perfectly so she could dole out the lecture they were in desperate need of. "And let me be clear . . . ?" she began, looking between the two.

When both boys were too cowardly to respond, she cast a glance over at the solemn-looking little boy who'd just taken to his feet.

The child cleared his throat. "Lord Whitley"—he stuck a little finger in the redheaded boy's direction—"and Lord Asher," he supplied, earning matching scowls from his bullies.

"Shut your mou—"

She glared away the remainder of that threat from Lord Whitley. "Let me be clear, Lord Asher and Lord Whitley. You may think you are tall. You may think you are strong. But you are both small in the ways that matter most. You are bullies," she said bluntly. "You are beasts. And you think you're clever, but your strength only comes from hurting others, which makes you the smallest of boys." She took a step closer, and leaning down and highlighting the height difference between them, she stuck her nose close to Lord Asher's. The boy's large Adam's apple jumped. "And no matter how much you might grow in meters? As long as you remain the same vile, heartless, ruthless beasts you are this day?" She shifted, fixing all her rage on the ringleader. "Then you will never grow to become a man."

Shamefaced, both boys dropped their gazes to the hardwood floor.

She clapped her hands close to their faces, startling their focus back to her. "Now go," she snapped.

The pair bolted, taking off running.

The moment they'd gone, Emma looked to the nameless little boy staring wide-eyed up at her. With those children gone, she now had her first real look at him. Thin to the point of gaunt, his skin pale and his green eyes enormous, he couldn't be more than eight or nine years of age. As one who'd been a frequent recipient of gossip and unkindness, her heart ached at the thought of this child fielding such cruelty so young.

Emma smiled gently at him, and his cheeks bloomed with color. She quit her place, walking with slow, measured steps until she stood beside him. The boy craned his head all the way back to look at her. Emma fell to a knee beside him. "Hullo," she greeted.

"You were rather rough on them," he whispered.

"*Too* rough?"

The child grinned, his lips moving up slowly until he revealed white but adorably uneven teeth, in his first smile since Emma had come upon him. "Not at all."

Returning that smile, Emma rescued the boy's spectacles from the floor. She used the front of her cloak to clean off the smudged lenses before returning them to his elfin face.

His smile widened, and a blush filled his cheeks. "Many thanks." The color deepened. "For my glasses . . ." That newly found brightness dimmed as he looked down at his fine leather boots. "And for rescuing me." That last part emerged more of a mumble, and her heart tugged again.

At what he'd endured.

At the lack of self-worth he felt in this moment, when the only ones who should feel shame were the boys she'd run off.

She scoffed. "You didn't require my rescuing," she said, and the child's head came flying back. "I should thank you for allowing me to speak up to such bullies. It is one of my favorite pastimes."

"Indeed?"

Emma offered a solemn nod. "Undoubtedly. I've fielded unkind words myself." One eventually developed armor, but occasionally, no matter how many a person fielded, those barbs found the weak spots within. She set to work collecting and stacking the boy's books.

The child joined her on the floor, watching a moment as she worked. "Why would anyone be mean to you?" he asked before handing over a copy of de Montesquieu's *The Spirit of the Laws*.

"Why is anyone mean to anyone?" she countered rhetorically.

"Well, they are mean to me because I'm a bastard," he said so matter-of-factly and unexpectedly that she lost her grip upon the book she held.

Emma fumbled, ultimately retaining her grip.

This was the reason for the cruelty he'd faced.

Even as her own father had been a loyal, devoted husband, the larger reality for most was that bastards were the way of Polite Society. Gentlemen joined their clubs, drank their brandies, and fathered illegitimate children upon the mistresses who'd never be their wives, but whom they'd bestow their affections and attentions upon.

She was ashamed to realize . . . until this moment? She'd never given proper thought to how those children were treated. What hardships they must know.

Was this what Charles's son faced?

Anger brought her teeth snapping together so hard that pain raced up along her jawline.

"I can leave," the child whispered, misunderstanding the reason for her silence, mistaking it for a rebuke of his birthright, factors beyond his control, ones she resented for him. He made to stand.

Emma shot out a hand, staying him.

"That is not the reason they are unkind to you," she said quietly. His brow dipped with confusion. "The truth is, cruelty is what fills heartless people with something other than the emptiness in that organ. Insults are merely the arguments employed by those who are in the wrong."

"That is splendid," he said in awed tones.

Emma rescued a copy of Rousseau's work and held it aloft. "Alas, those latter words belonged to Mr. Rousseau."

His features softened.

Eager to continue diverting his thoughts away from the meanness he'd known that day, she made a show of examining the title a moment. "This is a rather impressive collection of works to read." Emma gathered up another, studying the maroon lettering. "John Locke, *Two Treatises of Government?*" She glanced up.

"I enjoy it." His spine grew several inches, and he looked taller for the now proud set of his shoulders. "And I'm ten. Not so young. I am just"—he wrinkled his freckled nose—"small," he said under his breath.

Emma set Locke's work atop the neat stack they'd formed. "Bah. As I said, height has nothing to do with how tall a person truly is. Why, I was teased mercilessly when I made my Come Out because I was too tall."

"You were teased?" the boy ventured hesitantly.

"Mercilessly. Lesser people can and will always find some perceived flaw to bully a person over." Memories filtered in . . . of that meanness she'd met from other debutantes at Almack's, women who'd attributed Emma's height as just one of the many reasons her betrothed had wanted nothing to do with her. "Now, how one lives one's life? How he or she treats others? How he or she helps others in need of help? *That* is what matters . . . ?" She stared at him questioningly, seeking his name.

"Seamus," the child murmured. "My name is Seamus."

Emma held out her spare hand. "And I am Emma." The boy stared at it a moment before placing his fingers in hers and shaking. His hand was so very fragile and so very small, and for a moment, she wondered what it would be to have a child of her own. A tiny boy or girl who loved the same books she did. She'd thought of that once.

Before she'd fully appreciated just how very much her betrothed had despised her and the idea of a future with her.

Drawing back her hand, Emma forced aside thoughts of what was never to have been, and shifted her attention squarely to her new companion.

Lowering onto her stomach, she reached for the nearest book.

"Who is your favorite, Seamus?"

Chapter 14

THE LONDONER

A MEETING BETWEEN RIVALS

The dashing Earl of Scarsdale was seen beside the
sour Miss Gately. Society is abuzz with what the two
leaders of rival establishments might have been meeting on . . .

                                        M. FAIRPOINT

Having collected a not-so-very-small stack of books for his new club,
Charles deposited them at the counter and went off in search of his
nephew, knowing implicitly where he'd find Seamus. And even more
exactly, *how* he'd find him.

Seamus would be precisely as Charles had left him: sprawled upon
his stomach with a stack of books spread out before him. But for the
periodic turning of pages, he'd be absolutely silent, completely engrossed
in whatever title he read that day.

As it turned out, when he came upon the boy, Seamus proved not so silent, but still engrossed . . . just in a way different from all the previous times before it.

And also . . . not alone.

"He is quite possibly the most critical thinker, the most accomplished of all the Enlightened philosophers," Seamus said with more enthusiasm than Charles ever recalled of the boy.

"Oh, come," the young woman who lay shoulder to shoulder beside Seamus scoffed. "He is *highly* overrated."

From where he stood at the end of the aisle, Charles froze. That woman and her voice were both familiar. But it was impossible. It was more a product of him seeing her anywhere and everywhere. For there was no other accounting for how she'd come to be here, and with Seamus . . .

"Never!" Seamus said. "His is one of the most widely disseminated works of all the Enlightenment."

Angling a hand out before her, she proceeded to tick points off on her fingers. "Born into a prominent family. A family whose influence provided him with the *schooling* and *connections* to rise effortlessly?"

"Well, who do you *think* is the best?" Seamus challenged, that slight emphasis indicating whomever it was would never hold up against the philosopher whose work he supported.

"Do you want to know?" Emma kicked up her heels, rucking her skirts slightly below her knees, and Charles swallowed hard, certain there wasn't a more magnificent sight than she, conversing on matters of political philosophy with her shapely calves so exposed. At her side, Seamus brought his legs up, matching Emma's posture.

The little boy nodded vigorously, his glasses slipping down. And then with the tenderest of movements, Emma leaned over and ever so naturally slid those rims back into their proper place.

Charles's breath hitched, the sound thankfully lost to that unlikely pair so very engrossed in their debate.

"Le Rond," she said.

Seamus blinked. "Le *Ronnnd*?" The added syllable to that particular name highlighted the boy's incredulity and disappointment.

Emma nodded. "Yes."

There was a pause, and then Seamus burst out laughing. "You're ribbing me."

"Not at all," she said with a seriousness that penetrated through the boy's mirth. Fishing around a neater-than-usual stack of books, carefully piled and clearly a product of Emma's influence, she plucked one of the titles free and popped it open.

"Le Rond isn't as notable as the other Enlightened thinkers. But he also didn't have a fancy, fine upbringing, as so many of them did. He didn't come into the world with connections." As she spoke, Seamus sat absorbed in her telling, with a riveted awe and fascination that Charles understood all too well, as he'd been bewitched by the same spell she wove. Emma paused on one of the pages and pushed it over to the child at her side. "He was illegitimate," she said softly, and Charles stiffened, but he needn't have been worried on Seamus's behalf. With an almost reverence to his hesitant movements, Seamus pulled the book closer and looked down at whatever words Emma now pointed to. "He was left upon the steps of a church—abandoned. His education was paid for, but everything he did with that education? Well, that came because of him and being free of the powerful influence enjoyed by so many of these others."

As the pair launched into a discussion about the French thinker, Charles stared on, a silent observer. His mind raced, and it was physically impossible to leave. Even though he should. Even though his being here infringed upon this special moment Seamus had found.

Nay, this special moment Seamus had found . . . with Emma.

Charles tried to make sense . . . of any of it: How had the two come to be here, together? How had they struck up such a familiar discussion on a topic that was so dear to the boy . . . and apparently, to Emma? It was one more thing Charles had never known about her. So much of her remained a mystery.

Charles ran his gaze over her long, slender form. A mystery that he desperately wished to understand and uncover . . . and share in.

Here all these years, Charles and his family had spent the better part of his life keeping Seamus from the world. There'd been an even more concerted effort to keep him away from Emma Gately.

Only to now stumble upon the pair of them sprawled on the floor, conversing ever so effortlessly, as though they were not only the fastest of friends, but longtime ones at that.

Crossing her comfortable-looking boots behind her, Emma spoke animatedly, gesturing to the page as she did. Periodically, Seamus nodded, which only fueled the enthusiastic cadence as Emma spoke, her words lost, but not her excitement . . .

And in that moment, with Emma Gately lying on a bookshop floor, conversing freely and joyously as she did with Seamus, Charles fell head over heels in love with her.

He caught the end of the shelving unit, the world shifting under him.

The floorboards *also* moved under Charles's unsteady balance.

Fortunately, wholly engrossed in what she was sharing, Emma remained oblivious to Charles's presence, for which Charles would be eternally grateful. Everything spun and whirred. His thoughts all skidded together; his pulse raced. He'd known he wanted to marry her—too late, of course. He'd belatedly discovered she was a woman of wit and courage and confidence. But these past two days, he'd seen her in ways he'd failed to before.

But seeing her here, like this? It left him shaken to the core. This tangible, living, breathing proof of why his heart belonged to Emma

Gately, and why it wouldn't properly beat until he managed to convince her of the impossible—that he was deserving of her.

Seamus angled a glance over his shoulder, and his eyes brightened. "Scarsdale!" he greeted.

The book promptly slipped from Emma's fingers, landing with a dull *thwack*, as she whipped around to face him.

Her lips moved several times before any words emerged. *"Charlesss?"* Emma's beautifully sharp cheeks went through varying shades of red before arriving at a bright hue of crimson . . .

Charles hooded his eyes.

The same color of red she'd worn last evening when—

"You know one another?" Seamus blurted, effectively dousing the wicked thoughts Charles had no place having. At least, not here. Not now. And not with the young boy before him doing the questioning.

"Uh . . ." Charles doffed his hat. For it . . . felt . . . inherently wrong that he'd never before introduced Emma to the nephew whom he was raising as his son.

Slowly, Emma sat up but didn't rise. She drew up her legs, with her knees close to her chest. "We . . . do," she supplied for him, of course more courageous and capable of finding her words than Charles.

Alas, no child, particularly not his inquisitive nephew, would ever be contented with that veiled, incomplete explanation.

Seamus looked back and forth from Charles to Emma, then finally settled on Charles.

"This is Miss Gately," Charles said quietly.

His nephew's already big eyes bulged. *"This* is Miss Gately? But—"

As Emma's focus sharpened on the boy, Charles made a loud clearing sound, slashing a hand at his throat, cutting off the remainder of whatever ill-timed response the child might make. Emma looked back swiftly, and Charles hastily disguised that motion, scratching at his throat instead.

She narrowed her eyes, the suspicion there so very different from the unrestrained warmth and openness with which she and Seamus conversed. And Charles proved the miserable rotter Emma and society believed him to be, because he found himself envying his nephew the closeness he'd found with her. "And . . . you know one another," she stated, when Charles failed to own his connection to Seamus.

"Seamus is my son." He'd breathed the lie so much it had become truth to the world.

He braced for Emma to tense. To leave. As would be her right, given that to her knowledge, he'd been unfaithful to her, and in other ways Charles had been. It didn't matter that he'd done so to maintain a lie to spare his sister's reputation. Because she didn't know those details.

Because you never told her . . . But what if you had . . .

Perhaps then she wouldn't have looked upon him with wary mistrust . . .

What he was unprepared for was the warmth of the smile . . . this time, directed at Charles. "Your son is a clever young man."

Charles's heart filled.

The little boy grew several inches under that praise, beaming and proud.

And damn it all if Charles didn't fall in love with her for a second time that day. "He is," he said hoarsely.

Sitting up, Seamus sat with his ankles crossed and his knees folded close to him. He urged Charles to join them, but Charles hesitated, not wanting to infringe upon their meeting, and not wanting the brief moment he'd shared with Emma to end, and for them to find themselves in the place they always did . . . at odds and battling.

Seamus's smile wavered.

Emma waved Charles over.

And he would have followed her wherever she led in that moment.

Venturing deeper down the aisle, Charles joined Emma and Seamus, lowering himself to the floor.

"Miss Gately," the child began as soon as Charles had taken up a spot between Emma and Seamus.

"Emma," she corrected, tendering that use of her Christian name.

"*Emma* knows ever so much about the Enlightened thinkers. So. Much." Seamus lifted his hands and held them apart to signify the breadth of his new idol's knowledge. "And do you know what she said?" The boy didn't wait. "Le Rond was a bastard, Scarsdale. A bastard. And he was left on a hospital's steps and . . ."

While the child launched into a near word-for-word recitation of everything Emma had shared on the philosopher, Charles caught her eye.

They shared a smile, and he felt a buoyant lightness fill every corner of his being at the warmth there. At the connection between them.

This is what it could have been . . .

As she looked back to Seamus, the smile froze on Charles's face, tense and tight and painful. For this was what it could have been if he hadn't resisted a future with her. If he hadn't directed undeserved anger her way, over decisions their parents had made. Their parents, who had known better than Charles what he needed.

If he'd just taken the time to *know* her.

Nearly breathless, Seamus concluded speaking. "Scarsdale insists that Locke is the most clever."

Emma whipped another startled gaze up Charles's way. "You read the Enlightened thinkers?"

And his fingers twitched with the need to yank at a suddenly uncomfortably tight cravat. "I . . ."

"Oh, yes!" Seamus happily supplied for him.

He felt Emma's stare, the interest in her pretty blue eyes deepening. "Indeed?"

No one had looked to him for any form of intellectual discourse. They'd taken him for an athlete. A fellow given to a good jest. In fact, he'd been laughed at for his academic attempts at university. But with Emma . . . for the first time, he felt free in discussing topics previously denied him.

"I'm not nearly as versed or even half as intelligent in the topic as Seamus," he explained. Academics had never come easy and, as such, had never been any remotely strong suit of Charles. But proud as he was—nay . . . embarrassed as he was—he couldn't bring himself to admit any of that aloud. "Everything I've learned has been from this one." Leaning over, he ruffled his nephew's golden locks. "I wouldn't have even known anything of it, hadn't it been for him."

"*Bahhh.*" Seamus swatted at his hand. "Tell Emma what you told me about Locke and why you like him so much?"

Oh, hell, he felt exposed. And this time, Charles did wrestle with his cravat. "Miss Gately doesn't want to hear—"

"Oh, she does!" Emma exclaimed. She swiveled her attention back to the little boy. "I do."

"Once, I had a nasty tutor . . ." Seamus went on, happy to supply that which Charles attempted to withhold. "A mean, stern fellow. He rapped my knuckles"—he lifted his hand, displaying the sight of that old, now invisible wound for Emma—"and often."

She gasped. "The bounder."

"Worry not; Scarsdale sacked him." The little boy flashed a crooked-toothed smile. "But only after he'd punched him in the stomach."

Charles winced. "I didn't really hit him"—he managed a sheepish grin—"that hard?"

Clapping lightly, Emma laughed. "I shall always applaud the defense of another in need."

And with that dimpled, radiant smile trained upon him, Charles had an understanding of just how Seamus had felt, being elevated so by this woman before him.

Emma looped her arms about her knees and rested her chin atop them; she rubbed it back and forth over her skirts distractedly. "Now tell me, Lord Scarsdale, what is your opinion on Mr. Locke and his writings?"

Once again, Charles's mind went racing back to all the times at Eton and Oxford when he'd been marched to the front of the classroom and put on display, to fumble through some point that he hadn't fully understood. The damp palms, the churning in his stomach that had been eased only when he'd donned a grin and made up some jest or another to distract the class, and spare himself anything but the fury of the preceptors.

The gentle encouragement in Emma's eyes, however . . . proved different from the coldness of frustrated instructors who'd not known what to do with a marquess's son and failed student. That warmth radiating from her gaze pushed aside all the keen reminders of his failings and allowed him to continue. "I pointed out to Seamus that Locke spoke of learning by play and recreation, and as such, every child should be thusly so encouraged."

Emma stopped that distracted movement of her chin, and resting it there on her knees, she stared at him. "That is lovely," she said softly. And in this moment with her, he didn't feel like a failure of a student. He didn't think about all the details he didn't know. "I never thought of it in quite that way." Her nose wrinkled at the end in what he'd come to learn was an endearing indication of her in contemplative thought. And he wanted all those details about this woman. He wanted to know everything about her, and all the subtleties that made Emma Gately, Emma Gately.

Even as you are undeserving of one as clever and strong and witty as she is, a voice taunted. And it was . . . the first time in which he'd made himself own that reality, that she was entirely too good for him.

"My own governesses all sought to turn me into what society viewed as an appropriately serious student," she went on through the tumult of his thoughts. "Until I came across one who opened my eyes to the philosophers and deeper thought, and I just naturally came to expect that to consider scholarly topics, one need behave in a way that is considered scholarly." She straightened. And this time as she spoke, she did so almost more to herself . . . as if her eyes had been opened to a point she'd never considered, and as that thought took root, her excitement grew. "But why must it? Why should children be expected to be—"

"Miniature adults?" Charles supplied for her.

Emma nodded frantically. "Precisely!" She sat back. "Why, I think you are the one who has had the right of it all these years, Cha—" She slid a glance in a grinning Seamus's direction. "Lord Scarsdale," Emma substituted.

"I told you," Seamus said with a pride that Charles was undeserving of.

And damned if he didn't feel himself blushing like the schoolboy he'd once been. "Yes, well, as I said, my knowledge is less extensive than either yours or Miss Gately's. And that selection of Locke is only because I never knew of Le Rond"—Charles held Emma's eyes—"until Miss Gately."

"Do not diminish your own thoughts and opinions, Charles." Emma spoke with a quiet yet gentle insistence, and his mouth went dry as it hit him square between the eyes: she saw.

She saw and knew that he'd attempted to shift away praise and return their focus to his deficits—of which there were many.

It was too much. Too intimate. And it was all happening too quickly, in this very public place.

Charles cleared his throat and averted his gaze, bringing it over to his wide-grinning nephew.

And by that wide grin, the boy also saw too much. "You did not say how you and Emma came to meet?" It was a question that, the moment it left his lips, Charles wished he hadn't asked, because the light the boy had previously radiated . . . dimmed.

The boy's gaze fell to the tips of his boots, and he studied the leather as intently as he did the books he pored over in the late-night hours. "Miss Gately was kind enough to . . . help me when . . . when . . ."

"You make more of it than there was," Emma said quickly, resting a hand so gently, so naturally upon Seamus's shoulder that a cinch squeezed tightly about Charles's chest.

"I'm not."

"Then we shall agree to disagree," she said with a gentle but firm insistence. The pair exchanged a look, a warm, kind bond that only deepened the pressure weighing down on Charles.

"Emmma?"

They looked back as one to the trio standing there at the end of the aisle: Emma's sister, Miss Isla Gately; and her friend Lady Olivia; and . . . Charles sharpened his gaze on the tall, wiry fellow scowling back at him.

Emma scrambled to her feet. "Isla! Olivia! Owen!"

Owen?

Not taking his eyes off the gentleman still glaring at him, Charles stood more slowly.

The gentleman whom Emma had spoken to so naturally looked her way. In an instant, the hardness left the fellow's angular face, as he went instantly soft at the sight of her.

Charles's back went up.

He knew the look of a besotted man. Nay, a man besotted with Emma Gately. It was a look he himself had worn for the better part of two months. And who was to say how much longer this gent had . . . and how long he'd been squiring Emma and her sister and friend about?

And not for the first time that day, he felt the burning sting of jealousy as it sizzled to life and ran through his veins like an electric charge, that seething sentiment more potent . . . this time not for the easy companionship Emma had known with Seamus, but because of the man before him.

Yes, he also knew a rival when he saw one.

"Seamus, Lord Scarsdale, allow me to introduce my sister, Isla; my dearest friend, Lady Olivia; and her brother, Mr. Owen Watley." The gentleman, Mr. Owen Watley, dropped a stiff and reluctant bow. "This is Lord Scarsdale's son, Mr. Seamus Hayden," Emma finished.

Her pronouncement ushered in a quick, thick, and awkward silence.

Tension whipped through Charles, his own blistering resentment toward the younger gentleman's regard for Emma temporarily forgotten, and he slid closer to Seamus. He rested a hand upon his nephew's shoulder. From the corner of Charles's eye, he caught a slight movement. In a show of solidarity and support, Emma flanked the boy's other side.

God, she was . . . magnificent. Beautiful in her strength and support and honor.

What a fool he'd been.

The quiet abruptly ended.

Isla and Olivia, instantly smiles, came over to join them, exchanging pleasantries with Seamus. All the while, Emma facilitated a discussion between the boy and pair of ladies. Periodically, she'd nod, and say something that earned a blush or smile from Seamus.

Charles's skin prickled as Mr. Watley hung on the fringe, glowering once more at him.

Given the deplorable way in which Charles had behaved toward Emma these past years, he certainly wasn't exempt from the other man's disapproval. Even so, Seamus had no part of the decisions Charles had made, and as such, Charles hardly intended to let a young pup— and at that, a young pup who'd been making eyes at Charles's former betrothed—go about glowering his way like a stern Lady Jersey at Almack's.

Charles lifted a single eyebrow in the younger man's direction. Mr. Watley flushed and looked away.

Alas, Mr. Watley wasn't the only one to ice Charles with a single look.

Emma's sister pinned an impressive glare upon him. "We should be going, should we not, Emma?"

There was a brief moment of hesitation.

"Yes, we should be going," Emma murmured.

Or mayhap it was merely Charles's own yearnings for that slight pause, some indication, *any* indication, that Emma wished to remain here . . . as he so desperately wanted her to. But as they'd been with Seamus, before her small army of friends had arrived.

She held out her fingers to Seamus. "It was a pleasure, Mr. Hayden."

"The same, miss," Seamus returned, giving her palm a mighty shake.

Emma turned to Charles, her gaze softer than he ever remembered . . . at least as it had been directed to him. It was time for her to leave. And he hated it. He hated that this trio had come upon them and stolen the too-brief exchange he and Emma and Seamus had shared.

"Miss Gately," he said quietly.

She bowed her head. "Lord Scarsdale." And with a curtsy, she took her leave, and pausing at the end of the aisle, she cast one more glance his way.

Her sister said something, and then reaching back, she grabbed Emma and dragged her off.

The moment they'd gone, Charles continued to stare after the place she'd been.

His nephew came to stand next to him, and Charles reluctantly forced his attention away from that empty spot and down to Seamus.

"*That* was your Miss Gately," his nephew whispered.

"Yes."

"The very one you did not want to marry?"

Charles flinched. "Yes?"

Seamus gave his head a rueful shake.

"I know. I know." Charles swiped his hands over his face. "I *knoww*," he added for a third time. Because it really couldn't be stated enough, all the ways in which he'd made a blunder of it where Emma was concerned.

In the greatest reversal of roles, the small child patted Charles on the low of his back. "Better to have discovered it now, than never."

"No, you have me there." The right corner of Charles's lips tugged up. "Come," he said, shifting away from further talk of Emma that was only destined to lead to details too complex for the child before him. "As penance for my years of folly, I shall purchase this whole collection for you."

Seamus giggled. "No." He held aloft a small, brown leather volume. "I only want this one."

Charles scanned the title.

Le Rond.

Whether that philosopher was truly Emma's favorite thinker, or whether she'd merely been attempting to help a hurting boy, was unclear.

As he and Seamus returned the remainder of the books to their respective places upon the shelves, Charles knew only one certainty— he'd been thoroughly bewitched this day by Emma Gately, and he'd not been the only one.

Chapter 15

THE LONDONER

PROBLEMS ABOUND FOR THE MISMATCH CLUB

The Mismatch Club continues to go from bad to worse;
the group still struggles to find itself. How quick was
their rise ... and fall ...

M. FAIRPOINT

Despite Isla's earlier insistence that Emma hadn't put enough effort into her latest assignment with the Mismatch Society, those worries had been for naught.

Emma had spent the remainder of the week preparing. She'd mapped out various ideas on all manner of topics, from the rights women were denied and deserving of to the unrealistic expectations that existed for them. And having settled upon the latter, she'd taken copious notes, which she'd committed to memory so she needn't bore the other members with a dull recitation.

She'd rehearsed enough, with her sister and Olivia serving in the role of a pretend audience, and she had practiced her inflection and delivery to the point that even Isla couldn't have . . . and more importantly, hadn't . . . found fault with her performance.

In the end, standing in the meeting parlor on Waverton Street, all Emma's efforts appeared to be for naught.

Nay . . . not appeared.

In fact, were.

For their once large gathering had been reduced to their original numbers: Emma, Isla, Olivia, Sylvia, Annalee, and Valerie. Lila also remained.

"Where is . . . Clara?" Emma blurted. Not Clara, too.

"Oh, she is dealing with a problem with the music hall," Sylvia explained. "She wanted me to assure you all that she has no intention of—"

"Abandoning us?" Valerie drawled. Her smile faded to a scowl. "As all the others have done?"

"If ever there was a time for a drink, this is it," Annalee said into the quiet. Uncorking her silver-etched flask, she held it aloft. "Though in fairness, every time is an ideal one for a drink." The young socialite's laughter reverberated around the otherwise solemn room.

Nay, "morose" was a more apt description for their group.

Seated next to her, Valerie leaned over and rescued the flask from Annalee's fingers.

Annalee pouted. "This is hardly the time to encourage me to abandon my spi—"

Valerie tipped back the drink and continued downing the spirits in one long, slow swallow. When she'd finished, she set the flask beyond the other woman's reach. "There. They are finished."

Sylvia clapped once. "For the sake of the meeting, might I suggest we focus on new business? New business being our continued reduction in numbers."

And there went Emma's planned material for the Mismatch Society. She tightened her hold upon the small notebook on her lap, those pages filled with the details of her prepared speech. For the nervousness she'd felt at this new-for-her role, there wasn't a rush of relief, but only the sting of regret. Everything she'd prepared would fall by the wayside, forgotten. Not that it much mattered, anyway, if the other members weren't there to speak to.

While Valerie went about doing roll call, a hand rested on Emma's knee, and she glanced up.

"It was going to be magnificent," Olivia whispered with the support and loyalty only a best friend was capable of. "And it still will be. One day, when you share. Which you will." Valerie got to Olivia, and the other lady looked away, answering the call.

Frantic footfalls sounded outside the room.

They looked up, just as an out-of-breath Cora staggered into the room. "I'm here," she gasped. A moment later, she was joined by Brenna. "We're here!"

And then, the most unexpected of the missing members arrived. "As am I."

Everyone gasped. "Cressida!"

The young woman blushed, and head down, she rushed to join Emma.

"How . . . ?" Emma whispered to Cressida as the others around them chatted happily with the return of the three.

Stealing a furtive glance about, Cressida caught Emma's hands. "You mustn't say anything. He swore me to absolute secrecy."

"He?"

"The Earl of Scarsdale paid a visit to my brother and managed to convince him to allow me to return."

Floored, a jolt went through Emma. "He did . . . what?" she asked, earning a curious look from Sylvia.

"Hush," Cressida implored.

And as the group refocused, Emma's mind raced under the discovery of what her friend had revealed . . . and more, what Charles had done. Why? Why would he do that? Nay, it mattered not why . . . just that he had. Her heart beat wildly. As this day, which had started out as grim, suddenly brightened.

"Perhaps the others *are* coming as well?" Isla ventured, pulling Emma's head out from the clouds. "Mayhap we've been worrying for naught?"

"Oh, no." The Kearsley sisters spoke in unison, still lightly winded as they took their customary seats. "They aren't," Cora added, earning a put-off look from her younger sibling.

Or mayhap they hadn't.

Cora continued on anyway through that sisterly disapproval. "I have it on authority from Miss Dobson that she will not be attending. That is, not today."

Well, that wasn't so dire. Emma cleared her throat. "I am happy to report, however, today's reduction in members is unrelated to Lord Scarsdale," she offered, knowing so implicitly. After what they'd shared . . . And his sending one of their missing members back was proof—

"Oh?" Sylvia asked, fetching a newspaper off the table, and all eyes went to Emma. "Are you . . . certain of that?"

"Yes. I spoke to the gentleman." Butterflies somersaulted low in her belly with the remembrances of that night she'd visited him . . . and everything he'd done to her body. "And as such," she went on, feeling her entire body go warm, "I can say with confidence he has abandoned his plans for a rival league."

"Alas, it appears the gentleman did not get the memorandum," Sylvia said dryly, and handed off that heavily creased newspaper. It passed from remaining woman to remaining woman, until Isla reluctantly handed it over to Emma.

With a frown, she scanned the tiny print.

"Front page, center," Sylvia directed, and Emma's eyes went there. And then she promptly wished they hadn't.

Her entire body went stock still. She frantically worked her eyes over the article. "The Club du Livre is progressive and positive, the influence that Polite Society and all society *neeeeeds*?" Emma's voice climbed up on that last particular word. "The unlikeliest of lords, with the patronage and support of his respected mother, has brought both lords and ladies together in an original venture. The Earl of *Ssss* . . . Son of a swag-bellied bull!" She exhaled that curse through a sharp hiss of air between her tightly clenched teeth.

Oh, it was not to be borne. Where the Mismatch Society had been called into question as scandalous and condemned, Charles's society continued to be met with appreciation and fascination, and praise.

A growl worked its way up her throat.

"What is it?" Olivia gently prodded as Emma continued reading the article in silence, and as she did, her fingers clasped the pages harder and harder, noisily wrinkling the damning scrap.

"A need was identified," she made herself continue, fighting to speak past an ever-spiraling rage and shock. "Unlike another less respected, less regarded club, who took itself too seriously, and who set out to lecture young women . . . breaking down the tenets of a functioning society, this new club proves an innovative, welcome addition . . ." A sound of frustration escaped her, and she slapped the newspaper down on the rose-inlaid table. Oh, this was too much.

"We are *not* a club," Isla exclaimed.

That disrespect of what they preferred to be known as now seemed secondary when presented with this latest, and very real, threat.

And what made this moment of betrayal all the worse was the silence and the looks trained on Emma. She, who'd been so very certain that Charles would cease poaching her members and abandon his idea, which had been forged only to get to her. "That condemnation for the Mismatch Society comes because we are women," Valerie said quietly. "Had we welcomed men into our folds—"

"We *did.*" Sylvia pointed out the addition they'd made of her husband.

"Just one, and one who was highly respected." Annalee kicked out her legs atop the edge of the table. "Scarsdale's band of rogues," the young socialite drawled. "You have to admit, it would be enough to get nearly any woman in London into Lady Rochester's parlor."

"Not I," Valerie muttered.

"Ah." Annalee lifted a finger. "But just because you're clever, dear, doesn't mean all women are. And they aren't. Not where men are concerned, anyway," she added.

Lila sighed. "Unfortunately, Annalee is correct."

Another wave of silence came. All the while, Emma's mind spun, as did her . . . emotions. How could Charles do this? Why would he? And renege? Particularly after everything they'd shared?

The moment the thought slid in, a taunting voice at the back of her mind mocked her . . . for daring to make anything more of the wicked interlude in his chambers, or the chance exchange between her and Charles and his son. Once again, she'd let herself believe . . . more. *Because you wanted it to be more.*

When would she learn?

Olivia looked to Emma. "But . . . but . . . he never planned to cease his operation?" There was a hesitant question there from her friend.

"Apparently not," she seethed, crumpling the hated pages between her fingers.

Why must Emma always be a fool where Charles was concerned? This time, when the frustration and resentment surged to life, it was directed at herself . . . and not at the bounder who'd not quit his poaching.

"The injustice of it all!" she exclaimed, no longer holding back. Outrage brought her to her feet, and her notebook tumbled to the floor. "Had we convened meetings between men and women, we would have met with condemnation." She paced, stomping a path back and forth beside the stack of scandal sheets. "We are disparaged while they are praised. We are shamed while they are valued for what he created." It was the way of the world, the wrong way, and she was tired to her soul of it.

"I confess to not being entirely clear as to what he's created, exactly," Valerie ventured. "All the stopping and starting . . . no offense, of course." Unable to read another word in that scandal sheet aloud, Emma passed it back over, and the moment it reached the other woman's hands, Valerie read silently to herself. When she finished, she looked up. "It appears to be a *book* . . . club?"

Annalee took it from the other woman's hands and also skimmed. "Elucidating young minds . . . and more mature minds . . . through current works of literature," the young socialite said to herself. "Apparently they are reading Austen's *Pride and Prejudice* and discussing it as a social commentary on marriages and society." This time she looked up. "I do have to admit that it is very clever."

"Yes, it is," Emma made herself admit aloud, because she was angry, but she wasn't so very petty as to not see that Charles had come up with a rather brilliant venture. Not unlike the Mismatch Society, his establishment challenged existing social orders, but he'd chosen to do so by incorporating books young women enjoyed reading.

In short, everything he'd insisted about Locke and learning he'd cleverly applied to his new pursuit, creating an endeavor that was pleasurable. Whereas Emma? She'd been crafting lectures and taking notes. How were they to have ever competed with Charles's innovative approach? One that combined true learning and literature that women were eagerly reading?

"Our society is *enjoyable*," Lila said belatedly. "How dare they presume otherwise?"

"Yes, just because we take ourselves seriously does not mean the women who attended were not enjoying their time here," Isla piped in . . . before blushing, as the irony and truth became clear.

Had they truly appreciated their time with the Mismatch Society and the discussions and enlightenment that had occurred here more than what was taking place at Charles's, they'd not have defected in the first place.

Cora cleared her throat. "Well, I needn't frills and fluff to add to my enlightenment. I need nothing more than the stimulating discourse of my fellow women, who make me think." The young lady brought back her shoulders. "And if that wasn't, isn't, and cannot be enough for some women? Then I say it is their loss."

Murmurs of assent went up, and as one, the ladies all stomped their feet in a rolling applause.

With the exception of Emma . . . Emma, who couldn't even muster for herself false confidence or cheer or anything beyond this crushing . . . hurt.

And if it weren't blasphemy, she'd have cursed the late, great writer Jane Austen. After all, it was hardly Miss Austen's fault that her works were being used in ways that she'd likely not expected. Emma's lips pulled in a grimace. And by a man, at that.

How were they to compete with that great writer's works and all the women who wished to read them?

"What is it, Emma?" Sylvia asked gently when the room had settled once more.

Of course, their fearless, astute leader should have seen and known Emma's lack of enthusiasm. Emma folded her hands on her lap. "I don't disagree with Cora," she began, glancing at the older Kearsley sister, who smiled at that acknowledgment, "and yet, at the same time . . . our goal, our mission is to encourage women to think freely."

"And you're making the assumption they aren't doing that with Lord Scarsdale's society?" Sylvia asked, without inflection.

"Yes. No." Emma emitted a sound of frustration. "I don't . . . *know.*" And that was the honest truth where Charles was concerned. From their meeting at Regent Street to the Old Corner Bookshop with his nephew?

She didn't know how to make heads or tails of him. "I simply know that if we're only speaking to like-minded individuals who already believe in the advancement of women's rights and goals and dreams and aspirations, then . . . it is as though we are shouting into a like void, where those thoughts can never take greater root and grow and spread as we so hoped." Then she was the same woman she'd always been . . . on the fringes, raging only in her head at the injustices, all the while not really contributing anything of real import.

Sylvia, the eternal optimist who'd fought for their society from the start, persisted. "Just because some have left"—*Most. Most have.*—"does not mean they won't find their way back. Or that others shan't find their way to us."

"But will they?" Emma persisted. "Will they, when Lord Scarsdale's group not only affords them a similar setting, with similar goals as ours, and does so in a way that is thrilling because the men present"— Annalee's face pulled—"and their proper mamas and papas all approve?"

Sylvia held up a palm. "I do believe it bears pointing out that we aren't in competition with Lord Scarsdale and his members."

Emma firmed her jaw. Like hell they weren't. She agreed with the viscountess on much. Nearly everything. But not on this.

"As I see it," the viscountess said, "we aren't shutting them down. So we can either bemoan their existence"—the regal hostess glanced around, touching her gaze upon each woman, before speaking—"or we can focus on restructuring ours."

Restructuring . . .

"What, exactly, does that mean?"

"It means whatever it was that once brought women into our fold . . . we need to find that magic again," Valerie said quietly.

"But . . . but . . . we are magical," Isla moaned.

Except they weren't.

"I motion that we entrust our rebuilding where it belongs, with the woman responsible for the creation of the society," the viscountess suggested, and Emma directed her focus on that person who would lead them.

That same fearless leader who was staring directly back at Emma . . . Her skin prickled with the feel of several pairs of eyes, and she registered their intent. "Why are you looking at me?" she blurted.

"I think it should be obvious." Annalee withdrew a cheroot and touched it to her nearby candlestick, sparking a flash of orange. She took a puff on the scrap, then exhaled a little cloud.

"Actually, no. No, it is not at all obvious." Because the last person of any of the remaining women in the room who should be tasked with such an important charge . . . was her. She'd not the influence nor the ideas . . .

"You were leading our next discussion," Sylvia gently pointed out. "But it makes sense that the same woman who imagined the Mismatch should also be responsible for saving it."

"And going up against Scarsdale, no less," Olivia pointed out.

Emma opened her mouth to protest, looking to her sister and her best friend. Alas, their attention was on the group.

"I call for a vote. Emma to lead the charge," Cressida called out, earning nods from the other women around the room.

And as the members put it to a vote, Emma couldn't suppress a groan.

War had been waged this day for the very soul of the Mismatch Society.

And it would seem Emma had been nominated as the one to lead the charge . . . and against her former betrothed, no less.

She smiled.

Chapter 16

THE LONDONER

FROM RIVALRY . . . TO FEUD

Between Miss Gately's Mismatch Club and the Earl of
Scarsdale's Club du Livre, never before has London
been beset by a rivalry between two, since the War of
the Roses.

M. FAIRPOINT

After a fortnight of direct challenges to the Mismatch Society from
Charles, and the endless barrage of social scrutiny their rivalry had
received, Emma had resolved that day to not let herself dwell on him
or any of it.

She'd not focus on the praise being lavished upon Charles's venture, while disparagements rained down on hers. Or the fact that his
numbers continued to rise, while hers continued to fall. Or the fact that
he'd somehow ascertained topics of her discussion and incorporated
them into his meetings. Or the fact that he'd sent flowers and French
chocolates in the middle of a Mismatch meeting, effectively distracting

everyone from the day's agenda, because, really, which lady was capable of resisting chocolate?

She wasn't going to think of any of it.

Nay, none of it.

Alas, fate was a cruel, fickle mistress, who was surely born of Polite Society.

In the middle of Lady Rutland's soiree, from where Emma stood at the entrance to one of the hostess's card rooms, laughter filled the air, so strong it washed over her like a wave of hilarity.

"Are we . . . not in the card room?" Owen asked puzzledly.

Yes, because none would ever know it, given the sound echoing around the room. Not the laughter of Polite Society—practiced giggles tittered behind hands.

This was the belly-deep amusement roused only by a master story-teller and charmer.

"Oh, no. We are," Emma seethed. "We are precisely where we are supposed to be." It was everyone else, however, who appeared mistaken about what it was they were supposed to be doing in here.

The lanky lord, taller than most men, angled his neck in a bid to get a better view.

"Charles," she said between her teeth. Fortunately that bold claiming of his name was lost on another round of laughter from the people surrounding him.

From her, Isla, Olivia, and Owen's vantage in the doorway, it was hard to make out much of anything beyond the crush of bodies. None of which were seated at the card tables, and all of whom were surrounding one table at the very center of the room.

Emma narrowed her eyes. And there could be absolutely no disputing which charmer was at the center of that show. Was it any wonder? Was it any wonder at absolute all that Charles Hayden, the Earl of Scarsdale, had had the success he had in establishing his club amongst Polite Society? Any wonder at all?

Emma gritted her teeth.

Or that he'd done so with the *ton's* utmost approval and appreciation. When the Mismatch Society should be condemned. It was unpar-
donable. It was a crime against women.

"Let us leave, Emma," Olivia said softly, taking her arm to steer
their quartet away.

Emma gently but firmly disentangled herself and locked her feet to
Lady Rutland's drawing-room floor.

"Yes, we can go to the other card room," Isla urged.

The other card room, which was no doubt empty because nearly all
the guests had crammed themselves inside this particular drawing room,
filling up every space, like some kind of overstuffed armoire. And she
was half tempted to agree. That, however, would be an act of cowardice.
A concession in a battle with her former betrothed.

"Come, Emma," her sister insisted once more, and Emma ignored
her, squinting for a glimpse of the thief of her ideas.

And then she found him.

She narrowed her eyes.

Lords and ladies of all ages swarmed Charles's card table, where
he lounged comfortably, gesturing with his hands while he spoke. His
mirth-filled baritone rose over the noisy crowd. Most of his words were
lost, but not the infectiousness in them. He'd always possessed an absolute ease around all that she'd been in awe of. And secretly envied him
for. No person should be so unaffected when there was Emma who
was . . . well, *Emma*.

"And Lord Alvanley said—"

"I'll tell it, Scarsdale," Lord Alvanley interrupted, and several figures
shifted slightly, revealing a hint of the pair who held the entire room
enthralled. "You wanted me to join a club. I already belong to four . . .
and he said . . ." He paused, the room falling silent, and it was as though
the masterful storyteller who held the room enrapt with Charles knew
how to draw out the moment. "Not like this one, Alvanley. You see,

there aren't just gents present, but ladies, too, with the finest"—Emma's eyebrows shot up—"discussions."

Floored by the shock of that almost outrageously improper comment, it took a moment to register. And then the room erupted with their mirth.

Lady Jersey tapped Charles's shoulder with her fan. "You naughty boy, teasing so!"

Emma rolled her eyes. Only *Charles* could charm the most respectable matrons while behaving so wickedly.

"He snagged *Alvanley's* membership," Isla whispered.

Emma searched her gaze over the pair at the center of the crowd's attention. "Yes, I see that." The wittiest lord, more noteworthy and sought after than the late Beau Brummell, should have joined Charles's ranks? Bloody hell, this was dire. This was dire, indeed.

"Well, I vote for choosing any room but this one," Owen said indignantly. "I won't have us keep company with someone who'd so threaten your endeavor."

"Yes," Olivia agreed. "I am of the same opinion as Owen."

"No," Emma said calmly. Though appreciating those efforts on her behalf from each of her friends, she'd not be run off. And with her sister and Olivia pleading quietly behind her, Emma ventured into the room.

Not that she need worry about anyone having bothered trying to run her off; they were all fully engrossed in Charles and Lord Alvanley's telling. Grabbing the chair of a vacant table far from the night's entertainment, Emma seated herself.

Her friends hovered there, silent. Isla was the first to join Emma on one of Lady Rutland's Dutch Marquetry side chairs. The others promptly fell into the vacant ones.

"There," Emma said, reaching for the deck of new cards. "That is better." Feeling her friends' eyes on her, she paused and looked up. "The way I see it, we easily found a table, and no one is paying us any mind, which is how we prefer it."

"Really?" Isla said tersely. Emma should have known better than to expect her sister would allow her that self-delusion. "Is there anything better about any of this . . . ?"

"Demmed hilarious, you are, Scarsdale," Alvanley boomed, his high praise ushering in an echo of concurring opinions from the earl's adoring audience.

Emma tightened her mouth. Yes, hilarious.

She resumed shuffling.

Hilarious, the way he'd rescheduled his meetings so they coincided with her meeting times.

Hilarious, how he'd sent a small army of children to distribute information about his club all down Waverton Street to passersby.

The crowd shifted, putting Charles on display, just as a lady pressed herself against his shoulder.

The cards flew from Emma's fingers and rained down about the table in a wrinkled mess.

And, of course, Charles would choose that moment to look up. His gaze found hers, and she held his stare, because she'd be damned if she looked away first. Or at all.

He bowed his head in silent greeting.

The entire room's attention swung her way.

Oh, bloody hell.

Affixing a smile to her lips, Emma returned that greeting, lest any more be said about how cold and emotionless she was. She hurried to gather up the cards, stacking them. Alas, her shaking fingers made the task impossible.

"Here," Owen murmured, gently taking the sloppy stack from her.

"Thank you," she mouthed.

Olivia's brother smiled, then effortlessly saw to the shuffle, allowing Emma a chance to get her thoughts ordered. When he'd finished, he set them down, having Isla see to the cut. Collecting the deck, Emma distributed them, doling out thirteen for each . . . when a shadow fell over the table.

And she knew, implicitly, intuitively, born of her awareness of him. She fumbled her deal, revealing the king of hearts.

How perfectly suited, she thought.

Emma forced herself to look up, and as one, she and her tablemates rose, dropping respective curtsies, and a reluctant bow from Owen.

Charles's eyes, however—his gaze belonged to Emma. It was the manner of piercing stare that made a woman feel as if she were the only one in the room, and he was there to join her in that solitude, making the moment theirs. Which was utter romantic rot. They weren't the only two, and there was an entire room of *ton* members gleefully watching the charming earl and the gangly Gately girl, who'd not been able to hold him. Even so, their gazes remained locked, the moment belonging to only them.

"Miss Gately," he murmured in that smooth baritone that had likely brought many a woman to surrender and sin for him. "Would you join me in a turn about the room?" And not unlike that serpent who'd first tempted Eve, he offered his elbow as the apple it was.

"Shove off, Scarsdale," Isla snapped. "We're in the middle of something."

To Charles's credit, he displayed no outward shock or outrage at that greeting. "Miss Gately," he said with a smile. "A pleasure, as always."

"Only when you're gone," she said, returning that smile.

"Isla," Emma warned.

And when presented with the possibility of having her friends flay Charles, and in a public way, or accept that invitation and take on the attention herself, she'd always choose the latter. Hastily placing her fingers atop his sleeve, she allowed him to escort her off, and start their journey around the perimeter of the parquet floor.

"Have a care with that one, Emma-love," Charles said. "You're going to break his heart."

Puzzling her brow, she followed his pointed stare across the busy room, over to a glowering Owen.

"Owenn?" she asked, before lowering her voice. "He is a friend." Charles steered them right out of Lady Rutland's drawing room and onward to the other card room. The other empty card room. "Only *you* insist on making all matters between a man and a woman romantic," she said, her voice echoing around the large, vacant drawing room. Because they'd all gathered to listen to this man and Lord Alvanley.

"That gent is eyeing you with romantic eyes," he said bluntly as she slipped free of his arm and ventured deeper into the room. "Trust me as one who knows."

Envy whipped through her, green like a snake unleashing its poison. "Because you've made so many romantic eyes?"

"Yes, because they're my own these past months whenever I see you, Emma-love."

His words, smooth and low, rumbled through the room, and Emma trembled. "Don't call me that." To give her fingers something to do, she picked up a deck from the nearby card table. "You are so practiced with your words. A rogue through and through."

He strolled closer, his a languid glide, until he stopped on the other side of the table. "Not in this," he said quietly. "Only with you, Emie."

"Stop it," she ordered, dampening her mouth. "That is what my father calls me."

"Then Emma-love it shall be," he murmured in that deep, rich baritone, steeped in warmth and sin. How was it possible for a voice to bring a woman's body to tremble? Charles leaned across the table, and her breath quickened in her chest. "Never fear, I shall keep searching for the endearment you so choose."

It implied his resolve—one that had annoyed her in the initial months, but after their meeting over billiards in her family's household that not-so-long-ago day, had served only to . . . confuse her. "Why are you here?" she asked, gripping tightly the playing deck. All the while, she felt Charles's gaze upon her. "You studiously avoid soirees."

"You know that?"

Her fingers fumbled the shuffle, and she promptly righted the deck . . . and herself. "Of course I know that," she said, her cheeks heating at how much she'd inadvertently revealed. Unlike him, she had paid attention to how he'd spent his evenings, and to the events he preferred attending. Which was how she could say with enough certainty that she'd wager freely at all the card tables present everything she knew about Charles's affaires de coeur—and win.

"Yes, well, you are not incorrect," he murmured. "I despise them, Emma," he said. "I did come here with the express certainty of seeing someone."

Her heart lifted.

"Camille appreciates when I . . . attend the same events she does."

Camille.

His sister.

"You came . . . because of your sister?" And oddly, that garnered even more warmth than when she'd been foolish enough to believe he was here for her.

"Do you take me for a cur?" The right corner of his mouth crooked up. "Never mind. Don't answer that."

Except he'd already opened the door for her, and she slipped through. "Do you know, I think you are a cur, Charles Hayden," she said. Putting down the cards, she stepped around the table to confront him head-on.

He stiffened.

"But I do not think of you as a cur for the reasons you believe. You're a loyal brother, and a devoted son. And a good friend."

He grinned, a silly, dazed-looking, boyish smile that didn't fit with the completely confident rogue who moments ago had charmed Lady Rutland's drawing room. "Indeed."

"Do not"—she stuck a finger in his chest, earning a little grunt from the gentleman—"let it go to your head."

His smile widened. "Too late."

Yes, she could see that. "Who you are to your family, however, doesn't undo the fact that you are wreaking havoc on my society."

"How so?" He bristled with an over-the-top indignation that rang loud for the patent falseness it was.

"Chocolate, Charles." Emma folded her arms at her chest. "You sent *chocolate*?"

"Everyone *loooooves* chocolate. I thought it should please you."

She narrowed her eyes. "Do you truly expect me to believe that load of rot?"

He winked.

"You are poaching my members."

"Ah-ah-ah." He wagged a finger. "*Au contraire, mon amie*—I am welcoming *all* members. You see, I am not so . . . exclusive. So restrictive. So . . . narrow-minded," he continued over her gasp, "in who I allow or disallow. Men and women should be free to interact in society, not separate from one another, but free to challenge each other." He dropped a hip atop the card table and folded his arms. "You see, we're really quite progressive."

Which was precisely what the papers had called him. Her mouth went slack, and she sucked in a noisy gasp before expelling it in a noisy exhale. *"You?"*

His brow dipped. "What is that supposed to mean?"

He'd "what-is-that-supposed-to-mean" her? "You have *The Londoner* in your pocket." Emma jabbed her finger at his lapel.

He scoffed. "What rubbish. Of course I don't have them in my pocket." He paused. "I merely posted advertisements, nothing more."

She peered at him.

"My God," she exclaimed, shaking her head hard enough to send her chignon loose and several blasted strands free. "And this is why they're printing such horrid things about the Mismatch Society. They ceased their personal attacks on me but moved over to the Mismatch Society," she spat. "Now it makes sense."

"I would never pay for the spread of unfavorable words spoken about you or your society, Emma." His hurt was palpable, and was not any that even the best London stage actor could feign.

She managed a smile. "All that, I've managed to secure on my own?" He nodded. "Precisely."

The moment that affirmation left him, Emma's and Charles's eyebrows both went flying up. "No. That is *not*"—he made a slashing motion with his arms—"what I meant. Not you. There'd never be anything anyone could ever say about you," he said quietly, his words a physical caress.

"Just my society."

He nodded.

With a sound of disgust, she made to step around him.

"I'm making a blunder of this, I am," he said quickly, hurrying to put himself in her path.

Emma stopped short, and again, crossing her arms, she glared at him. "Indeed, you are. For someone so very urbane and smooth."

Charles turned up his hands sheepishly. "I told you, love; I'm not capable of any pretense around you."

And she hated her heart for reacting as if that solemnly delivered vow actually meant something to him.

"You would challenge my society, Charles? Suggest it is somehow inferior."

"I've done no such thing!"

"All the while, you pass yourself off as—"

"Progressive," he finished for her.

Emma burst out laughing.

She laughed so hard the tears came running, streaming down her cheeks. She tried to speak, opening her mouth, and then, shaking her head, she leaned into her amusement all the more. Good Lord, it was just too much. *Too much.*

Charles frowned. "What is so amusing about *that?*" he demanded when her laughter subsided.

"It means that I'd hardly think a man who consigns desperate women to the role of mistress to see to your pleasures is so very progressive."

His color turned an interesting shade of red she'd never before seen human skin turn. "I . . . I assure you. My . . . my . . ." Oh, now this she was rather enjoying, the smug, assured Lord Scarsdale stammering like every last lady, from debutante to dowager, he'd charmed the pantalets off.

"Mis-tress," she clearly enunciated for him, and his cheeks went crimson. And here, before talking to Charles at various points in the last several months, she'd not believed scoundrels and rogues capable of that feat.

"First, Emma, I would have you know that those women were—"

"In need of funds to secure their futures?"

His frown deepened. "I was going to say 'quite pleased with the arrangement.'"

That blow landed, no doubt, exactly as he'd intended, like a sharp barb between the breasts. "Oh, undoubtedly," she drawled, heaping all the sarcasm she could into those two words. Emma headed for the door.

"Never tell me you've not thought of that night we shared."

His words brought her up short, halting her in her tracks. He'd gone there . . . that place she'd no chance of holding the upper hand over. Even so, Emma brought back her shoulders and faced him anyway.

It was a mistake.

He smiled slowly, then pushed away from the table and, letting his arms fall, began a slow, languid stroll across the room. Toward her. His steps sleek, his movements even sleeker. He stopped between her and the doorway out.

She knew what he was doing. She knew exactly what he intended, and knowing should have made her immune to it, and yet, God help her, he moved like a panther she'd once watched in fascination at the Royal Menagerie.

He stopped, a fraction apart, so close she felt his breath, a hint of brandy and the whisper of chocolate, an unexpectedly sweet flavor upon him, that begged to be tasted.

⌘

Her opinion of him was so very low.

And for only good reasons.

Why, he'd spent years giving them to her. Glad she resented him as much as he resented her. Until now. Hating it with all his soul . . . that he'd not been better for her.

In this moment, everything he wanted to do with her and to her marked him the very scoundrel she took him to be. But God help him, with her eyes fiery and her cheeks flushed with that bright color, and those long, straight strands falling over her shoulder, she seduced him more than any scandalous garment she could have donned.

Reaching behind her, he brought the door shut, and turned the lock. *Click.*

Emma followed his actions with her eyes. "What are you doing?" Even as he brought a hand up, cupping her cheek, and her lashes slid shut, and she leaned into him.

"I have thought of only you and that night, Emma."

"And destroying my club," she added. But her hands crept up, and she gripped the front of his jacket.

"Well, building up my own." He ran a trail of kisses down the curve of her cheek.

"It is the s-same thing." She moaned, the little wanton spill of her desire from her lips fueling his, and Charles filled his palms with her lush buttocks, drawing her close to his shaft.

"I thought you were a society?" he asked, nipping lightly at her neck.

"D-did I not say that?" Emma reflexively moved her hips against him, and Charles buried his face in her shoulder. His breath grew faster, as with her every undulation, his passion swelled.

"You didn't." And then he shifted his head, hovering his mouth along the bodice of her dress, that pause a clear signal that this moment was for her to decide. That Emma would be in charge of where this night should go. This time. Emma lifted her lashes and looked him in the eyes.

"We shouldn't be here. Not a-alone." Her voice quavered, but neither did she make a move to leave or end this forbidden exchange they stole on the fringe of Lady Rutland's revelries.

"Lord Alvanley has quite secured the attention of everyone present." He lowered his mouth close to hers, and Emma lifted her head to meet his. But Charles stopped. "Do you want to leave, Emma-love?"

"No," she whispered, and then her eyes slid shut as he kissed a path along her neckline. "Wh-what is it about you th-that I cannot w-walk away?" she rasped.

"Because you're learning what I learned too late . . . that we are meant to be together, Emma."

"You infuriate me."

"You captivate me, so it cancels out."

She laughed softly, her amusement fading to a husked groan as he slipped her bodice down and freed her breasts to his attentions. Charles lifted one of those gentle swells and lowered his head to worship the peak.

"*Ohhh . . .*" She panted, those desperately quick intakes of air a symphony of the same hunger he carried for her.

Outside the room, beyond the door panel, the tinkling laughter of guests passing by filled the room, but lent an even greater, forbidden wickedness to what they did here, just a stone's throw from discovery, and that heightened the sexual tension of this moment. He suckled on the shell of her ear, and she moved against him, knocking the door slightly with that restive thrusting.

Those footfalls outside slowed.

"Shh." He urged her to silence, and Emma went motionless in his arms, and as she did, Charles laved the tip of her left breast.

Her breath caught.

"Shh," he said again, challenging her as he made love to her.

The murmurings of the guests drifted by and away until it was just the two of them once more.

Dragging her skirts up around her waist, Charles slid a knee between her legs. She immediately sank onto his thigh, and with a primitive rocking as old as time, she rode him. "That's it, love," he encouraged, his voice harsh and low. Charles rotated his leg in a smooth, slow circle that brought another moan spilling from Emma's lips.

"This is wicked, isn't it?" Except she sounded enlivened by that revelation.

"Oh, yes, love." The manner of naughtiness that saw them dancing with scandal, and never more had he wanted to waltz than he did in this moment, with her thrusting upon him, her breath noisy and wantonly wonderful. "Very, very illicit. I can show you more," he vowed.

That hoarse promise seemed to fuel her even more. She moaned, and pushed herself against him harder, clinging to his jacket as she did, grinding herself onto his thigh. With each thrust, there grew a frantic desperation to her exertions.

Her eyes locked with his, her golden eyebrows stitched, her glistening features a study of concentration as she attended to her own pleasure. And never more did he wish he were, in fact, the cad she and the world accused him of being, because he ached to lay her down on Lady Rutland's floor and plunge himself into the welcoming heat that surely pooled at her center.

Even the thought was too much. He needed to feel her.

Charles reached between them and slid a finger inside her damp curls. "You feel so good," he praised, moisture slicking the way as he stroked her. Reluctantly, he pulled away, knowing what she needed to attain that level she sought.

Emma resumed riding his thigh. This time with a greater frenzy than before, the rocking of her hips uneven and jerky. She stiffened, and he anticipated her surrender before she even gave herself fully over to it. She climaxed, moaning and crying out her desire over and over. Until her hips ceased rocking, and she collapsed, limp, against him.

Charles smoothed his palm over her lower back. "Good?"

Emma tilted up her face. "You know it was, you scoundrel." The smile in her voice softened that rebuke.

He grinned in return.

"You're so very arrogant, aren't you?" she said with a roll of her eyes as she made to step out of his arms. But Charles caught her, keeping her anchored against him longer, unwilling to let the moment end.

"Not arrogant," he murmured, roving his gaze over her face. He brushed a damp strand back behind her ear. "Only pleased that I could bring you that bliss." And he wanted to show her more than this. He wanted to have a whole future with her.

Except, inevitably, desire faded, and they were left with the reality of what they were. Or what they weren't. But more importantly, what had come before this.

Emma stepped out of his arms, and this time, he let her go.

Her satin skirts fell in a noisy rustle down her legs, and she made a show of smoothing the front of them.

They both spoke at the same time.

"Em—"

"Charles."

He motioned for her. "You first."

"I . . . don't know what to make of you," she said, her voice pained. "I enjoy being with you."

He nodded frantically. "Yes, and I enjoy—"

"But everything I know, every part of me scared of being hurt, says to not trust you."

"I hurt you," he said solemnly. "And I don't expect that to be something so easily forgotten. It is just my hope, in time, that you can see I do"— her eyes locked with his, those enormous blue pools growing wide—"care about you." But he'd never be worthy of her. That he couldn't promise.

Did he imagine the regret there? Had she wished for him to say more?

"If you care about me, you can stop making a jest of the Mismatch Society," she finally said.

"It's not my intention—"

"But that is what you have done," she interrupted with a quiet insistence. "Regardless of your intentions, battle lines have been drawn, and society is playing out their favorites, of which I will never emerge triumphant."

"You do yourself a disservi—"

She released a sound of frustration. "Charles, I *know* who I am, just as I know who you are."

He stiffened, knowing implicitly the manner of person she believed him to be.

"You are charming," she said, knocking him off balance with that praise. "You are personable and witty and clever . . ." With every bit of unexpected praise she heaped upon him, his spine grew, and his heart swelled along with it. "Whatever you do will be a success because of who *you* are."

"No one has ever felt that way about me," he said past a thick throat.

Her eyes softened, and her lips formed a wistful smile. "Then those people don't know you."

Her words would suggest his own parents didn't. That she some-how saw in him something the world—his parents, his siblings, his friends—never had.

"I should go." She lingered.

"Yes."

But oh, how he wanted her to stay. He wished for the world to melt away so that it was just they two together. There wasn't a past. There wasn't this present. There was only the future he dreamed of for them.

Alas . . .

Emma turned to go.

"Emma!"

She paused, sliding a questioning glance his way.

"I will stop soliciting on Waverton Street. I'll move that to some area not near where you hold your meetings. But you have my word." His gaze locked with hers. "I would never disparage you or seek to hurt you or your venture."

"Thank you, Charles," she said with a quiet solemnity, and grati-tude underlining it.

And then she was gone.

The moment she slipped out, Charles closed his eyes. God, he wanted her. In his bed. In his life. In every way. He'd alternated between wanting her, in spite of his failings, and thinking he had no right to a future with her, because of them. Only, with the words she'd spoken here this night, she'd opened his eyes to the fact that he was more than his failings. That she saw worth in him, because there was worth there.

And it firmed his resolve to earn her love.

As if her thoughts had led her back, the door opened, and he quickly turned. "Emm—" The greeting died as he faced not the golden-haired nymph who'd just left his arms, but the scowling, spectacle-wearing

Mr. Watley. "Oh, hello, chum," Charles said, affecting a grin for the other man's benefit.

"I'm not your chum," the gentleman said stiffly. The young man's eyes went to Charles's cravat. He followed his stare. Nay, to Charles's wrinkled cravat that Emma had undone a short while ago, as she'd been coming undone. Mr. Watley balled his hands into fists. "Stay away from her." He clipped out that command.

So they'd get right to it, then, would they? Charles winged up an eyebrow. "You speak for the lady?"

"I know what she wants," the bold pup shot back with a daring that would have raised him in Charles's estimation if it weren't Emma the young man proclaimed to know. And what was worse . . . he did know her. And Charles hated him for it. Hated him with the fire of a thousand burning suns as he acknowledged his unlikely rival for Emma's affections.

"And if you think she wants you speaking for her," Charles said coolly, "you know the lady a good deal less than you think you do."

Mr. Watley blushed, but then found his voice again. "Who do you think she came to when she wanted out of your arrangement?" The boy didn't wait. "It was me. I am the one who gave her the guidance."

Ah, one of the barristers had been his rival for her affections. Charles hadn't stood a chance. "I wouldn't presume to decide for her, and I suggest you do the same."

"You hurt her before, and I'll not see you hurt her *or* the Mismatch Society again." Any more than he already had. "Good day." Turning on his heel, the young man left.

The moment he'd gone, Charles let go of the thought of him, refusing to allow himself to think of anything about this night but what he and Emma had shared.

Chapter 17

In the following days, Emma poured herself into that which had saved her two months earlier—the Mismatch Society.

Recommitting herself to the group and its salvation and success, she'd openly canvassed for new members, and drafted topics to be spoken about.

And she'd felt . . . enlivened, for the first time in longer than she could remember where the society was concerned. Charles had been, with her, what no one else—certainly not her friends and other society members who were entirely too close to the Mismatch—had: honest. He'd challenged her to not expect that there should be members as their due. Simply because they'd been first did not mean anyone owed her or any of the other ladies anything.

And as enraged as she'd been, Charles had ultimately challenged her to look at herself and her creation . . . and demand better of both.

Annalee banged the gavel. "This meeting is called to order."

"It comes as no surprise to those of you present that we are fighting for the very soul of the Mismatch Society." As Emma spoke into the quiet, the focus of each person present was on her. "Lord Scarsdale's society is new. A novelty. However, he has also highlighted that perhaps our exclusivity has been a detriment." As he'd taken such delight in pointing out to her their last evening together.

"It wasn't," Valerie muttered to herself.

"Hence," Emma went on, "the addition of our newest members." Male members of the society. The room's attention shifted from her over to the three men crammed together upon the too-small-for-them satin settee. Morgan, Pierce, and Owen each lifted a hand in greeting . . . that was met with a stark silence. "If we can provide a Mismatch welcome."

Except only silence reigned.

"I cannot believe we've stooped this low," Isla bemoaned, sinking in her seat. "Men. We're allowing men to join us?"

"If one can even call them that." Annalee laughed uproariously at her own jest.

"I beg your pardon," Pierce shot over in Isla's direction. "Need I point out that it was we who were asked to come here?" He nudged his twin. "Isn't that right?"

Morgan nodded.

"Please, do go; we wouldn't want to have you if you've more pressing things to do." Seated on the King Louis XIV chair at the elbow of

Morgan's seating, Annalee leaned over and exhaled a puff of smoke in his face.

Indignant, Emma's brother waved away that little plume. "I beg your pardon?"

"You and your brother are doing a lot of that," Valerie shot back. "And with good reason."

"Very well, I think I will leave." Pierce shot up. "And I'll take these other two with me."

Emma raced to put herself between that trio and the exit. The last thing they needed was for Charles to learn that she couldn't even hold on to her own brothers as male members. "No one is going anywhere."

Owen cleared his throat. "I'm not! That is, I'm staying. I want to be here."

Grateful for that loyalty, Emma spared him a smile.

"Very well," Morgan shot back. "Then Owen can stay and—"

"No one is leaving," Emma said firmly, and when her other brother made to speak, she said it again. "No one is leaving." *Oh, bloody hell.* This was dissolving into a disaster, and fast. Feeling Sylvia's stare, Emma focused her energies on bringing order to the group.

Everyone immediately ceased their quarreling. "Now," she began calmly, "that I have everyone's attention . . ." Her fingers shaking, Emma hurried to gather up the notes she'd assembled. "I have recently been task—" She winced. Wrong word choice. "Assigned the responsibility of coordinating our upcoming meeting, and having lost some of our key members and heard the concerns, concerns I shared, about echoing only to like-minded women—"

"Ahemmm." Pierce gave her a look.

"And now men," Emma corrected, "that if we cannot rely on a growing membership to provide new perspectives and new topics we'd not previously considered, we should thereby bring in outside perspectives on topics that we've spoken on . . . or mayhap not spoken on."

"I'm confused," Annalee said with her usual bluntness. "You were the one who was most adamantly opposed when Sylvia suggested male membership."

"Yes," Brenna agreed. "And that was just one man, and him being granted a temporary membership."

"And this, this would be a permanent change?" asked Annalee.

The eight sets of female stares trained on Emma were incriminating, and guilt brought a heated blush to her cheeks. Her friends weren't wrong. She had been most outspoken when, just a few weeks prior, Sylvia had recommended adding Lord St. John, and that had been with the intention of securing societal approval so the women would be free to meet without being yanked out by protective guardians.

And yet . . . they were deserving of the truth . . . the whole truth. The reason for her evolution in thought belonged to one person.

"Lord Scarsdale raised the point to me," she allowed.

Gasps went up.

"Of course he did," Isla muttered under her breath.

Emma rushed to speak, reassuring her friends that this wasn't because of any weakening on her part toward Charles. "He pointed out there was no reason women and men cannot come together. We are continually separated. In Parliament. In the household. Why, even after dinner. And in that separation, we can never achieve a status where we are seen and treated as equals." He'd helped her see as much. Her resentment for how she'd been treated had filled her with such anger toward men that she'd simply wanted them barred from any venture she was part of. "Mayhap more good could come in pushing for an equal place in society."

"And so your brothers and Olivia's are our token members?" Annalee quipped.

Emma wrinkled her nose.

"It is just . . . they have everything," Isla moaned.

Pierce's brow dipped. "I don't have every—"

"Not you! Men on the whole." Isla spoke over her brother. "Men in general. They have clubs. They have streets where they carry out their separate lives. This is ours. I . . . vote for a female-only society."

"Well, it's a sad day indeed when a chap has to say he's driven women to driving all men out," Pierce said, making to climb to his feet once more, when this time Annalee rapped him on the knee and stopped him.

"Ouch," he grunted. "What was that for?"

"You don't get to decide when to leave, pup." The socialite leaned over and glared Pierce right back into his seat. "Everything is put to a vote, including your presence here."

Emma's brother swallowed visibly, but was wise enough to comply.

"What are you proposing, Emma?" Sylvia asked for clarification.

"I'm proposing, unlike before when we invited Lord St. John solely and with the lone benefit of lending his respectability to our venture, now we actually consider welcoming men within our folds."

Valerie paused in her note keeping, and looked to Emma. "A temporary invitation, again?"

"Only until we reconvene and decide whether to move forward as Isla wishes, with a female-only society. I'm just saying that perhaps we should consider it," she finished weakly.

"Ahem."

Everyone looked to Owen.

"I-if I may?" he began, waiting for permission to speak, and when none was forthcoming, he continued to hesitate before finding his voice. "I want to begin by saying how very honored I am to be included in your ranks."

Pierce and Morgan snorted, twin expressions of mockery effectively silenced by the glare of every woman in the room.

Owen continued. "I would greatly welcome the opportunity to come and discuss whatever matters you may have. As a barrister, I can provide guidance on legal matters members might have."

And just like that, every woman sat up a bit straighter and attended the young man all the more.

"However, I am . . . suspicious of the motives."

Emma frowned.

"Not yours, of course," he said, his voice rising a decibel. "But rather, it is just . . . Lord Scarsdale."

A pall fell over the room.

"If he is suggesting your society invites male members, then . . ."

"He's doing it for a reason," Isla murmured.

Owen's spectacles slipped forward, and he pushed them back into place. "P-precisely. That is what I'm worried about."

The room fell quiet as everyone contemplated those fears raised. "We invited Lord St. John because he was respectable and lent that respectability to our society. We cannot afford to be anything but selective," Valerie pointed out.

Because of Caroline, the lone widowed mother amongst their group. Where it had been a concern for Sylvia before, she no longer had that worry in quite the same way, having been afforded the luxury of protection that came from being married to one of London's most honorable lords.

"To invite the *wrong* man," Owen went on, "is to invite peril to the ladies who are here, and I fear that is why he's urging you in this direction."

Murmurs rolled around the parlor.

Emma frowned. There would have been a time once where she'd been of the same exact wariness where Charles was concerned. She'd believed him to be heartless. She'd thought him incapable of thinking about anything beyond his own self-interests. And yet . . . these past weeks, he'd proven himself to be . . . different . . . in ways she had never expected. "I do not believe Ch—" The eyes of every person in the room sharpened on Emma. "Lord Scarsdale's," she substituted, "motives are dishonorable in this."

"That is certainly a shift," Annalee noted without inflection.

"He's agreed to cease distributing pamphlets on Waverton Street," Emma felt inclined to point out. "No one was out there today."

"And stealing our members?" Olivia demanded. "Is that the act of an honorable man?"

She'd been of the same opinion. She'd been angry and resentful for every woman who'd been a member of the Mismatch who'd instead found her way to Charles's group. Only to realize pride had been the reason for those sentiments. "Is it really stealing if they left of their own volition?" Emma put the same question to the members that she had made to herself.

Morgan shot up an arm. "If I may, as a valued member, offer my opinion?"

"You are neither, pup," Annalee quipped, and this time, she leaned over and ruffled the top of Morgan's dark curls. "Not yet, anyway," she added with a wink.

A dazed glimmer lit his eyes, and Emma suppressed a smile. Yes, any person, man or woman, was more than a bit besotted by the free-spirited socialite.

"You were saying, brother?" his twin nudged.

Morgan blinked several times, and then a bright blush filled his cheeks. "Er . . . uh . . . yes, I was merely pointing out as—"

"An unvalued maybe-member?" Pierce supplied.

His brother, however, continued on with his train of thought this time. "—a gentleman who knows Lord Scarsdale, he's not so very bad. He's, in fact, quite a decent fellow."

"Aside from the part of his breaking your sister's heart?" Valerie asked, her expression deadpan.

Morgan nodded enthusiastically. "Precisely."

His concurrence was met with a series of groans, and it was the moment Emma knew her brother had lost the attention of the Mismatch. Yet again she'd been possessed of the same outrage over that disloyalty. But it wasn't really disloyalty. Morgan, just as much as her parents and Pierce, spoke of Charles with a knowledge that came from a lifetime of knowing him.

"She was jesting, brother." Pierce's whisper was loud enough to be picked up by anyone in any corner of the room, which Emma would wager was no coincidence on the part of the younger twin. "She was jesting."

"Oh," Morgan said weakly.

And whatever brief truce he'd arrived at with Annalee died a swift death as she leaned away, putting distance between them.

"I don't believe a person is all good or all bad," Emma ventured, and she received such a pitying look from her sister that it took a physical effort to hold her disappointed gaze.

"You're singing a very different tune," Isla remarked.

"Ahem, if I may?" Owen called out, and Emma was grateful for that unwanted attention being shifted his way.

Except . . . this time, as he spoke, he made a point of avoiding her eyes. "I took it upon myself to make inquiries into the increasingly vitriolic words being spoken about the Mismatch Society." Bending down, he retrieved several folded missives from the small leather satchel at his feet.

The ladies arched their necks collectively, attempting to look at those notes.

"I'd noticed a shift in the tone," he explained. "Frequently disparaging, the attacks appeared to become more"—this time, he did slide a glance Emma's way—"pointed."

Her belly churned. Yes, there had seemed to be a change . . . one that she'd not paid too much attention to until now. Until Owen sifted through those notes . . . and refused to look her way once more.

"I made inquiries at *The Londoner* and found a certain earl, the Earl of Scarsdale, has been paying for certain placements."

Emma's entire body went whipcord straight, and around her, Owen's pronouncement was met with a silence that made this revelation all the worse.

Charles . . . paying to have those negative articles about her appear in every London household. It was . . .

Emma and her brothers spoke as one.

"Impossible."

"No."

Their denials, however, were lost to the din of outrage that erupted amongst the members.

Whatever her friends said, however, rolled together in a hum in her ears. It was impossible. He wouldn't do that.

Ever.

Yes, they'd reached a truce.

And yet . . . she'd been the first to declare war upon *him*. Granted, since then, she'd thought they had arrived at a truce of sorts, but what if they hadn't? What if they were still at war and had been all along? And if it was an all-out war . . .

"I . . ." *Don't believe it? Or don't want to believe it?* A voice taunted her for that weakness. Except this time a different war waged, an internal one, one that insisted the man Charles was, was not one who'd do . . . what Owen was proclaiming he'd done. The man who'd made love to her the other evening, and agreed so easily to cease operating on the streets where her own club operated. Emma pressed her fingertips against her temple. It . . . didn't fit with who she'd believed Charles Hayden, the Earl of Scarsdale, was.

Emma registered the stark silence and stiffened her spine. "I will have answers for us," she promised. "You will see . . ." That she and Pierce and Morgan were correct in their defense of Charles.

Because the alternative—that he'd deceived her again—was a betrayal her heart could not recover from.

Chapter 18

"You are lousy company, you know."

Given he'd only just arrived at Forbidden Pleasures, and hadn't even seated himself across from his friend and fellow rogue Lord Landon, Charles rather did *not* know that. Nor, for that matter, was Landon's the amicable greeting a fellow wished to receive upon joining a friend for drinks.

"Why, thank you, Landon," Charles said dryly as a footman drew out a chair for him and set down a glass. Charles poured himself a snifter from Landon's bottle. "That's quite the welcoming." But then, neither should it come as a surprise. For the better part of a fortnight, his attentions had been strictly on Emma, who'd bewitched him, and the new club he'd founded. A club that had taken society by storm, and not in a scandalous way.

Of course, Landon would take exception with either.

"I'm being truthful." Landon passed his half-empty glass back and forth between his palms. "With St. John married, you're all I have, and I'd prefer to have you"—he paused to wave a hand in Charles's direction—"not *this*."

Not this? He glanced down at himself.

"Distracted. And rumpled. You're rumpled."

"Yes, well, my state is a product of my time working on my club," he protested. He'd been shut away for the better part of the day, poring over books that would serve as the basis for future discussions with his club, until his footman had paid a call to Charles's rooms to remind him of this current meeting. Charles gave a pointed look to Landon's skewed cravat. "What can you say for yourself?"

"Oh, shove off. This is different. This"—he indicated the white pleated fabric at his throat—"is affected. Your mess has nothing to do with fashion or design, and everything to do with the miserable state you're perpetually existing in."

Charles frowned. And here he'd been doing vastly better than in those initial days of his breakup. Granted, his thoughts had still been as consumed by Emma—nay, even more so—since her visit and their meeting at the Old Corner Bookshop, and their meeting in Lady Rutland's—

Landon snapped his fingers before Charles's eyes. *"Hullllo,"* he called, waving his hands wildly. "And you are woolgathering, man. Woolgathering."

Charles frowned. "I—"

"You're not," Landon said flatly.

"I didn't even finish my thought."

"You're thinking that you're doing immensely better than you were, but you're probably more like . . ." Landon adjusted his thumb and forefinger several times, assessing the hairbreadth space between them. "This much. Which is really not at all. You're entirely distracted, and everything you're doing is only because of her."

Charles frowned. Yes, well, his friend had him there. Only . . . "Not entirely."

"You're telling me you didn't start your book club because of the lady?"

Actually, she was the very reason he'd been inspired. Charles's gaze moved out over the crowded gaming floor, and he saw himself in a different place, a different setting. Seated on a floor with Emma—

Landon thumped the table, calling back Charles's attention. "Hullo, there it is, again. That is the distractibility I'm speaking of. And as St. John is busy being in love, I'm all you've got to intervene."

"Ah, and that is what this is?" Charles drawled, taking a sip of his drink. "An intervention?"

"Precisely."

At that moment, a voluptuous beauty sidled up to the table, interrupting the other man's lecture.

"Hullo," she purred her greeting, and wrapping her arms around Charles's shoulders, she glided her talonlike fingernails under his jacket, and caressed the flat of his stomach, and then lower still.

Tall, and in possession of loose golden curls that hung down about her shoulders, the woman's coloring put him in mind of another, one also with blonde hair, but drawn back severely, and as stubborn as the woman herself in its refusal to curl. That woman, whose lithe frame was too gaunt to ever be considered lush, and—

As the woman pressed a trail of kisses along his neck, the thick, overpowering jasmine scent of her made him slightly queasy, and he found himself preferring . . . longing for . . . a brighter, richer scent that conjured summer.

She wrapped a hand around his length, and Charles shifted in his seat, swiftly angling away from the persistent beauty.

Emitting a breathy laugh, she took it as some manner of game, and edged back his cravat to touch her rouged lips to the front of his throat. His mouth pulled in a grimace, and he hastily disentangled her hands from his person. "That will be all," he said quickly, completely unsettled, and likely more alarming, unmoved by his absolute disinterest in her attentions. "I'm not interested tonight." He softened that rejection with a coin.

The young woman pocketed the sovereign, and with a pout, she sashayed on over to the next table, where she took a perch on Lord Waters's lap.

Feeling Landon's stare on him, Charles looked over. "You were say—? *What?*" he asked, putting a different question to the man.

"That was unbearable."

"I know." Charles shifted in his seat and adjusted the even more wrinkled cravat the woman had mussed on him. "She was a bit clingy, wasn't sh—"

"I meant you!" Landon knocked his head against the table softly. "I meant *you*."

Charles's ears went hot. "Oh." But then, this was the effect Emma Gately had on him. She climbed into his head and muddled his thoughts and distracted him from . . . everything and anyone.

Sitting up, with his drink in hand, Landon leaned forward across the table. "*This* is what I'm talking about."

"My disinterest in being seduced by a woman in the presence of a friend who summoned me for drinks?"

"*That!*" Landon exclaimed, pointing his glass so quickly in Charles's direction he sloshed droplets over the rim.

Charles puzzled his brow. "I do not follow."

"You sent that pretty thing away," his friend charged. "When any other time, you would have happily dangled her on your lap and at least availed yourself of some of her charms."

Yes. The other man wasn't incorrect—when Charles had been a lad, doing that which his family had wished . . . playing the role of rogue. And shamefully, he had enjoyed it. More than he should. And in so doing, he'd betrayed Emma. Pushing away useless regrets that would change nothing, he shook his head. "I'm struggling to follow, Landon," he began.

"I see that."

Charles continued over Landon's mutterings. "You summoned me for a meeting, and then expect I should dally with some woman while we speak." Of course, it wouldn't have mattered either way. Charles hadn't been interested in what she'd offered. He'd sooner cut out his own tongue and never form another word than admit as much to Landon. "And you'd now be offended that I should turn her away. My God, I'm not some randy youth who . . ." His words trailed off as he looked from Landon to the beauty, then settled finally once more on Landon. Charles narrowed his eyes. "*This* was the intervention, wasn't it?"

His friend shifted on his seat. "It was more of a test," Landon mumbled. "One that, I'll have you know, you failed."

Charles gave his head a disgusted shake. "The only reason you summoned me is to try and get me bedded?" God spare him from the well-meaning intentions of rakes and rogues.

"No. Yes." Landon cursed. "Hell, I'm trying to shake you from whatever this Miss Gately has done to you," the other man whispered. Not that he needed to have bothered, as every last lord present was thoroughly foxed and obscenely loud in their bawdy jests and laughter. "She has made you miserable."

"But . . . we could have been happy together," Charles said quietly. He'd realized that, too late. Which was likely for the best, as she was entirely too good for him.

"Well, you're not. With her, or happy with her, and it's time to move on . . . beyond your book club and efforts to snag the lady's attention," Landon added more emphatically when Charles attempted to speak.

Charles stared into his drink, gave the contents a counterclockwise swirl, and then reversed course, the turbulent little whirlpool he created a perfect metaphor for him and Emma. He'd not even given them a chance as a couple. And he'd failed to appreciate her wit, and strength, until it had been too late. Until he'd cost himself the possibility of them.

"You didn't even like her," Landon said with the blunt directness that only one's best friend was capable of.

Frowning, Charles looked up. "I liked her . . . enough." He'd resented her. He'd blamed her. Realizing too late how unfair it had been to place any of those sentiments at the young lady's feet.

"You avoided her for *eighteen* years."

"That's not true. It was more like seventeen. And prior to that, I visited her in the nursery, and we played spillikins together, and she wasn't all that—"

Landon looked at Charles as if he'd lost the remainder of his head. "Have you gone mad? Or are you making a jest?" Landon pleaded with his eyes and his words. "My God, man, please tell me you're making a jest, because if not, I think you're very well beyond even my help."

It was likely the former. Fortunately, Charles was saved from answering.

"Either way, that is my very point, Scarsdale. You're not yourself, and we need to get you back to being yourself."

Perhaps it was that at the ripe age of three and thirty, with all the years since Seamus's conception spent *carousing*—or playing at it—he'd begun . . . to tire of the lie and the lifestyle. Charles glanced around the pleasure palace; most of the drunken men laughing uproariously and shouting bawdy jests among their friends were ten years or so younger than him. And another handful were men thirty years older—dissolute, disreputable lords who'd never tired of the life.

Was that what he wanted to be?

He could say unequivocally it wasn't.

Until recently, he would have said he was perfectly content with letting the world think whatever they would about him, and would have wanted just that.

But that had been until Miss Emma Gately had snapped their betrothal and freed him of that boring future he'd thought awaited him.

Landon had called Charles here to talk to him about getting back to himself. The rub of it? At thirty-three, Charles was only just realizing he didn't have a damned clue as to who, exactly, he was.

The rogue. The scoundrel. The dutiful son, attempting to make amends. The miserable betrothed.

He'd become all those rolled together, and was now left trying to figure out who and what he was.

And had it not been for Emma and her influence, he'd have never even looked.

"God, for a charming rogue, you're deuced bad at this." Landon shoved back his chair. "Now if you'll excuse me, I'm off to steal that delicious golden beauty you sent over to Waters."

Charles stared after Landon's retreating figure as he headed over to Lord Waters's table, and then the men proceeded to . . . share the young woman.

Landon hadn't been wrong about much this night. Quite the opposite. And watching on as the two dissolute lords sampled the Cyprian's wares, Charles felt . . . an ennui.

He'd never much gotten the carousing . . . not the way Landon did. Oh, in his university days sowing his oats, Charles had enjoyed the favors of skilled courtesans. Enough that when the time had come to save his sister's reputation and fall on the sword of his own indiscretions, he'd been able to do so without society batting an eye. They'd seen what he and his family had hoped they'd see: a young, careless lord who had sired a babe out of wedlock.

As such, the world had not looked closer than that. They'd not seen a then-romantic Camille's folly in trusting her heart to the last man she should. To a spendthrift scoundrel who'd seen in Camille nothing more than a path to a large fortune, and when it had been clear the bounder wouldn't see a bit of her dowry, he'd moved on . . . and Charles's family had been left picking up the pieces.

Charles finished off his drink, and stared at a lone teardrop bit of brandy clinging to the bottom of the glass.

Nay, he'd been the one to pick up the pieces. And it was the least of the sacrifices that he could make, given the lousy brother he'd been. One so absorbed in his own pursuit of happiness that he'd failed to protect the sister who loved him . . . who'd needed him.

The rub of it was, even as he'd change nothing, his sacrifices hadn't been sacrifices at all . . . He was still left in this in-between state, where he didn't truly belong to anything. Or fit in anywhere.

He wasn't Landon or Waters or any of the other gents here . . .

And yet that was how the world saw him. And because that was how he was viewed, neither was he truly a member of the respectable circles . . . frequented by the likes of his former betrothed.

He'd come to peace with . . . all that. Or he'd thought he had. Perhaps it was the late-night hour, or the lingering conflict between him and Emma, but he found himself oddly restless with his circumstances.

Which was why, when all the fashionable and unfashionable sorts still had hours left of their night's revelry, a short while later, Charles found himself leaving his club and entering his rooms to seek out some much-needed rest. Dismissing his valet, Charles instead shrugged out of his jacket, and not breaking stride, he tossed the black article atop his desk as he made his way to his bed.

Seating himself on the edge of the mattress, Charles tugged off one boot.

He tossed it aside and was reaching for the next when he froze; his gaze collided with the crimson-cloaked figure seated in the corner, blanketed in shadows.

"Hullo, Lord Scarsdale," Emma said softly. "We meet again."

Chapter 19

They met again.

And yet as Charles had entered his chambers and set to work disrobing, she'd interrupted him . . . because the last thing she wanted, needed, or intended to let happen was a repeat of their last exchange in these very rooms . . .

With him naked, and her breathless.

Nay, there was to be no breathlessness. Or butterflies. Or any weakness.

"Emma," Charles murmured.

He didn't stand but remained seated there, and she was grateful for it, as his six feet two inches and broadly muscular frame invariably shrank any space.

Except with him seated upon the bed, it only raised all manner of intimate thoughts about again feeling his mouth upon her, but this time with that feather bedding under her.

All the moisture left her mouth, leaving her parched like a woman stranded in a desert, attempting to find herself.

And mayhap she was.

From the moment she'd taken part in that mock wedding ceremony as a child, Emma had been left searching for herself.

"This is a surprise . . . but a welcome one." He smiled slowly, displaying his perfect, pearl-white teeth, a rogue's smile, cocksure and arrogant with a bold confidence that could come only from knowing the effect he had upon women.

Women such as the one with whom he'd had a child.

Or the ones who'd rushed to join his society, while abandoning hers.

That brought her back to the reason she'd sought him out.

"Oh, it shouldn't be, Charles," she said, climbing to her feet and marching over so that she had him cornered on the bed with an advantage over him . . . so that he had to crane his head back to meet her gaze. "If you knew what was wise for you, you'd know that there was nothing welcome about my being here." Emma stuck a finger into his chest, making her first misstep of the night, as the material of his shirt served as little layer between her and his rippled pectoral muscles. She swiftly drew back her arm, letting it fall safely to her side.

It was too late.

The damage had been done.

Charles's rogue's grin deepened, and lowering himself onto his elbows, he stared boldly up at her.

"This is generally where you inquire about the reason I've snuck into your household," Emma said, proud of the steady strength to her voice.

"I am impressed at your having done so."

Of course he would be. Though in truth, she was as well. After all, it had been no small feat, gaining entry and sneaking to his rooms while avoiding detection. It had required her waiting at the kitchens until the last of the staff had vacated before finding her way inside.

With the languid grace of a sleek tiger, Charles pushed himself up. "But, Emma-love," he murmured, slipping a hand about her waist. And parting his legs, he drew her to stand between them. Emma's heart somersaulted. "How have you not realized that anytime we meet is a welcome pleasure?" He wrapped that last word in deep, husky tones, layering it with silk that could never be misconstrued for anything but the seductive whispering that it was.

Emma cursed the weakness within that brought her lashes drifting down. "Y-you are loose with your words."

"Only with you," he vowed.

It was an absolute lie. A rogue with his reputation could melt the heart of the iciest dowager. She should say as much. She wanted to. But . . . his tongue teased the lobe of her ear, and her breath caught. Her pulse quickened. He flicked that slice of flesh against her, a scorching brand that surely marked her.

Stop.

And yet, no matter how much she commanded herself to step away and out of his arms, and focus her thoughts, once more she was reduced to heightened sensation and feeling that her body craved. That it hungered for.

Emma drifted closer.

Or perhaps Charles's other hand, which had found its way about her waist, had guided her closer?

Then he drifted his mouth down her neck, lightly kissing that flesh.

Her body heated several degrees as he licked a path along the top portions of her breasts that had been lifted and put on display by the gown she'd donned.

"Y-you still do not intend to ask me why I've c-come?"

"Should I?" he asked huskily in between each worshipping kiss he placed upon her breast. "I was just happy to find you here."

"O-oh, yes." Then she couldn't fight it. Not any longer. A little moan spilled from her lips.

"'Oh, yes,' you like that, love?" He paused, blowing lightly upon her skin. "Or 'Oh, yes,' I should ask?"

Ask . . . what? What was he saying? What had she been saying? "I . . ." She was too confused. Clouded by the same haze of desire she'd vowed to never fall prey to. Not again. Her eyes drifted open.

His gaze worked a path over her face. "Have you suffered some kind of harm?" he asked.

"No."

"Has someone hurt you in any way?"

"Yes." That grounded her, and she managed to step away.

He'd already taken to his feet. "Who?" If a single word could be a threat, then the icy syllable he clipped out now achieved that goal.

Emma didn't want it to matter that he should care either way . . . And yet it did. She squared her shoulders. "You."

He blinked. "Me?"

"You," she repeated. In fact, over the years he'd made something of a habit where she'd been concerned. She bit the inside of her cheek to keep from leveling that bitter charge at him.

"Me . . . ?" Charles shook his head.

Returning to the spot she'd staked out earlier, Emma fetched the same paper she'd committed to memory, which had also kept her company while he'd been off doing whatever it was he'd done with the women at his clubs. She hurled her copy of *The Londoner* at him, hitting Charles square in the chest.

He caught it to him. "What is this?" he asked, already reading.

"That is actually the question I have for you, Charles. What is this?"

"I am afraid I do not follow," he said slowly, lowering the newspaper to his side.

"Your society is still functioning." And worse, thriving.

"We are a club."

Emma's eyebrows went flying up. My God, was he making a jest about any of this?

"At no point did I agree to disband."

Emma searched her mind, replaying every last word of the discussion they'd had in this very room, and rocked back on her heels. He'd not said it. And yet . . . she instantly found herself. "Your meaning was clear."

"Apparently it wasn't," he said dryly. "Otherwise you wouldn't be here, offended and calling me out for some imagined slight."

"This is no imagined slight, Charles!" she cried, her voice climbing, and she briefly closed her eyes, fighting to get control of her rapidly spiraling resentment and outrage. "This is a very real affront," she said, this time calm and quiet in that delivery.

"Because I cannot have a club of my own."

The fact that his wasn't even a question only added to the rage threatening to simmer over once more. "It is a society," Emma gritted out.

He smiled. "Well, there you are. They are different, after all."

At that poorly timed jest, she narrowed her eyes. Why, he thought he could simply charm away their conflict. He must have seen something, however, for his grin faded.

Charles took a step toward her. "Emma, I am sorry if you misunderstood, but I didn't promise to disband my club." She backed away from him, lest he attempted to weave more of his sorcerer's magic over her.

"You only started this to goad me, Charles."

Something flashed in his eyes. "It may have begun as one thing, Emma." And he continued forward once more, refusing to allow her the physical barrier of space. Well, she'd be damned if she retreated any more. Emma dug in her heels and locked her feet to the floor. Charles stopped with only a pace between them; he roved his eyes over her face, and then his fingers came up in a distracted caress of her chin. "But my reasons for establishing my club? They have since changed."

Frustration pulled an exasperated sound from her lips. He expected her to believe that his motives were honorable. "I want you to stop."

Charles immediately let his hand drop.

"I mean poaching my members, plagiarizing my meetings, Charles," she clarified.

His knuckles came up once more. "So I can touch you?"

A pained laugh escaped her, only to die a moment later as he tenderly cupped her cheek; all the while, the tips of his fingers resumed the caress he'd previously abandoned.

And something shifted in that moment.

Passion flared to life, hovering in the air around them, the fans of it deepening by the slightest touch, one that somehow still managed to conjure all the wanton moments that had been born in this very room, and at the hand of this man who now stroked her cheek.

And Emma turned into his touch, angling in a way so that she leaned into him, wordlessly, silently, and secretly wanting more of him.

Why does it need to be a secret? Why was it wrong for a woman to find pleasure when and where she wanted, while men were afforded the luxury of assuaging their needs without any explanation needed? Free to feel.

I want to feel . . .

"You should go," he said hoarsely.

"Why?" she asked curiously.

"Because this time"—his already low baritone dipped, emerging a shade deeper with a passion she recognized—"this time, I want to make love to you in every sense of the word."

"So you'll send me away . . . ?"

"It is the right thing to do." And there was a faint entreating quality to that admission.

Emma studied the sharply beautiful planes of his face, each chiseled contour tight and tense. The corners of his perfectly formed lips white from the manner in which he clenched his mouth.

Now he would show principles. Now, when she didn't want him to. But then Charles had always proven contrary, wanting her only after she had left him.

Charles made to draw away once more, but this time, Emma quickly caught his hand and kept it there, pressed against her cheek, and then, curving her palm over the top of his hand, she guided it lower. She directed him lower, leading his touch to where she wanted it, pressing it against the bodice of her low-cut gown, the vast expanse of exposed flesh bare against his naked fingers.

He groaned. "You don't know what you're doing, Emma. You're playing with fire."

Yes, she was. And for the first time, she wanted to be burnt by it. She wanted to be consumed in a conflagration of passion, coaxed by his touch. "What if I said I wanted you to do . . . more of those things to me? All of them."

Charles's gaze locked with hers, and she braced for his continued moral resistance. But then he took her mouth under his, in this, her first kiss.

Passion exploded to life, sparkling like the Kent earth right after a lightning strike, and Emma found herself as immobilized as if one of those bolts had streaked down from the heavens and caught her where she stood.

She came alive all at once. Smote by desire, and reborn in passion. Gripping his shirtfront, she leveraged herself closer, coming up on tiptoe to better meet his mouth, and she kissed him in return.

He growled, a low, raw, primal sound born of desire that thrummed against her lips, and she reveled in this newfound power that came of being a woman.

Emma turned her head a fraction so she could better avail herself of his mouth.

Removing the combs from her hair, Charles let those strands free so that they cascaded like a waterfall about them. All the while, he licked at the seam of her lips, tasting that flesh with the tip of his tongue, and a wet, hot heat settled between her legs.

Hungry for more of him, for all of him, Emma parted her lips and let him inside, and in he swept, all silk and warmth, with a tantalizing allure which contained a promise of the more she desperately craved. She lashed her tongue against his, set free by the eddy of desire he'd awakened within her.

Charles swirled his tongue about hers in a teasing manner that turned the kiss into a passionate game where she sought, and he withheld, part of himself.

Gripping him hard by the nape, she held him in place, ultimately taking what she needed, making all of his mouth hers.

He groaned, the sound of his desire reverberating in their kiss, and that light thrumming sent a deeper throbbing to her core.

"Charles," she panted.

And at last, it was as though he surrendered himself completely to Emma.

His hands were on her everywhere, making quick work of her cloak, shoving it free of her body; then, cupping her at the waist, he steered the both of them until he perched himself on the edge of the mattress and pulled her between his legs once more.

Christi Caldwell

With a deftness that should have infuriated for the skill it evidenced, Charles had the buttons of her gown free and her dress down as it fell in a shimmery, shuddery heap of noisy satin.

Emma stepped out of it, kicking it aside. There would be time for reality later. Now, she just wanted this.

All of this.

Charles closed his mouth around the tip of her right breast, and she gasped.

Her fingers came up reflexively as she clenched and unclenched the dark-blond strands, holding him close as he worshipped her, laving that tip, suckling the bud until her hips moved wildly, undulating.

He drew away so abruptly she cried out from the loss.

"You are so beautiful," he whispered, diverting his masterful attentions elsewhere, pressing a path of hot, wet kisses along her neck.

"Mmm." Incapable of the speech needed to encourage his attentions there, she dropped her head back to let her body show him what she needed.

She'd gone through her life believing the lie society had told her— that she wasn't beautiful. Her features were too sharp. Her teeth more than slightly crooked. Her hips and breasts not lush . . . but when he spoke so and laid worship to her body as he did, she had her eyes opened at last to the lie as she was awakened instead to the truth of her femininity and beauty.

Her breath caught on a gasp as he filled his hands with her buttocks.

Emma reflexively tightened her limbs; the drag of the fabric of his trousers against the coarse hair of her womanhood pulled another moan from her, and she rubbed herself against him.

Charles squeezed her buttocks, molding that flesh in his hands, and that illicit touch, paired with wicked words, forbidden ones he whispered against her ear, encouraged each rise and fall of her hips.

Pressure built between her thighs, sharp and keen, and with each thrust of her body against his in a bid to assuage the ache there, the more desperate this yearning to find the same fulfillment he'd brought her to became. Her speech dissolved to wordless little grunts as she ground herself against him, the enormous length of his shaft rigid as steel, and she hungered to feel that flesh at last.

Then he moved a hand between their bodies, and slipped his fingers into her drenched center.

Emma cursed, bucking her hips harder, and Charles laughed quietly, that low rumble which shook his chest reverberating with male triumph.

And she didn't care. Because her pleasure was as much her triumph as it was his. Nay, it was more. She wanted this moment, and took it boldly and unapologetically. The real weakness would be for her to deny herself all this. Any of it.

Emma bit her lip sharply enough that she tasted the metallic tinge of blood, and with his fingers still stroking through her sodden channel, she mimicked his earlier movement, reaching between them and gripping his length through his trousers.

Charles hissed sharply between his teeth, his already impossibly hard length surging even harder and higher under her touch.

And she knew the very same triumph he had moments ago, and celebrated this new discovery of her power over him.

"Do you like that?" Emma teased him with those same words he notoriously loved to ask of her, and with his eyes squeezed shut and his neck muscles struggling through the motions of swallowing, she took her torment further. Sliding free the front placard of his trousers, Emma bared him . . . to her eyes. And her touch.

His hips shot up. "Hell," he groaned.

"Is that a no?" she asked huskily, already knowing the answer, but playing the same game he'd insisted she play.

"Nooooo." Charles angled his neck about, searching for her mouth with his.

Emma, however, continued to deny him, withholding what he wanted. "You have to be more clear, Lord Scarsdale," she breathed against the corner of his mouth, and the moment she removed her hands from his shaft, he cried out.

"Yes," he hissed, his eyes flying open, those dark irises burning her with the heat there. "I love your hand on me. I want it."

And her breath caught at the rawness of that unrestrained avowal.

In one fluid movement, he reversed them, flipping her over, so that she lay under him and the mattress was at Emma's back. Sliding down her body, he rested with his head between her legs and put his mouth on her, devouring her.

He alternately nipped at the swollen flesh of her lips and tongued her channel.

Emma melted under him; she moaned her approval, letting her legs splay, and tangling her fingers in his hair, she anchored him in place. Thrusting her hips up, and pushing herself against that wicked kiss.

And then, in a devious turnabout, he abruptly stopped.

Her entire soul screamed at the loss of him. *"Charrles."* Emma wept his name, blending it with a plea for him to continue.

"Lay your hands beside you, love," he ordered, a command that sent a new hungering through her, and she complied. Doing as he bade. Then he picked up where he'd left off. He laved that oversensitized bud. He stroked her with his tongue.

All the while, she did precisely as he'd bidden. Emma forced her arms to remain at her sides; her fingers curled into the sheets, and she gripped the satin fabric tightly to keep from touching him. The pressure mounted, that merging of pleasure and pain, two conflicting feelings that—when making love to Charles—only made sense.

She closed her eyes, and her head lolled back and forth of its own volition.

This made sense between them. This, when nothing else seemed to. When they were at odds in so many ways.

Refusing to let that encroach upon the splendor of this, her first time making love, Emma shoved herself up onto her elbows. It was too much. "Charles?" she pleaded, and he immediately ceased tasting of her.

He quickly shucked off his shirt and shoved down his trousers until he stood naked before her.

Emma worked a hungry gaze over him, taking a moment to worship every defined, contoured muscle of his chest lightly covered with tight, golden coils. The equally firm, muscled wall of his belly. And then she dipped her appreciation lower, to the length of his shaft that sprang proud and hard from a nest of golden curls, the smooth plum tip of him gleaming.

Her breath caught. "I want you," she breathed, owning her need of him. For him . . . and what only he could give her.

His eyes darkened, and she held up her arms for him.

Leaning over, he yanked open his nightstand drawer and removed a small sheath. Their gazes locked as he slid the French letter over his length, and then he covered her body with his.

Emma wrapped her arms about him and let her legs spread.

He buried his head in her chest, suckling fiercely at the peak of her right breast, and there was a hedonistic pull to the wet sounds of his mouth upon her. All the while, he ground the heel of his palm to her center, the tight thatch of her curls soaked from her desire.

Why were women taught this was wrong?

She panted.

Why, when there was no greater bliss . . . no greater magnificence than this? All this.

Suddenly, he stopped, and she cried out . . . silently? Aloud? It was all confused as to what was real.

"Is this what you want, Emma?" he asked gruffly. "Are you certain?"

Emma touched her fingers to his lips, silencing the remainder of that noble question. She moved her eyes, hazy from the passion he'd awakened, over the strained muscles of his face.

His brow gleamed with perspiration, and she lifted trembling fingers up to brush those droplets away. What must that question have cost him? That restraint?

Emma finally let her gaze rest, meeting his stare directly. "I have never been more certain of anything," she said with a strength that brought Charles's lashes sweeping down like a glorious golden blanket.

With a groan, Charles shifted, lowering himself between her legs, and he moved his hand, replacing it with his hard length. Her pulse escalated, and panting, she reflexively lifted her hips, urging him to continue.

And then he gave her what she begged for, sliding himself slowly within her; her body was tight, but her channel so wet it slicked the way for his entry.

Emma wrapped her arms around him, running her fingers up and down his back, and undulating beneath him, she urged him onward.

Charles's eyes locked with hers, and the searing depth of emotion there robbed her of what little breath she had left in her lungs. "There is no one like you, Emma." He thrust home, and she knew there was supposed to be pain; everything she'd ever learned and been prepared for said the moment would be marred by discomfort. And yet there was none of it. Closing her eyes, she panted fast and hard at the exquisite sensation of his enormous length buried inside her.

Charles placed a butterfly-soft kiss just above her brow, and her eyes fluttered open. "Did I hurt you?" Worry roughened his voice.

Emma arched her head back and twined her hands about his nape. "Only when you stopped," she breathed.

His eyes darkened, and he claimed her mouth.

He moved slowly, withdrawing and then pressing deep, repeating that tantalizing motion, as he rocked within her.

Emma followed his lead, matching each downward thrust by lifting up into him.

Their movements took on a frenzy, more frantic and desperate as they strained against one another. Her sweat mingled with his. Their breaths grew shallow and raspy as they moved in perfect time.

The ache between her legs became so acute she was tunneled to that desperate sensation, and more, to the need to assuage it.

"Charlessss." She hissed his name, digging her nails into his back, leaving crescent marks upon his flesh as she climbed higher and higher, closer to that glorious cliff she'd dived from days before.

"That's it," he encouraged harshly. He sank his fingers into her thighs, using her limbs to leverage himself forward, deepening his strokes.

Emma stiffened. Throwing her head back, she screamed. She screamed his name, endlessly, over and over as she knew a pleasure unlike any other she'd ever known before. This bliss made all the fuller by having him inside her. He pumped harder and faster, his thrusts growing almost jerky from the force of them, drawing out Emma's climax.

Then he froze. With a low, animalistic groan, he buried his face against her neck and joined her.

She felt his length shuddering and throbbing as he thrust over and over again.

They collapsed at the same time, against one another, clinging to each other, with him buried to the hilt deep inside.

Charles abruptly reversed them, so she lay sprawled atop his chest.

Until their breathing resumed a normal, even cadence and the fog of desire lifted, and Emma made a slow descent back to Earth and the same reality awaiting her when she did—the same reality which had driven her here this night. Only she'd proven once again not strong in the ways that she wanted to be, for she was reluctant to let go of the magic and return to what they were, what they'd always been—a woman and man, always at odds with one another.

Now, they were two lovers at odds.

She lay there with her cheek pressed against his chest, absorbing the sound of his heartbeat, rhythmic and strong, pounding underneath her ear.

"Are you happy?" he murmured, smoothing a palm along the small of her back, just over the curve of her buttocks, rubbing in a delicious, soothing circle.

Emma propped her chin atop his chest. "Very much so."

They shared a smile, which eased back reality's inevitable arrival.

"We'll marry," he said quietly.

And with that, the cold rush of the present she'd been avoiding found its way into this stolen interlude. Emma swung her legs over the side of the bed. "What is that? An offer? A statement?" And a sharp ache needled her chest at what his words were.

Or rather, what they were not.

He frowned. "Of course we'll marry, Emma."

"Because of what we've done here?"

Color rose in his cheeks. "Yes," he said tightly. "And because . . ." Her ears pricked up as she waited for him to say more. "It is the right thing for us to do. And I want to marry you."

There it was. Only as tacked on as she'd always been to him and his life. An afterthought.

The mattress groaned, indicating he'd moved. From the corner of her eye, she caught him removing the sheath from his shaft and tossing it aside as he hastily cleaned himself.

"You needn't marry me, and I needn't marry you," she said calmly, as she might deliver a lecture to the Mismatch Society. "I am a grown woman, and you are a grown man, and we are both entirely capable of . . . of . . ."

"Making love?" he supplied.

Her cheeks went warm. "Yes . . . that." Somehow, despite everything she'd done with this man, a blush was still possible. "Making love," she made herself say. "And there needn't be anything more."

"You'd deny how very compatible we are, love?" He folded an arm around her waist and drew her close so that Emma's back rested against his chest. Charles kissed the place just behind the shell of her ear, his breath fanning her skin. Her eyes grew heavy from the desire his touch always roused, and she resisted melting against him and pleading for him to make love to her—again.

"Not in the ways that matter, Charles," she said tiredly, and with a strength she didn't know she possessed, she stepped out of his arms. Except that wasn't true . . . She'd since discovered his affection for his son, and their shared love of political philosophy . . . and now they shared joint ventures. Her society. His club. Avoiding his eyes, she rescued her garments littering his floor.

Charles stopped her, resting a hand lightly upon her arm. "There is nothing I can say to convince you of this."

There were any manner of things he might say . . . if he felt them. "I do not want your words summoned because I require convincing." Emma sifted through the tangle of garments, searching for her dress—and then froze.

With numb fingers, she bypassed her dress for the white lawn shirt.

That was, white in all but one particular spot.

The crimson rouge of a woman's lips upon his shirt, the red stark and vivid as sin upon white—a shade of innocence at odds with a man whose name and every deed and act were synonymous with sin. And it proved more sobering than when her sister had flipped their boat and knocked Emma into the crisp Kent waters.

The thick scent of jasmine that clung to his shirt. The rumpled quality of his garments when he'd entered his rooms.

Tears clogged her throat and blinded her eyes, and she cursed herself for that weakness. "Ah, how easily you scoundrels move from the bed of one woman to another." She hated that her voice emerged as a whisper.

Confusion lent Charles's brow several wrinkles, and then he followed her stare. His eyes bulged. He hastily yanked the garment from her fingers and stuffed it behind his back, as if that might somehow undo what she'd seen. "It is not what it looks like." Shockingly, he had the good grace to blush.

Emma began frantically drawing on her undergarments. "Or smells like?" Because the scent of whomever had been in his arms lingered on those articles, too.

"I wasn't with a woman. I was . . . but not . . . as you're thinking. I was at one of my clubs."

She forced a laugh, a cynical, sharp bark of humorless mirth. "I take it White's and Brooke's are still not permitting women members?"

His flush deepened, and he dragged a hand through his hair. "Not that manner of club."

Emma paused mid-dressing. "Ah," she said, feigning a dawned understanding. "A *wicked* club."

He winced. "Yes, but I was just visiting Landon for drinks. She pressed herself against me. She offered herself. I didn't want her. I didn't want—"

"What you want and who you want isn't really my concern," she lied, hating the thickened quality of her voice, praying he didn't look closely and see it for the hurt it was. Hating herself more for caring how he spent his nights. Hating herself for having believed him.

"Emma," he called frantically, dragging on his garments. "Please, just let me explain."

And knowing he intended to convince her once more, and fearing she'd believe those lies, Emma bolted.

She raced through his townhouse, not breaking stride until she reached the waiting hackney. Out of breath from the pace she'd set, she banged on the ceiling. The carriage lurched forward, and Emma peeled back the curtain a fraction and peeked out at Charles, running bare-chested after the departing conveyance.

She swiftly let the velvet fall.

She'd made so many mistakes where Charles was concerned, and she'd do well to put her energies and efforts where they belonged—on the Mismatch Society.

Chapter 20

THE LONDONER

SCANDAL!

Yet another scandal has erupted between the Mismatch Club and Club du Livre. This time, shocking though it may be, the scandal belongs to the Earl of Scarsdale!

M. FAIRPOINT

Last night hadn't marked the first time Emma had rejected Charles.

Even so, in the immediacy of making love to Emma, he'd been fairly certain his feet would never find their way back to Earth.

Until they had.

Until she'd seen his garments and believed every worst thing about him.

And why shouldn't she have? The evidence had been damning.

And there was no going back this time, the truth of that ushering in a wave of finality that left him bereft.

"Egad, man, you've returned to woeful, heartbroken chap," Landon bemoaned. "But then passing on the buxom beauty last evening, which"—Landon held his cue stick aloft—"by the way, I should thank you for. She was magnificent. That being beside the point, of course. Now you've let your billiards game go to hell?" The other man jabbed the bottom of his stick on the floor, thumping it several times. "This isn't to be borne."

Had it not been for Landon's setup, as he'd called it, there wouldn't have been the rouged shirt, and things with Emma last night would have ended very differently than they had. "Enough with the mention of the damned woman," he growled. Except it wasn't Landon's fault. Not really. Charles had continued visiting those illicit clubs . . . ones where women were put on display. Desperate women, as Emma had pointed out . . .

Emma . . .

Charles's eyes slid shut briefly until Landon spoke, forcing Charles's focus back to the marquess.

"*Hmph.* Seems someone is still resentful. Regretting your decision," Landon persisted, nagging as only he could.

Charles slammed down his cue stick. "It's not because of . . . of . . . her." But rather because of the one woman he wanted in his life and in his heart and in his bed. None of which he could say. None of which he could admit, because to do so would be to acknowledge he'd been with Emma. Charles's shot went wide.

"Oh, dear," Landon murmured. "You are in a bad way."

"I thought you should welcome your win," Charles shot back testily.

"Ha-ha, yes, of course," Landon quipped. "Let us all make light of my depleted coffers."

Coffers all society knew the other man had himself depleted. Reaching inside his jacket front, Charles withdrew a purse and tossed it across the table.

Shooting up a hand, Landon closed a quick fist around it, the coins rattling with a clink. The debt-ridden lord gave the bag a little shake. "And as appreciative as I am for the winnings, it is hardly enjoyable to fleece a distracted man, particularly a distracted friend."

"Another game? Double the odds?" Charles offered instead, invariably knowing the best way to divert his bothersome, if well-meaning, friend's attentions.

Landon wagged a finger. "I know what you're doing, chum." He grinned. "And I'll allow it. I was teasing before. I know very well what has you out of sorts. That this has something to do with your Miss Gately."

Bloody hell. Charles made a show of rearranging the twelve balls, and took the first shot, with Landon following . . . and securing the right to play first for points.

The other man gave him a knowing look. *"Hmm,"* he said pointedly, and Charles's skin flushed hot.

He never admitted his friend Landon was correct about anything.

The largest reason being the other man was generally wrong when it came to most matters.

But not a small reason also being the other man was outrageously obnoxious when he did find himself in the right.

And in this, there was no disputing it—Landon had been on the mark.

And what was even worse . . . the other man knew it.

Yes, there was no other explanation for Lord Landon's sudden propensity for being correct—hell hath frozen over. Or mayhap it was really just that the marquess was more perceptive and an even better friend than he'd credited. Charles, however, still couldn't bring himself to confide the absolute nightmare that had been last evening. While he wished only thoughts of her in his arms, in his bed, and under him were all he could think of, the fact remained it was what had come after that gripped him. For when she'd fled, there'd been a sense of finality to her leaving. She'd seen that stain, and that crimson mark had resurrected every barrier that he'd managed to break down.

Landon made a study of the table, periodically eyeing his next play too long, then taking his shot. While the other man made quick work of the balls, Charles applied chalk to his stick.

Landon's next shot went wide, and he motioned for Charles to begin his turn.

Leaning over the table, Charles eyed the scattered balls, and squinted, focusing in on his target. The last thing he needed any more of was Landon's ribbing. Or worse . . . probing. Charles's cue stick slipped forward, scraped the table, and missed the target ball entirely.

He and Landon stared in silence at the scraped velvet table, and then Landon burst out laughing.

Charles stuck up two fingers. "Oh, go to hell," he muttered, and his faithless friend only howled all the more with his hilarity.

Dashing tears of mirth from his cheeks, Landon bent over his cue stick. "Not distracted, my arse. You've the look to you. The same look you've worn for weeks."

"I don't have a look," Charles repeated . . . unconvincingly to even himself.

"Like a lovesick pup," Landon squeezed out past his still-noisy amusement.

He bristled. "I'm not a lovesick *pup*." He'd not been a pup in years.

"But you are not denying you're lovesick, though?" Landon chortled.

Charles lifted his palm and gave another two-fingered V.

"Who is in love?" a voice called into the high-ceilinged room, that question echoing.

Oh, bloody hell.

Landon immediately ceased laughing as he and Charles faced Charles's mother. She swept forward, Charles's brother, Derek, close behind.

The two men promptly lowered their cue sticks to their sides and greeted the marchioness at the same time.

"Mother."

"Lady Rochester."

"Phineas," she greeted warmly and affectionately as she tucked a loose strand of longer-than-fashionable hair behind his ear. Alas, Charles's mother had been the only one permitted by the other man the use of a name Landon despised. "Is it you?"

Ever the rogue, for debutantes to dowagers alike, Landon caught her fingertips with his spare hand, and bowed, promptly dislodging that curl, and undoing her efforts of righting him. "As your scoundrel of a husband stole you from me before I had a chance, my heart can belong to no other." And grotesque as his friend flirting with his mother in fact was, it was a good deal more preferred than had Landon outed Charles's feelings about Emma.

She snorted. "A rogue since the day you were born, Landon." The marchioness softened that with a smile, and holding on to his hand still, she raised her spare one to affectionately pat the fingers covering hers. "And a charming one, at that."

"You've always been so wonderful to me, Lady Rochester. But I still have never had that waltz I vowed to one day steal from you." Releasing his hold upon her, Landon brought his arms into position.

Oh, right, that, however, was a line too far. Charles jabbed the other man in the back with the tip of his cue stick. "Enough already," he said tightly. It was one thing to bear witness to the marquess going about charming every lady around London, and saving Charles from her probing. It was quite another when it was Charles's own mother.

"Rest assured, dear, no one is going to seduce me away from your father." She gave a little snap of her skirts. "I'm quite content in—"

Releasing his cue stick, Charles promptly slapped his hands over his ears. *"Ahhhhhhhhh,"* he said loudly in a bid to blot out those assurances he had no desire of hearing.

His mother collected his palms and forcibly lowered them to his sides. "My marriage," she finished. "I was going to say *my marriage.*" Passing a look over to Landon, she followed that with a wink, which pulled another laugh from the entirely-too-affable rogue.

Charles and Derek turned scowls upon the other man.

"Pick better friends," Derek said out of the corner of his mouth.

"There's St. John," Charles felt inclined to point out for his younger brother. Anyone would be hard-pressed to find offense with the proper viscount.

"Ouch." Landon staggered back and pressed a hand to his chest in false, wounded affront. "That hurts, gentlemen. *Hurts.*"

His mother did a glance about the billiards room. "I take it this is not the chosen location for your next meeting," she said dryly, retrieving the forgotten cue stick from the floor.

"Our next meeting," Charles corrected, as she was an integral part of the club he'd formed . . . one whose presence had allowed it to occur without scandal ensuing.

"Very well, as you are allowing me some ownership of your new venture, dearest son of mine—"

"I beg pardon." Derek bristled with indignation.

The marchioness paused long enough in her tirade to pat her youngest son gently on the cheek. "I'm only using it in this instance to accentuate displeasure, dear."

Derek beamed. "Carry on, then." He dropped a hip on the edge of the billiards table, and crossed his arms at his chest. "This I'm happy to hear."

"Fabulous," Charles said under his breath.

"Continuing on," she began.

He'd rather she not. At all. "Don't," he entreated. The last thing a grown man wished for was a parental lecture . . . and delivered in front of his younger brother and best friend, no less. He nudged his head imperceptibly toward the pair. "Please, don't."

Derek and Landon spoke at the same time.

"Ah, please do."

"Oh, do."

Alas, Charles's declination was destined to be overruled by Landon's and Derek's encouragement.

The matriarch of the family and society, in general, obliged Charles's faithless brother and friend. "You have a room full of young ladies scheduled to join us in"—his mother plucked the chain from his waistcoat and consulted the gold timepiece—"a quarter of an hour." She let the fob fall. "You don't have a room arranged. I have no idea what discussion is taking place today—"

"I'd wager neither does Charles," Derek pointed out.

"*Et tu*, brother?"

His younger sibling blushed. "I didn't mean any offense."

Which only made it all the . . . more offensive. That general expectation that Charles didn't have a proper organized thought in his head. In fairness, he hadn't. Before now, that was.

Landon raised his cue stick in the air, calling everyone's attention his way. "If I may also point out . . . he has his head in the clouds. Still."

Derek laughed, and Charles slid another sharp look his way. His brother immediately coughed into his fist.

There it was. Point. Point. Point. Point. And point. They weren't wrong . . . the lot of them. And yet . . . "I know what I'm doing." At the three matching and very pointed stares, he grimaced. "I'll allow, since its inception, the club may have appeared . . . somewhat disjointed."

"Whatever would make you say *that*?" Landon drawled, applying chalk to the end of his stick. "The varying iteration of names?"

His brother jumped in. "The continually different meeting locations. The Green Parlor. The Drawing Room."

"What is next?" Landon let his arms splay. "The billiards room?"

Charles frowned. "Well, that doesn't make sense," he said, thumping the other man on the back. "We're not a billiards club, nor do we discuss . . ." Giving his head a shake, cursing that blasted inherent tendency of having his mind wander off, he forced himself to focus. "Either way, I believe I have . . ." *Nay* . . . "I have found my way. Firstly, I'd have it clear, our members are not solely young ladies."

"Just most of them." Landon touched a finger to his forehead to chest in an abbreviated cross.

Charles frowned. He'd not have anyone, friends included, make anything salacious out of his club. "I'll point out there are gentlemen also interested in—"

His mother waggled her eyebrows.

He blanched. "What we are discussing," Charles said, exasperation pulling those words from him. Good God in heaven, what hellish reversal was this that he, the rogue, had to suffer through scandalous thoughts, ones freely expressed by his damned *mother*.

"Your brother and some of the gents he calls friends hardly count," Landon said, chuckling. "Why, I'd wager you ordered the poor lad to join in, and he, in turn, twisted their weaker arms."

"Well, it is a good thing for you, you don't have any farthings left to lose," Derek shot back.

Actually, despite that opinion and assumption, Charles hadn't coerced or coordinated anyone. Everyone had come—and more importantly, stayed—of their own volition. Brother included.

Landon narrowed his eyes. "That is a low blow, young Hayden."

Derek surged forward, but the marchioness slid herself between them. "Boys!" She clapped once, and much the way they had as the children they once were, Charles, his brother, and his boyhood friend immediately stopped sparring and drew back their shoulders, standing at attention. "We are now at . . ." She grabbed Charles's timepiece, and he grunted; lest she break the piece, he allowed her to draw him over to consult the fob. She released it quickly. "Ten minutes away, and there's no meeting place set up. I just visited the parlor, and I know this is your venture, Charles, but this is also a reflection of—"

"I've taken care of it." Charles had gone back and forth over all options, and had arrived at the only place that made the most sense for his club centered around books.

"You have?" his mother asked.

"I have."

This time, Charles's pronouncement was met with like stupefaction, and from this, his greatest *supporters*. And that collective shock proved somehow even more . . . hurtful than the early words voiced aloud between Landon and Derek. Those, even if they had contained traces of truth, had been delivered in good-natured jest. This awkward silence from all of them was just one more indication of the lack of faith they had in his abilities . . . and in his capabilities. Nay, what was truly worse? They were entitled to their reservations. At what point had he demonstrated himself a man capable of focusing and carrying out . . . anything of import?

"Seating has already been arranged, and an agenda already laid out in preparation. Refreshment trays should be out, even now."

"Miss Dobson—"

Charles interrupted his brother, anticipating the remainder of that question. "I've instructed Cook to avoid any inclusion of almonds due to Miss Dobson's hypersensitivity to the food." Yes, that had been . . . a rather unfortunate and ignominious start to their last meeting. The young woman had consumed a ratafia cake, baked in bitter almonds, and her face had immediately swelled while her throat had closed. "I also solicited Camille to send around inquiries about potential food sensitivities to our other members. I've seen to the purchase of copies of the text and seen they've been distributed to . . . those members whose family are not in the position of parting with the funds." As was the case with Camille's closest friend, Miss Fawcett, and several of the young lords who came from notoriously impoverished families.

The trio looked among one another.

"What?" he asked gruffly, fiddling with his cravat.

Tears shimmered in their mother's eyes, and he tensed.

"I'm sure I've forgotten something, but . . ." Charles's words trailed off as she came forward, and much the way she had when she'd first sent him on to Eton, she tenderly adjusted his cravat.

"I *never* doubted you."

Landon shot up a hand. "I did."

The marchioness turned her famous pillar-of-Polite-Society glare upon him, and the gentleman had sense enough to drop his gaze to the floor.

"'Pologies," he mouthed, lifting a palm.

Returning her attention to Charles, his mother dabbed the drops from the corners of her eyes. "Now, let us go, as the members are surely arrived and are being shown to the library."

With a sigh, Landon returned his cue stick to the wall and reluctantly joined Derek.

Charles made to follow after them, when his mother stayed him with a hand on his arm.

He glanced down.

"I am proud of you, Charles."

I am proud of you . . .

He'd never doubted her love. Not for a single moment. Nor his father's. Oh, he'd resented him for controlling his life and maneuvering him into marriage as a boy, but he'd also known there was love there.

But pride?

Those were words that had not fallen often—if at all—from either of their lips. In fairness, he'd never given them reason to be proud.

"These . . . things have not come easy to you, as they do Camille or Derek, but it never meant you weren't clever or capable."

It meant all that. Bitterness filled his mouth and soured his tongue.

She framed his cheeks in her hands, directing his gaze to hers. "You've never believed in yourself, Charles, but that doesn't mean I never did."

He'd not had any reason to believe in himself. He'd not excelled in his schooling. He'd not met any of the expectations his father had of him. And now, the one thing his mother could and would find pride in? Well, it had all been conceived for reasons that hadn't been motivated for the reasons she thought. Unlike Emma, who had set out to create something, he'd simply followed along in a bid to woo her.

His mother searched her gaze over his face, her brow furrowing. "What is it?"

Of course, because a mother saw, and a mother always knew.

Charles shook his head. "You're making more of . . . this than it is."

"I don't believe I am."

"I only did it because Emma called me out," he exclaimed, owning the real motivation behind what he'd done. "She insisted that I didn't take anything seriously." And she'd not been wrong. "And I . . ."

"And you set out to prove you were capable?"

Rubbing four fingers across his forehead, Charles nodded. "Yes. That is why." That was what it had begun as, anyway. Heat pricked his skin at the attention his mother trained on him.

The silence his admission ushered in left him hollow; it heightened his sense of shame. "Do you know what I think, Charles?"

He gave his head a tight, curt shake.

"I believe she called you out because she saw there was more to you than the world saw. She encouraged you to do things she knew you could do."

Charles chuckled, the sound wry to his own ears. Seating himself at the side of the billiards table, he scrubbed a hand over his face. "And you also believed we would have been happily married." He thought of the shock of betrayal in Emma's eyes as she'd fled last night, and he closed his eyes tightly.

"I did." Her eyes twinkled. "And I still do."

His lips curled up at the corner in a wry twist. "She doesn't even like me."

But what about that moment in the bookshop . . . on Regent Street, or at Lady Rutland's? When it was so easy and so very natural to be with her? And speak to her about topics you both care about and share an interest in . . .

His mother rested her hand on his, pulling Charles back from those wishful and, worse, delusional musings. "When you were children, Emma lit up the moment you entered a room. She adored you . . ."

Until she hadn't.

Until he'd taken all his resentment out on the person who'd been least deserving of it. The very person whom he'd shared a bond with. Or what would have been a bond, had he not gone and severed the ties of it with his meanness and disinterest. Charles stared blankly at the opposite wall. What was worse . . .

"She doesn't trust me." He released a curse. "Nor should she." Because of his role in concealing Camille's fall, and because of whom he'd allowed himself to become thereafter.

His mother's features buckled, and she touched a hand to her mouth. "We didn't think enough about you, Charles," she said on an aching whisper. "We didn't think about how what your father . . . and I asked of you should affect you and Emma, and that was wrong."

Yes, it had been wrong. But it would have been more wrong had Charles not done everything in his power to protect his sister from the suffering and fallout which would have come following her indiscretion.

As it was, he'd not called out the bounder who'd deceived her, the man with false intentions to elope with her.

"It was my choice," he said tiredly. Tired of it all. Tired of the deception. Tired of the sins of another man, who had left so many lives altered. And tired of being powerless to win the one woman he wished to. "And regardless of what you asked, I didn't need to throw myself into that part as I did. And because of that . . . I don't deserve her." He spoke quietly, to himself. "I didn't appreciate her when I had a chance of a future with her. I drank too much. I wagered often. I was not"—his cheeks went hot—"faithful."

His mother gently cupped his cheeks. "Who you were yesterday, Charles, isn't who you will forever be. And I know Emma. I trust in Emma. She will one day soon see that."

Not when what she'd seen last evening had been rouge on his shirt. Not when he should have long ago stopped visiting such establishments.

"Now, come," his mother said, pulling him from his thoughts. "Punctuality is the politeness of kings."

As they made the walk to the library, Charles considered everything his mother had said. He'd taken for fact that Emma would never want a life with him because of his past sins. But perhaps his mother was correct. Perhaps the times he and Emma had bonded these past weeks indicated there could be more . . . that she might see him in a new light. And with every step, a lightness suffused him, spreading what felt like a good deal of hope he'd not had for them.

Charles reached the library, and abruptly stopped. His entire body jolted as shock ran through him.

The room was filled, noisy with chatter, and yet it was not the size of the crowd of ladies and gentlemen nor the success of his club that held him motionless.

It was two women.

Two women who'd become recent additions to his club.

As of today. None other than Miss Lee and Miss Linden.

Emma wouldn't have.

The women gave simultaneous waves in Charles's direction.

"We received a note from Miss Gately encouraging us to join one of your meetings, Lord Scarsdale!" Miss Linden said, explaining their presence.

And yet as those two women, whose names he'd been linked to and quite scandalously, ventured deeper into the room, that very truth was confirmed—Emma had done just that.

Bloody hell.

His former betrothed had gone too far.

Chapter 21

THE LONDONER

A LADY SPURNED!

Whispers abound that the scandal which has shaken Le Libre Club was nothing more than a tawdry orchestration on the part of Miss Emma Gately. For shame!

M. FAIRPOINT

Emma had always wished to receive a note from her former betrothed.

It was a secret she'd carried and shared with no one for the sheer foolishness of having it.

It had been just one of many private longings she had harbored where the gentleman was concerned.

She had let herself to thoughts of pretty sonnets, or even bad ones. Verses drafted just for her, a secret between the two of them.

And at last, he had written.

But once more, in yet another way, it was nothing she'd ever hoped for from him.

Meet me at the Serpentine at dawn. Same place as our
last meeting.

—Scarsdale

Seated on the bench of her carriage, she lingered her gaze upon two details: the absence of her name and the addition of his formal one.

It was silly to be disappointed still, in any way, over Charles. Given the rouge-stained shirt that had lain atop garments she'd shed in his room, there shouldn't ever be any illusions again on her part about who he was. A vise squeezed painfully about her heart, proving the damned organ still wasn't done bleeding where he was concerned.

It was far better, far safer, to see him for the threat to the Mismatch Society that he was.

Folding the missive along its heavy crease, which had been made all the heavier from the constant reading and rereading she'd done of that scrap, Emma tucked it back inside her reticule. She stole a look across the bench to where Heather snored softly, and quietly let herself out of the carriage. Emma closed the carriage door with a careful click so as to not awaken the young woman she'd dragged along at this ungodly hour, and set off to meet Charles.

Nor did she have any illusions about what this meeting was about.

Or the gossip that had ensued.

And yet none of it had felt like any form of triumph. She'd felt only . . . all the worse inside.

Their truce, if it had ever really been that, had come to an end . . . after they'd made love, when she'd seen the evidence of his deeds that night contained upon his shirt and been reminded of all the ways in which she was still a fool for Charles.

She'd already crafted a response, one constructed on everything he would no doubt say. And focusing on that, as she made her march through the serene grounds of an empty Hyde Park, proved steadying.

Lifting her skirts to keep them from dragging on the dew-slicked earth, Emma found her way along the same path she had when she'd ended it with Charles. As such, there was a poignant familiarity to the impending exchange, a different confrontation that was also not so very different—two people who'd almost been wed, destined to be at odds forevermore.

Emma crested the slight rise and stopped, her gaze instantly finding him; his hands folded at his back, Charles stared out across the serene Serpentine, the faintest traces of the sun just creeping over the horizon bathing that river in an orange light, the water set afire.

Taking a breath, she continued the remainder of the way.

She reached him and opened her mouth to begin the scripted exchange she'd arrived here with this day, when, his back to her still, Charles spoke into the quiet. Cutting off her attempts.

"Do you know, Emma," he said quietly, his focus still directed out, "I came here knowing exactly what I planned to say to you." She bit the inside of her cheek under the evidence that they'd been alike, even in this. Charles let his arms fall to his sides, but made no move to look at her. "I'd planned what I intended to say about your sending Miss Lee and Miss Linden to my family's household." He spoke as if more to himself. "I arrived earlier, and I just . . . stood here. And do you know what I saw, Emma?" At last, he cast a glance her way, his eyes containing so much emotion, too much to ever make sense of without any deciphering from him.

Dampening her mouth, Emma shook her head.

"I saw you here . . . and myself, marching over that same rise you just walked." He pointed beyond her to the path she herself had been so reflecting on in the very same way. "I thought of that day you broke it off. And why you did." He paused. "It was something I've understood from that day. Why should you have wanted a life with me? Why, when you don't even respect me?"

"I . . . respect you, Charles," she said, joining him at the very edge of the shore. At the look he slid her way, she clarified. "Perhaps not before, but these past weeks . . . I've seen—"

"Precisely." He pointed a finger at her. "That is precisely it. You didn't know me, and I didn't know you, and it was because I never allowed for it." And this time an emotion she did recognize and knew all too well flashed in those dark brown irises: regret. "Instead, you've been left to form whatever opinions you have based on what you do know of me." His lips pulled. "None of which are . . . honorable."

What was he saying? What was he trying to say? She hung on, her breath bated, wanting to understand what exactly he was saying, a puzzle of a mystery she couldn't solve without his explanation.

He sighed. "And so I initially came driven by anger that you'd dare send Miss Lee and Miss Linden to me. But then as I stood, waiting for you to come and thinking of the day you severed our arrangement, it hit me—you don't know anything about my relationship with them." Those words cleaved her in two, left her splayed in ways she hated because she cared about him. "You don't know about my relationship with Seamus." His features spasmed. "Hell, Emma, you didn't even meet him . . . because of me. Because I never let you in, and that was wrong."

I never let you in . . .

She bit down hard on the inside of her cheek. "Why?"

He stared questioningly at her.

"Why was it wrong?" she clarified, her arms wrapped about her middle in a solitary embrace she didn't recall making. "It was ordained by our parents. You were never required to have to let me in or want me in your life. There was no fault in your not wanting me." It had taken until just recently for her to realize as much.

His throat moved. "Because I never gave us a chance, and I failed to see you as you deserved to be seen. I failed to appreciate you as you deserved to be appreciated.

"And mayhap it wouldn't have changed anything," he continued, running his eyes over her face. "Mayhap you still would have chosen the very path you have . . ." He looked to the graveled one they'd both traversed this day, and another before it. "But the truth remains, I've shared nothing with you. I've let you to your beliefs. About Seamus. About Miss Lee and Miss Linden."

He'd let her to her beliefs . . . which implied not everything was as it seemed in terms of those people in his life.

"I know you are a good father to Seamus," she said quietly. "I saw you with him but once, and know you are the manner of parent to build him up and celebrate his interests and indulge them when most parents of the peerage"—her own included—"do not bother with them in that way." As for Miss Lee and Miss Linden? Her gut clenched. Coward that she was, Emma didn't want to know about the women in his life. The named ones she'd spent all her adult life resenting as much as Charles for what they had shared. The knowledge all society had of their identities had made their realness and his betrayal all the more acute.

"Miss Lee and Miss Linden," Charles began in solemn tones, and every muscle in her body tensed. She was not to be spared talk of those women whom he still had dealings with.

"It isn't my business, Charles." Not anymore. Emma took a step away from him, but he shot out a hand, catching her fingers, holding them gently, asking her with that slight action to stay. To listen.

Oh, God. She was not to be spared this, then, after all.

"No. I want you to know. I need you to." His features were strained, a physical exertion of a man who'd less wish to share the next details than Emma. "It began with Camille."

Of anything he might have said about the women to whom he'd been publicly linked . . . mention of his sister was not what she'd expected. "I don't . . ." She shook her head.

"My sister lost her heart . . . and . . ."—hatred flared to life in his eyes, a vitriol so strong it sent gooseflesh rising on her arms—"and her virtue to a man. She was just seventeen."

Emma gasped. "My God." Not a whisper or a word or a hint of impropriety clung to the young woman. And in a society that found its sustenance on the falls from grace and heartbreak endured by its members, they'd somehow missed those morsels.

"There was no god in this," he said with so much bitterness dripping from his tones it oozed off his words. "He was a rake of the first order. And I was oblivious to the attentions he was bestowing upon her, and the meetings he'd coordinated on our family's Kent properties." His lip curled in a snarl, giving Charles the look of a feral wolf eager to shred the man who found himself the subject of his telling. "He bedded her with only the intention of securing her dowry, and when he presented her ruin to my father, and my father made clear he'd never see a pence, the cad left." His features collapsed. "And I let him. I was her brother, and I should have fought for her honor."

Emma moved quickly, placing a hand on his sleeve. "Calling him out would have not changed what happened to your sister, Charles," she said, willing him with her words to see. "It wouldn't undo what he did. The hurt he inflicted. It would have only led to one of you perishing on a dueling field"—and knowing the shot Charles was, likely the bounder would have paid the price with his life—"and everything exactly as he left it."

He balled and unballed his fists at his sides. "I was her eldest brother," he said harshly. "I failed her."

She tabulated the details of what he'd shared. "Charles, you were at university. You were a boy yourself."

He turned quickly toward her. "I wasn't a boy, any more than you were a girl at the age of twenty-two, Emma."

Fair point. He was right on that score.

She tried again. "Murder isn't a mark of honor, and that is what it would have been," she said with a gentle but firm insistence. "Men are taught that duels are merely a matter of good. They are not, Charles."

A muscle rippled along his proud, noble jawline, the only indication he heard her. "I couldn't help my sister before she was ruined. My parents came to me, after the fact . . . and revealed . . ." His words trailed off, and yet that punctuated pause ushered in a thick tension.

She waited, allowing him the time he needed. All the while, she ached to be closer to him, to take him in her arms and give him the strength necessary to finish what he *needed* to say.

Charles glanced around, searching the empty grounds, before landing on a point just over the top of Emma's head. "She was with child."

My God. Emma's eyes slid closed once more, and she made herself open them, thinking of how young Camille would have been . . . and what terror and heartbreak she would have known.

Through it, Charles spoke, his words rolling together rapidly, his voice still hushed so that she edged closer to hear every one of them. "A girl who'd just turned seventeen? With child? In this world? She would forever be an object of scorn. Her future settled by society. Her life uncertain."

But a gentleman . . .

Those three words lingered in the air, a whisper that percolated, and then the realization hit her square in the chest, rocking her back on her heels. Emma's breath caught on a noisy gasp that sent a still-gliding pelican off into flight. Incapable of words, she urged him with her eyes to confirm what could only be imaginings in her head, because the alternative would mean so much about Charles and her belief of him had been . . . wrong, in all the worst ways.

He nodded tightly. "He is Camille's son."

All the muscles in her legs turned to putty, and she sank onto a nearby boulder. Unblinking, she stared up at him as he spoke, his words a whir in her ears.

With that, he continued on, quickly, almost as if he delivered a rote telling he knew too well and was eager to have done. "I'd already been a wild student. Society knew I was reckless and given to mischief; as such, my parents . . ."—his lips formed another of those wry twists— "encouraged me to fulfill those expectations. That any ill behavior on my part would feed into the perception." Twisting at the sides of his Oxonian, Charles glanced down at the article. "Until the perception became the reality. I would go to gaming hells and dens of ill repute, and I lived that part, Emma. That was true. It became true anyway."

A wave of hurt rushed through her; it brought her to her feet. Burning with jealousy at what those nameless women had known with him . . .

"Some years ago, I was at one of those clubs, and there was a woman there." He paused. "Miss Lee."

"Oh." She wetted her lips as Miss Lee became more real, with a beginning with him. And a tale between them.

"Her father was a merchant." His jaw tensed. "He sold her on a losing hand to some dissolute lord."

Another gasp escaped her, but Charles continued over that interruption.

"She was the same age as Camille when Camille had been so used. I helped free her from that man." He took a step toward her. "I gave her the funds to maintain a townhouse, and provided a stipend over the years so she might survive, but that has been the extent of my connection with her." He lowered his brow to hers. "From that night on, I returned to my clubs, and I searched for hints of women in those same straits . . ."

"Miss Linden," she whispered.

"Miss Linden." He grimaced. "I didn't pay enough care to being discreet in the help I was providing until it was too late. For them . . ." He held her eyes, the intensity of his stare piercing through her. "And for you." Charles ran his knuckles along her cheek. "But you were the first for me since that night I . . . vowed to change my life." With a last, lingering caress, he let his hand fall and returned to the edge of the river.

Her chest rose and fell quickly, and Emma ran a hand over her brow. She took a step nearer and then stopped, her world knocked out of kilter by everything he'd revealed.

He'd taken his sister's child as his own . . . He'd rescued women who'd been wronged and in peril. All the while, he'd let the world believe the worst of him when he'd only been giving the best of himself to the sister he loved.

She looked to him, her heart stricken. "My god, I doubted you," she whispered. She'd been so blinded by jealousy she'd not allowed herself to believe in him. "I saw the rouge on your shirt." Emma's eyes slid shut briefly. "And I believed every worst thing about you."

Charles took several angry steps forward, closing the small distance she'd put between them. "Don't do that," he said harshly, splotches of red suffusing the sharp planes of his chiseled cheeks.

She moved her eyes over his face. "Don't . . . ?"

"Do not make me out to be more honorable than I am. I'm not, Emma," he said bluntly. "I still did . . ." His color deepened, and when he spoke, he did so in a furious whisper. "All of those things you've hated me for doing." As if he were unable to meet her eyes, Charles directed his gaze out on a pair of pink pelicans gliding to a graceful stop atop the water.

Emma stood there, studying Charles, her mind putting together all the pieces of the puzzle this man had been to her. His parents had come to him, a young man at university, and thrust the weight of their family's broken world upon his shoulders. And he'd done as they wished, agreeing to live a lie to protect his sister.

And in that moment, she fell in love with him. Her eyes slid closed as she staggered under the weight of that discovery. She'd always been in awe of him. Enamored and charmed. But this? This was deeper. She fell in love with who he was, a man who'd love Seamus, fostering the boy's love of learning. She fell in love with him for having allowed her the freedom on Regent Street to stand up for herself.

And she loved him for all he was.

A noisy splash of the fowl at play on the river brought her eyes open, and her heart lurched at finding Charles frozen, immobile in the same way he'd been.

These past weeks, she'd come to see Charles in a new way, but she'd still been left with more questions about the man he truly was.

All along, she'd resisted what her eyes and heart had been showing her about who he was. She'd been so blinded by her own hurt pride . . . until this moment. For in this moment, she understood him.

At last.

⁂

Emma's silence was far worse than any words she could have spoken. It was heavy and vague, and he didn't know how to make sense of what she was thinking. About him.

Even with that, however, having shared with her the truths that had tormented him filled Charles with a lightness he had been missing.

At last, someone knew.

Nay, *she* knew. He'd wanted to share it with her. From the moment they'd been betrothed as children, their lives had intersected in ways that had brought them to this very moment.

As such, she'd been deserving of not only the history he'd withheld, but his fidelity as well.

He pulled his gaze from the Serpentine and made himself at last look at Emma.

She hugged her arms about herself and glanced out at the sun creeping higher upon the horizon. That orange orb bathed her features in a soft light, burnishing the tightly drawn-back strands of her golden hair, and his breath hitched. One day, just one day, he wished to see her as she was, with the sun about her, in this very spot, without the world falling down around them . . . or without either of them resurrecting past pains. He wanted it to have been different.

Forcing himself away from the hungering of that thought and those wishful yearnings, Charles directed his attention forward once more. "I know none of what I shared really matters," he said, his voice hollow to his ears. He returned his hat to his head. "It doesn't undo . . . anything." Nothing would. "But I . . . wanted you to know anyway."

There came several beats of silence.

The crunch of gravel filled the morning quiet, blending with a noisy splash as one of the pelicans dunked its head under the water's surface in search of its morning meal.

He stiffened, feeling Emma's presence even before she took up a place directly beside him, so close their arms brushed, and she stared out with him at the river ahead.

"Of course it would have mattered," she whispered, and his entire body stiffened. Emma slid her fingers into his. "It *does* matter."

It does matter . . .

And with that, she held forth an absolution.

Her words hinting at a future, and not a broken past. "You played the part you were asked to, Charles," she said with a gentleness he didn't deserve. "Because it was asked of you. You played a part, Charles," she said firmly, capturing his hands and tightening her grip when he made to pull away. "You became the part."

"And I fell into it entirely too easily." He couldn't hold back the trace bitterness at his own moral failings. Of which there were so many.

She sighed, and leaned her head against his shoulder. "We always *see* ourselves through the lenses of how the world views us, until it distorts our vision and . . . we can't even truly see clearly who we are. But you . . . ?" Emma's eyes roved over his face. "I have learned these past weeks, and in these past minutes, who you are."

"And who am I?" he entreated, because he'd been lost so long he felt like a mere facade of a man, an empty shadow of a person.

"You really don't know?" she said softly.

Some emotion stuck painfully in his throat, something that felt like tears, and he struggled to swallow around it.

"You're a man who has put his family first when most any other man would have never made that sacrifice. You are a man who would storm across streets to save women."

"You didn't need saving," he pointed out. She'd been gloriously in control, and marvelous in her spirit.

Her expression grew contemplative. "There are different ways to save a person, Charles. You have done far more than you ever give yourself credit for."

Because it had been so very easy to focus on all the ways in which he'd failed his sister. "I stole your idea."

Emma smiled wryly. "Yes, well, there is that. Perhaps don't remind me of that," she said, startling a laugh from him, transforming dark into light as she did. Her teasing smile faded, and a glimmer lit her eyes. "You made the idea your own."

"I'm rubbish at it," he said in honesty. For with Emma, it was somehow easy to speak of his failings.

Emma scoffed. "You're rubbish at it? Charles"—she framed his face between her palms and squeezed slightly, shaking his head back and forth—"you managed to call the interest of some of the most respected women, friends I hold dear."

"Because of . . ." He winced, unable to complete the rest of that thought.

"What?" Emma released him, that twinkle back in her eyes. "Because you and Landon are dashing rogues whom ladies are eager to interact with? That may have been part of it"—she paused—"*at first*. But many of them are women I know. And respect. If curiosity about two rogues running a club drew them in, whatever it was you shared at your meetings? It kept them there." She pressed her palms against his chest. "*You* created a forum for people to come together, and did so in a way that uses literature they love." Emma darted out her tongue, the tip of it trailing along that flesh that continued to torment his days and his nights with equal fervor. "That is the manner of gentleman who is honorable, Charles." She paused. "The manner of man I could see myself spending my life with."

His heart forgot its function was beating. He frantically moved his gaze over her face. "What are you saying?"

Emma smoothed his lapels the way a devoted, loving wife might, tempting him all the more with that promise. "I am saying I want us . . . to try. To be a couple without our parents' interference. Not because of the arrangement they had, but because . . . we want to."

He briefly closed his eyes. And just like that, she offered him all he'd ever wanted, and had discovered he wanted only after she'd gone.

Her expression wavered. "Unless you don't—"

"I do!" he blurted, and touched his brow to hers. "I want that very much, Emma."

She smiled and tilted up her head.

Charles lowered his to meet her, but she drew back.

He stared at her questioningly.

"I will have you know that this does not mean I don't intend to woo back my former members, Lord Scarsdale," she whispered against his lips.

"You may try, Miss Gately." Charles nuzzled at her neck, laving the place where her pulse beat.

"O-oh, I intend to do far m-more *thannn*"—Charles suckled on the shell of her lobe—*"Mmm."*

"What was that?" he teased.

"I was going to say something about . . ." Charles kissed the remainder of that admission from her lips in a brief meeting of their mouths.

Her lashes fluttered, and when she opened them, a dazed little glimmer shone within those blue depths, one he reveled in. "What was I going to say?" she breathed to herself.

"That you'd won the battles, but I would win the war."

And then twining her arms about his neck, she drew herself up on tiptoe and pressed against him. "Yes, but in the reverse, Lord Scarsdale." And with that bold, husky whisper, she kissed him.

And he was fairly certain he'd never been happier than he was in this moment.

Chapter 22

THE LONDONER

FROM A RIVALRY TO . . . LOVE . . . ?

Inconceivable though it may be, from the ashes of a rivalry has sprung . . . a courtship between the unlikeliest of pairs: Miss Gately and the Earl of Scarsdale.

M. FAIRPOINT

Over the next fortnight, Emma and Charles were a courting couple in every sense of the word: with their public strolls through Hyde Park with Seamus, the gossips had printed freely and spoken loudly about them, and the new and unexpected seriousness of Emma and Charles's relationship.

They'd had ices at Gunter's and visited the Old Corner Bookshop— also with Seamus.

In all, it was precisely everything she'd ever secretly dreamed of and wished for a relationship with him.

Or . . . almost.

There was, of course, the matter of interfering members of the *ton*, who'd begun gossiping once more about her.

As well as . . . interfering parents.

"This is . . . how romantics do things these days?" Her father's noisy whisper sounded in the hallway.

Or if a lady wished to be technically correct on the whole thing . . . *still* interfering parents.

Over the tops of the two desks they'd placed across from one another, Charles and Emma picked up their gazes from the notes they'd been taking on their respective topics for their clubs and shared both a look and smile. "Perhaps if we are quiet, they'll go away," he whispered.

"Unlikely," she said in hushed tones while her maid embroidered in the corner.

As if to prove that very point, her father continued on with his lamentations. "I almost preferred when I was having my weekly billiards visits with the boy to . . . to . . . *this*."

"They are enjoying themselves," Emma's mother said, making less of an effort to disguise her voice. "And that is what matters."

"In my day we managed to escape chaperones, and—" Emma and Charles collectively winced, and at the same time covered their ears.

"I hate when they do that," she mouthed.

"I know. Vile," he concurred, completely soundless.

They both remained seated with their hands locked in that position several moments, then lowered them back to the table.

From the other side of the door panel, her father continued with his bemoanings. "What is it, even? An academics session? As if they are two university students studying their Latin."

Emma cupped her hands around her mouth and lowered her voice, her words intended for Charles only. "I despise Latin," she confided.

"I as well, love."

As if on cue, her father spoke: "That isn't romantic, love . . ." There was a pause. "Perhaps we should speak to her?"

Emma recoiled. "Oh, God, no," she cried out. "Absolutely not," she reiterated, repeating that declination loudly toward the doorway so there could be no doubting on her parents' part just whom she spoke to. "No. Talks."

Alas, her horrified shock served also as her salvation. On the other side of the oak panel, there came a flurry of curses and the pattering of footfalls as her parents scattered.

Charles brought his palms together in a rhythmic, quiet clap. "Well done, love. Well done."

Sweeping her right hand in a small circle at her brow, she dipped her head in acknowledgment of that credit.

They shared a smile before each returning to their work.

Or rather *Charles* did.

Click-click-click-click.

The frantic knock of his pen atop his page filled the quiet. Emma peeked over the top of her notes, and engrossed as he was, she simply observed him while he worked.

He'd caught the left corner of his lower lip between his teeth, and several curls hung loose over his brow as he wrote. He was a study of concentration, and she couldn't have been any more enamored.

To the world at large, how she and Charles spent their time together here would never be considered romantic. And yet, never had she felt closer to another person. There was nothing more she wished to do than be here with him, sharing ideas and discussing the two similar ventures they'd struck.

His flourishing, while hers was floundering. That reality crept back in.

Just a short while ago, that realization had left her riddled with resentment. And though she felt regret and frustration now at the ways in which the society was struggling, she'd also come to see and appreciate that what Charles had created—whatever his motives had initially been—mattered to him.

She didn't begrudge him his success. That didn't, however, make the troubles the society now faced any easier to accept.

Her gaze slid over to the copy of *The Londoner* resting at the side of her desk. Even as she reached for it, Charles intercepted her efforts. "Don't," he said quietly and firmly.

The unfavorable words and, worse, the warnings about the Mismatch Society as an evil influence had persisted. Charles, she knew, had nothing to do with those words. Despite the misgivings still held by her friends . . . and sister.

Concern spilled from his gaze. "I didn't—"

She cut him off. "I know you didn't." Even when they'd just been rivals, she'd still not believed him capable of what Owen professed he was guilty of. Emma threw down her pen, and abandoned all pretense of work. "I care less about who is responsible and more for the fact that the Mismatch Society is struggling," she confided, and it felt so freeing and wonderful to have someone from outside of that sphere to commiserate with. Someone who'd also created something from scratch, and cared about it as she did.

"Perhaps . . ."

When he stopped, she dropped her elbows on the surface of her desk. "Yes?" she urged. She didn't want him to have to measure words with her.

"Perhaps you're worrying too much. Trying too hard."

She wrinkled her nose. "How is it possible to try too hard?"

"Well, when you began the Mismatch Society," he said, "did you worry about who would join your ranks and who would not?"

Emma's brows came together. For in actuality, she hadn't. It had been more about a place where she could go and meet with just the handful of fast friends she'd found . . . Only when it had grown, so had her expectations for what she wanted them to be. But what if he was correct? What if the reason for their recent struggles was because they'd gotten so very far away from what they'd started out as? A group dedicated to discussions that evolved in a natural way. In a way that wasn't scripted or . . . in a way that they tried so hard.

Now, most of their meetings were spent worrying after their decreased numbers. Over the years, she'd spent so much time listening to society's condemnations and worrying about them . . . even when she herself hadn't realized as much. She'd prided herself on being boldly assertive, but all the while she'd listened to the critics: what they'd said about her betrothal. About her relationship with Charles. About . . . even the Mismatch Society.

Emma shoved back her seat as the truth hit her. She stared at him with unblinking eyes. "You're right," she said on an exhale. "We've been so focused on a competition with your club that we've failed to see the reason ladies were leaving was because discussions ceased happening. You provided what we've recently been unable to."

His brow furrowed. "And what is that?"

Did he really not know? "A stimulating place where women can speak on topics that matter to them, while using literature as a vehicle to do so."

He blushed. "I . . . It just evolved. I didn't set out with that specific goal in mind."

Resting an elbow on the table, Emma dropped her chin atop it. "It just came naturally to you, Lord Scarsdale," she praised.

And then wonder of wonders . . . he blushed. "No! That isn't what I was saying. Rather—"

Emma stretched her hands across the table and covered his ink-stained fingers with her own. "You didn't say it," she agreed. "I did. It is what you did."

She'd always taken him as self-important and arrogant. He'd erected a flawless facade of a man so urbane and unaffected. Or mayhap it was simply that she had failed to look close enough to see the real man. And in that, he'd been entirely correct in some of those earliest accusations he'd hurled at her. Emma let her arm drop and leaned forward, erasing some of the space between them. "It comes naturally, and there is no shame to be found in that." She stared wistfully down at her collection of crossed-out lines and failed lectures. "I would give anything to have a bit of that talent."

"You conceived something from nothing, and are direct in your studies and devoted to your members. And I . . ."

His gaze locked on her face.

The door burst open, killing that declaration on his lips.

"Fraternizing with the enemy," Isla muttered, stalking forward. "I never thought I'd see the day." Close at their younger sister's heels, Morgan and Pierce came trotting in. The two young men who'd always been enamored of the earl studiously avoided his gaze.

"Get up," Isla said without preamble. "We have a meeting—"

Emma glanced down at her notebook. She'd been more dazed than usual, but she'd not yet resorted to confusing her days. "We don't—"

"It is an emergency meeting. You remember," her sister shot back. "When there are crises that merit us gathering as a society outside of our usual hours."

"Oh." And it was surely wrong to feel this rush of disappointment at having her time with Charles ended.

Emma's father immediately stumbled into the room. "Billiards!" he exclaimed breathlessly. "If Emie is rushing off, won't you join me for a match?"

Previously, that devotion to Charles had grated. Now, Emma had come to appreciate that mayhap her father's taste in friendship with Charles had less to do with Emma and her betrothal, and more to do with the simple fact he enjoyed the younger man's presence. Because in fairness . . . who didn't?

"Alas, I must decline. I have important matters to attend to regarding my own club."

"Important matters to attend," Isla muttered. "Speak plainly and say, plotting further against the Mismatch Society, will you."

Emma gave her youngest sibling a sharp look . . . which Isla ignored.

"Uh . . . yes, well." Charles cleared his throat and returned his attention to the bereft bear of a man, who looked like a child who'd dropped his Gunter's ice. "As I was saying, I'm unable to join today; however, if you'd welcome some company tomo—"

"I would," the viscount boomed. "Bring your father—"

"And brother," Morgan and Pierce said at the same time.

"Men," Isla muttered with the vitriolic fury only a loyal, loving sister could manage. "Well, then, come along." Alas, for all the ways in which Emma had proven happy, her sister had been far less easy to trust Charles. Nor could or would Emma ever dare violate his confidence. In time, her friends and the family not already besotted with Charles would see him as she did.

Emma hesitated, hating for this moment with Charles to end.

"Go; we will meet later."

Seeming to realize she marched alone, Isla stopped in the doorway. "Well, then, you, too, brothers. You are part of the society," she snapped. "Thanks to this one," she added under her breath with a scowl for Emma.

Their twin brothers instantly fell back, their expressions abruptly a whole lot dourer.

A short while later, they arrived at Waverton Street and were shown to the parlor. Emma settled herself on the window seat overlooking the streets below, with her sister joining her on the upholstered cushion.

The room immediately quieted, with Annalee gaveling them in. "Emergency meeting, called to order."

And it certainly was a testament to Emma's distractedness that she'd no idea what the latest trouble to face the Mismatch Society in fact was.

"There have been . . . some concerns raised by several of the members, Emma," Annalee said gently.

It did not escape her notice that Owen, Olivia, and her brothers directed their stares up at the ceiling—Emma narrowed her eyes—or that Isla stared angrily back. "Concerns?" she asked slowly.

"Because you are cared about, of course," Valerie rushed to assure her. Of course.

"You have been distracted, and you are not even caring about our sinking numbers and his rising ones," Isla exclaimed.

And there it was.

Emma stiffened. *This* was the reason for the emergency meeting? Because of her relationship with Charles. Granted, her resentment of the gentleman in question was one of the whole reasons she'd found most of her friends and started the Mismatch Society in the first place. But this? This . . . felt like a betrayal. And yet she was as much responsible for the misgivings anyone had of Charles.

"It occurred to me just this day that we have worried entirely too much about who is leaving of their own volition," she said quietly. "We are so focused on competing with Lord Scarsdale we've gotten away from what our mission is." And yet so much of this was her fault. "I take responsibility for that," she said to the room at large. "*I* have made this a competition, but it is not," she implored, placing a slight emphasis on that last word, willing the women and men present to understand. "At least, that is not what it should be."

"She is lost," Annalee whispered.

"She is in love," Lila and Sylvia corrected in time.

"And blinded because of it." Those bitter words came from Owen.

"I am not blind," Emma said, sailing to her feet. She clasped her hands about her, and as she spoke, she briefly held the gaze of each member. "At least not in the way you are thinking. Charles is a good man." She spoke on a rush before anyone might seek to interject their own opinions—and erroneous ones at that. "He is clever, and he genuinely cares about what he has created as much as we do." Emma drew in a deep breath. "My pride, however, was hurt, and because of that, it led me here, and it fueled the rise of the Mismatch Society, but then it also steered me down a path where I lost focus on what our mission should be." Her gaze came to rest on the leader of their group, and in the other woman's eyes was something missing from all but Clara and Lila—understanding.

They knew what Emma had just herself found out. She loved him.

Her heart jumped.

Love.

It was certainly what it was . . . on her part. But what of what he felt? Was it . . . the same? He'd of course not spoken those words to her, but his actions—

Crasssh.

Pandemonium erupted, shouts and screams going up from the members as the windowpanes broke, exploding in a spray of splintered glass.

Emma jolted, shock knocking her off balance.

Wait . . . no . . . that was not shock.

She touched a shaky hand to the back of her head; a sticky warmth oozed onto her palms. Dazed, she studied the near-black liquid. Nay, not liquid. It was . . . blood.

"Emma?" her sister asked haltingly, and she looked up to meet Isla's eyes.

Or she tried to.

It was just too hard.

Impossible.

Her lashes fluttered, and her legs wavered, and Emma collapsed . . . remembering no more.

Chapter 23

THE LONDONER

DANGER!

Society is abuzz with questions as to which member amongst Polite Society should prove a vengeful villain of the Mismatch Club? No one is safe.

M. FAIRPOINT

Charles was going to marry her.

That was, if she agreed to wed him. If she wanted to. As he wanted her.

And these past weeks, she'd given him every hope that her answer this time might be . . . would be different.

But it also meant other aspects of his life needed to be different, too. Change had been due long before this moment.

"You summoned me, chap." Landon strolled into Charles's office ahead of the butler, cutting off the formal introduction with only the ease of one who was very much at home in this household.

Coming to his feet, Charles motioned to the wingback chairs situated at the front of his desk. "I have."

Tomlinson backed out of the room, and Landon plopped down in one of the seats. Slumped in the chair with his legs spread, he'd the look of bored calm personified. And yet the other man's astute gaze took in everything: the ledgers and notebooks stacked on Charles's desk. The room in general. "Not your usual place of play," he remarked.

"No," Charles said. Over the years, he'd really not committed himself to endeavors and matters as he should. Oh, he'd handled the finances for Miss Lee and Miss Linden. He'd not been a wastrel, but neither had he devoted his efforts to business. Not as he should. "I'll not be joining you at Forbidden Pleasures anymore."

"Is this about the buxom beauty and my attempts to help you?" Landon sat up straighter in his seat. "Because it wasn't my intention to offend you."

"No, no. It's not about that." At least, not directly. "I've come to see that my attending a place such as that is . . . wrong. Through my attendance, I've lent support to an establishment that has harmed women."

Landon stilled, then released a groan. "You're doing *it*."

As in marriage. "It," however, was the way the other man had always referred to matrimony when his finances had been at their most dire and he'd had to entertain the possibility of finding a wealthy wife. Thus far he'd been saved by windfalls at the gaming tables. He wouldn't always, however. It was Charles's hope that some honorable, loving, good woman would rescue Landon from himself. "I love her," he answered, not pretending to misunderstand.

"She's worthy of you?"

At least, this time, it was a question from his friend.

"Even more so," Charles promised.

Landon sighed again, this one more resigned than the one to precede it. "Yes, well, I've fought you on that from the start, but someone who brings you this much happiness can't be all bad."

Charles gave him a look.

"Very well. At all bad," the marquess allowed. Landon glanced about the room. "And then there was one."

Charles waggled his eyebrows. "Perhaps not for long?"

Landon burst out laughing.

KnockKnockKnock.

They looked to the entrance of the room, and Landon pointed. "Perhaps that is my future knocking, even now?"

The door burst open; Charles and Landon stood.

Seamus came sprinting forward, with Camille following along at a more sedate pace behind him.

"As I said," Landon called. "Fate was knocking."

Glaring at his friend, Charles moved out from behind his desk. "Don't even think about it," he warned before turning his attention to the little figure hurtling his way.

Landon winked.

"Scarsdale!" Seamus cried happily, rushing into Charles's arms, and he caught the boy to him, pretending to stagger back under his slight weight.

"Grown a stone in the week since I've seen you, you have!"

"I know what I am," Seamus said, as if remembering himself, and with the need to be a mature figure in the presence of older gentlemen, he stepped stiffly out of Charles's arms.

Camille rested a hand upon her son's shoulder. "You are a strong, mighty boy."

"The fiercest!" Landon exclaimed, and made a show of squeezing Seamus's biceps.

The little boy giggled.

His friend shifted all his focus to Charles's sister. "Lady Camille! The only sunny spot in—"

"England," she said drolly. "You must find some new material, Landon."

He staggered back. "Never tell me—"

"You've used that before? Indeed. Several times, in fact." Going up on tiptoe, she kissed her brother on the cheek. "Charles."

"He's becoming rusty in his doddering years, isn't he, sister?" Charles asked, vastly preferring having fun at his roguish friend's expense to the earlier flirting he'd been doing with Camille.

"No. No!" The other man clucked his tongue like an angry rooster. "Not doddering. I'm like a fine bottle of brandy, richer and better with age."

"Hardly richer." Charles couldn't resist, and his boyhood friend threw up his fists and boxed at the air.

Landon let his arms fall to his sides. "I always enjoy having my reputation as a rogue and gentleman challenged. Alas, I will leave you to your family business." Lifting a hand in salute, he waved to Charles's assembled family and left.

The moment he'd gone, Charles started for the bellpull. "I'll ring for refreshments."

"No. No!" Camille called quickly. "That will not be necessary."

"For Seamus, then."

"I am fine," his nephew insisted.

Even so, Charles continued, and rang the bell. A young maid appeared almost instantly. "Have a tray brought of the Bakewell tart that Master Seamus prefers, please."

Seamus's face lit.

"I said no, Charles," his sister admonished, settling into the mahogany two-seat settee in the middle of the room, Seamus taking the place beside her.

Charles opened his mouth to make a quip, but something stopped him—the serious set to her features. The tension at the corners of her mouth and eyes. All earlier levity faded as he pushed the door shut and joined the pair. "What is it?" he asked quietly after he'd sat on the Gainsborough chair closest to his nephew.

"I told Mother and Father I was coming. That I wished to speak with you"—Camille glanced over at the child next to her—"about . . . Seamus."

He immediately tensed. "Is everything—"

"Please," she interrupted.

"She's planned out her speech," Seamus said on a loud whisper, and that teasing camaraderie in his nephew's playful voice drove back some of the tension.

"We should let her continue, then," Charles said with a wink.

"Ahem. As I was saying." His sister favored each of them with a frown. "Seamus is a clever boy."

"The cleverest," Charles said automatically, the words born of truth.

"There's never been any matter he couldn't solve," Camille went on. "He sees everything, and knows even more."

All earlier lightness aside, his nephew stared down at his lap, and a sense of dread returned and grew within Charles. "What is it?" he asked for a second time.

Camille looked at the boy. "Tell him," she urged in gentling tones, maternal ones.

At last, Seamus looked up. "I know you're not my father," he said with a bluntness that knocked Charles back on his leather upholstered chair.

It had always been . . . understood. But neither had it been anything the family spoke of.

Charles found his voice. "I love you as if I were." He spoke in solemn tones.

The little boy nodded. "I know that. I also know she is my mother." As if there were another woman in the room and the statement needed clarification, Seamus pointed to Camille.

There it was. At last, they'd spoken the truth aloud. It was a conversation that had come about two decades earlier than Charles had anticipated. As such, he'd not put time into properly preparing.

"It was what I wished to talk about," Camille explained, clasping and unclasping her gloved hands. "I have asked you to live a lie, and I know what this has done to you and Miss Gately."

He shook his head, looking pointedly at his nephew.

"He deserves to hear and know everything, Charles," she insisted with far greater strength than Charles could manage in this moment.

"Of course," he said on a rush, nodding his head. "But I have no regrets," he implored the both of them to understand. Not over caring for them. The only regrets Charles carried came from the fact that he'd not shared with Emma. And even so . . . the struggle had been that it hadn't fully been his story to tell. "I would have you each know that."

"But we have regrets," Seamus admitted with an honesty that threatened to cleave Charles in two. "I don't like living a lie. It is hard enough being a bastard," he said with a bluntness that sent pain stabbing in Charles's gut.

Camille reached for her son's hand and held it tight. "It's worse when you're lying, too."

Warning bells chimed. *Oh, God.* What was his sister saying? He was already shaking his head.

"I'm claiming him as my own, and acknowledging that you are not, in fact, his father."

"No!" The denial exploded from him. There would be too much. Too much pain. Too much gossip. Too much of everything, when she'd already endured far more than any woman should.

A sad little smile wreathed her lips. "I'm not asking you, Charles. I'm doing this for me and Seamus. It is time that Seamus and I . . . and you . . . be set free. My mistakes were not yours to own. It was wrong of Mother and Father to ask you to make this sacrifice, just as it was wrong for me to allow it."

"I didn't—"

"Ask," she murmured, interrupting his hoarse exclamation. "I know that. And I know you never would. But you have cared for me and Seamus."

"And I will always care for you," he vowed. His eyes burnt from the sting of moisture there, and he blinked several times as he looked to the solemn, silent little boy. "I will always care for you," he repeated, more insistent, willing his nephew to hear that and believe it. Charles had been there for Seamus since the moment he'd entered the world and would be there until he took his last breath.

"I know," his nephew said with the quiet, calm confidence only a child could be capable of.

Tears filled Camille's eyes. "We *both* know." Exhaling softly through her lips, she brushed back the tears slipping down her cheeks. "But it is time I do the same as his mother."

She'd be shredded by society. Seamus, as well. And their parents. He grimaced. "Mother and Father—"

"Are not pleased." Camille smiled her first real smile since she'd entered his offices. "But they know I am determined in this." She stood, and stretched out a hand for Seamus. The little boy slipped his fingers through hers.

Charles exploded to his feet. "The tart."

"I promised Seamus a visit to Gunter's. There will be more for you," Camille said gently but firmly, her meaning clear. Her refusal of that baked treat had more to do with her at last claiming her role as mother to Seamus and making the decisions for him.

Charles stared after the pair walking off hand in hand.

Seamus cast a lingering glance over his shoulder, and with one final smile for Charles, he was gone.

They both were.

The moment Camille and Seamus left, Charles sagged against the settee the mother-son pair had occupied. He raised trembling hands and ran them over his face. For so long, he'd been set on protecting

Camille. She'd been right in her charges, that he'd been so intent on saving her that he'd not allowed her to be fully involved in decisions that had directly affected her and her son. He'd underestimated her, as he'd underestimated women until Emma. Until Emma had opened his eyes to everything he'd failed to see. And yet, though he was confident in Camille and sure of her strength, it didn't erase the fact that there would be scandal . . . and struggle. The scandal he could give two rots about. But if he could spare her pain . . . he would.

Frantic footfalls pounded outside in the corridor, and he let his arms fall, facing the door. She'd changed her mind.

And yet—

"St. John," he greeted. "A pleasu—" His greeting immediately cut off as he took in the other man's strained features, etched in an expression he'd seen him wear only when their friend, the late Earl of Norfolk, had died. A different worry churned in his stomach. "What is it?"

"There was an accident . . ." The viscount's throat moved as if he struggled over the emotion caught there to make the remainder of those words.

He tensed. Everyone knew of the Kearsley curse, and it had come to fruition . . . again. Charles took a quick step toward the other man. "Lady Sylvia—"

"She is fine." His friend doffed his hat, and twisted the brim in his hands.

She is fine. "Thank God . . ." Except St. John arriving here in his cloak and hat and speaking those words meant . . .

Someone else was hurt.

Someone who had sent the other man fleeing here to Charles. Someone he cared about.

His knees knocked together, and he wrapped a hand over the curved back of the settee, gripping it so hard the carved wood dug into his palms.

No.

Charles shook his head, willing the other man to silence, edging away to ward off what was coming. What he couldn't hear. Because nothing could happen to her. She was all that was joy and genius, and his happiness and very existence were inextricably twined to hers. *"Mm. Mm."* There was no world for him without her in it.

St. John nodded slowly, his expression pained. "Someone threw a brick through the Mismatch Society window." *No.* Charles continued shaking his head, but St. John's words continued anyway. "Emma was struck."

A keening wail better suited to a wounded beast spilled from Charles's lips, and he caught his head in his hands, ripping at his hair. And he tried to breathe. To speak. And failed successfully at both, so that only a garbled combination of raspy, incoherent words left him. "Is she . . . is she . . . ?"

"Unconscious when I came here. Her brothers carried her home. I don't know —"

Whatever the rest of those words his friend intended to utter, Charles didn't stick around to listen.

He took off running.

Chapter 24

THE LONDONER

QUESTIONS CONTINUE!

Who was the father, brother, guardian, or worse . . . former betrothed responsible for the attack on Miss Gately?

M. FAIRPOINT

Emma's parents had always been contrary.

When she'd wished to gallivant freely over the countryside, they'd insisted she attend her studies.

The moment she'd devoted herself to more scholarly pursuits, they'd insisted her interests were too rebellious.

It only made sense that the moment she discovered she was head over heels in love with Charles, they should resist her relationship with him.

It was also why, even with her head throbbing and the world still more than slightly unsteady, she burst into the drawing room to demand the meeting they'd refused.

Her parents, locked in one another's arms, immediately broke apart, both of them flushed and more than slightly disheveled. "Really?" she demanded. "This is how you're spending your time?" Emma locked her gaze on the mural overhead, ultimately knowing the image of her mother righting her neckline was one that would burn her eyes and sear her mind forevermore.

"Why are you out of bed?" her father asked in a display of his usual bluster and concern that would have warmed her heart if she weren't outraged out of her damned mind with him and the traitorous woman beside him. "It is late, and you are unwell."

"I am fine," she gritted out. At least enough to take umbrage to everything Isla had shared the moment she'd awakened a short while ago. Emma stalked over, her strides too quick, and she made herself adjust them. "You are forbidding me from seeing Charles?" she demanded, ignoring the way her head pounded. The discomfort was easy to forget when presented with this . . . nonsense.

Her mother rushed forward and wrapped an arm about Emma's waist. "Come." She guided her over to the same seat where all that ugly sin had just been committed between Emma's parents.

She'd burn that sofa herself before sitting in it again. Emma folded her arms. "Now?" she snapped. "Now is the time you opt to let Father have control of a situation?"

"I beg your pardon?" her papa grumbled.

Both women ignored him.

"Now is as good a time as any," her mother said. "Given that you were nearly killed."

Her father frowned. "And furthermore, it is more that I'm forbidding him from seeing you."

"That is the same thing," she said bluntly.

"Is it?" He hemmed. "I don't see it that way."

"Very well." Emma clasped her hands before her. "Then I'd like to see Charles."

Her father's nostrils flared. "No."

Emma threw up her arms, and immediately regretted that sudden movement. She winced and reflexively touched a hand to the knot at the back of her skull.

"You really should not be out of your bed, Emma," her mother chided as if she were still the small girl who'd sneaked from her chambers and wandered the household in the dead of night, when everyone else was sleeping, in search of the night's pastries that hadn't been eaten.

"I am fine," she snapped, then promptly winced at the dull throbbing from the place at the back of her skull where she'd taken that rock.

"That!" her mother exclaimed, pointing at Emma. "That is precisely why you should be abed." Wrapping an arm about Emma's waist and another around her shoulders, she guided her toward the door. "Help me see her abovestairs, dear heart."

Emma dug in her heels. "I am not leaving." She ground her feet to a stop, so that if her mother continued forward, she'd be forced to drag her down. "And I do not want to be shown to my rooms."

Her parents exchanged a look, and then reluctantly, Emma's mother shifted course and led them over to a different chair, and Emma sat. They stared at one another. "Are you mad?" she demanded.

They gasped.

"And I am not asking or using that word as any manner of insult. I am just trying to understand, because nothing else could explain how you, the both of you who know Charles as you do, who have been pressing me to wed him, should somehow come to believe that he could hurt me."

When she'd finished her tirade, her father made to speak, but his wife held up a hand, and commanded the floor. "He has hurt you, Emma."

Emma stared back, waiting for her to say more. "When?" she cried out.

"By not honoring your commitment years ago. By establishing a rival club. Should I continue?"

Her father cleared his throat. "Because she can," he interjected, and promptly sank back in his seat when mother and daughter sluiced glares his way. "As you were."

"Now is the time when you decide to hear things that I told you years ago?" Emma asked incredulously.

"Your father has it on the authority of someone he trusts, whom our *family* trusts," her mother corrected.

"Who?" she demanded.

There was a beat of silence, the faintest look passed between them, and Emma narrowed her eyes.

"We've sworn to secrecy," her father finally admitted.

This time her vision blurred, and it wasn't her injury but rather the bright flash of rage that blinded her. Someone had come to her parents with information that affected her future and her happiness, and they would withhold that name?

Emma took a deep breath, and tried again to reason with her parents. "This is Charles. Your godson. The man you played billiards with, Papa." She switched her focus to her mother. "The man whom you once told me scraped his knees and you helped tend him when he was a babe." For a moment, her mother's expression wavered, and Emma thought she'd reached them. "He wouldn't do what you are accusing him of." She pressed her point.

And apparently pushed too hard.

Her papa grunted. "Then the investigation will yield as much."

"The . . ." *My God.* Emma couldn't even make herself finish that. But she had to. "You hired an investigator."

"We are not necessarily saying he is guilty," her mama hedged. "Just as we are not saying you can never see h—"

Emma cut her off. "When?"

"And we weren't rude. We were very polite."

A humorless laugh spilled from her lips. "Oh, I hope you are prepared to lose your lifelong friendship with Lord and Lady Rochester, because they will *never* forgive this affront." Nor should they. This was an unforgivable slandering of a man who was good and who was honorable.

Emma's warning managed to leach the color from their cheeks.

"Then so be it." Her mother spoke quietly. "If they cannot understand, then our friendship is not one that should be saved."

"We have issued no public declarations," Emma's father insisted. "We are simply saying we wish to be sure he wasn't. We want to be sure that if you intend to marry him, that he is someone who is absolutely safe."

The viscountess smiled gently. "When you have a daughter someday, Emma, you will discover that you will protect your child at any costs."

"Even at the cost of her happiness?" she spat, unable to keep the bitterness from that query.

"Yes," her mother said evenly. "Even that."

She came to her feet. "At every turn, you have decided what is best for me."

"Emma—"

"No!" She shouted her father into silence. "You will listen to me. You chose my future when I was but a child. You decided who I should wed without a regard to how I might one day feel, or what I might want." Her entire body shook from the force of the resentment burning through her. "And then finally, when I realize it is Charles I love and want in my life, you would keep me away . . . once more deciding that you know what is best."

Her father made to speak, but the viscountess lifted a hand.

"We are finally hearing you, Emma," her mother said with a calm that belied the lingering echo of Emma's cries around the room. "We failed to see you were hurt before. Now, we are looking with clear eyes: after you ended it, he started a rival society. After all his scandals, this is going to be humiliating, and we would protect you from this humiliation."

That quiet pronouncement brought Emma rocking back on her heels.

For that had been the same thought and fear she'd carried—that in giving herself to Charles, she'd be opening herself up to humiliation. Only to see . . . how very little that had mattered. "I don't care," she said softly, the truth coming to her at last. "I don't care what people say or how it might look." And there was something so very freeing in that truth. A lightness suffused her chest. So much of what had caused her humiliation had been the absolute absence of control . . . but this? Deciding her own heart, taking ownership of who she wanted to spend the rest of her life with, was the greatest control she'd ever had over herself. She smiled. "I love him," she said simply. And to hell with anyone—her parents included—who might judge her for it. With that, Emma started for the door.

"Emma," her father called out imploringly.

Emma ignored that plaintive entreaty.

"Let her go. She needs some time," her mama said as Emma brought the door shut behind her.

Time was what they thought she required?

She was done with it. Done letting others choose her course. Done letting her parents decide her future.

She knew what she wanted, and more specifically who she wanted . . .

Her heart lifted in her chest, with the sense of absolute rightness . . .

A short while later, she had a bag packed and her crimson cloak donned, underestimated by her family, as she'd always been. Emma found her way outside and went in search of a hackney . . . finding one stopped just across the pavement. She bolted for the carriage. Calling up instructions, she let the driver take her bag, and accepted his hand up.

The moment the door shut behind her, she settled onto the bench and gasped.

A tall figure sat in the shadows, and she immediately brought up her reticule to bring it across the stranger's face . . .

"Don't!" he cried out, holding up his arms protectively. "It is me."

Through the shock of discovering someone in her conveyance, Emma slowly lowered her reticule and stared at the familiar person opposite her. *"Owen?"* she asked incredulously as the carriage lurched forward. Oh, thank God.

"I thought you might be in need of . . . assistance."

God love him.

"You scared the devil out of me," she said, tugging off her gloves and pushing back her hood. "I am ever so relieved it was you."

"Your parents are not happy," he ventured, adjusting his spectacles.

"With good reason."

Good reason being . . . the erroneous thought that Charles was somehow guilty in what had occurred this day? A healthy dose of annoyance replaced any earlier relief at finding him here.

Emma had reached for the curtain, to tug it back and peer out, when Owen spoke.

"They are worried about you, Emma . . . as am I."

Something in his tone froze her efforts, and she gripped the edge of the fabric before releasing it. And even in the dark of the carriage, she saw a hardness she'd never before seen in Owen's eyes. A manner that she would have said him impossible of possessing . . . and it chilled her from the inside out.

Have a care with that one, Emma-love . . . You're going to break his heart . . . That gent is eyeing you with romantic eyes . . .

Oh, God. Dread swirled in her belly.

And this time, she did grab for the curtain, and peered out at the passing scenery. "Where are we going?" she demanded; fury lent a tremble to her voice.

"He is not right for you, Emma. He never was. A man who would create a rival league to challenge yours, and who would"—color flooded his cheeks—"defile you in public as he did at Lady Rutland's."

Lady Rutland's? Then the memory of what she and Charles had done and shared returned.

She blanched and dropped the curtain as if burnt.

"Yes, I heard the both of you," he said matter-of-factly, drawing off his gloves. "And you should be fortunate I did. I sent our sisters on their way and stood guard to ensure no one discovered you so."

Mortification brought her toes curling. That he'd listened in on something so intimate, something so special, left her physically ill. "Oh, my God." Horror pulled that whisper from deep within her chest.

"You needn't worry," he said with a casual matter-of-factness. "I do not blame you. I know he seduced you."

Emma considered her reply, and the man across from her. He believed he was right in this. He believed he acted out of friendship. He thought she was a woman incapable of knowing her own mind. Unlike Charles, who challenged her and embraced the fact that she made her own decisions. "I wanted to be with Charles," she said. "I want to be with him still. And I intend to, Owen." Emma rapped on the roof, urging the driver to bring the conveyance to a stop.

The hack, however, continued rolling along at a brisk clip.

"He is not going to do that," Owen explained.

Her heart kicked up a beat as for the first time—in this moment and in all the years knowing Owen—she became genuinely afraid of him.

Emma made another attempt. "I command you, stop this carriage and get out this instant."

"You don't want me to do that. I know you are just proud, and like to be in control of your own decisions, but—"

God save her from interfering people. Only Charles had applauded the self-control she'd allowed herself these past months. "You presume to tell me what I want?" she demanded.

He chuckled. "Yes. It is funny, that. He said the same thing to me." At the questioning look she gave him, Owen clarified. "Lord Scarsdale. After I confronted him, warning him away from you."

"You confronted him," she whispered.

Owen's spine grew several inches, as if she were praising him for that interference.

"I did."

And all the while, Charles had said nothing. He'd let her to her friendship with Owen, not interfering or seeking to influence her relationship with him.

How she wished he had.

But would she have listened? Could she have believed Owen would prove to be this man before her?

And here all these years she'd passed judgment upon Charles, and held Owen in the highest esteem. Pride—yet again it proved her pride which had been so blinding.

"Where are we going, Owen?"

"Scotland."

"Scot . . ." A chill scraped along her spine as she frantically looked out the window at the passing landscape of the London scene. Familiar streets had since given way to fewer familiar ones on the fringe of London.

"What are we doing there?" she asked, even as she already knew.

"Why, I'm saving you."

"Saving me?" she echoed.

"We are going to Gretna Green. I am marrying you."

Bloody hell.

Chapter 25

THE LONDONER

DEVASTATED!

The Earl of Scarsdale was purported to have been in-
consolable over the attack upon his former betrothed.
Perhaps soon the courting couple shall find themselves . . . as something *more*?

M. FAIRPOINT

If Charles hadn't left a hole on the path he'd paced over his Aubusson
carpet, there'd be one there by the end of the night.

This was hell . . .

He'd been barred from seeing her. Oh, the rejection had been polite
enough. They'd insisted Emma required rest, and that they would send
word for him when she awakened. But there could be no doubting . . .
they were keeping him from her. He gnashed his teeth. And along with
that, they believed Charles had harmed her. As if he were capable. As

if he wouldn't gnaw off his own arm with his teeth if it meant to spare her any suffering.

"I'm sure they weren't really sending you away," Landon said, supportive as always.

"Their butler told me to leave," Charles responded.

"Well, that is pretty decisive, then," the marquess allowed.

Yes, it was.

The irony wasn't lost on him that he, who'd been capable of charming anyone, should find himself at odds with the viscount who'd called him friend.

"I'm sure you can reason with them. Eventually," Landon said from where he sat alongside St. John. "No one is being logical. They are worried about their daughter."

He stopped abruptly. "Worried I will hurt her," he finished for the other man.

Landon scoffed. "They aren't thinking rationally. Of course you didn't hit your Miss Gately with a brick. Why, that doesn't even make sense." The marquess looked to St. John, and pointedly.

The viscount knitted his brows, and then nodded. "Of course he didn't. Absolutely preposterous." He paused. "Not to mention I was with him when he learned of the news. No one who was haunted and suffering like Scarsdale could have possibly been guilty of harming the lady."

"Well, I wasn't, and didn't require that proof to know my friend isn't a lady-killer." Landon grinned. "At least, not in the literal sense."

Ignoring that jesting, Charles resumed pacing. Frustration ate at him. A restlessness that came from the fact that he could be and was kept from her. That it was beyond his—and her—power.

What if she's of the same opinion as her parents? a voice taunted. As soon as the insidious thought slid in, Charles thrust the thought aside. She knew him. As he knew her. She'd not doubt him in this.

A knock sounded at the door, and he abruptly stopped. He'd given word he wasn't to be disturbed unless it pertained to— "Enter!" he called out, already striding across the room.

Tomlinson cleared his throat. "Mr. and Mr. Gately," he announced, and then backed out.

The twins streamed into the room, speaking in synchronization. "Where is she?"

Oh, God in heaven. "What?" he asked dumbly.

Emma's brothers shared a look. "She's not here?" Morgan's was a plea, one that Charles recognized all too well, one that contained the raw agony of a brother who'd failed his sister.

Charles moaned. *Not again. No. No. No.*

Pierce erupted into a stream of cursing.

"You lost her!" Charles demanded of the pair, even as he knew the guilt they carried, too fearful and furious to realize it was wrong to hold them to blame and yet . . . "She was attacked today, and no one thought to secure the damned house." *Me. I should have done it. I should have staked a place outside her family's and demanded to be seen.* Even if they'd thrown him out.

Morgan winced, his features spasming. "You are right."

"Hey, now," St. John murmured, resting a hand on Morgan's shoulder and squeezing.

Charles struggled to order his thoughts and breathe.

"Of course we don't think it is you," Pierce rushed to assure him. "Even if—"

Their parents did. Charles had been correct. Either way, their ill opinion of him meant nothing right now.

Another knock sounded, and this time, Tomlinson reappeared . . . with a woman at his side.

Hope sprang in Charles's chest as he took in the cloaked figure beside his butler.

Emma!

And yet . . .

She shoved back the hood of her cloak.

Not Emma.

"Olivia!" Morgan exclaimed. Desperation wreathed the gentleman's face. "Is she with you?"

The young lady hesitated, and then silently, she shook her head.

Numbness settled around Charles's chest as hope died once more. An ever-growing dread resurfaced, boiling inside.

"I am here about Emma." That voice came soft and small, a pleading whisper, hoarse with grief, and he nodded to Tomlinson.

The servant immediately stepped out of the room.

"It was my brother." The young lady's voice broke, and she fisted her hands at her sides. "It *is* my brother. He is in love with her. I learned he intends to elope with her."

⌘

Charles rode for two hours.

And with every bit of roadway traveled, the hell of the past merged with the present so that it became conjoined and twisted in his mind . . . Camille and Emma. In the end, Camille had been ruined but spared of marriage to the cad who'd hurt her. But also a man who'd been singularly interested in the wealth she could bring him. There'd been no love involved. No emotions at all.

Unlike Mr. Watley . . . Mr. Watley, who this day had been driven only by those sentiments . . . those volatile emotions that made a person unpredictable. And dangerous. And a man who could orchestrate an entire scheme to portray Charles as guilty in the hopes of driving a wedge between him and Emma? That man was capable of any number of dark deeds . . . as had been proven this day.

Leaning forward, Charles urged his mount on all the faster. His breath came hard, little to do with the pace he'd set and everything to do with the numbing panic that had followed him as he'd galloped through the streets of London . . . until the cobblestones had given way to the green countryside, marking the moment he'd left.

The shift from soot and mud and stone to overgrown roads, lined by trees and lush emerald earth, forced his mind back.

To the time he'd loved the countryside. To the time when there'd been no greater joy than riding and running wild over the land. And for some of those days, he'd entertained a little girl at his side. Chasing her and being chased in return . . . until they'd grown up and he'd come to associate those lands and that place with resentment over his lot.

He wanted to go back and live there with her . . . Hell, he wanted to do everything with her. Go everywhere with her.

And yet a sense of hopelessness threatened to swarm him, riding hard, pushing his horse harder than he ever had, because there was no future without Emma in it.

He was lost—

Charles yanked hard on the reins; a downed tree blocked the middle of the road.

Rascal reared, pawing at the earth before settling.

Making a soothing noise, Charles patted the chestnut mount on his withers. When the skittish creature was at last calmed, Charles dismounted. His horse promptly wandered to the side of the roadway and found a patch of overgrown grass to chew on.

Stalking over to the blockage, Charles cursed, assessing the path. Upon inspection, it wasn't a downed tree, but rather a series of branches. He frowned, skimming his gaze over the road. Ones that appeared as if they'd been strategically placed.

Where in blazes were they?

They couldn't have been so far ahead. Watley's sister had come immediately, and according to Emma's brothers, she'd been in the midst of arguing with her parents over the right to see him not long before she'd been abducted. Gretna Green was the end goal for Watley. Speed would have been his concern. Unless he had taken one of those less-traveled roads, in which case, one of Emma's brothers or—

A rock landed on the tip of his boot, and he jumped, from not the pain but the surprise of it.

"You're late, Scarsdale."

And then he heard it. Nay, he heard her. Or . . . he thought he did. Perhaps it was just the hungering to see her that had led to him hearing her.

Emma.

Another pebble caught him square on his other boot, bringing his eyes flying open, and he grunted. No, there was no imagining that.

"It took you long enough, Charles-love," a voice called down.

Angling his head back, Charles scanned his gaze, frantically searching . . . and then finding. He squinted at the beloved figure high overhead, perched as comfortably as in a seating room, only in the nook of a branch.

"You were once very skilled at climbing trees to escape me, Charles. Never tell me you won't scale one to find me," she teased, and a dizzying lightness suffused his chest, leaving him buoyant, and he felt his lips form the first smile he'd managed since they'd been together yesterday morn.

Catching the low-hanging branch, he drew himself up, and he scaled the old oak until he reached the place just below the perch she'd made for herself. "You knew about that."

A twinkle lit her eyes. "I had the tree across from you," she whispered, and then winked.

His eyebrows went flying up. "You—"

"Were there? Yes. Heard everything?" She nodded. "Indeed. I climbed down before you or your parents saw me."

His mind raced back, recalling all the remembrances of that day, the words he recalled speaking . . . and then a small figure, in the distance, hovering beside the lake. Emma. She'd been near enough to hear all. His chest tightened. "Oh, God, Emma. No wonder—"

"Oh, hush." Emma tapped the tip of her boot against his shoulder. "I was hiding, too. You didn't have a market on 'child wishing to escape their betrothal' that day."

Some of the tension eased from his shoulders. "We were always of a remarkably similar thought," he said wistfully. They'd just been too proud and filled with resentment to see that they were meant to be together.

"It just took us some time to see it." She spoke that thought aloud. Snapping her notebook shut, she returned it to the valise she'd set up in the crook of an enormous curved branch.

"I'm sorry." About so much. For betraying her. For not seeing her as she'd deserved to be seen.

"I'm sorry, too. For the lost time," she murmured.

"I don't want to lose any more with you," he said, his voice hoarsened by the tears stuck in his throat. "I've wasted so much . . . and yesterday, today . . . thinking I'd lost you—" The agony of that brought his eyes shut. As every ugliest nightmare and possibility battered him. "It was as though it were happening again, and I was hopeless to stop—"

"*Shh,*" she whispered, and her palm stroked his cheek, the tenderness of that loving touch making it possible to look at her once more. "I didn't doubt you'd find me."

"I feared I wouldn't." His voice broke as he, at last, surrendered to the pressing fear that had gripped him since they'd been separated and since he'd set out after her. "I just rode, imagining all the while that I would be too late. That you were lost to me, and I didn't . . . I couldn't live if you were."

Emma pressed a finger against his lips. "I didn't doubt you would be here." She glanced the eight paces below to the blockage in the road. "Your work?"

She lifted her head in proud acknowledgment. "Of course. But I had my reticule and was prepared to walk if I needed to save myself." She paused, a twinkle sparkling in her eyes. "Completely, that is."

He chuckled, his chest rumbling, that mirth coming more from the relief of knowing she was here with him.

"How did you find me?" she asked.

He hesitated. "Olivia came to see me. She . . . learned of her brother's intentions and came posthaste. She was . . . is . . . devastated by his betrayal and believes herself responsible."

"No! I would never—"

"I assured her as much. Guilt, however, isn't always rational." He knew that from all he carried about Camille's struggles, a remorse that would always remain with him, no matter how much Emma had helped him see that he wasn't to blame.

"You were right about him," Emma murmured, her voice soft and sad, and he set aside his own tumult because it didn't really matter. She did. What she felt and what she'd suffered, and the hurt of a lost friendship that had been important to her.

"I am so sorry," he said quietly, and finished his climb until he'd found a seat directly next to her. "I wish I hadn't been."

"Me too." She lightly swung the leg she'd hung over the side. "For not listening to your warnings. My pride," she muttered, and her face pulled in a grimace. With a sigh, Emma rested her cheek against his shoulder.

Charles placed a lingering kiss upon her forehead. "So how'd you handle the pup?" he asked, and Emma's smile was back in place.

"He underestimated me."

"Of course he did. *Foolish man.*"

Emma turned so she sat facing him, her knees drawn up to her chest, with an ease but also a precariousness that sent another swell of panic cresting. "The Duke of Wingate taught the Mismatch Society some clever skills in putting a man to sleep." She lifted her right hand, angling it. "You just hit with the edge in this portion of the neck"—Emma demonstrated a slow slashing movement toward the upper portion of Charles's neck—"and it puts a man to sleep."

He ran his gaze over her face. "My God, you are breathtaking."

She laughed. "I swear, Charles Hayden, you are the only man in London who'd be impressed by a lady knocking out a gent, and not absolutely horrified."

"You are a glorious warrior, Emma Gately, a woman that I would be honored to spend the rest of my days attempting to make gloriously happy."

Emma stilled, then let her legs fall so they hung over the side of the branch. "What?"

She didn't know? How could she not know every wish he carried for a future that included them two together in it? Lowering himself onto his stomach, he scaled back down. The moment his feet hit the ground, he dropped to a knee. "Emma Gately," he called up. "Will you marry me? Will you give me the gift of living only for your happiness?"

There came the rustle of leaves, and a moment later, Emma lowered herself to the ground, her eyes wide circles of emotion. Her mouth trembled, and she touched her fingers to those lips he would never tire of kissing.

Charles turned up his palms. "I love you endlessly and to distraction, Emma. My life is empty without you in it, and if you'd have me—"

A sob burst from her, and Emma lunged forward.

Charles already had his arms open, and he let himself fall back until they lay there with the yew leaves fluttering overhead. He brought up both hands to smooth the cherished planes of her face. "Is that—"

"Yes," she cried against his mouth, a blend of tears and laughter. "That is a yes."

Charles smiled.

Epilogue

That same summer

There was a rumble in the gardens.

A rumble that could belong only to discontented parents.

Perched in the same yew tree Charles had taken shelter within seventeen years ago, Emma suppressed a giggle.

Leaning near, he placed his lips close to her ear, the sough of his breath sending delicious shivers from where it fanned. "*Shh*, love. You'll give us away."

The voices grew increasingly closer, the blending of their parents and siblings as they stalked the marchioness's prized grounds.

"They've changed their minds." Emma's mother's forlorn wail could likely be heard across the Leeds countryside . . . if the entire Leeds countryside hadn't already been installed within the Marquess and Marchioness of Rochester's sprawling manor for the wedding of the season.

As it had been written of, in all the papers.

"They've not changed their minds," Emma's father said, all hint of exasperation effectively ruined by the trace of uncertainty there. "In fact, if it's either of them who's had a change of mind, it would be my Emma."

"Yes, given she's done it befo— *Owww*." Pierce's mutterings ended on a sharp wail. "What in hell was that for, Isla?" he demanded of their youngest sibling. "She did end it, and as such, it's not beyond the realm of possibility that she's doing it again."

"Because she's not flighty," Isla snapped. "She knows her mind."

Charles cupped Emma's nape, and pressed his lips to her neck. "She's right," he whispered.

Warmth settled in her belly, and Emma's body came alive as it always did under the power of his touch.

ClapClapClap. "No one is changing their minds," Charles's mother called. "Now, I trust they're likely returned to greet the guests, so we might call off the search."

The voices of that search party grew fainter and fainter as their family pulled away.

"Ten minutes, Charles," his mother called up.

"Thank you, Mother," Charles rejoined.

Emma peeked down at the marchioness below. "Thank you," she whispered to the smiling marchioness.

She winked. "I never saw you." With that, humming softly, Lady Rochester hurried off.

When they were at last alone, Charles reached for Emma's hem, and ever so slowly, with painstaking care, he slid up the garment. She shivered, lifting her hips slightly to aid his efforts.

"Lord Scarsdale, whatever are you doing?" she breathed, her voice quavering. For she knew. Oh, how she knew what he intended. Then he glided his fingers along the expanse of her calf, and higher, stroking her thigh. A little sigh spilled out, and she used the enormous trunk for support; closing her eyes, she lay back and gave herself over to the exquisiteness of that tantalizing caress.

"I think you know, Lady Scarsdale," he teased in his rogue's whisper.

"*Shh!*" That secret, that they'd continued on to Gretna Green before returning, was one they'd kept between them.

"No one is here," he pointed out. "They've all been driven off." He massaged the length of her leg, his fingers climbing up close to the juncture between her legs, that place that ached for him. That always did.

And releasing a little sigh, Emma lay there and let herself revel in his ministrations. "I'll be disheveled for my wedding."

"Your second wedding," he reminded her, and he pressed the heel of his palm against her center, teasing her with that masterful pressure.

"Th-third." Her breath grew steadily erratic. "It is our th-third. A-as such"—Emma bit her lip as he caressed her, letting her legs splay wider—"I b-believe it is fine if we are just a touch late?"

Charles grinned. "I couldn't agree more."

And on that day, Emma and Charles were wed . . . for a third time. In a marriage that, this time, would be . . . *forever*.

Acknowledgments

To Cheryl, Sarah, and Kellie, whose eyes and insight I could never do without. Thank you for catching all you do, and for keeping me breathing through the editorial process.